THE SKY LORDS

THE SKY LORDS

a novel

JOHN BROSNAN

St. Martin's Press
New York

Library of Congress Cataloging-in-Publication Data

Brosnan, John.
    The sky lords / John Brosnan.
       p.   cm.
    "A Thomas Dunne book."
    ISBN 0-312-05964-7
    I. Title.
  PR6052.R585S5   1991
  823'.914—dc20   90-29262
                                               CIP

First published in Great Britain by Victor Gollancz Limited.

First U.S. Edition: May 1991
10 9 8 7 6 5 4 3 2 1

To my Mother

Contents

PART I

Lord Pangloth

Chapter One:

Not far away, something began to shriek in terrible agony. Jan looked at the guard. The guard shrugged her tanned shoulders and said, "Sounds like a big reptile's been caught by a whip tree."

Trying to ignore the nerve-jangling screeching, Jan turned her attention back to the panther. "I've told you," she called down to it. "We don't need a cat, but thanks anyway."

The black panther made no move to go but remained sitting on its haunches looking up at her. "I work good for you, catch vermin, patrol your walls at night," it said in its high-pitched, hissing voice.

Jan studied the animal more closely. It was a powerfully built beast seemingly in good health. Conditions in the blight lands must be getting really bad if such an animal was willing to demean itself by offering to work for humans. She noticed a long scar down its right flank. It looked fresh.

At her side Martha said nervously, "Don't like. Make go away. Martha don't like . . . ."

Jan patted the chimp on the head. "Don't worry. It can't hurt you." The guard hefted her cross-bow. "Shall I put a bolt through its shoulder to speed it on its way?" she asked Jan.

Before Jan could answer the panther turned its head towards the guard and said, "Fire weapon and I be up wall very fast. Take your throat away with me. That mesh like grass to my claws." Then, in a calculated display of indifference, it sprawled on its side, exposing its belly to them. Jan saw that it was male. She raised her hand to the guard, who had reddened at the panther's threat and was likely to do something foolish. "Don't, Carla. Leave this to me." Martha, meanwhile, had started to whimper.

The panther eyed Jan with what might have been feline amusement. "You very young to be boss-man."

11

"I'm not a boss-*man*," said Jan. "I'm the daughter of Headwoman Melissa and it's my turn to be in charge of the wall defences this week."

The panther gave a human-like shrug of its powerful shoulders and said, "Like I say, you boss. So why you not let poor cat into settlement?" Its pronunciation of the word 'settlement' was preceded by a long hiss.

"We have a strict policy as to what animals we allow to live with us," Jan told the panther. "You must know that."

"Times are hard. Getting harder. We need to work together. Like old days. When my forefathers served your forefathers."

"Fore*mothers*," corrected Jan indignantly. "And that was a long time ago. When you big cats could be trusted."

"You don't trust me?" The panther tried to look innocent.

"Of course not. I'd be foolish to. In the same way that a carrot could trust me not to eat it."

"So," said the panther. It quickly got up. "You make mistake," it said as it turned and, swishing its tail in annoyance, stalked off down what remained of the trail that had led to the corn fields before the blight lands had overwhelmed them. The panther soon vanished from view. Martha jumped up and down with excited relief. "Nasty cat. *Nasty*. Martha don't like . . . ."

Jan sighed and wiped the sweat from her forehead with the back of her hand. A glance at the sun revealed she had at least another hour of duty to go. She looked at Carla, who was frowning. "You should have let me shoot it, Mistress," she told Jan. "Arrogant beast. Arrogant *male* beast."

"You think it'll come back?" Jan asked her.

"It had better not. It'll get my bolt between its eyes instead of its shoulder."

Jan doubted if Carla would find it so easy to despatch the sly carnivore, but she didn't voice her reservations. The wall guards needed to indulge in such bravado — Jan knew it helped to keep up their morale in what was an increasingly discouraging task.

"Sound the alarm if it returns," Jan told her. "I'll be on the east side."

Carla gave her a perfunctory salute as Jan, followed by the still excited Martha, headed off eastwards along the wooden parapet.

12

It was only then that Jan realized that the reptile, if that's what it had been, had stopped screaming. She wondered why the encounter with the panther had disturbed her so much. *It was a bad omen*, she told herself and whispered a quick prayer to Mother God.

There was only one more incident during Jan's last hour of duty. An elephant creeper had penetrated the mesh barrier on the east perimeter and was threatening to bring down a section of the wall. Jan had supervised the squad of fifteen guards who, with flame throwers and axes, had destroyed the slowly writhing tendril, which measured over four feet in diameter at its widest point. Afterwards she watched as Martha and the other chimps clambered up the mesh fence and, with their customary speed, repaired the damage caused by the vine. Just as they were finishing, Alsa arrived to relieve Jan. Jan was only too glad to hand over to Alsa the gold-plated branch of authority which she'd kept tucked in her belt.

"It's all yours," she told Alsa gratefully. "I'm exhausted."

Alsa surveyed the repair work in the fence. "Been busy?"

"No more than usual." Jan beckoned to Martha who scurried down the mesh, putting her pliers away in the tool-bag tied around her waist as she came. "We go home?" she asked.

"Yes." Jan patted her on the head. Then to Alsa she said, "You may have a visit from a smooth-talking panther. Wants to work for us in return of shelter. Be careful of him. He's not a happy cat. He may try something desperate."

Alsa smiled at her. "Don't worry. You know me. I never take chances. Coward to the core." She leaned forward and embraced Jan, kissing her on the lips. "Take care, little one."

As Jan climbed down the ladder leading from the parapet she couldn't help bridling over Alsa's use of that embarrassing term. She knew that, as always, it had been meant affectionately but she was sensitive about her size. It hadn't been bad when she was younger; she'd believed her mother when she'd said that she would eventually catch up with her contemporaries but now that she'd reached eighteen it was clear she was not going to grow any taller. Alsa and her other friends towered over her by some four or five inches. It was galling for her to be the same height as the average man.

The sky was clear of clouds and the sun was hot as Jan and Martha cut through the vegetable gardens that were crammed into every available space between the wall and the outer buildings of Minerva. Martha, Jan noticed, kept glancing nervously upwards.

"He's not due for another two weeks," Jan said, "so relax."

"Can't help it. Sky Lord scare Martha. Don't like."

"You're not alone there," said Jan grimly. She was dreaming about the Sky Lord almost every night now. The dream took the form of her first childhood memory of the Sky Lord *Pangloth*. It had seemed to fill the entire sky above Minerva and, as it descended closer to the town, its great eyes had fixed on the five-year-old Jan as she cowered beside her mother on the official dais in the tribute square. She had screamed and screamed in terror and had tried to bury herself under her mother's kilt . . . but in the dream her mother disappeared, leaving her alone.

Jan found herself automatically scanning the empty blue sky. *I'm being as silly as Martha*, she told herself guiltily. *Pangloth* was nothing if not punctual. It was, as her mother said, all part of the Sky Lord mystique.

A shrill, shouted obscenity distracted her. They were passing near the male chimp compound and several of the male chimps had come to the bars to shout insults. Most of them were directed at Martha but a few of the more reckless chimps hurled abuse at Jan as well. Martha chittered angrily back at them, jumping up and down and waving her arms. Jan said, "Don't waste your time on them. Come on, I'm in a hurry. I badly need a wash and a cold drink." She continued on. Martha, after a final, angry riposte complete with gestures, followed her. It was a pity, Jan reflected, that the male chimps, unlike the female ones, became so unpredictable after a certain age. Not all of them, true, but enough to ensure that every adult male had to be segregated for safety's sake. It hadn't always been like that, she knew; once male chimps had remained as reliable as the females, but about forty or fifty years ago things began to change and the first signs of male chimp unpredictability had appeared.

How unlike human males, she thought. They remained totally predictable all their lives. Every man she knew was of a placid and cheerful disposition, forever being relentlessly optimistic. Even the approaching crisis with the Sky Lord didn't seem to bother them over much. Why, she wondered — not for the first time — had the Mother God made Minervan men such *uncomplicated* creatures compared to women? When She had removed the evil from their souls surely She could have made them a bit more interesting at the same time.

As if to prove her point she saw Simon ahead of her. He was one of a party of six men working on a small potato patch. Seeing her he dropped his hoe and hurried to meet her, a wide grin on his handsome and totally open face. "Jan! How good to see you! How are you?"

She felt a flush creep up her neck. Simon was the only male she'd ever made love to. The experience had been interesting but not especially exciting, yet the memory of her intimacy with him made her uncomfortable. "Hello Simon," she said brusquely. "Sorry I can't stop to talk. I've just got off the Wall and I'm dead tired."

"That's okay. Maybe we can meet in the tavern tonight." He was staring at her with such undisguised pleasure he was making her feel even more uncomfortable. She frowned. "Have you forgotten the Council meeting tonight?" she asked him irritably. "There won't be any time between it ending and your curfew."

He looked momentarily crestfallen, then the grin was back on his face. "Tomorrow, then?"

"Possibly," she said and walked past him. In two weeks Minerva might be destroyed and all he could think about was socializing. *Men . . . .*

She and Martha entered the town and hurried along the narrow, alley-like streets. There had been much more space until about four or five years ago when the inhabitants of the outer farming settlements had been finally forced to move into town after losing their long battle with the blight lands.

Now newer, and smaller, wooden dwellings jostled next to the older stone buildings, destroying the careful architectural harmony of the original town. But otherwise everything looked

15

deceptively normal. There was no visible sign of all the preparations that were feverishly taking place throughout the town.

Jan and Martha parted company when they came to a long, low building with no glass in its many windows. It was the female chimps' dormitory, housing over forty of them as well as several baby chimps of both sexes. They said their farewells and Jan continued on towards her home near the centre of Minerva.

Her mother was there when she arrived. She was hunched over a map of the town spread across the kitchen table. As Jan entered she looked up, brushed her silver-dyed hair from her face and gave Jan a weary smile. "Hello, darling. How were things on the wall today? Any problems?"

"Nothing serious." Jan leaned over her mother and kissed her on the cheek. "I'll tell you later. First I must change out of these smelly clothes." She poured a mugful of water, drank it quickly, then filled a bowl and took it into her bedroom. She wished there was still sufficient water for baths or showers but now that Minerva had been reduced to only three wells such luxuries were out of the question.

She hurriedly pulled off her thick gauntlets and then thankfully unstrapped and removed the heavy, steel breast plate. Next came the weapons belt with her short-sword, dagger and hatchet. Followed by her knee-length boots, vest, kilt and underwear. Then she washed herself all over using a wet cloth and one of her few remaining pieces of precious soap.

She didn't have to towel herself dry. It was still so hot that the moisture swiftly dried on her skin, but by the time she donned her favourite blue cotton robe she was feeling greatly refreshed.

When she returned to the kitchen her mother had put away the map but the look of strain remained on her face. As she prepared a meal of potato cakes and salad Jan told her of the day's events on the wall. She dwelt on the incident with the panther and her mother noticed her uneasiness. "What was it about the beast that troubled you so much?"

Jan frowned. "I don't know. It was as if it was an . . . ." She didn't continue. She didn't want to tell her mother that she believed the black panther was an omen. It would only upset her and make her angry. She would again accuse Jan of being weak

16

and negative, of letting her down in this time of crisis. Instead she asked Melissa how the preparations were coming along.

"On schedule. Just." She rubbed the sides of her forehead with her fingertips. "The only problem now is getting the final decision from the Council. If it goes against us tonight everything will have been a waste of time and Minerva will be doomed."

Hesitantly, Jan said, "I know you're right, mother, but all the same I wish there was another way. When I think of what's going to happen I get so, so . . . ." She stopped but it was too late.

Melissa came over to her and held her face between her hands. "Jan, you are my daughter. You have a position to uphold in Minerva. You cannot afford to be frightened. You mustn't *let* yourself be frightened. And you *must* give me your full and total support!"

"But of course I will support you, mother. You *know* I will vote on your side tonight . . . ."

Her mother's eyes were fierce. "That's not what I mean. You must be behind me *all* the time. A few words of doubt to one of your friends and those same words will be used as ammunition against me in the council hall."

"I haven't said anything to anyone, mother," protested Jan. She tried to pull free of her mother's grip. "Mother, you're *hurting* me . . . ."

Melissa released her but her eyes remained fierce. "I have to win the vote tonight otherwise all is lost. Don't you realize that?"

Jan gave a fearful nod. "Of course I do. Don't worry, mother, you'll win the vote. I know it."

"If I don't we will return here after the meeting and fall on our swords together. Better a clean death such as that than what will happen to us if Minerva falls to the *Lord Pangloth*."

Jan stared at her mother. Was she really serious about their committing suicide? She *couldn't* be! . . . But the look in her eyes told Jan that she was.

After an uncomfortable meal eaten in silence Jan retired to her room. She'd intended to have a few hours sleep but found that impossible. Finally, she got up, put on a leisure tunic and went out. It was dusk now. In two hours' time the Council meeting

17

would begin but Jan wanted to put it, and its implications, out of her mind for a while.

She went to the men's compound. She found her father in the workshop. He was soldering the seam along a sheet metal tube that was about six feet long and four inches wide. He put down the soldering iron when Jan approached his bench and smiled broadly. He was a handsome man with a wide, expressive mouth; attractive grey-blue eyes and thick black hair. Jan knew that, physically at least, she took after him more than she did Melissa. Her mother, under the silver dye of her office, was blonde and her body was long and slim, whereas Jan was short and dark like her father, with the same coloured eyes and black hair.

"Hello Jan," he said happily and reached out to hug her. She didn't resist his quick embrace even though physical contact between fathers and daughters was socially frowned upon. In fact, *any* contact between them was socially frowned upon. It was never actively discouraged — that would have gone against the constitution of Minerva—but there were subtle, hidden pressures that Jan had been aware of ever since she was a small child. She knew that her mother disapproved of her relationship with her father even though Melissa had never explicitly said so.

Her father looked closely at her. "You're tired," he told her in a gently accusing tone. "Aren't you sleeping properly?"

"I've been on wall duty. It's always hard to relax afterwards. And there's the meeting tonight . . . ."

For a few moments her father looked uncharacteristically troubled. Then he smiled reassuringly and said, "I'm sure everything will turn out for the best. Melissa and her supporters will win the day, you'll see."

Jan nodded. She wanted to tell him of Melissa's threat to have them both commit suicide if she lost the vote but decided against it. He wouldn't know how to handle such information. "Yes, I suppose so. But what then?" Jan ran her hand along the metal tube. "You really think these are going to work?"

Again he looked momentarily worried. Then he said firmly, "I have every faith in Melissa. She knows what she's doing. If she said we can destroy the Sky Lord then we will. And don't forget, we have the Mother God on our side. She will deliver us."

18

"Of course she will," said Jan, but without conviction. She knew the thought was blasphemous but she couldn't help wondering why the Mother God had waited so *long* to deliver Minerva from the reign of the Sky Lord. It had lasted over three hundred years now.

Her father put his hand on her shoulder. "Poor Jan. You're so young yet you act as if you carry the cares of the whole world on your back."

She managed to give him what she hoped looked like a brave smile. Poor father, she told him silently. I may be only eighteen and you are over eighty but you are the child. And you always will be. She envied him the security of his trusting naivety and wished she'd been born a man.

Jan told her father she had to return home and prepare for the meeting. He embraced her again and repeated his belief that everything was going to be all right.

Outside it was getting dark. As she hurried homewards she couldn't help glancing up at the night sky, expecting to see the stars blotted out by the bulk of the Sky Lord, who had somehow learned of their planned rebellion and arrived ahead of schedule to punish them.

Out in the blight lands something screamed. Whether from pain or rage she couldn't tell.

Chapter Two:

The fungus that was slowly killing Headwoman Avedon was deceptively pretty. It was a bright red growth that covered the left side of her face like peach fuzz. Jan couldn't help staring at it as Avedon, the oldest of the Headwomen and therefore leader of the Council, was summarizing Melissa's plan and the opposition faction's case against it. Jan forced herself to look away and transferred her gaze to the spectators' gallery that encircled the

19

Council chamber. She spotted Simon in the Men's section. He was staring down at her with his usual puppy-like grin fixed on his face. She sighed inwardly.

Avedon completed her summing up and handed the Speaker's baton to Headwoman Anna, who was Melissa's chief opponent. Jan's stomach gave a queasy flutter as Anna began to speak. If she managed to persuade the Council to overthrow Melissa's plan Jan didn't want to think of the consequences, yet at the same time she shared Headwoman Anna's misgivings about the proposed action against the Sky Lord.

But Jan's immediate survival was her main concern. Incredible as it seemed in the familiar surroundings of the Council chamber with its ancient murals on the walls, she knew that her mother was serious about them killing themselves that night if she lost. Jan thought about trying to drive the point of the sword, that now hung by her side, into her chest . . . No, she could never do it. It would be impossible! And when she refused what would Melissa do? Surely her mother wouldn't kill her? It was unthinkable! But these were not normal times. Anything was possible . . . .

She suppressed a shudder and tried to concentrate on Anna's words. Anna was standing in the centre of the circular floor of the chamber and pointing an accusing finger at Melissa, who glared back at her with grim eyes. ". . . And I say again that Headwoman Melissa's plan will bring about the destruction of Minerva!" Anna was saying in ringing tones. "It is foolhardy in the extreme to think we can bring down a Sky Lord, or even drive him away. If it was possible it would have been done before by either our foremothers or by some other community. No, the Sky Lords have ruled the world for nearly three and a half centuries and it's going to take more than Headwoman Melissa's fireworks to alter that fact. I say we should scrap her plan immediately, halt the preparations and destroy the rockets before it's too late!"

There was a murmur of approval from both the inner circle of seats where the Headwomen sat and from the outer circles where their daughters sat. Melissa's expression grew more grim and for a second she locked eyes with Jan, who was sitting

20

almost opposite her. Jan found herself looking into the eyes of a stranger. Her mother had vanished and in her place was someone else. Someone frightening.

Melissa raised her arm and was granted permission to speak by Avedon. She stood up and said, "We have no alternative but to follow my plan. Otherwise we will all die of starvation during the coming winter. You all know that if we meet the Sky Lord's customary quota of tribute all our grain bins will be empty. As for the so-called invincibility of the Sky Lords, that is a *myth*. We all know that some fifty or sixty years ago a Sky Lord crashed during a storm in the north lands. It was struck by lightning. Well, we will strike *Lord Pangloth* with our *own* lightning!"

This brought Melissa her own murmur of approval and Jan saw several heads nodding in agreement throughout the chamber. But Anna waved the Speaker's baton, which gave her the right to interject whenever she wanted. "We don't know for *sure* that ever happened. It was just a rumour spread by travellers. But even if it did happen it was through the grace of the Mother God, who used her natural forces to destroy the Sky Lord. How can you know that your rockets will do *Lord Pangloth* any harm?"

Melissa turned to Avedon. "Permission for Sister Helen to address the chamber?"

Avedon nodded and Melissa then gestured to Helen, who was sitting in the front row of the gallery. Helen rose, looking uncomfortable. Small, though not as short as Jan, and wiry, she was in charge of the foundry and had been instrumental in making Melissa's plan reality. She knew much arcane lore, including, it was suspected, too much about the forbidden and evil sciences of Man. As a result she was not popular, but this never seemed to bother her.

"Tell the Council again what I have tried to tell them on past occasions," commanded Melissa. "Perhaps hearing it from you, the expert, will finally convince the doubters amongst us."

Helen swallowed nervously and, in a thin voice, said, "The Sky Lords are kept aloft, as you know, by gases which are lighter than air. There are two such gases — hydrogen and helium. Once the Sky Lords were filled entirely with helium because it is safest. It is an *inert* gas whereas hydrogen is flammable. Over the years the

21

Sky Lords have lost much of their helium, through natural leakage, accidents and so on, and haven't been able to replace it. They've been forced to use hydrogen as a substitute in many of their gas cells. Hydrogen, unlike helium, can be manufactured relatively easily by means of a process called 'electrolysis' which is — "

Melissa cut her short with a wave of her hand. "Never mind the details," she said. "What we want to know is whether the Sky Lords contain a great deal of the dangerous gas."

Helen's face went bright red. "Uh, yes, Headwoman Melissa, I would say that all the Sky Lords now contain much more hydrogen than helium."

"Which makes them very vulnerable to fire?"

"Very vulnerable."

"So our rockets with their fire bombs in their tips will inflict serious damage?"

Helen cleared her throat and said, loudly, "I believe we stand a very good chance of destroying the *Lord Pangloth* completely."

An excited murmur spread through the chamber. But it stopped when Anna interjected with, "Can you be sure they haven't found a way of making the safer gas? The helium? If they can make the other gas why can't they do the same with the helium. Or maybe they have invented an entirely new gas?"

"No," said Helen firmly with a shake of her head. "That's impossible. Scientifically impossible. If you'd let me explain — "

This time Avedon herself interrupted her. "Enough talk of Man's science in this chamber. We will take your word for it. Sit down, Sister Helen."

She sat down hurriedly, her face redder than ever. Anna took advantage of the moment to declare loudly, "*Man's science . . .* that is our problem here. Melissa's plan is tainted with it. *Rockets!*" She spat out the word contemptuously. "Such weapons are not only against the constitution but are blasphemous. The Mother God will turn her face from us if we use Man's weapons!"

"The same thing was said when we started using the flame throwers but there is no sign we have affronted the Mother God," said Melissa.

"Really? If that it so how is it that our crop-lands have been overrun by the blight? What good did those weapons do us?" asked Anna.

"If we hadn't used them the fungus would be growing all over the town by now. The flame throwers are the only effective weapon against the spores. Not to mention against many of the larger beasts that threaten our perimeter in increasing numbers."

"Yet still Minerva is faced with destruction," persisted Anna.

Melissa sighed. "If we can defeat the Sky Lord we will have enough grain to see us through the winter. Perhaps by then we will have managed to reclaim some of our land from the blight. But if we succumb to the Sky Lord our fate is sealed."

"We could try talking to the Sky Lord. We could explain our situation. It will, after all, be obvious to him from the air!" cried Anna. "We offer him, say, only a third of the expected tribute and promise to make it up to him later. We throw ourselves on his mercy."

Melissa gave a bitter laugh. "When has a Sky Lord ever shown mercy? You know how they regard us land dwellers. Literally as the *scum of the earth*. We are less than human to them. Just a part of the blight left by the Gene Wars. Better to ask mercy from one of the giant lizards. No, our only chance is to burn the *Lord Pangloth* out of the sky. It is time that we, the sisters of Minerva, freed ourselves from the reign of Men!"

That did it. Jan could physically feel the tide of emotion in the chamber turn irrevocably in Melissa's favour. She had won. And, a short time later, the vote confirmed it. A count of hands gave her a majority of twenty-three. Jan relaxed. She was not going to die. Not *yet*, anyway. She had at least another two weeks.

The two weeks went by with frightening speed. Jan had wanted to savour them but there had been no time. Melissa had kept her, and everyone else, working to exhaustion on the final preparations. Jan had been put in charge of one of the many three-woman groups that would fire the rockets. They practised the firing routine endlessly, positioning the rockets in their stands, removing the camouflaged netting that concealed the launchers and pretending to light the fuses before taking cover behind a makeshift barrier.

The rockets were, according to Helen, fairly simple devices. They were propelled by gunpowder and were capable, as the series of test firings had proved, of reaching a height of about a thousand feet. When they hit something a plunger was depressed, which activated a chemical fuse. This set off a charge that ignited the alcohol in the nose cone and spread it over a wide area. No one asked, publically anyway, how Helen came to possess the knowledge to make gunpowder, a substance that was high on the proscribed list. Jan suspected that Helen had probably invented the stuff from scratch.

Even though Melissa was now theoretically in charge of Minerva Anna kept up her campaign of opposition almost to the very end. The most significant confrontation between them occurred at the start of the second week. Anna, her daughter Tasma, Headwoman Jean and Adam, spokesman for the men, appeared that evening at Melissa's house. Melissa admitted them with ill grace and told Jan to fetch drinks. Anna said not to bother as this was far from being a social call, so Jan remained in the hallway.

"Is it true," Anna asked Melissa accusingly, "that you told Avedon you want the men armed?"

"It is true," said Melissa, and waited.

"Is there no limit to your blasphemy?" cried Anna. "For a man to carry a weapon within the borders of Minerva is against everything we hold sacred. The founding sisters of Minerva must be crying with shame in heaven!"

"The founding sisters of Minerva were realists," replied Melissa. "And so am I. We're going to need everyone available to defend Minerva next Monday. Even if we set the *Lord Pangloth* on fire there may still be time for units of Sky Warriors to descend upon us."

"Better that than to offend the Mother God in this fashion!" cried Anna. She turned to Adam, who was trying to keep behind Jean and Tasma. "Tell Headwoman Melissa that you, as the spokesman for all the men, refuse to bear arms."

Reluctantly, Adam emerged from between Jean and Tasma.

24

He regarded Melissa worriedly. "It's not so much that we refuse, Headwoman Melissa, it's that arming us would be a waste of time. The men of Minerva, as you well know, are not fighters. The Mother God saw to that. What good would we be in a battle with Sky Warriors?"

"You're going to find out," Melissa told him brusquely. "When a Sky Warrier comes at you with the intention of splitting open your skull with an axe or skewering you on a sword you will have the choice of trying to stop him with a weapon of your own or letting him do what he wants to you. Don't expect the sisters to protect you. We will be too busy defending ourselves so it's up to you. The choice is yours."

Adam had gone pale. "But . . . but all our lives we have had it instilled in us that it is absolutely forbidden to touch a weapon or to use a tool in a threatening way. You can't suddenly expect us to overcome such training."

"He's right," said Anna. The other two women nodded.

Melissa shrugged. "All I know is that I have the authority in these circumstances, according to the constitution, to take whatever extraordinary measures I see fit to ensure the survival of Minerva and that I am ordering the distribution of weapons to every male over the age of twelve. Whether they use them or not is up to the individual himself. And that is that."

Anna scowled and opened her mouth to protest but obviously thought better of it. With an angry swirl of her robe she headed for the front door. The others followed her, with Adam bringing up the rear. He was the only one to mutter an apologetic "Good night" as they went out.

When they'd gone Jan said to her mother, "Do you really think any of the men will fight?"

Melissa shrugged again. "Some may do. Self-preservation is a strong drive. We shall see. But I'm hoping it won't be necessary. With any luck the *Lord Pangloth* will be destroyed before the Sky Warriors can be deployed."

"If some of them *do* fight," said Jan slowly, "then they might develop a taste for it, mightn't they? We'd never be able to trust them again."

"Superstition," said Melissa. She walked out of the hallway

25

and into the front room. She sat wearily on a puff-ball sack. Jan followed her inside.

"But isn't that the reason they've always been forbidden to handle weapons?" she asked her mother. "For fear of awakening the taint of the Old Men that still dwells within them?"

Not looking at her Melissa said, "The Mother God changed them for good. They can't revert back."

"Then why the law against weapons? Why the separate compound? Why the curfew? Why are we still afraid of them?"

"Tradition. And that is how it should be. Even the men of Minerva, changed as they are, cannot expiate the sins their ancestors committed against our foremothers for untold millennia, or the sins that the Sky Lord *Pangloth* commits against us now. That is why the men must worship in the Cell of Atonement in the cathedral every Sunday. They lost the right to be our equals a long time ago and can never retain it. Now go to your room and leave me be. I have much to think about."

Jan did as she was told. As she sat cleaning her sword for the third time that day she pondered what would happen to the men after Monday if Melissa's plan to destroy the Sky Lord was successful. Would there be a movement among the sisters to expel the men completely from Minerva? It was highly likely, and highly likely that she herself would support such a movement, but at the same time she didn't like to think of her father being banished from Minerva. Or even Simon, for that matter. And what would the future of Minerva be without any men at all? The next breeding time was less than three years away . . . .

That Sunday — the day before the coming of the Sky Lord — the cathedral was packed with worshippers. None prayed harder to the symbol of the Mother God, carved from the trunk of an ancient and sacred oak tree, than Jan. She prayed that she would wake up the following morning and find that everything was back to the way it had been when she was younger; when the crop-lands hadn't been overrun by the blight, when the rooftops of the town were not concealing weapons to be used against the Sky Lord . . . but most of all she prayed that the cold and ruthless woman that Melissa had become would vanish and that her mother would return.

Jan did not sleep that night. At first she spent the time restlessly pacing about the empty house — Melissa was out conducting a final inspection of the rocket positions — looking and touching familiar household objects in an attempt to convince herself that everything was normal, and would *continue* to be normal, even after tomorrow. Then, at around two in the morning, she heard a distant bellowing followed by a thunderous crash. There were shouts, screams and then came the strident clanging of one of the wall alarms. She hastily buckled on her armour and weapons belt and, taking one of the cold light lamps with her, hurried outside.

The narrow street was already filling up as other sisters rushed out of their homes and headed towards the source of the alarm. Jan joined in the rush. As she ran she speculated on the nature of the emergency. From the sound of the crash it was obviously serious — one of the big reptiles perhaps. She hoped the wall hadn't been breached. Since her last tour of duty she hadn't given much thought to the dangers beyond the perimeter defences, being too preoccupied with other worries. It would be ironic if Minerva were to be overrun by the denizens of the blight lands before the arrival of the Sky Lord.

She gave a start as something touched her bare thigh. She looked and saw that it was Martha. The chimp, her tool bag secure around her waist, was keeping pace beside her. "Martha, you scared me."

"Sorry . . . Mistress . . . ." She panted as she ran, using all four limbs. "You know why . . . alarm?"

"No. Probably a lizard. A big one."

Jan was proved right. When they arrived at the wall they saw that the massive west gate had been flattened and lying in the splintered wreckage was the monstrous form of one of the giant reptiles. It was tangled in the steel mesh from the upper barrier and it was this that had obviously prevented it from getting any further into Minerva. Cross-bow bolts protruded from its body but it continued to jerk and writhe. Jan saw that it was of the type

27

that walked on two legs like a human — a type noted for its ferocity.

She pushed through the growing crowd, looking for Alsa, who she knew was on wall duty tonight. She spotted her friend with a group of guards. They were gathered round something on the ground.

As Jan drew closer she saw it was a body covered by a blood stained robe. "Who is it?" she asked Alsa fearfully. Alsa turned and gave her a dazed look. She didn't seem to recognize Jan at first, then her expression cleared and she said, "Oh, it's you, little one," then turned her attention back to the body on the ground.

The dying reptile gave a tremendous thump with its tail, causing Jan to jump with alarm. As she turned she saw one of the wall guards step dangerously close to the beast and put a bolt into one of its eyes. It gave a convulsive shudder and went quiet, though its chest continued to rise and fall. Jan turned back to Alsa. "Who is it?" she asked again.

"Carla," said Alsa. She leaned down and pulled back the blood-sodden robe a short way. Jan felt her stomach turn over as she looked at what lay beneath the robe. Carla's one remaining eye seemed to stare at her from her ruined face. Jan was suddenly filled with the irrational conviction that Carla was still alive, even in that terrible condition, and could feel everything that had happened to her body. Jan wanted to run screaming back to her house and hide under her bed covers until the world returned to normal — returned to what it had been like when she was a child, when she didn't have to see things like this . . . when she didn't have to know such things even happened. She had actually taken a step backwards before she managed to regain some control of herself. You're the daughter of Headwoman Melissa, she told herself, you can't disgrace yourself!

"We were together on the gate," Alsa said as, to Jan's relief, she covered up the thing that had been Carla again. "I jumped clear just in time but she stayed at her post. She was crushed under the collapsing gate when the lizard broke through."

"What happened?" Jan asked her. "What made it charge the gate that way? The big lizards have been known to blunder into the wall occasionally but none has ever acted like this before."

28

Alsa massaged the side of her face. Jan saw that a large purple bruise was forming there. "I'm not sure . . . but I think it was *chasing* something."

"Chasing something?"

"I only got a glimpse but I think it was a cat. A big cat. Black. It was running just ahead of the lizard, then it sprung to one side and just disappeared."

"A big cat?" said Jan. "A panther?"

"It could have been. I told you I only got a glimpse."

Jan remembered the day the panther had asked for sanctuary. It had been at this very gate. And Carla had been with her at the time.

Giving the reptile a wide berth Jan went to the gaping hole in the shattered gate and peered out into the darkness beyond. "Careful," warned a nearby guard. "No telling what's been attracted into the vicinity by all the noise, not to mention the smell of blood."

Jan ignored her. She was intently scanning the trees for any sign of movement. And then she saw the eyes. They were staring down at her from a high branch, glowing green in the reflected light from the many lamps, but the panther's body remained completely invisible.

"Give me that!" snarled Jan, snatching the cross-bow from the hands of the startled guard. She raised the weapon towards the branch where she'd seen the eyes, but they were gone now.

"What's wrong? What's out there?" asked the guard.

Jan didn't answer. She was listening for a sound — any sound that would give her an indication of the panther's position — but all she heard was the rumbling of distant thunder. Then, on the horizon, she saw lightning flicker.

After a long pause she handed the cross-bow back to the guard and muttered, "There's a storm coming."

29

Chapter Three:

The storm had come and gone but the sky was still grey with low cloud. It was cold too, and Jan pulled her cloak tighter around her as she stared anxiously from the rooftop into the town square below. The square was the traditional place where the Sky Lord picked up his tribute and now, an hour before noon, its perimeter was piled high with bales. Except that Jan knew on this occasion that the bales contained not grain but sand and straw.

Melissa and the other Headwomen were gathered in front of the dais where, in the past, they sat to give group obeisance to the representatives of the Sky Lord. This time the dais would provide the signal for the launch of the attack when Melissa sent a red flare into the air.

Jan looked around. People were visible on many rooftops but this was normal. A visit from the Sky Lord customarily brought out many spectators; the *Lord Pangloth* may have been loathed and feared by the sisters of Minerva but there was no denying that the spectacle he presented was hard to resist.

She looked at her watch. The Sky Lord was due at noon. Less than an hour to go. At her side Martha fidgeted nervously, toying with her tool kit. There was no reason for the chimp to be on the rooftop but she pleaded with Jan to be allowed to stay with her and Jan had relented. Martha, bedraggled from the rain, looked very unhappy indeed and Jan gave her a reassuring rub behind the ears. Martha made a half-hearted sound of appreciation then said, "Martha scared, Mistress. Very scared."

"Don't worry," Jan told her automatically. "There's no need to be. Everything is going to be all right."

"The men-chimps say not. The men-chimps say Sky Lord make Minerva no more. Say Sky Warriors come down, kill sisters . . . *rape* sisters . . . ."

"Shush!" cried Jan, shocked. It was the second time she had heard that blasphemous word this morning. "You know it is not permitted to say that word, Martha!"

Martha hung her head. "Sorry, Mistress."

Jan sighed. "Just don't do it again." She still hadn't recovered from the first occasion she'd heard that blasphemy earlier in the morning, nor from the shattering circumstances surrounding its utterance.

It had been just before dawn when Melissa came home. Jan was in the kitchen toying with her breakfast while at the same time trying to erase the ghastly image of Carla's remains from her inner eye. What little appetite she'd had vanished completely when she saw the expression on her mother's face. Melissa looked more exhausted than anyone Jan had ever seen before but at the same time she wore an expression of terrible resolution. It was the sort of look, thought Jan fearfully, that a corpse, brought back to life for some unholy purpose, would wear.

Melissa stared down silently at Jan for several moments then placed a small metal tube on the table in front of her. It was around three inches long and about an inch in diameter. Jan looked at it and then at her mother's disturbing face. "What's that?"

"A fire bomb. Helen made it. She made several. She's very clever," said Melissa in a dead voice. She picked up the device and showed Jan one end of it. "See this section? You twist it in the direction of the arrow and thirty seconds later it will explode."

Jan took the cylinder and studied it. She tried to look impressed, as Melissa obviously expected her to be, but couldn't comprehend what possible use such a small weapon could be against the Sky Lord. She held it out for Melissa to take back but Melissa shook her head.

"That's yours. You will keep it with you from now on."

Jan frowned. "But what will I do with it. I mean, do I *throw* it at the Sky Lord or what?"

Melissa gave a sigh that was more like a shudder. "If things go wrong this day and we lose the battle then that little bomb will be our final chance of achieving vengeance. If you are still alive you will let yourself be captured by the Sky Warriors and taken up to

31

the Sky Lord. Then, at the first opportunity you get, you will place that device in a spot where it will cause the greatest damage to the Sky Lord, preferably next to an area containing the inflammable gas, hydrogen."

Jan's mouth dropped open with astonishment as she listened to Melissa's words. "Mother, you can't be *serious*!"

"Of course I'm serious, you little fool!" snapped Melissa, making Jan flinch.

"But I couldn't do that!" she protested, her mind reeling at the implications of what Melissa had said. "I could never let myself be taken alive by the Sky Warriors! It's unthinkable! And the idea of going up into the Sky Lord itself . . . ." She shook her head.

"The choice is not yours," said Melissa coldly. "I am *ordering* you to do as I say. If you survive the battle, and I want you to take great pains to ensure that you *do*, you will surrender. You *must*, do you understand?"

Jan started to tremble. She looked again at the small cylinder she held in her hand. "It's ridiculous," she said in a weak voice. "Even if I were taken up to the Sky Lord how could I hope to destroy it with something as small as this?"

"Hopefully you won't be alone. I told you, Helen has made several of these bombs. They have been given to selected individuals, of whom you are one."

"But why me, mother? Why *me*?" she cried.

"That should be obvious. You are my daughter. If my attempt to destroy the Sky Lord fails today it is crucial that *my* daughter be involved in our final act of rebellion. You will be avenging not only Minerva but your mother's honour."

Jan looked into her mother's eyes and saw that there was no hope of reasoning with her. But just as despair began to overwhelm her a possible way out occurred to her. "Mother," she said slowly, "even if I *were* able to survive the retribution of the Sky Lord if our attack fails today, and even if I were taken up into the Sky Lord as a prisoner, how could I possibly conceal this from the Sky Warriors?" She held up the bomb. "You know how thoroughly the Sky Warriors search our bales of grain before they're hoisted into the Sky Lord. They would be sure to find this in my clothing."

A tic had appeared in Melissa's left cheek. She said, "It won't be in your clothing, it will be in *you*."

"You expect me to *swallow* this? But — "

"Don't be obtuse!" snapped Melissa. "A second's thought will tell you how you will conceal it within you."

Jan almost dropped the cylinder, but remembering that it was a bomb managed to keep hold of it. A wave of disgust spread through her as she stared at the object, seeing it in a new light. "I couldn't . . . ."

"You *will*, like all the others who have been chosed to try and smuggle these devices on board the Sky Lord. It's doubtful that the Sky Warriors would think to carry out such an intimate search but let us pray none of them tries to rape you."

"Mother!" gasped Jan, profoundly shocked at hearing the obscenity of obscenities spoken aloud.

Melissa leaned forward and gripped her shoulders hard. "Jan, you can't afford to be squeamish. You must face reality. This is war. Things that are better left unsaid, or not even contemplated, in normal times *must* be faced up to now. You are no longer a child!"

"And you are no longer my mother." She had said these words without meaning to, but they had come out of her mouth even as they formed within her mind. She was not surprised when Melissa's hand caught her a stinging blow across the cheek. Tears filled her eyes. She wanted to apologize; to beg her mother's forgiveness, but now her mouth wouldn't work at all.

"Go to the bathroom and do as I have instructed, *now*," said Melissa in a voice that trembled with either barely suppressed fury or barely controlled pain. Without a word Jan got up from the table and went into the bathroom.

She could feel the bomb now as she stood anxiously on the rooftop of the tavern; it was uncomfortable and heavy, and it made her feel sick. She had been tempted to throw the thing away as soon as Melissa had gone but felt so guilty over what she had said to her mother she couldn't bring herself to disobey her. Even now, as she watched her mother's distant figure in front of the dais, she wanted to rush down to her and ask her forgiveness.

33

Instead she squared her shoulders and turned to face her rocket team, which consisted of Paula, a wall guard, Lisa, who worked in the bakery, and Peter, a man. The latter was still looking very sheepish about the hatchet he was obliged to carry in his belt. Jan had mixed feelings about the weapon; she doubted that Peter would be capable of using it and would therefore be useless if it came to hand to hand fighting, but at the same time the idea that he *might* be capable of using it profoundly disturbed her.

She gave them what she hoped looked like the calm and confident smile of someone relaxed in their authority and said, "Well, do we all know what we're supposed to be doing, or shall we have another run-through?"

Paula answered for the others. "I don't think it's necessary, Mistress. Besides, it might not be wise to remove the camouflage at this late stage. The Sky Lord might be early."

Jan winced mentally. The guard was right and had shown her up in front of the others. Yet more proof that she was unsuited for command. If her mother hadn't been Melissa she'd probably be a weaver or a seamstress instead of walking around in armour pretending to be a warrior.

She nodded benignly at Paula. "I take your point. The *Lord Pangloth* has always been punctual in the past but you can't be too careful." Then she went and made a show of inspecting the rockets in their earthenware launch tubes under the fabric screen, which had been painted to resemble part of the roof when seen from the air. When the signal was given the camouflage would be removed, the wooden frame supporting the launch tubes put into a vertical position and then the fuses would be lit . . . .

Behind her she heard the hatch in the roof being opened. She turned and saw Alsa emerge on to the roof. "What are *you* doing here?" she exclaimed in surprise. "You should be at your post." Jan knew that Alsa's launching position was near the alcohol-producing plant on the other side of the town.

Alsa smiled at her. The bruise that Jan had seen forming earlier in the morning was now a purple stain that stretched from her right temple to her jaw. "I had to come and see you, little one. To wish you luck, to tell you to be careful." She embraced Jan and kissed her.

Jan let herself enjoy the comfort of those familiar arms. Alsa had been her first lover and she remained the closest of her friends despite her often patronizing manner towards Jan of late. But then, as their kiss lingered, Jan felt herself losing control. She was in danger of bursting into tears; of clinging to Alsa and begging her not to go . . . .

Jan disengaged herself from Alsa's embrace and took a step backwards. She forced herself to smile at her, though she could feel her lower lip trembling. "Be careful yourself, Alsa. And when it's all over let's meet downstairs for a drink."

"It's a date, little one. But only on condition we have the drink in one of the private rooms. We've been apart too long."

"I'd like that," Jan said, sincerely. She and Alsa hadn't been lovers for nearly a year now but suddenly all of Jan's old sexual feelings towards Alsa had come back with a rush. Her need for Alsa was positively intense. She couldn't wait for the next few hours to pass and for the moment to arrive when their bodies would be entwined beneath the covers of one of the tavern's large and cosy beds. But even as she relished this thought, a cold, dispassionate voice, coming from a dark recess of her mind, was saying: "You will never see Alsa again."

Masking the anguish that this premonition caused her she smiled at Alsa and said, "Until later then. Take care."

Alsa gave her an affectionate kiss on the cheek. "You take care too, my little one."

As Jan watched Alsa climb back down through the hatch she couldn't help wondering if she was also carrying a hard and heavy cylinder of death within her.

It was one minute to twelve. Everyone was looking west towards the range of low hills on the horizon. It was from behind these hills that the *Lord Pangloth* always appeared but today, because of the low cloud and the showers of rain that were falling on the blight lands between Minerva and the hills, it was difficult even to distinguish their outline.

Jan fiddled nervously with the hilt of her sword as she peered in the direction of the hills. Merciful Mother God, she prayed silently, send us a miracle. Don't let the Sky Lord appear. Let him be gone forever, struck down by lightning in the storm like that other Sky Lord of years ago . . . .

Twelve o'clock.

There was still no sign of the *Lord Pangloth*.

And then Jan felt a strange sensation. The air around her suddenly felt different. It wasn't like a breeze but more as if the air had abruptly become *heavier*.

Instinctively, she looked up. "Mother God . . ." she murmured.

The *Lord Pangloth* was directly overhead. He was descending through the layer of low, grey cloud. As his vast bulk emerged from the cloud it swirled around him in agitated streamers. Seeing him made Jan feel as insignificant and helpless as when she'd first seen him as a little girl. *How can we possibly destroy something that is so big*? she asked herself despairingly.

"Mother God, save us . . . ." That came from Lisa. The others were looking up as well. From neighbouring rooftops came similar exclamations of surprise and fear. Martha huddled herself in a corner of the roof and wailed.

There was something very wrong, thought Jan, as she watched the *Lord Pangloth* continue to descend. His mile-long body began to fill the sky, blotting out everything else. Why had he changed his traditional way of arrival? Why hadn't he come from the west as usual? Did he suspect what they planned to do?

As he came ever lower Jan was gripped by an atavistic fear that she'd experienced before on these occasions. It seemed that the *Lord Pangloth* was going to settle right on top of the town, crushing them and their buildings under his weight. Jan fought to control a growing sense of panic. Martha's high-pitched keening didn't help.

The *Lord Pangloth* stopped descending. He remained suspended some fifteen hundred feet above Minerva, his great eyes staring down. As usual Jan believed they were staring straight at her.

There was a loud hiss, then a crackling sound. Then a voice that boomed like thunder began to speak:"I AM THE LORD PANGLOTH, MASTER OF THE SKIES AND ALL THAT LIES BENEATH MY SHADOW. SEE ME AND TREMBLE! (*Click!*) YOU ARE MY SUBJECTS TO DO WITH AS I PLEASE! I COULD DESTROY YOU LIKE THE EARTHWORMS THAT YOU ARE BUT I AM MERCIFUL.(*Click!*) IN RETURN FOR THE TRIBUTE YOU ARE ABOUT TO OFFER UP TO ME I SHALL SPARE YOUR LIVES. THEREFORE MAKE THE SIGNAL THAT YOU ARE READY TO OFFER UP THAT WHICH IS RIGHTFULLY MINE. (*Click! Crackle!*) FAIL TO DO SO AND MY RETRIBUTION WILL BE SWIFT AND TERRIBLE . . . TERRIBLE . . . TERRIBLE . . . ." The voice stopped abruptly.

Jan frowned. *Lord Pangloth*'s ultimatum was the same as usual but the clicks and crackling sounds, as well as the repetition of the last word, were new. These additional changes from the normal pattern of events bothered her as well.

She tore her gaze away from the Sky Lord's frightening mass and watched Avedon light the fire on the dais that was the signal to the *Lord Pangloth* that the tribute was ready to be picked up. Her heart began to pound. Not long now.

As the smoke rose from the symbolic pyre she returned her gaze to the *Lord Pangloth*. She tried to remember what her mother had told her, that first time when she was a little girl: "Don't be scared, dear. It's only an airship. A left-over toy from the Age of Man's Wickedness. It looks big and powerful but there's hardly anything inside it — just a few men and a lot of gas."

It's only an airship. Jan repeated those words to herself. But in vain. The *Lord Pangloth* may have been only an airship but it was an airship over five thousand feet long and nearly a thousand feet wide. Jan knew its dimensions only too well. And telling herself that its awesome bulk was a kind of illusion — that it was mostly filled with gas — didn't help. It had when she was a child but no longer.

An airship? No, it was a floating city. A floating *fortified* city. She could see the barrels of the death machines called cannons protruding from various points of the hull like stubble on a giant's chin. She could see rows of windows, decks, hatchways — and the barrel-shaped engines, each one the size of a wheat silo, which made a powerful, disturbing hum that was almost like the rumble of distant thunder. How many sky people lived within that monstrous flying machine? No one knew for sure. A thousand, perhaps. Or even two thousand.

The sound from the *Lord Pangloth*'s engines changed pitch. Jan saw the engines suspended beneath the great stabilizing fins at the rear swivel round on their axis . . . .

The Sky Lord stopped descending. Jan estimated it was now at an altitude of only six hundred or so feet. Well within the range of the rockets. She glanced down at the dais again. Any moment now.

"Get ready," she told her team. Her voice sounded like a stranger's. "Martha, shut up."

"Here it comes!" cried Lisa. Jan looked up. A large section of the *Lord Pangloth*'s hull had become detached and was being lowered towards the ground on cables attached to its sides. Jan knew that it was the 'tribute' cradle. She also knew that it would contain a squad of armed Sky Warriors whose job it was to search all the bales of grain before they were hoisted upwards. She could see one of them leaning over the rail and looking down. The cradle appeared to be dead on target for the centre of the square even though it was swaying about in a stiff breeze that had sprung up. Jan hoped the wind wouldn't affect the rockets. It certainly had no apparent affect on the Sky Lord, who hung rock-steady above the town. She guessed its many engines served to compensate for all but the strongest of winds.

The descending cradle was now only about a hundred and fifty feet above the ground. The Sky Warriors, looking like giant crustaceans in their layered, carapace-like black armour, could be plainly seen. Jan glanced anxiously at the dais. What was her mother waiting for? Had she lost her nerve . . .?

There was a flash on the dais and then something was rising into the air trailing red smoke. For a few seconds Jan just stared at it, her body paralysed, then she managed to turn and scream at her team: "Now! *Now*!. . ."

They ripped away the camouflaged cover and hauled the launching frame upright while Jan worked frantically at her flint wheel, trying to get a good spark. "Ready, Mistress!" cried

Paula. Just then Jan succeeded in setting light to her taper, to her intense relief. Shielding the flame with her hand she knelt down at the base of the tubes and applied the taper to each fuse in turn. When she was sure all three were spluttering she yelled, "Take cover!"

The others, including Martha, were already huddled behind the wooden barrier at the far end of the roof as Jan skidded round its corner and flung herself flat.

For a few long moments nothing at all, and then came a deafening *whoosh*!

As the sound faded away Jan, ignoring the sparks that were showering down on the roof, got to her feet and looked up. The air seemed filled with rockets as they rose from every part of Minerva. Hundreds and hundreds of them, and all heading directly for the Sky Lord.

She saw two of the rockets hit the bottom of the cargo cradle. They exploded and suddenly the cradle was on fire.

We're going to win! she told herself joyfully. *We really are*!

Chapter Four:

They made their final stand at the hospital.

Partly because it was the only sizable building in Minerva still more or less intact but mainly because it was where all the survivors had automatically headed after the bombing.

Strategically, it was an ideal place to stage a last stand, if the word 'ideal' could be applied in such circumstances. It was set in its own grounds — one of the few buildings in Minerva to enjoy that luxury — and surrounded by a low wall; both hang-overs from the bad old days when quarantines had been necessary.

Altogether there were eighty-six Minervans within the hospital and its grounds. Forty-seven of them were suffering serious injuries and were unable to fight. Of the remaining thirty-nine, all of whom bore injuries of varying degrees of severity, eleven were men who couldn't be depended upon to fight. That left twenty-eight women, of whom only eighteen were professional warriors. One of the latter was Jan.

She stood at the hospital wall watching the Sky Warriors approach up the avenue. She held a loaded cross-bow. Blood was running down the side of her face from a gash on her head and there were lacerations on her arms and legs. Her ears were still ringing from the explosion that had sent her falling through the roof of the tavern, so she didn't hear the warning yelled by the woman next to her. It was only when the woman yanked sharply on her elbow that she turned and saw that everyone else had taken cover behind the low wall. Slowly Jan sunk to her knees and rested the cross-bow on top of the wall. Everything seemed unreal. So much had happened during the last hour that her senses had become overloaded. The series of shocks had left her numb and feeling disconnected from what was going on around her. She felt no fear as the front line of advancing Sky Warriors halted and aimed their long-barrelled, single-shot rifles at the Minervan defenders. Jan knew about guns and was well aware of their destructive power but it was only when the woman beside her gave her arm another hard jerk that she lowered her head beneath the wall.

The sharp *cracks* of the rifles penetrated the buzzing in her ears. Chips of stone exploded from the top of the wall less than a foot away from Jan's head. Further along the wall she saw a woman clutch at her face with her hands and fall backwards.

"Now!" yelled someone very close by. Jan remembered what she was supposed to do. She raised her head above the wall again and picked up the cross-bow. The Sky Warriors were approaching at a run. Many had attached knives to the ends of their rifles. They were yelling as they came. Jan placed the butt of the cross-bow against her shoulder and picked out a target. She waited. The armour worn by the Sky Warriors wasn't made of metal but it was strong enough to deflect a cross-bow bolt unless it was fired at very close range.

. When her target was about twenty feet away she pulled the trigger. The cross-bow twanged and kicked her shoulder and her target was slammed backwards. *I've just killed another human being for the first time in my life*, she told herself but the realization drew no emotional response. Then she saw that her target wasn't dead after all. He was writhing about on the ground, the feathered end of the bolt protruding from his left shoulder. His blood looked very bright against his black armour.

There were several Sky Warriors on the ground along with Jan's victim, many of them not moving at all. Their companions were already retreating back down to the avenue. The women behind the wall gave a brief cheer. Someone yelled out something that was obviously a rude comment about the Warriors, though Jan couldn't make out the words, and a few women actually laughed.

Jan thought that was very strange as she mechanically reloaded her cross-bow. More and more Sky Warriors were pouring into the avenue and she knew there was no hope of stopping their second charge. She looked round for the Sky Lord. It was now some two or three miles to the east of the town, hanging low in the sky like some vast fish. A break in the clouds illuminated the silvery, scale-like objects that covered the upper half of its hull and added to its fish-like appearance. The one great eye she could see at the bow seemed to have an anticipatory gleam within it. She wished she could fire the bolt from her cross-bow all the way to that terrible eye and blind it forever. But even if she had such a powerful weapon she knew the bolt would never reach the Sky Lord, just as none of the rockets had.

After the bombs had fallen and Jan had been in the square trying to find Melissa she had stumbled into Helen, who appeared to be walking aimlessly in circles. She had lost her right arm below the elbow and though someone had tied a tourniquet tightly around her upper arm the stump still dripped blood. She was clearly in shock but that did not prevent Jan from seizing her by the shoulders and shaking her roughly.

"What happened?" cried Jan, then choked as another cloud of thick black smoke came drifting across the square. On all sides the buildings were burning and the heat from the crackling fires came in waves whenever the smoke briefly cleared. When Jan

41

got her breath back she again shook Helen. "What *happened*, damn you?"

But the only response from Helen was a blank look. Jan let her go and she staggered away into the smoke. Jan gave a sob of frustration. It wasn't fair. She had to know what had gone wrong when victory had seemed so certain . . . .

The rockets had behaved perfectly, with the exception of a few that had spun off out of control shortly after take-off. But these few duds, which Helen had calculated for, didn't matter, for the majority of the rockets were clearly going to hit their target.

And then, when the first of the rockets was less than a hundred feet or so from the hull of the Sky Lord, everything went wrong.

Beams of light — very bright beams of turquoise light — flashed out from numerous points on the Sky Lord's hull and every one of them made contact with a rocket. That was the really uncanny thing, that every beam of light touched a rocket. What kind of people were they who could aim weapons — for it quickly became clear that the beams of light *were* weapons — with such unerring accuracy at moving targets? For even as Jan was asking herself this question the rockets exploded. Each and every one of them — instantaneously.

A glowing fire-ball marked the position of each rocket and then she saw burning debris start to fall from the sky. The Sky Lord, meanwhile, had started to ascend. The loading cradle, which was still burning fiercely, was no longer being winched upwards. As she watched she saw a Sky Warrior, enveloped in flames, jump over the side.

"What happened? What were those lights?" asked a stunned voice. It was Paula. The question served to snap Jan out of her paralysis. "Reload the tubes!" she orded briskly. "Quick, before the *Lord Pangloth* is out of range."

As her team hurriedly prepared another three rockets for firing nearby whooshing sounds told Jan that others had reacted more quickly than her. She glanced down towards the dais but there was so much smoke about from the rockets' exhausts she couldn't make it out. She wondered what was going through her mother's mind at this instant.

Something crashed down on to the roof beside her and she

jumped back with a cry of pain as her left leg was spattered with sparks. She saw that it was the burning tail section of a rocket. She used it to light her taper then told the others to take cover as she applied the flame to the fuses . . . .

As she'd feared it was all a waste of time. Again the turquoise beams of light flashed down from the *Lord Pangloth* and again the rockets, far fewer this time, disappeared into balls of fire too far from their target to do any harm.

The Sky Lord continued to rise. As it did so the burning loading cradle was cut loose — either that or the cables supporting it had burnt through — and it fell, trailing sparks, to earth. Jan watched it crash behind some houses on the other side of the square.

For a time after that, perhaps five minutes, nothing happened. The Sky Lord reached an altitude of about four thousand feet and stopped ascending. Partly obscured by the low cloud it just hung there motionless in the sky, a malign, silent presence.

"What are we going to do now?" asked Paula, a tremor in her voice. Jan had been asking herself the same question. She looked again towards the dais in the square in the hope that somehow her mother would pull a last minute miracle from her sleeve even though she knew that no such miracle existed. Martha emerged from her hiding place under the discarded camouflage screen and wrapped her arms around Jan's legs. "Mistress, Mistress," she wailed as she buried her face into Jan's kilt.

Irritated, Jan tried to pull herself free from the chimp's powerful grip. She was feeling too frightened herself to spare the time to reassure Martha.

"Look!" It was the man. He was pointing up towards the Sky Lord. Jan looked and saw several small dark objects tumbling downwards. As they got closer she could hear them making a whistling noise . . . .

When the first of them landed in the square directly in front of the tavern and sent a geyser of smoke and soil high into the air Jan knew that the objects were bombs. She had heard stories about these weapons of the Sky Lord when she was a child — they were the means by which the Sky Lords had subdued the ground dwellers after the Gene Wars — but she had never seen them being used before.

More bombs landed and suddenly the whole universe seemed to Jan to be filled with nothing but noise and blinding lights. She was knocked off her feet by a shock wave. It felt like being hit with a huge, invisible pillow. She lay stunned, on her back, for an indeterminable amount of time before she was able to roll over on to her hands and knees and crawl to the parapet at the front of the roof. Her eyes swam with tears at the sight that greeted her.

Minerva was being murdered. Fires were raging in every part of the town and still the bombs kept falling. She saw a great ball of fire rise up on the other side of town and knew that the alcohol plant had been hit. "Alsa . . ." she whispered to herself. The square was a mass of craters. Where the dais had been was just a pile of blackened, smoking timber. She had to get down there; she had to find her mother.

"You bloody cowards!" someone shouted behind her. She turned and saw Lisa, the wall guard, standing and brandishing her sword at the dark bulk of the Sky Lord overhead. "Come down, you male bastards! Come down and fight us like women!" Because of what happened next that image — of the muscular, golden-haired warrior making her brave but futile gestures at the monster above them — was imprinted in Jan's mind . . . .

She actually saw the bomb hit the roof. It was just a dark blur of movement and then a hole appeared magically in the roof behind Lisa. The bomb didn't detonate immediately. It must have passed all the way through the tavern until it hit the stone floor of the basement and exploded. Jan saw the rear section of the roof leap into the air then vanish. Lisa vanished too. Then Jan began to fall as her section of the roof collapsed beneath her. As she fell she heard Martha shrieking with terror. She never saw the chimp again, or any of the others who had been with her on the roof.

Her fall was broken by something soft. It was a bed. One of the tavern's famous large and cosy ones. It might even have been the same one that Alsa and she would have had for their rendezvous that evening — if the day had turned out as Jan hoped it would. Later, when Milo, during one of his many discourses on bizarre topics, told Jan of the concept of alternative universes she often thought afterwards that somewhere, in one of these near-

44

identical worlds, she and Alsa did keep their romantic rendez-vous that evening.

She didn't stay on the bed for very long because it started to tilt as the floor began to give way. She jumped from it and clung to a window ledge. Looking over her shoulder she saw that the whole rear of the tavern no longer existed. It was as if a great blade had come down and cut the building in half.

The bed picked up speed, slid to the edge of the sagging floor and disappeared. She heard it crash into the basement. She looked up and saw she had fallen two floors from the roof. Rubble was continuing to fall through the gaping hole overhead. She had to get out.

She climbed on to the window sill and looked down. The roof of the verandah that extended along the front of the tavern was only feet below her. She lowered herself on to it, then swung down from the guttering until she was standing on the verandah balcony and then jumped the rest of the way. And was immediately knocked over again by the concussion wave of an exploding bomb. She lay at the foot of the verandah, her face pressed into the dirt and hands clamped to her ringing ears, until the bombs ceased to fall. Only when she was certain that the bombing had really stopped did she rise and head across the ruined square to search for her mother. It was here that she encountered the dazed and stumbling Helen.

She never found Melissa's body. Or if she did she failed to recognize it. There were parts of bodies scattered about but she didn't have the stomach to examine these too closely. She did, however, find the corpse of Headwoman Avedon. Her face was badly burnt but the fungus on the side of her head was still plainly visible. Better to die this way, Jan reflected, than suffer a slow, painful death from the fungus. At least one of us has got something good from this foul day.

The square was filling up now. People who had nowhere else to go to escape the flames of the burning town. Jan saw Head-woman Anna in the distance and, relieved to see someone she knew well, even if it was her mother's chief rival, hurried over to her. "Anna!" she called as she ran, not caring about formalities in such grim circumstances.

Anna turned as she heard her name being called. She frowned when she saw it was Jan. As Jan drew close to Anna she was astonished to see the Headwoman draw her sword and rush towards her, intention plain. "Filth!" cried Anna. "Spawn of the mother-devil who has murdered us all. Your mother may be dead but at least I will have the satisfaction of spitting *you*. . .!"

Filled with dismay, Jan retreated and drew her own sword just in time to parry Anna's first vicious swing at her head. "Anna, don't! I don't want to fight you!" Jan pleaded but she could see it was no use. Anna's eyes were wild and frightening. There was no way that Jan could reach her. She parried another blow — so strong it jarred her whole arm — and continued to retreat. She realized she stood a very good chance of being killed by Anna. Her hysterical rage was providing her with unnatural strength.

"They're dropping more bombs!" screamed someone nearby. This and cries of alarm from other people were enough to make Anna cease her attack and look up. Jan felt momentarily safe to do likewise. The Sky Lord was moving, and as it moved it issued out a cloud of small black objects into the air, like a female frog squirting eggs into the water of a pond. At first Jan thought too that these were more bombs but then she saw strange shapes blossom out above each object which had the effect of slowing down their rate of fall.

And as the objects drew closer to the ground Jan saw that they were Sky Warriors. Hundreds of them.

It had been Jan's hope that many of the descending Sky Warriors would land in the fires started by the Sky Lord's bomb and burn to death but they were obviously very skilled at manipulating the black canopies of cloth that billowed out above them. None of the Sky Warriors landed within the town itself but around it, in the space between the edge of the town and the wall. Then they had begun to move in on foot from all sides at once.

"Here they come again!"

A solid wall of black armour was rushing up the wide avenue towards the hospital wall. Jan knew it was hopeless but she still felt no fear. Her only emotion was an unfocused hope that it would all be over soon and that her death would be quick. She aimed her cross-bow again and waited. The black tide advanced. She fired, saw her target fall along with many others but this time the Sky Warriors kept coming. Some were firing their long rifles as they ran. Jan could hear the fizzing noises the bullets made as they hurtled through the air. One of them seemed to pass by her head very closely. There was not going to be enough time to reload the cross-bow so she dropped it and drew her sword and her hatchet, backing away from the wall as she did so. The others were doing the same. The woman on Jan's right suddenly grunted and fell backwards. Jan could only spare her a quick glance. There was a neat, round hole in her forehead. Jan envied her the quickness of her death.

The Sky Warriors were coming over the wall. It was the closest Jan had ever been to them before. She could even see their eyes behind the narrow slits of their shiny black face masks. They were yelling very loudly as they came. Jan, her hatchet in her left hand and her sword in her right, went to meet them.

Chapter Five:

A weight was lifted from her lower body. Then a boot, planted against her left side, rocked her back and forth. She groaned and tried to open her eyes but the lids were crusted shut. The throbbing in her head was more than she could bear and she was terribly thirsty.

"This one's still alive," said a voice. A man's voice.

"Not for much longer by the look of it. Might as well do the earthworm a favour and cut her throat." Another voice, also male. She groaned again, more loudly this time, and tried to sit up but her body refused to move.

There was a creaking sound and then she felt her chin gripped by gloved fingers and her head was turned roughly from side to side. She waited for the knife blade to slice into the exposed flesh of her throat.

But then the hand released her chin and the fingers began to prod her in her stomach at the base of her breast plate. "Can't see anything serious. All that blood can't belong to her," said the first voice, very close now.

"Probably came from this poor bastard here," said the second voice. "See, looks like she got him in the armpit with a lucky thrust."

It wasn't lucky, thought Jan resentfully through the red haze of pain that filled her head. *When the Sky Warrior had raised his arms to brain me with his rifle butt I made a perfectly good lunge.*

"So what do you think?" asked the first voice.

"I still say we cut her throat."

"The orders were to bring back prisoners and so far the pickings have been slim."

"The orders were to bring back some *important* prisoners so that the Aristos can punish them personally for their treachery. Does this bitch look important to you? Besides, she's too young."

"Well," said the first voice slowly. "She *might* be important. Maybe under all that blood she's an earthworm princess. That armour looks expensive, sort of."

There was a long pause before the second voice said, "If she's a princess I'm Lord Pangloth, but I guess we might as well take her. If she's not important enough for the Aristos to play with we can claim our rights and sell her as a slave." Gloved hands gripped her wrists and she was hauled roughly to her feet. The violent movement made the pain in her head explode into even greater intensity and she cried out. She still couldn't open her eyes and, overcome with dizziness, she would have fallen if her invisible captors hadn't held her upright. Then her wrists were pressed together and she felt rope being tied around them. "Come on!" commanded the second voice and there was a jerk on the rope. Blind, sick with pain and shock, Jan had no will to resist and took her first stumbling steps towards her uncertain fate.

It wasn't until they reached the square that she was able to open her eyes. It had begun to rain, quite hard, and the cold water had washed away the dried blood that had sealed her eyelids. She found herself looking at the black armoured back of a Sky Warrior. The rope binding her wrists was slung over his shoulder. Beside her, on her right, was another Warrior. He turned his head toward her when she looked at him. "See again, can you?" he asked coldly. She saw blue eyes peering out from the ugly helmet. "Good. A blind slave isn't worth two cents."

She tried to answer but her throat was too dry. So she tipped her head back and opened her mouth to the rain. The cold water tasted so wonderful she briefly felt glad to be still alive. Then she glanced about and the crushing despair returned.

Little that was recognizable remained of Minerva. The fires had been extinguished by the rain but they'd had long enough to do their work. What hadn't been blasted apart by the bombs had subsequently burnt down. She could see Sky Warriors poking about in the ruins, looking for salvageable loot. By the look of the piles of different items in the square they'd already had good fortune. She even saw several grain sacks lying about, which meant they'd found the underground storage bins. Sky Warriors were loading their loot into two loading cradles identical to the one that had earlier been destroyed. Jan guessed that the Sky Lord was directly overhead again but the downpour made it impossible to see. The cables on the loading cradles just seemed to fade into nothingness some fifty feet above the ground.

Jan saw that she was being taken towards a large wicker cage that looked very crudely built. Tied to its top was a single rope that, like the cables on the cradles, vanished upwards into the greyness. There were about twenty people in the cage. As she drew nearer she saw that none of them were relatives or close friends. In fact she recognized only a few of them. If these were truly the only surviving Minervans it meant that everyone she'd ever loved or been close to was dead. Her mother, her father, Alsa, all her friends . . . even Simon was gone. It was all too much to comprehend. Until now she had only lost one close relative through death and that had been Pola, her older sister, who had been born at the breeding time before Jan's. Pola had died in a battle with a band of marauders while on guard duty at one of the outer farming areas some six years ago. It had taken

Jan a long time to come to terms with Pola's death. Now she was faced with the death of her whole world.

"What have you got there?" asked a Sky Warrior standing by the cage as her two captors came to halt. The one who was holding the rope began to untie her wrists.

"Not sure, sir," said the other Warrior, the one she thought of as 'first voice' and the slightly more sympathetic of the two. "By the look of her armour we thought she might be a high ranker. Maybe even a princess, sir."

A third Warrior made a sniggering sound as he stepped nearer for a closer look at her. "The amazons don't have princesses, soldier. Or rather they *didn't*. Liked to pretend they were all very democratic. But they did have a ruling class of sorts . . . ." Jan saw, as he thrust his helmeted face close to her own, that he was dressed differently to the other two and was obviously an officer. "Well, what about it, amazon?" he demanded. "Were you anyone important in this earthworm town?"

The rain water had eased the dryness in her throat and she was able to answer. "No," she said hoarsely. "I was just a warrior." Then she remembered that around her neck she wore the chain and medallion which signified that she was the daughter of a Headwoman. It was hidden under her armour but this officer seemed knowledgeable about customs.

"Just a warrior," repeated the officer sneeringly. Then he grabbed her by the arm and pulled her to the side of the cage. "You in there!" he bawled. "Do any of you know who this girl is?"

The Minervans, who were all sitting slumped against the sides of the large cage, looked at Jan. Their faces were grey with shock and fatigue. She saw that more than half of them were men. "Well?" demanded the Sky Warrior.

The occupants of the cage all shook their heads. Jan felt relieved. She still didn't care whether she lived or died but from what the other two Warriors had said she didn't care to fall into the hands of the 'Aristos', whoever they were. The thought of torture terrified her.

"That's that then," muttered the officer, sounding annoyed. "Get that armour off her and stick her in the cage with the rest of the earthworms." He gave her a shove towards the other two.

They unbuckled her breast plate. A flutter of panic stirred in her lower belly. The officer was certain to spot the medallion around her neck. And as the armour fell free he did.

He stepped close to her and took hold of the medallion in his gauntlet. "Now *that's* interesting," he said. "Looks like solid gold. What's its significance?"

She swallowed dryly. "It's . . . it's a medal. I won it. For bravery. On the wall. I stopped one of the big lizards getting in . . . ." As she spoke she felt a wave of self disgust. Lying pathetically to these bastards to save herself. If her mother could hear her . . . .

She gasped as the officer unexpectedly pulled the medallion from her neck, snapping the chain. He slipped it in a pouch on his belt. "Quite the brave little amazon, aren't you? And you *are* little, for an amazon. You're about the same size as one of their eunuchs."

"Er, we thought we'd put a claim on her ourselves if no one else wants her," said 'second voice' hesitantly. "See if we can sell her to one of the slave guilds."

"I see no problem," said the officer. "Though I'd expect a percentage."

"Oh, of course, sir," said 'second voice'. "Goes without saying, sir."

"I'm glad to hear it," said the officer dryly. "Now finish with her and rejoin your unit. We'll be pulling out soon."

"Yessir." They made her remove her gloves, boots and weapons belt, then 'second voice' ran his hands over her clothes, presumably searching for any hidden weapons. She recoiled at his touch, fearing that this might be a prelude to rape.

The bomb was still there inside her. She could feel it tightly secure within its cloth wrapping. She wished that she had somehow lost it during the battle, or when she was unconscious.

But the search was quickly over and then she was being pushed towards an entrance in the side of the cage that one of the Sky Warriors had opened. She was shoved through it and heard the door swing shut behind her. "Make yourself comfortable with your friends while you can. Very soon you'll be going on a very interesting ride," said the officer and laughed.

51

Thankfully Jan sat down between two of the women. She felt very weak and her head still throbbed with appalling pain. As the officer and the two Warriors walked away, one of the latter carrying her breast plate and other equipment, the woman on her right said, "You're the daughter of Headwoman Melissa, aren't you? The one responsible for all this."

Jan looked at her. She was vaguely familiar but Jan didn't know her name. For a moment Jan was about to deny being Melissa's daughter but decided against such a cowardly action. "My mother wasn't responsible alone. The majority of the Council voted with her on two occasions."

"All the same, it was her idea to defy the Sky Lord. And look what it's gained us." The woman raised a limp hand to indicate the smoking ruins of the town.

Jan sighed. She didn't have the strength to argue. "Why didn't you tell the Sky Warrior who I was?"

"I wasn't sure at first. Now I am." The woman's glazed eyes regarded Jan with a cold contempt. Jan remembered the way Anna had looked when she'd attacked her. If it hadn't been for the distraction afforded by the arrival of the Sky Warriors Anna would have surely killed her. Jan felt the weight of her despair increase even further. Not only was she in the hands of her enemies but she was hated by her own people. She glanced around the cage. Those who had overheard the woman's words were staring at her with the same contempt, even the men. She closed her eyes. Let them do what they wanted.

It wasn't fair, she reflected bitterly. It wasn't fair that she was still alive. By all rights she shouldn't be. She had been certain that she was going to die in the final battle at the hospital. The defenders had been swiftly overwhelmed and she had suddenly found herself alone in a sea of Sky Warriors. One of them was in front of her, raising the butt of his gun to club her, and she had lunged. After that she couldn't remember anything. She presumed the butt had hit her as he fell, knocking her unconscious. With his body and blood covering her she'd been taken for dead until the heat of the battle was over and the Sky Warriors had started thinking about prisoners. She wondered what had happened to all the helpless wounded in the hospital, and then shut her mind to what she knew must have occurred . . . .

After about half an hour the rain eased off. She opened her eyes and looked up. The Sky Lord was still concealed in the grey murk but she sensed it hovered very low above them and she fancied she could hear the hum of its many engines. There were very few Sky Warriors in the square now and only one loading cradle remained. She guessed it wouldn't be long before they would be leaving. She was puzzled why the cage hadn't yet been hauled up into the Sky Lord. She looked again at the single rope tied to the top of the cage. It was thick but frayed. She didn't relish the idea of it having to support twenty-one people, even for the short trip up to the Sky Lord.

A short time later the remaining loading cradle lifted off, carrying with it the rest of the Sky Warriors and their loot. But the cage continued to sit there in the bomb-ravaged square. Jan found this disturbing. What was in store for them?

With a protesting creak the wicker cage finally rose into the air. Jan and the others had to grab quickly for handholds as the cage began to rotate back and forth on the end of the rope which was also making creaking sounds of protest. One of the men cried out in alarm. Jan didn't blame him.

Very soon they were enveloped in the greyness of the low cloud. Jan couldn't even see the woman next to her. She clung harder to the wicker bars as the rotating got worse. She felt dizzy and shut her eyes but that didn't help. As much as she feared having to go on board the Sky Lord she prayed to the Mother God that the journey up to it wouldn't take much longer.

After what seemed a very long time the cage emerged from the cloud. Jan opened her eyes and looked up. Overhead, as frightening as ever in its sheer immensity, hung the *Lord Pangloth*. It was some two to three hundred feet above them. The rope attached to the cage looked as substantial as a piece of cotton trailing from the belly of the vast airship. Then Jan realized something that nearly made her void her bowels in terror.

The cage was rising as the Sky Lord continued to rise but it wasn't being winched upwards. The cage was being allowed just to dangle at the end of the rope. A look down at the receding surface of the cloud layer below the cage confirmed this fear. They were rising rapidly above the cloud but not getting any closer to the Sky Lord.

The others had begun to notice this as well. "What's wrong?" wailed one woman. "Why aren't they pulling us up?"

The cage, still spinning back and forth, continued to make its alarming creaking noises. Jan wouldn't have been surprised if the whole thing fell to pieces around them. The woven floor, through which she could see the clouds below, looked especially insubstantial. She decided to climb a short way up the side of the cage and hook her arms and legs through the gaps of the weave. It wasn't very comfortable but she felt more secure.

"We're still not moving!" cried someone. "What are those bastards up to?"

"They're going to cut the rope! I know it!" cried another, her voice rising in panic. Someone else, a man, began to sob.

Jan had been thinking the same thing. Either that or Sky Warriors intended leaving them down here in the cage until they died of thirst, hunger, exposure or all three. But what had been all that talk of selling her into slavery?

Her teeth were chattering. It was getting colder the higher they went and she, like the others, was soaking wet. *Oh well*, she told herself, *I'm going to get my wish after all. I'm going to die . . . .*

But when, a few minutes later, the woman who had recognized her said: "One of us should climb up there and untie the rope. Better to die at our own hand than at the hands of those male monsters" — Jan had quickly objected. She still wanted to die but not that way. She couldn't bear to think of the long drop down through the clouds to that final awful impact far below.

The woman sneered at her. "So much for the honour of Melissa's family. Her daughter is a coward."

"I'm not! You don't understand . . . it is for the honour of Minerva and my mother that I must reach the Sky Lord alive."

"Oh yes?" said the woman, giving her a sceptical smile. "And why is that?"

Jan already regretted her words but she had no choice but to go on. "My mission is to . . . destroy the *Lord Pangloth*." As soon as she spoke she knew how absurd she sounded. She wasn't

54

surprised when the woman laughed, as did a few of the others who were within earshot.

"You're going to destroy the Sky Lord? And how will you achieve that small feat, daughter of Melissa?"

"I . . . I have the means hidden . . . on my person. A weapon. Made by Helen . . . ." She felt foolish. She knew she was saying all this just to stay alive a while longer. She didn't really think there was any chance of doing even minor damage to the Sky Lord with Helen's tiny fire-bomb. She never had. Besides, the plan had been for several Minervans carrying such bombs to get on board the *Lord Pangloth.*

The woman laughed again. "A weapon? What kind of weapon? And where is it? Perhaps it's a pin hidden in your hair. You plan to use it to let all the gas out of *Pangloth?* Fool! You are as mad as your mother, girl!"

Before Jan could think of a suitable reply one of the men cried, "We've stopped rising!"

Jan saw it was true. The Sky Lord was no longer ascending but was now starting to move forward at increasing speed. Very soon the cage was being buffeted about in a strong wind, making speech impossible. And ahead of the Sky Lord Jan saw something that made her feel certain that the flimsy cage wouldn't stay tethered to the sky giant for much longer. It was a huge, black thundercloud and the Sky Lord appeared to be heading straight for it.

Chapter Six:

The flight through the thunderstorm was the most frightening thing Jan had ever experienced. It was already getting dark as the Sky Lord approached the seething mountain of storm clouds but once inside them everything became pitch black. The buffeting the cage and its occupants suffered was staggering in its intensity.

Sometimes the cage was lifted in a violent updraft only to drop with a sudden, sickening lurch. On each occasion Jan was certain the frayed rope had snapped and she screamed.

Then came the appalling thunderclaps followed by the flashes of lightning. To Jan it seemed they were in the very centre of the storm and she expected to be struck by lightning at any second. She had never in her life felt so insignificant and helpless, her arms and legs locked together through the wicker-work of the cage, her eyes screwed shut, prayed and prayed to the Mother God for salvation as she was blown by the winds, drenched by the rain, deafened by the thunder and dazzled by the lightning.

When she had convinced herself that the rope had snapped long ago and that the cage was on its own within the storm clouds to be endlessly tossed about by the winds without ever falling to earth the buffeting suddenly ceased. She opened her eyes to see that the cage was now suspended in clear, still air and she could again hear the powerful whine of the Sky Lord's engines. She looked up and saw that the vast underbelly of the airship was ablaze with rows of lights. She unlocked her hands and legs from the wicker-work and let herself drop to the floor of the cage. It was freezing and her limbs ached but she was too exhausted to care. She slept.

She awoke in bright sunshine. Through the cage floor she could see that the ground was very close. They were passing over blight land, with its deceptive riot of bright, clashing colour. The tops of the trees and the bigger fungi seemed only feet below her.

She sat up and found that every muscle in her body was stiff and exceedingly painful but the sun on her skin felt wonderful. And she realized she was very hungry. How long since she had eaten? Twenty-four hours at least.

She was hemmed in by sleeping forms, or so it seemed at first, but when she touched a nearby man on the shoulder to wake him up she discovered, with a shock, that he was cold and stiff. Dead.

For a moment she was under the impression that she was the only one left alive but, to her relief, when she shook the shoulder of a woman she found it warm. The woman stirred and groaned, then opened her eyes. "Oh, it's you," she said. "The mad daughter of Melissa. Leave me alone and let me sleep, fool." Jan hadn't recognized the woman as her accuser. The woman's face seemed to have shrunk during the night. It was gaunt and her eyes were ringed with black. Jan wondered if she looked any better.

"This man," said Jan hoarsely. "He's dead."

The woman raised herself with difficulty into a sitting position and gave the dead man a brief look. "He's lucky," she said. "I envy him. He's with the Mother God now. If he's led a blameless life she will give him rebirth as a woman and he will be a step nearer to paradise."

Jan knew this to be true but it made her feel no better about being wedged next to a corpse. She reached over the dead man and tentatively touched the leg of the woman lying alongside him. She recoiled immediately. The woman was dead too.

The cage gave a lurch. Jan gasped and grabbed for a handhold. It lurched again. She looked up. "We're moving!" she cried. "We're going up!"

As the cage was hauled up towards the great belly of the Sky Lord several others stirred and sat up in the cage. Jan saw that seven didn't. She guessed it was the cold that had killed them, or possibly shock. And once again she found herself among the living. Perhaps it was meant to be. Perhaps she *did* have a mission after all. Was the Mother God keeping her alive in order to carry out Melissa's instructions? Jan didn't find the idea reassuring.

The survivors eyed one another fearfully as the bulk of the airship filled the sky above them. Jan could see that they were being drawn up into a square opening in the hull. Her heart thumped painfully as her apprehension increased. What awaited them within the Sky Lord? What new horrors did the servants of the *Lord Pangloth* have in store for them?

The cage was pulled up through the opening in the hull and Jan saw that they were in a large, darkly-lit room with a high ceiling from which were suspended several pieces of machinery, including the winch that had hauled up the cage. As Jan's eyes adapted to the dimness she saw that there were a large number of people in the room.

With a sighing sound the opening in the hull slowly closed and then the cage was lowered, with a jarring thump, to the floor. The figures in the shadows converged on the cage and Jan saw that they were all men. Several were dressed in black and carried weapons; they were obviously Sky Warriors without their armour. The others wore baggy one-piece suits of varying colours but all drab. Overcome with fear, Jan couldn't help trembling. Intellectually she had known that the Sky Warriors were men, but hidden behind their armour and face-masks she was able to keep that awareness repressed; now, however, she had no choice but face up to the knowledge that she was surrounded by *men*. Men who were not like the men of Minerva but men who were the unchanged descendants of the Old Men — the monsters who had subjugated and brutalized women for thousands of years, who had raped the world with their greed, aggression and evil technology and then finally all but destroyed it with the Gene Wars. All her life she had been taught to fear and revile these creatures and now she was at their mercy.

The Sky Warriors and the other men were regarding the occupants of the cage with a mixture of contempt and amusement. "Yo, Amazons!" called one of them. "Lost your taste for fighting now, have you?"

"Let us out of here and we'll show you!" called back the woman who was Jan's accuser. Jan wished that she had possessed the courage to say those words.

Then, from among the Sky Warriors, emerged two people whose appearance was very different from those around them. Jan was also surprised to see that one of them was a woman. The man, who led the way, wore a blood red jacket with sleeves that ballooned out all the way to the wrists. The jacket stopped just below his waist and instead of trousers he was wearing what appeared to be very fine, and very tight, white stockings that showed up the musculature of his legs. Jan was sure that the shape of his sexual organs would have been revealed too if they hadn't been covered by a prominent red pouch made of hard leather. His black hair hung to his shoulders and his long, arrogant face seemed to be covered with a white powder while his lips were the same colour as his jacket.

The woman looked even more bizarre. She too was dressed in

red, but her gown was of a type that Jan had never seen before. It was so tight around her waist that Jan wondered how she could breathe. The unnatural narrowness of her waist served to accentuate her hips and her upper torso, of which Jan could see a great deal thanks to the front of the gown being cut so low that it exposed most of her rather prominent breasts. And to add to Jan's bemusement she saw that under the gown the woman was wearing some kind of restricting halter that pushed her breasts upwards and together.

Like the man the woman also had her face covered with white powder, and her lips painted red, but her hair, which was blonde, was piled high on her head and kept in place by a number of jewelled pins.

It was only when the man began to speak that Jan managed to tear her eyes away from the apparition that was the woman. "I am Prince Magid, the *Lord Pangloth*'s High Chamberlain," he announced in a high, reedy voice. "I am here to inform you of the *Lord Pangloth*'s decision regarding your fate. For daring to rebel against the just rule of the Sky Lord you have, of course, forfeited all the rights the *Lord Pangloth* generously graced you with. Your community first broke the prime law of the Sky Lords, by making devices capable of flight when you knew that the sky is the sole domain of the Sky Lords and forever barred to you groundlings. And then you dared use these devices against the *Lord Pangloth* in a treacherous attempt to destroy your sovereign. That the attempt was doomed to failure in no way diminishes the enormity of your crime.

"The other members of your community have already paid the price — now it is your turn. You have two choices: death or slavery for the rest of your life. What is it to be. You have a minute to make your decision."

There was silence. Jan turned and looked at the others. Of the original twenty only thirteen remained alive. Nine women and four men. Of the seven who had died during the night five had been men. As Jan expected, her accuser was the first to speak. And Jan knew what she was going to say even as she opened her mouth. "I say we choose death," she said. "For the honour of Minerva's memory and for our dead sisters."

"Yes, let it be death!" agreed another woman loudly. Three other women murmured their agreement with less enthusiasm. The four men looked anxious. "Well, what does the daughter of Melissa say?" demanded the woman coldly as she turned towards Jan.

Jan didn't know what to do. Her wish to die had vanished when she had awoken that morning to the sun's kiss on her skin, yet at the same time she dreaded the idea of submitting herself to the men of the Sky Lord for even a minute, much less the rest of her life. And then there was her mission to consider. She doubted she had even a small chance of success but now she felt honour-bound to make the attempt.

"Just as I thought," said the woman when Jan didn't reply.

"Your time is up," said the man in red. Two Sky Warriors stepped forward and unlocked the cage door. Others drew their swords. "Out, and announce your decision."

Slowly they climbed out of the cage and formed a line in front of it on the shouted orders of the Warriors. Jan cast a brief glance back at the seven pathetic forms lying in the cage.

"Well, what is it to be?" demanded the High Chamberlain with his high, strained voice. It was as if he was not used to talking so loudly. "Those who choose death step forward."

Jan's accuser stepped forward without even a moment's hesitation. Four other women followed after only a brief pause. Then one by one, and with obvious reluctance, the remaining four women joined the others, leaving only Jan and the four men standing in the original line. Jan felt humiliated. She wanted to take that crucial step forward but couldn't.

Her accuser looked over her shoulder at her. She said nothing but the contempt in her eyes was plain. Jan looked down at the floor.

"So many of you eager to die?" asked the High Chamberlain. He sounded surprised. And from the surrounding Sky Warriors came disappointed mutters. Jan guessed they had a financial interest in the outcome. Yet if the Sky Warriors wanted them as slaves why had they been so careless with their lives in the cage?

"Better death than the ultimate dishonour," said Jan's accuser. Jan continued to envy her. If she had said those same

60

words she was sure she would have sounded merely silly. "All we ask is that our deaths be clean and that our bodies are not despoiled by your touch beforehand."

"Your deaths will be clean," said the High Chamberlain, irritably. "And you won't be molested. But what of that one? Why does she not share your irrational desire for destruction?"

Jan looked up and saw he was pointing at her. Jan's accuser glanced at her and said coldly, "She's our secret weapon. She is going to destroy all of you and your Sky Lord single handed. At least, that is what she told us . . . ."

The High Chamberlain, his female companion and all the other sky men laughed and Jan felt her cheeks grow hot. She wanted to die — but she didn't want to *enough*, she knew shamefully, to step forward and join the others.

When the laughter subsided the High Chamberlain sighed and said, "Very well, let us end this distasteful matter. Those of you who choose death will get back into the cage."

Jan avoided the eyes of the nine women as they filed slowly back into the cage. The four men also stood with their heads bowed. Then Jan was pulled to one side by a Sky Warrior. He had a large black beard. Jan had never seen a beard like it before. Minervan men rarely grew beards.

There came a whine of machine from overhead and the cage rose a few feet from the floor. As it swayed on the rope there was a rumble and the opening appeared beneath it again. Jan felt even sicker. She knew what was going to happen. So did those in the cage. Some of them began to pray aloud to the Mother God. Jan shut her eyes.

"Daughter of Melissa!"

She opened her eyes and saw her accuser glaring at her through the bars of the cage. "Daughter of Melissa! Why are you so modest about yourself? I'm sure that your masters would be flattered to know that you are — "

The cage dropped. There was no warning. It just seemed to vanish. Jan guessed that someone had simply hacked through the flayed rope. She swayed dizzily and for a few moments thought she was going to pass out but the feeling passed. Suddenly she found herself face to face with the High Chamberlain. Waves of a very strong and sickly-sweet perfume filled her nostrils, making her want to gag. The woman was close behind him, staring over his shoulder at Jan with intense curiosity.

"What's your name, girl?" he demanded.

"Jan. Jan Dorvin."

"What was that woman talking about just then?"

Jan shook her head. "I don't know. She didn't like me. She thinks . . . thought I was a coward."

The High Chamberlain stroked his small, pointed beard thoughtfully then said, "For your sake you had better be a coward. For that way you will remain alive. Commit any act of disobedience and you will immediately share the fate of your late compatriots. Understand?"

"Yes," said Jan in almost a whisper.

"Good." The High Chamberlain then turned to the four Minervan men. "The same applies to you, though from what I know about you eunuchs disobedience is not in your nature. Even so you have been warned. Understand?"

They all nodded. Jan had a feeling of contempt for them which she quickly stifled. She was in no position to accuse others of cowardice. Nor could she be sure they *were* cowards. She had seen several Minervan men fighting alongside the sisters during yesterday's battles. They hadn't fought well, and had been swiftly cut down by the Sky Warriors but they *had* made the effort and she had respected them for it. At the same time, however, the sight of Minervan men wielding swords had filled her with deep unease . . . just as she had expected it would.

The High Chamberlain was glancing about enquiringly. "Presumably some of you have claimed slave rights on these survivors? If so, state your claims."

"I, Gregory Tanith of the Third Battalion, and on behalf of Warrior Martin Sundin, also of the Third Battalion, claim the slave rights on this female Minervan," said the Sky Warrior with the black beard who was still gripping her by the arm. Jan, surprised, realized he was 'first voice'.

The High Chamberlain nodded impatiently and said, "Do you have official verification of this claim?"

"I do. Officer Kaplan of the Third Battalion will verify the claim."

"Very well, the claim is recognized. Who do you intend selling her to?"

"We were thinking of Guild Master Bannion. He's had some losses among his glass walkers."

The High Chamberlain gave an approving nod. "Good. If there is still any fight left in this amazon, working with Bannion's mob will soon knock it out of her."

"Oh Basil, it seems a *waste* to put her among Bannion's louts. She's such a pretty creature. Why not buy her for me? I could have her trained to be my maid." It was the woman, who hadn't spoken before. She spoke in a very cautious way. To Jan it seemed as if she was trying to imitate a little girl.

"Don't be ridiculous," said the High Chamberlain irritably. "I'm not letting you have an amazon for a maid. Besides, we don't know yet if she's carrying any infections. If she is, let Bannion's scum be the sufferers."

The woman nodded meekly and said no more. The High Chamberlain then turned his attention to the claimants on the four Minervan men. Jan was distressed to hear that they were being sold to different 'Guild Masters', whoever they were. She didn't want to be separated from the only other surviving Minervans, even if they *were* men. But suddenly she was being pushed through the crowd by her black-bearded 'owner' and all at once she felt very much alone.

She was marched to a wide doorway that had a sign saying DECONTAMINATION above it. In the room beyond a bored-looking man with very pale skin sat at a table. On one side of the table was a pile of clothing. A spark of interest showed in his eyes as he saw Jan. He leered at her. "And what have we here? One of those Minervan amazons?"

"The only one," said Tanith. "The rest of the women opted for the drop. Apart from her there's only four of their men left."

"Wasteful," said the man at the desk with a disapproving shake of his head. "So who's she going to?"

"Bannion. Joining one of his hull crews."

63

The pale-faced man grinned when he heard this. It was not a pleasant grin. The more she heard about Bannion and his people the more her anxiety increased. "What's your name?" he asked her.

"Jan," she muttered.

"Well, Jan, get your clothes off. Everything."

It was what she had been dreading. "You're going to . . . to — " she forced herself to say the hateful word — "rape me."

The two men exchanged a glance and laughed. "Don't flatter yourself, earthworm. Do you think we're crazy? God knows what vermin you've got crawling about inside you," said the man at the desk scornfully. "My job is to make sure that at least the outside of you is clean. So get your clothes off."

Slowly and reluctantly Jan removed her kilt, vest and underclothes. Apart from her acute embarrassment she was terrified that they would subject her to an intimate search. She was painfully aware of the bomb inside her. It seemed to have expanded in size.

"Jeez, look at those muscles," said the desk man as he got to his feet.

"All the amazons are — *were* — built like this," said Tanith, trying to sound blasé. "But she's smaller than average."

The desk man kept running his eyes up and down her. Jan wanted to do two things — to punch him very hard in the face and to vomit. "Pity to waste this on Bannion's creeps," he told Tanith.

"Yeah. Look, I got to get back on duty soon so could you hurry things along?"

"Well, I don't *want* to but I will, soldier." He gave Jan a wink then, taking a stick with a hook on the end of it, picked up her clothes and dumped them into the opening of a chute in the wall beside his desk. He pulled a lever. Jan guessed that her clothes were now fluttering towards the ground. "Go through that doorway, girl — *move*," he ordered, pointing at a narrow door at the end of the small room. When Jan hesitated he said, "Go on, you won't come to any harm. Not in *there* anyway." He laughed.

Jan approached the door warily and opened it. It led into a long shower stall. She felt relieved that they had made no attempt to search her. Being thought of as a disease ridden savage had its advantages.

She went and stood under one of the shower nozzles. She looked up at it expectantly and suddenly she was hit in the face with a jet of white liquid that both stung her eyes and smelt horrible. She gasped, rubbing her eyes, and stumbled blindly towards the door. All the nozzles in the stall were obviously spraying out the vile liquid and some of it got into her mouth, making her retch. She reached the door and turned the handle. The door wouldn't open. She banged on it. "Let me out!" she cried. "Help!" The fumes were getting worse. She was finding it hard to breathe. She sagged, coughing and retching, to her knees.

The hissing from the nozzles died away. Jan looked about with streaming eyes. The white liquid was draining away through grills in the floor but she was covered with the stuff. She got up and tried the door again but it remained locked. The nozzles came to life again and she turned round in alarm but this time it appeared they were spraying out ordinary water.

Experimentally she extended her hand under the nearest stream, then licked it. It tasted musty but it was definitely water. She stepped under the spray and gratefully washed the stinging, and stinking, white liquid from her body. When she had finished the water stopped and the door sprang open.

She walked back into the room. Both of the men were regarding her with malicious amusement. She spat on to the floor, partly to clear her throat of the lingering taste and partly to express her anger. "Bastards," she said. "You could have warned me. What was that stuff?"

Tanith walked over to her and casually hit her across the face with his gloved hand. The force of the blow knocked her down. "Rule number one," he said, looking down at her. "You must never be insolent to a Sky Warrior or any Freeman. You can behave however you like with your fellow slaves but if you deliberately insult a Freeman again it will be the drop for you. Understand?"

Jan nodded silently as she clutched her throbbing cheek. Blood trickled from a slit lip. "The white liquid was just a powerful disinfectant," continued Tanith. "Your skin and eyes will remain

65

sore for a few days but you will suffer no long term ill effects." He bent down and helped her up.

The desk man approached, still grinning, with a bundle of clothing in his arms. He handed it to Jan. "Put this on."

She let the clothing fall open and saw that it consisted of one of those baggy, one-piece suits she'd seen earlier. As she climbed into it — marvelling at the strange fastener down the front of it that didn't feel sticky but joined together like magic — Tanith said to her, "How old are you, Jan?"

"Eighteen."

He put his hand on her shoulder. "Is that all? Well, it's time to see your new world. The place where you'll be spending your remaining one hundred and eighty-two or so years — if you're lucky."

Chapter Seven:

It was the smell that made the most powerful impression on Jan initially. Never before had she encountered so many unwashed human bodies in such close proximity. And there were other smells too — all of them bad. She noticed piles of animal dung on the straw matting that made up the surface of the 'road' and wondered why the people didn't bother to gather it up and simply throw it out of the airship.

As she followed Tanith along the road she had to keep reminding herself that she was indeed on the Sky Lord. If it hadn't been for the low ceiling with its bright-as-day lights she could have been walking through the main thoroughfare of some crowded but incredibly dirty town. There were shop fronts and a variety of other building façades with entrances and windows built into both sides of what she realized was a very wide corridor. And it was also a very long corridor — Jan felt as if she'd been walking along it for hours but knew it was probably

66

only fifteen minutes ago that she and Tanith had emerged from the small, moving room that had carried them up from the decontamination section.

Her first close look at how people lived within the Sky Lord had come as a shock. None of her many imaginings since childhood about what went on inside the vast airship prepared her for the squalor or filth that greeted her when she stepped out in to the 'street'. Apart from the crowds of people in their drab clothes — some wore little more than dirty rags — there were many animals; goats, pigs, chickens and even sheep. There were also numerous children about, to add to her surprise, and of varying ages, which meant that the Sky People didn't have a fixed breeding time . . . .

Jan attracted attention along the way, most of it antagonistic. Men, and quite a few women, jeered at her, calling her 'amazon', 'earthworm', 'earth-scum', and worse. At one point an angry man stepped in front of Tanith and demanded by what right he brought a disease-ridden earthworm into the centre of their town. Tanith put his hand meaningfully on the hilt of his sword and told the man to get out of their way. The man did so, but not before spitting at Jan.

A short time later Jan was caught off her emotional balance when a woman stepped up beside her and said to Tanith, "The child looks famished, soldier. May I give her this?" And she extended a large, red apple to Jan. Jan's stomach immediately started to rumble, though at the same time she was suspicious of the gesture. Was there something wrong with the apple? Was it poisoned?

Tanith gave a shrug. Jan took the apple and mumbled her thanks to the woman. She studied the apple suspiciously but her stomach overruled the misgivings of her head and she bit hungrily into it. It was full of juice and tasted delicious. At that moment she didn't give a damn if it *was* poisoned.

She was just finishing the apple when Tanith came to an unexpected halt in front of her and she bumped into his back. He took hold of her wrist and said gruffly, "Through here . . . ."

They had stopped in front of an open doorway which had a sign above it reading: THE GUILD OF GLASS WALKERS. Jan realized that this might be her last chance to try and escape from Tanith; despite her weakness from lack of food she was confident she was still capable of knocking him unconscious with a quick, surprise blow. The problem was where could she possibly escape *to* after that? Swift recapture would be almost certain, and then would come the long drop . . . .

So she allowed Tanith to push her through the doorway and into a dimly-lit lobby. Two men were lounging on a low bench against a wall while a third sat behind a big desk made of wickerwork. All three men were heavily built and dressed in black one-piece suits. Unlike the other sky people Jan had seen so far they were heavily tanned.

The one behind the desk put down the cup he'd been drinking from and said cheerfully, "Is this our new earthworm, Warrior Tanith?"

Tanith gave her a shove forward. "She is indeed."

The man looked Jan up and down in the same slow way as the man in the quarantine room had. This time, at least, she wasn't naked but it felt as if his eyes could see right through her clothing and her skin crawled just the same.

"Benny," said the man. "Take them through to the boss."

One of the men sitting on the bench got up and beckoned that they should follow him. Jan noticed that his only weapon seemed to be a small club hanging from his wide leather belt. He led them down a short corridor, then through a doorway and into a large room filled with a haze of perfumed smoke. The walls were hung with crude tapestries and large cushions covered most of the floor. Sitting on a pile of these cushions in the centre of the floor was the fattest man Jan had ever seen. To be totally accurate he was the *only* fat man Jan had ever seen — obesity being unknown among the Minervans. She supposed he must have weighed at least two hundred and fifty pounds. His one-piece garment, decorated with coloured designs, revealed massive rolls of fat around his stomach, chest and thighs, and his neck was so fat he seemed to have no chin at all.

But he wasn't the only odd sight in that room. Kneeling behind the fat man on the pile of cushions, and gently massaging the back of his huge neck, was a young girl who, at first glance, appeared to Jan to be entirely naked. However Jan then saw that

68

the girl was wearing a very small loin cloth that was little more than a few strips of leather. Her lack of clothing, and the obsequious expression the girl wore as she kneaded the fat man's neck, made Jan feel both ashamed for her and disgusted.

"Aha, the amazon!" exclaimed the fat man in his deep voice as Tanith pushed her forward. "And a meaty little item she is too, by the look of her."

As he leered at her Jan had the horrible thought that he was going to make her undress as well but to her relief he simply chuckled and said to Tanith, "She'll make a dandy glass walker. Are there any other amazons to be had?"

Tanith explained what had happened. The fat man made sounds of regret then reached under one of the cushions and brought out a small leather bag that jingled metallically when he shook it. "Your agreed price, soldier," he said and tossed the bag to Tanith. "You may go now."

Tanith slipped the bag into his belt pouch without checking the contents. "Thank you, Guild Master," he said then turned and exited quickly from the room. Jan felt a mild regret to see him go. He may have been her captor but he had been a tenuous link with her former life. She stared anxiously at the fat man, who had now picked up a wooden implement from a bowl in front of him and was sucking on it. Smoke poured out of the end, to Jan's wonder.

"Well, amazon," he said, "I hope you appreciate your position and don't intend any displays of disobedience. I trust the consequences of such behaviour have been explained to you?"

She nodded and tried to look meek.

"Good. You look as if you'll be a valuable worker. I'd hate to lose you too soon. And mind you obey whichever of my male slaves ends up with you. I hear you've been trying to keep up any of that Minervan foolishness and I'll have you whipped. You live in a man's world now, amazon, where women have no power at all." He suddenly laughed. "Not that my late wife ever did accept that fact of life."

The other man laughed too but abruptly stopped when the fat man's expression grew serious again. "Hmmm, it occurs to me that a spicy little piece of meat like this may cause trouble among the slaves. Benny, when you take her to the quarters you'd better stay awhile and supervise the argument over who gets her. Try and make a decision that will cause the least friction."

"I understand, boss."

Jan was wishing now that she had gone back into the cage with the other women. There was no way she was going to become the carnal property of some brutish male slave. She would have no choice but to defend herself, an action which would end, sooner or later, in her death. The sooner she could find a way of setting off her bomb, the better.

The fat man was reaching again into the bowl from which he'd extracted the smoking implement. This time he took out a small metal rod with a star on the end of it. The star was glowing red. He sighed. "I'm afraid there is a slight unpleasantness to attend to before you can be on your way, amazon. Please come here and kneel before me."

Jan saw at once what he intended to do, though she didn't know *where* exactly he intended to do it, and took an instinctive step backward. Immediately a powerful hand closed around the back of her neck and she was stopped from moving any further.

The fat man shook his head, making all the fat beneath his mouth wobble obscenely, then said sadly, "You must never *ever* disobey me, girl. But as you have just arrived I shall be lenient. Benny, just a quick touch of your razzle stick, if you please."

Before Jan knew what was happening she saw, out of the corner of her eye, the man apply the tip of what she had thought was a club to her upper right arm. She discovered instantly it was no club. Every nerve cell throughout her entire body seemed to burst into flame. She experienced agony infinitely beyond anything she thought the Mother God would allow to exist in Her universe. She screamed . . . .

Then the pain was gone and she was on her knees and retching fluid on to the floor. She'd emptied her bladder too, she realized, but nothing mattered now that the terrible pain was gone. And when Benny then dragged her closer to the fat man, who deftly applied the red hot, star-shaped brand to her right cheek, she didn't even make a sound. She just stared into the empty eyes of the other girl who continued to massage the fat man's neck even as he applied the brand. Jan no longer felt contempt for her. To

70

avoid being touched again by that black stick she was prepared, at that moment, to take the girl's place and do exactly the same.

The fat man put the glowing metal rod back into the bowl and said, "You are now marked as a slave. For life. Like her. See." He indicated the naked girl's face. For the first time Jan noticed the small black star on her right cheek. She thought it actually looked rather pretty. "You can only enter and move about within those parts of the Sky Lord that are marked with similar black stars," continued the fat man. "If you are ever discovered outside these designated areas you will immediately be ejected from the Sky Lord. Understand me, amazon?"

She said yes, anxious not to upset him again.

"Good. Benny, you can take her to the slave quarters now."

As Benny pulled her to her feet the fat man added, "Hopefully, if you turn out to be clean, we can get to know each other much better. Would you like that?"

Jan swallowed and said, "Yes. I would." The girl, showing her first sign of independent life, frowned at her. The fat man chuckled and made a dismissive gesture with one of his pudgy hands. Jan was hurried out of the room by Benny. She glanced down and saw that the black stick was, thankfully, again hanging from his belt.

He took her into a very narrow corridor that was more like a tunnel. It was badly lit and smelt foul and Jan had to hunch forward to avoid hitting her head on the roof. They hadn't gone far when Jan saw a large rat ahead of her. It watched them approach with no sign of fear and then, when Jan was only a few feet from it, suddenly vanished into a hole in the floor.

Finally the tunnel widened out and became better illuminated. It ended at a kind of junction with different corridors leading away in different directions and one that led straight down. Coming out of the latter were the sound of raucous male voices and dreadful cooking smells.

"Go on, climb down it," ordered Benny, indicating the ladder that led down into the tunnel. Jan did so, with Benny following her. After a short distance the ladder emerged from the ceiling of a narrow but very long room. Jan hesitated and looked around at all the faces that were staring up at her. A silence had fallen over the room as she'd made her appearance but then someone, a man, yelled loudly, "Don't be bashful, darling. Come on down!" Then came a burst of laughter, followed by jeering and catcalls. Jan's initial reaction was to climb back up again, but when Benny gave her a sharp knock on the top of her head with the heel of his boot she had no choice but to descend the rest of the way.

There was another brief spell of silence when the occupants of the long room saw Benny emerge from the hole in the ceiling after Jan, but as she reached the end of the ladder the jeering and laughter broke out again and she was immediately caught in a press of male bodies. For a moment she thought the room contained only men but then she glimpsed several women on the edge of the throng. From their expressions they were definitely not as happy as the men to see her.

She was relieved when Benny joined her at the base of the ladder and cleared a space around them simply by unhooking the black stick from his belt and pressing a switch in its side. The jeering and laughter subsided again. Then a man called out, "Hey, Benny, who's your pretty little friend?"

"She's from that amazon town we flattened yesterday," Benny told them cheerfully. "And she's come to join you . . . ."

There was a roar of laughter that made Jan flinch. Benny held up the black stick for silence. "Now the thing is, you bunch of hull scrubbers, that the boss doesn't want you fighting over this little amazon. Too many of you have died, or been maimed, in brawls during the last year and he's not happy about it. You're valuable to him and he doesn't like losing his valuables for no good reason. Are you with me?" He looked around.

There were mutters of assent. Benny continued "Right, so let's do this sensibly. Hands up all of you who think you deserve this little item here."

A lot of hands shot into the air and there was a great deal of laughter again. Benny scowled. "I haven't got forever, you idiots, so give me a break." He pointed the stick at a man almost directly in front of him. "You, Barth! What are you holding your hand up for? I know for a fact you have *two* women. What do you need another one for?"

Barth, a big man with a spectacular growth of beard, grinned and said, "Why do you think?"

More laughter. Even Benny smiled briefly but the scowl was soon back into position. "Put your hand down, Barth," he ordered. "And the rest of you who have women, no matter how much you think you deserve a spare, pull your hands down as well."

Reluctantly and slowly a lot of hands went down. But a lot still remained. It was obvious that the slave quarters contained many more men than women. It was then that Jan noticed a man standing apart from the rest. He was leaning against a wall next to two women who were looking at Jan and muttering to themselves. He had his arms folded and was watching her with studied indifference. She had noticed him because, unlike the other men, he was not only beardless but completely bald as well.

Her attention was wrenched back to her immediate predicament when one of the men stepped forward and grabbed hold of her left buttock, giving it a painful squeeze, "Only checking the goods," protested the man when Benny waved him away with the pain stick. "Hard to see what she's like under those overalls. Why not make her take them off, Benny?"

There was a chorus of bellowed agreement from the surrounding men. Benny didn't look amused. Frowning, he scanned their faces then seemed to come to a decision. He pointed the stick and called out, "Hey, you, *Buncher*! Come here!"

The throng parted as a huge man stepped forward. He had an unusually long lower jaw and reminded Jan of a chimp in the way he looked and moved. "Yeah, Benny?" he said in a low voice.

"You don't have a woman any more, do you? Not since what'shername did the long slide a few months back when her safety rope broke . . . ."

"Ol' Buncher cut that rope himself," said someone and laughed.

"I did not!" said Buncher angrily, turning to see who had made the accusation.

"Never mind that!" snapped Benny. "I told you I haven't got all day to waste in here. Buncher, you want this item?"

There were cries of protest. Benny waved his pain stick

meaningfully and said, "You idiots would take forever to settle this so I'm making the decision for you. Buncher gets the amazon. You got any complaints, take them up with the boss." He turned back to Buncher. "I'm presuming you *do* want her, Buncher?"

Jan looked at the huge man with a sinking feeling. He was staring at her. His eyes were small and unintelligent. In fact, Jan had seen more intelligence in the eyes of the average chimp. He nodded slowly. "Yeah, I want her."

"Good," said Benny. He gave Jan a push towards him. Buncher took hold of her upper arm with one of his large hands and grinned down at her. There was applause, more jeering and several obscene suggestions. "You others leave this happy couple alone," ordered Benny. "I hear there's any trouble I'll be back to give those responsible more than a quick taste of the old razzle stick." Then he was climbing quickly back up the ladder. Once again Jan felt a sense of abandonment, even though she had feared Benny and his pain stick much more than she had Tanith.

"Come on, we go now," said the man called Buncher. He propelled her through the laughing crowd and down the long room. She glimpsed a row of what were obviously open ovens. Steaming pots were sitting on most of them but one had a young pig cooking on a spit. Her gorge rose. As she'd always feared, the Sky People were meat-eaters . . . .

"Back off, you hear!" bellowed Buncher suddenly, swinging round and almost jerking her arm from its socket. He was yelling at the group who were following them. They laughed and called out insults but when Buncher pulled her along again she noticed they stayed where they were.

After a long open section Jan saw that room abruptly narrowed because of a series of makeshift cubicles on both sides constructed out of a variety of materials but mostly consisting of dyed cloth stitched together into patchworks. She guessed that these were individual living quarters and was proved correct when Buncher stopped at one of them and pulled open the blanket that concealed the entrance. "Inside," he ordered and gave her a shove that sent her sprawling on to the dirty straw matting. A chicken gave a squawk of alarm and ran out past her. Jan looked around. The cubicle was about eight feet by ten. There was a dirty mattress against one wall. The only other large item of furnishing in the place was a large wicker-work trunk with a padlock on its front. The floor was strewn with unwashed food utensils, soiled clothing, bones and other food scraps. The smell was foul.

Buncher let the blanket drop back into place, listened suspiciously for a time for any sound from outside then came and stood over Jan. "You're pretty. I like you," he told her in a flat, emotionless voice.

Jan got up. She saw there was a spark of light in his eyes now and knew what it signified. This time there was no way of avoiding the inevitable. "You want to make love to me?" she asked him shakily.

He frowned. "Make love . . .?" Then his face cleared. "Oh, yeah, yeah, we're going to make love." He reached out for her. She stepped back. "What if I said I didn't want to?"

Now he looked profoundly puzzled. "Eh? I don't get you . . . ." He reached for her again. This time she didn't back away. One of his beefy hands gripped her shoulder, the other began to tug at the opening of her suit. She moved closer to him and brought her right knee up very sharply into his groin. He made a whooshing noise and started to double over, his face twisting up with pain and shock.

As he folded over she rammed her fist into his chest above the heart then pulled free of his now weakened grip. He fell on hands and knees to the floor, wheezing and groaning. She stepped quickly around him, kicked him in the side of the stomach then raised her arm to deliver what she hoped would be a death blow across the back of his exposed neck. But before she could bring the edge of her hand hurtling down towards its target her wrist was suddenly seized by someone behind her.

An amused voice said, "Very impressive but not very smart, little amazon."

Chapter Eight:

She turned quickly. It was the bald man she had noticed earlier. He was smiling at her as he continued to grip her by the wrist. Despite her shock and anger at his sudden appearance she was surprised to see that his eyes were of different colours. One was blue, the other green.

She drove her free hand, the fingers out stiff, at his throat. The next thing she knew he was holding her by both wrists. He was only lightly built and not much taller than she, but he was much stronger than he looked.

"Calm down, little amazon, and use your head," he told her gently. "That way you may get to keep it. Trust me, eh?"

"Trust *you*?" she hissed contemptuously. "Why should I?"

"Because, for the time being at least, I'm your only hope of staying alive." He released her left hand. "I'll let your other hand go if you promise not to try and hit me or do anything silly like running off. All right?"

After a pause she reluctantly nodded. She had, she realized, no choice at the moment. "Good," he said and released her. He went over to Buncher, who was still on his hands and knees and groaning, and helped him to stand. When Buncher's pain-racked eyes focused on Jan his face contorted with rage. "I'll . . . *kill* her!" he gasped and tried to rush her but the bald man held him where he was with what seemed little effort. Jan's first impression was confirmed. He *was* stronger than he looked.

"Easy, Buncher," cautioned the bald man as he guided Buncher over to the mattress and sat him down on it. "Kill her and Bannion would be pissed with you."

Buncher, clutching at his groin, glared at Jan with rage-filled eyes. "Okay, I won't kill her . . . I'll just break all her joints, slowly."

"Well, I'm glad you're starting to use your imagination, Buncher," said the bald man lightly. "But if you give the matter some further thought you will see that the outcome will be the same. A glass walker who can't walk is no use to Bannion. No, I have a much better solution. Give the amazon to me."

"What?" Buncher turned and looked at the bald man, his eyes narrowing with suspicion. "Why?"

"Well, you're obviously not compatible while I, on the other hand, have had experience with such females in the past. I know how to treat them. Don't worry, I'll soon have this one broken, but without having to break her body. She'll still be able to do her work for Bannion."

"You try and break me and I'll kill you," Jan told the bald man angrily.

"Shut up," he said without looking at her. "Well, Buncher, what do you say?"

Buncher shook his head. "No way, Milo. Benny gave her to me. And I'm keeping her."

The man called Milo sighed. "Well, that's unfortunate, because I'm taking her, Buncher. And I want to take her with your blessing." He sat down beside him on the dirty mattress and put his arm around the big man's shoulders. Buncher tried to pull away. He looked alarmed. "None of your tricks, Milo. I know you . . . ."

Milo smiled sadly at him. "I don't think so. But don't worry, Buncher, no tricks. Just tell anyone who asks that the amazon was too much trouble and you gave her to me."

"No," said Buncher. He was still trying, and failing, to dislodge the smaller man's arm from around his shoulders.

"Be reasonable," said Milo in the same quiet tone of voice. "Do what I say and I'll owe you a couple of favours. And you know how useful my favours are, don't you, Buncher? On the other hand . . ." Milo's grip tightened. Buncher winced. Jan saw his face go white and then the veins stood out on the sides of his thick neck. "You're a sorcerer, Milo!" he gasped. "Everyone hates . . . you. We'll kill you one day . . . you'll see . . . ."

"How many times has it been tried? My safety rope has been cut three times and I'm still here, aren't I, Buncher? Even the poison in my food didn't work, and as for that clumsy attempt by Bronski in the latrine . . . ." Milo shook his head in mock sorrow. "I wonder whatever did happen to good old Bronski. But enough of nostalgia, back to the matter at hand." His grip tightened. Jan heard something go *snap* inside Buncher. He made a high-pitched mewling sound then he nodded frantically. Milo let him go. Buncher shrank away from him and wrapped his long arms about himself as if he was cold.

"Take her, take her . . ." he muttered, not looking at Milo.

Milo smiled at him, and even Jan felt a shiver of unease as she sensed the *wrongness* of that smile. Perhaps Buncher was right; maybe this man Milo *was* a sorcerer.

Milo said, "And you *will* say, if anyone asks you, Buncher, that you gave me the girl of your own free will?"

"Yeah, I will. I swear it."

"Good man." Milo gave him an approving pat on the shoulder. Buncher flinched at his touch. Milo stood up and smiled at Jan. "We can go now."

"I'm not going anywhere with you," Jan told him.

"You want to stay here? With him?" Milo indicated the dazed Buncher, who continued to stare at the floor, his arms still wrapped about himself.

"No," admitted Jan. "But I certainly don't want to go anywhere with *you*."

He sighed, then asked what her name was. She told him. "Well, Jan, be reasonable. You have no choice but to trust me. I'm your only chance of survival. I've already saved your life once. If you'd killed Buncher here the others would have torn you into pieces. And I mean that literally."

"Why do you want to help me?"

"Because you can help *me*."

"How?"

"That we can discuss in more private circumstances. Come on." He held out his hand to her. After a long hesitation she said, "All right, I'll go with you, but I warn you that if you try to touch me I'll kill you."

He smiled at her. "Long-lasting relationships have been established on even less romantic initial understandings." He

78

seemed to think he'd said something amusing but Jan didn't get the joke.

His own cubicle was almost at the end of the long room. Compared to Buncher's hovel it seemed immaculate. It had furniture too. A bed, a small table and a chair; all made of intricate wicker-work. The straw matting on the floor was relatively clean and there was no sign of any food scraps. There was even a painting on one of the 'walls'. It was suspended from the cane rod that supported the cloth partition. It was a strange painting. It was a swirling jumble of colours that seemed to form a specific pattern but Jan couldn't distinguish what it was. It was like seeing something out of the corner of your eye.

Milo sat down in the wicker chair, which creaked loudly, and gestured at the bed. She sat down cautiously, keeping her eyes fixed suspiciously on him.

"Relax," he told her. "I'm not going to spring on you and rip your clothes off."

"I know you're not. You'd soon be dead if you tried." She said this with a conviction she didn't feel. After what she'd just witnessed in Buncher's cubicle she knew she would be powerless against him.

He was obviously thinking the same thing because he seemed amused, then he said, "Poor little amazon, you've certainly been through the wars by the look of you. That's a bad gash on your head. And that bruise on your cheek. Who gave you that? It's fresh, isn't it?"

She told him about the Sky Warrior punching her. He made a sympathetic sound. "Any other injuries apart from the visible ones?" he asked.

"Just some cuts on my arms and legs but they've stopped bleeding."

"And what about internally? Any pains or other symptoms?"

"My stomach hurts," she admitted. "It's been sore ever since I threw up after that man Benny touched me with that pain stick."

Milo scowled. "He used a razzle stick on you?"

"Yes. It was horrible. How does it work? Is it magic?"

"Of a kind." He ran one of his hands over the top of his bald

79

head as if brushing back hair. "Look," he said, "I know quite a lot about medical matters. I could examine you if you like."

Her guard, which she'd lowered slightly at his display of sympathy for her, immediately went up again. "I told you you're not going to touch me. Not for any reason."

"All right, all right," he said hurriedly, holding up both hands to ward off an invisible blow. "Forget I said it, okay? Let's change the subject to food and drink. Are you thirsty? When did you last eat anything."

She was thirsty, and very hungry. Reluctantly she admitted as much to Milo. He went to a wicker chest similar to the one in Buncher's cubicle and unlocked it. He took out a canteen and tossed it to her. It was half full of water. She drank from it greedily.

"Nothing fresh to eat, I'm afraid," he told her as he rooted about in the chest. "How about some dried salt beef?"

She put down the canteen. "Is that meat?"

He gave her a quizzical look. "Let me guess. You're a vegetarian."

"Of course I am. All Minervans are . . . ." She paused. For a moment she'd forgotten that Minerva no longer existed.

Again he must have sensed what she was thinking, because he said gently, "I have some biscuits here. They're quite nourishing. No meat in them." He tossed over a small package. Her eyes brimming with tears she undid the greasy wrapping and took out one of the biscuits. It was crudely made but tasted fine.

As she was starting on a second biscuit Milo said, "Would it bother you too much to talk about what happened?"

She shook her head. "I'd like to."

"First tell me something about Minerva. I confess I know little about its more recent manifestations; I'm only familiar with its historical origins. I'm even surprised you still speak basic Americano. I'd have thought you would have evolved your own feminist language by now."

She frowned at him. Little of what he said made any sense to her. In the months to come she would find this a very familiar situation. "Minerva's historical origins . . .? What do you mean?"

"Don't you know how Minerva started?"

"Of course. After the Mother God punished the Old Men for ruining the earth she set up Minerva so that women could be truly free."

Milo looked at her then said quietly, "Jesus Christ."

"Who?"

"It doesn't matter. I'll tell you another time. Look, didn't you have any history books in that town of yours?"

"Books?" she said blankly.

He sighed. "Yeah, some hope. The fungus would have destroyed all the paper ages ago. But what about other records? Electronic stuff. Computers. You have any computers down there?"

"I don't know what a computer is but we didn't have any of Man's evil devices down there."

"So you don't know anything about anything." He shook his head in wonder. "My God, you're even more innocent than you look."

She wasn't sure but she felt she'd just been insulted. "So how do *you* think Minerva began?" she asked him huffily.

"I don't think, I *know*. It was a state in old America. Or rather it was one of the main states that old America broke up into in the period leading up to the Gene Wars. You have heard of the Gene Wars, I trust?"

"Of course I have."

"But you've never heard of the United States of America?"

She admitted she hadn't.

"America," he began to explain, "was once a great empire. With another huge empire, the Soviet Union, it formed a powerful alliance — the Soviet-American Alliance — which practically ruled the entire world for over fifty years in the twenty-first century." He paused and looked at her. "Do you understand any of this?"

"No," she said truthfully.

He sighed but continued anyway. "Well, the Alliance finally ended and the two empires began to break up into a number of autonomous states. Minerva was one of them and it was quite big. Within Minerva was a smaller state that was exclusively female but Minerva at large permitted male citizens. However, men could only become citizens if they agreed to certain conditions — they had to agree to undergo a complete genetic modification of their bodies and brains. This genetic 'rewiring' had the effect of softening, not to mention eradicating entirely, certain unwelcome masculine traits. One of the changes they underwent was that they became smaller, while at the same time Minervan females were modified to grow larger. Thus at a stroke the natural physical superiority of the human male — and the prime cause of the traditional exploitation and subjugation of women by men throughout history — was el— " He stopped.

Jan was yawning.

Milo said, "You're not interested in the origin of Minerva?"

"That's not how Minerva began. You're talking nonsense."

"Talk of the Mother God setting up Minerva Herself *isn't* nonsense as far as you're concerned?" he asked, with amusement.

"No, of course it isn't."

"If that's the case — that the Mother God established Minerva so women could be truly free — how do you explain this?" He gestured at their surroundings. "For hundreds of years Minerva, along with all the other ground communities throughout the world, has been under the thumb of the Sky Lords. That's not what I call freedom. Your goddess seems to have short-changed you."

"She's not our *goddess*," protested Jan, annoyed. "She's the one, true Mother God, creator of everything. And she didn't give absolute freedom to Minerva — she left the Sky Lords as a symbol of Man's evil so that we would never be complacent about its danger."

"Some symbol," murmured Milo. "It pulverized your town into the dirt yesterday."

She winced. "You don't have to remind me."

"I'm sorry, but I'm just trying to make my point. Your Mother God seems to have gone to unnecessary extremes to make her point about Man's evil. I presume not many of you survived."

Jan bowed her head. "No," she said in a subdued voice. "I'm the only one. The only woman, that is. There are four Minervan men on board as well . . . ." She covered her face with her hands and began to cry.

Milo waited patiently while she cried for a time, then said, "You don't know for sure you're the only female survivor from your town. The Sky Warriors aren't infallible. They more than likely missed quite a few when they were searching the ruins."

She took her hands away and stared at him. "You really think so?" she asked hopefully.

"I believe there's a very good chance of it. And there's something else for you to keep in mind — your Minerva wasn't the only one of its kind."

She stared at him in confusion. "What are you talking about?"

"Didn't you know? There's more than one Minerva. I know of at least one other town almost the same size as yours which is within the jurisdiction of the *Lord Pangloth*. It's also called Minerva and lies less than a quarter of a day's flying time to the east of here. And I have heard there are other such Minervan communities." He leaned back in his chair and smiled at her expression of astonishment. "So you see, you're not as alone as you thought you were."

Chapter Nine:

The communal latrine was as bad as Milo had warned her it would be. A long, foul-smelling place with rows of dirty sinks, urinals and sit-down toilets in cubicles without doors. Fortunately, there was only one other person in there as she entered, a woman who was just leaving one of the cubicles. She gave Jan an unreadable look as she hurried past her.

When she had gone Jan stepped into a cubicle. She was nervous and hoped Milo would be as good as his word and stay by the entrance to the latrine. She'd told him she didn't want any man to see her naked — which was true — but the other reason was that she intended to remove the incendiary bomb.

83

She just couldn't carry the thing inside her any longer. It had become much too uncomfortable.

She quickly climbed out of the one-piece baggy suit and, feeling exposed and vulnerable, extracted the bomb. Then, sitting on the bowl to evacuate her bowels, she unwrapped the cloth from the bomb and examined it. When it was inside her it had felt huge but now, resting in the palm of her hand, it seemed ridiculously small for the task it was supposed to achieve. She sighed and put it in one of her suit's many pockets.

Despite her anxiety about her immediate fate on the Sky Lord she was feeling in better spirits now. The revelation from Milo about the other Minervas had changed everything. At first she couldn't bring herself to believe him. It seemed impossible that no one in *her* Minerva knew about these other Minervan communities but Milo was convincing in his explanation. "I told you that originally Minerva covered a very large area. As the blight began spreading across the country the state of Minerva, like all the other states, became fragmented with the various parts becoming isolated from each other. As you Minervans didn't believe in using such 'evil' devices as radios I imagine communication ceased between your different communities ages ago."

The thought that somewhere there existed another Minerva, even though it was full of strangers, made all the difference. *Somehow* she would get there . . . some day. But first she had to perform the simple task of destroying the *Lord Pangloth*, not to mention trying to stay alive long enough to make the attempt.

Beside the toilet there was a worn looking lever protruding from the floor. When she was finished she pulled it, presuming it worked the flush. But there was no flush; instead there was a hiss of air from the bowl. The lever, she realized, operated some kind of air pump that sucked out the waste matter and no doubt ejected it from the Sky Lord to be deposited on the ground below.

She dressed hurriedly and emerged from the cubicle. The latrine was still empty. She went to one of the filthy sinks and turned on its tap. Only a trickle of brown water appeared. Milo had told her that water was scarce on the airship and strictly rationed. This water was for washing with only. She yearned to take another shower — as Tanith had warned her the white liquid had made her skin itch and feel uncomfortable — but had to be satisfied with just washing her hands and face.

As she headed back towards the latrine's entrance she heard the sound of raised voices. In the passageway outside she found Milo facing three men. They looked angry but she noticed they kept their distance from him.

". . . You heard Benny's order, Milo!" one of them was saying. "The amazon was to go to Buncher. What are *you* doing with her?"

"I told you," said Milo in his usual calm voice. "Buncher said I could have her. He changed his mind. I guess he's scared of picking up an infection."

"Balls!" cried another man. "You forced him to hand her over, admit it!"

"Why don't you go ask Buncher if you don't believe me?"

"We already have. He said the same as you."

"Well, there's no problem then."

"Something's wrong with him, Milo. He doesn't look good. We reckon you hurt him."

"Me? Hurt Buncher?" Milo laughed. "Nonsense."

"We know how you operate, Milo. You're going to have to give her back to him."

Milo folded his arms. "No. She's staying with me. And if anyone tries to take her from me I'm going to be very displeased. And we wouldn't want that, would we, lads?"

Each of the three men was bigger than Milo but none of them made a move towards him. There was a long, tense silence then one of them said angrily, "Sooner or later we're going to get you, Milo. Your luck can't hold and you know it. And then *she* goes back to Buncher." He pointed at Jan. "And when he's finished with her the rest of us will have some fun with her. We're not having an amazon around here who hasn't been taught her place."

"You can leave the lady's education in my capable hands," said Milo. "And now if this stimulating social exchange is over we'll be on our way. Come on, Jan."

For a few moments the three men didn't move then, as one, they abruptly turned and left the short corridor. "They're scared of you," Jan told Milo quietly as they followed the three men back into the main room.

"They're superstitious," he said. "Just ignorant fools. Most of the slaves here were originally marauders. Having had enough of the struggle for life in the blight lands they signalled the *Lord Pangloth* that they wanted to come aboard, even though they knew it meant slavery."

They returned to his cubicle. Jan could now hear sounds from the adjoining cubicles through the thin partitions. The speakers seemed to be deliberately keeping their voices low.

Again Milo motioned for her to sit on the bed while he took the chair. "You look better," he told her approvingly.

"I feel better, thanks to you," she replied, her tone guarded. Suddenly the bed tilted slightly and she had to grab hold of its edge to keep her balance. "What's happening?" she asked, alarmed.

"It's all right, just a change of course," he assured her.

The floor levelled out again. Jan relaxed. "It's incredible. Until then I'd hardly felt anything. I have to keep reminding myself that we're in the air . . . ."

"Most of the time the Sky Lord is a smooth ride, even in fairly turbulent conditions. Of course, when someone makes the stupid decision to fly it straight through the centre of a thunderstorm, as happened last night, it can get pretty rough."

"That was terrible," she said, shuddering at the memory.

"And it was all for your benefit," he told her. "You and your fellow Minervans, that is. The aristos were putting on a show to knock whatever stuffing you still had left in you well and truly out. However, they have more faith in the Sky Lord's anti-lightning system than I have. And I've heard the buffeting caused damage all over the ship. They won't do that again in a hurry. But you Minervans gave them a hell of a fright with your rockets yesterday so I guess their over-reaction is understandable."

"Our rockets," said Jan bitterly. "A lot of good they were."

"It was an admirable effort and it almost worked. Though I would have had mixed feelings about the outcome if it had," he added dryly.

86

"But it *didn't* work. Those beams of light destroyed every single rocket. We didn't have a chance."

"You weren't to know of the existence of the Sky Lord's automatic laser defence system. In fact it came as a big relief to a lot of people on board that it still worked. It's been years since it was last activated."

She frowned. "I don't understand."

"The beams of light are called lasers. They're a special form of light that doesn't exist naturally. They make good weapons. The Sky Lord's are under the control of a computer — a mechanical brain, let's say — which uses them to shoot down anything approaching the Sky Lord that the computer decides presents a danger."

Jan struggled to understand what Milo was saying. The idea of a 'mechanical brain' seemed especially far-fetched, as did the notion that light could be used as a weapon. But she had seen for herself the rockets being destroyed by the turquoise beams. "But if the Sky Lord has such terrible power," she said slowly, "why didn't he use it to destroy Minerva? Why drop those bombs on us instead?"

"Like I said, the system is automatic. It's not under the control of the aristos, as much as they'd like it to be. The computer that operates it is sealed off and hidden somewhere. It's separate from all the other computer systems — those that are still working, that is — and if the technos in the original group who took over this airship never succeed in getting into it then this lot of technological regressives don't stand a chance."

Jan stared at him blankly.

He took a deep breath. "Okay, let me put it this way — the beams of light are purely defensive weapons that operate independently of the Aristos. Also the beams only work against inanimate objects — non-living things like missiles or other projectiles. They wouldn't destroy a bird, much less a human being."

"Why would the Sky Lord behave so mercifully in this respect and so cruelly in all others?" she asked, totally baffled.

"Because, my innocent little amazon, in their original form the Sky Lords performed a very different service for mankind . . .

and womankind too," he added hastily. "In fact they used to be called Sky Angels, partly because of the nature of their work and also because of their origin in the heavens."

"The heavens?"

Milo pointed towards the low, grey ceiling. "The heavens. Outer space, to be exact. They were built in a giant orbiting space factory nearly a thousand miles above the earth's surface."

Jan gave him a suspicious look. Was he making fun of her or did he really believe in these fairy stories he was telling her? "How would anyone have managed to build a factory so high in the sky, and what would have prevented it from falling to the ground?"

Milo rolled his eyes in an exaggerated mime of exasperation. "I don't have the time to educate you in the basic laws of nature right now. You're going to have to take my word that in the old days we had the means of getting into outer space. In bigger versions of those rockets you fired at us yesterday. And you'll also have to take my word on the fact that if you go up high enough you no longer feel the pull of gravity. It was the lack of gravity that led to the Sky Angels being constructed in outer space. The special alloys and materials that go to make up the airship's skeleton and outer skin could only be manufactured in weightless conditions. They are incredibly strong but ultra-light."

"I see," said Jan, nodding.

Milo chuckled and said, "Do you? I doubt it. You Minervans have been living in your cosy cocoon of ignorance for centuries. And I'll tell you something else that you will find fantastic. We not only had factories in space but cities too. In orbit around the Earth and also on the moon and Mars."

"I'm beginning to think you've been drinking some very strong beer today."

He laughed again. "Well now, so you know about beer. I'm glad to hear you amazons have one vice at least. Did much beer-drinking go on in Minerva?"

"Quite a lot," she admitted. "Though when the grain supplies grew short we had to stop brewing it. There wasn't much left in storage by yesterday and rationing had been imposed. We did have an alcohol-manufacturing plant but it didn't make the kind you can drink. We used it for fuel. For cooking and heating and so on."

"Propanol, was it? Or butanol?"

She shrugged. "We just called it alcohol. It came out of these big vats in the plant. They were filled with brown stuff that was alive. You fed in anything — like leaves, grass, food scaps or whatever — and this stuff would turn it into alcohol."

Milo nodded. "Yes, I know what that was. A genetically engineered synthetic bacterium designed to convert organic matter into either propanol or butanol. Pity genetic engineering is a lost art these days. A bit of tinkering with a few of those bacteria and you could have had a vat that produced ethyl alcohol as well. The kind you can drink."

Jan was shocked. "You think we would have committed the blasphemy of doing such a thing, even if it was still possible?"

"I don't see why not. You were already taking advantage of 'evil' science by continuing to use your production plant all these years."

"But I'm sure no one knew in Minerva that the plant was the work of genegineers . . . " protested Jan.

"Originally, someone *must* have known it was."

"No Minervan would ever deliberately make use of anything that had been produced by the genegineers — those men were more responsible than anyone for turning the world into what it is today."

"What hypocrisy!" laughed Milo. "For one thing a lot of those genegineers were women. And Minerva used genetic engineering extensively in its early years, the results of which are still around. Look at your Minervan men . . . look at yourself for that matter."

"Myself?"

"You're what used to be called a Prime Standard according to the United Nations Genetic Ruling of 2062. That gives you a lot of advantages over all the previous generations of humanity. For one thing you have a life-span of two hundred plus years, and you'll never get any older physically than thirty-five — and you won't even reach that age for at least another forty years. You'll thus be spared all the horrors of old age while your eventual death, barring unforeseen circumstances, will be quick and painless.

"You also have a phenomenal immune system," Milo continued. "You are immune to all conventional infections and to the diseases, such as cancer, that plagued humanity for so long. Admittedly you are vulnerable to most of the more insidious designer viruses unleashed during the latter stages of the Gene Wars, and to some of the mutated species of fungi that are spreading at the moment, but those are handicaps you share with all the Prime Standards and overall you're very fortunate. You have incredible powers of recovery — your bones knit very quickly when broken and your central nervous system has the power to regenerate. Injuries that could paralyse a pre-Prime Standard type for life you are capable of shrugging off in a matter of weeks. And on top of that you don't menstruate, except at twenty-year intervals, if you don't become pregnant during your period of fertility."

Jan's mind was reeling. "I don't — what?"

"Menstruate," said Milo, smiling at her confusion. "In pre-Prime Standard times women menstruated every month from puberty to the menopause." When he saw she wasn't understanding what he said he paused. "What did they teach you back in Minerva? About your body, I mean?"

"I was taught to harmonize with my body," she told him. "By meditating and letting the spirit of the Mother God flow . . . ."

"No, no," he said quickly, interrupting her. "I mean were you taught about how your body *works*?"

"Yes. Of course I was."

"You know about your reproductive system, then? That when you're born you're carrying eggs inside you?"

Jan nodded that she did.

"Do you know how *many* eggs."

"A hundred or so, I think."

"Correct. But in pre-Prime Standard days a female child was born carrying *half a million* eggs in her ovaries."

"Oh, *really* . . ." she said, disbelievingly.

"It's true. And when a pre-Prime Standard girl reached

puberty, which in those days meant the age when her reproductive system had become functional — an egg was then released *every month* into her uterus to be fertilized. If the egg wasn't fertilized within two weeks it was ejected from the uterus along with the lining. This was called menstruation, and though it affected women differently most found it an unpleasant experience. Apart from the bleeding involved it could also be painful, as well as emotionally upsetting. Hormones were the culprit, as usual. When the egg was in the uterus hormonal changes caused an alteration in the surface of the uterus in preparation for the fertilization of the egg. These drastic hormonal changes were the cause of all the discomfort that women suffered."

"I can't believe any of this. The Mother God wouldn't have let women suffer so much."

"Your Mother God wasn't around in those days," Milo said drily. "God the Father was running the show and he evidently had it in for women."

"The Mother God has *always* existed, and always will," Jan told him firmly.

"Whatever you say. Anyway, when the genengineers around the middle of the twenty-first century finally solved the problem of how to switch off the molecular timer that caused the cellular self-destruction known as the ageing process it meant immortality was within reach at last. But, of course, if all humanity became immortal the Earth's resources would have been rapidly depleted so it was decided to impose a limit on just how long anyone could be genetically re-programmed to live. The debate went on a long time before the United Nations finally imposed the two hundred year plus law. In those days the United Nations still had weight, because it was backed by the Soviet-American Alliance."

"What was the United Nations?" she asked.

He waved an impatient hand. "Another time. The point was that if people were going to be allowed to live a two hundred year plus life-span they couldn't be allowed to breed as freely as before because, once again, the world's resources would be endangered. So it was also decreed by the United Nations that women could only become fertile for one year in every twenty."

91

Jan frowned at him. "Are you saying that before that time women were fertile *continuously*?" she asked in amazement.

"That's *exactly* what I've been trying to tell you. And these two decrees by the United Nations not only changed women's reproductive systems but the world itself."

"How come?"

"Because of all the opposition to the decrees. Much of it came from religious fundamentalists . . . The Islamic nations were dead set against the whole idea of genetic meddling with the human body. It was, they said, against the law of Allah . . . ."

"Allah?" asked Jan.

"Another very masculine God. You wouldn't have liked Him. Anyway, it wasn't just the Islamic nations, there was fierce opposition from the Western religious fundamentalists as well, Catholic and Protestant — and don't ask me what *they* were; it would take too long to explain. Just take my word for it that the whole argument got pretty bloody.

"You see, when the United Nations made the two hundred year plus decree they decreed at the same time that *every* individual in the world, provided they weren't too old to be genetically modified, was entitled by international law to have their life-span thus expanded. So you can imagine the result — people living in a country that had vetoed the longevity treatment for religious reasons were understandably tempted to move to a country where it *was* allowed. Well, all hell broke loose, and when the dust finally settled all the maps of the world had to be redrawn. Most of the bigger nations, including the Soviet Union and America, had fragmented into a number of new, autonomous states, such as your Minerva."

"You make it all sound so convincing," said Jan wonderingly.

"It's convincing because it's true," he told her. "Minerva owes its existence to genetic engineering despite whatever myths about its origin you've been fed. And Minerva's inhabitants weren't just satisfied with the Prime Standard model — they added all the modifications that they could under the then still-existing international laws. The early feminists, for reasons of dogma, were loath to acknowledge that most of the psychological differences between men and women were genetically inspired. The idea smacked too much of 'biological determinism', a very politically unpopular concept at the time.

"However, by the end of the twentieth century research into the working of the human brain had proved that biological determinism was a much stronger force in human affairs than anyone had previously wanted to accept. And, of course, the feminists took full advantage of these discoveries when they came to set up Minerva decades later . . . ."

Jan shook her head. "I'm sorry. You've lost me completely now. I can't even understand half the words you're using. What, for example, were these *feminists* you keep mentioning?"

To her annoyance this question amused him greatly. He threw back his head and laughed so loudly he provoked angry muttering from the surrounding cubicles.

Finally he said, "Very well, we'll leave it for the time being. I shall continue your belated education in the history of our unfortunate planet at a later date. Now let's talk about something else — the price for my on-going protection and support."

"Price?" she asked, puzzled.

"Yes, *price*, my little amazon. I told you before we would make a deal. In return for my help you will help me. By giving me something I need."

"But I don't *have* anything to give you."

"On the contrary. You have yourself," Milo said and smiled at her in the same way that he'd smiled at Buncher.

Chapter Ten:

"You're saying that you'll only continue helping me if I agree to have sex with you?" Jan asked angrily. She felt shocked and betrayed. After all his apparent sympathy for her she had begun to trust him.

He shrugged. "You have to be realistic, Jan. You can't get something for nothing in this world. Especially in *this* world up here. And as much as I feel sorry for you I am not, by nature, an altruist. Now I find you very attractive and charming and I feel that, despite your appalling ignorance, you might make a stimulating companion. To be frank, I need a woman. But I am fastidious in such matters and, as you have already seen, the women in this floating zoo leave much to be desired." He sighed and continued, "Since being captured three years ago I have had only a few brief and unsatisfactory couplings. I need something more and I believe you can provide it for me."

She had shrunk back on the bed. "You intend to have sex with me even though I don't want to," she accused him.

"That's putting it rather bluntly, but, well, yes . . . ."

"That's *rape*."

"No, no, not at all," he protested. "I'm not going to *force* you to make love to me. It won't be rape."

"What do you call it then? You're saying you'll hand me over to the rest of the animals in here if I don't allow you to penetrate me. That's rape as far as I'm concerned."

He regarded her coolly. "I assure you there's more to my love-making than mere penetration, young woman. But again I stress I will not be taking you by force."

"Just because you won't be using *physical* force doesn't make it any less a case of rape," she told him.

He ran his hand over his scalp and said, "Look, think of it merely as a business proposition. You have to do something you don't want to do in order to get something you need."

"I see. I let you rape me and you let me live. Is that what you call a business proposition?"

He looked annoyed. "I'm *not* going to rape you and, yes, selling your body *is* a business proposition. It's called prostitution and it's one of the oldest businesses in the world. Women — *and* men — have been selling their bodies for money or food or other favours for time immemorial."

"If someone doesn't want to have sex with someone else but is obliged to do so for reasons of survival then that's rape," she said firmly.

"No, you're being too pedantic," he told her. "Take, for example, a woman who wants a more comfortable way of life and who therefore sleeps with a man in order to attain it even though she feels no sexual attraction towards him — that's not rape, is it?"

Jan frowned. "Perhaps not, but I said 'for reasons of survival' and that's not the same as your example. A woman obliged to sell her body just to stay alive is being raped by the men who take advantage of her situation, no matter how much money or food they may give her. They are rapists, pure and simple."

"I don't think . . ." he said, and faltered.

"What you're offering *me* is the survival proposition," she said quickly, pressing home her advantage, "sex or death. In other words, rape."

He glared at her. "Enough of your Minervan dogma," he said irritably. "What we have here is a problem of semantics and further argument is futile. I will give you my ultimatum. You have exactly a week to decide whether or not to accept my proposition. If you agree to it you will give yourself to me *willingly* with no talk of rape or any other Minervan nonsense. If at the end of the week you do not accept my proposition I will withdraw my protection and you will be on your own here. And you know what that will mean. Do you accept the terms?"

Jan was silent for a time, then she said, "I have a week to make my decision?"

"Yes. I guarantee it."

"Very well. I'll tell you in a week." She leaned back against the flimsy wall and folded her arms. He seemed to relax. "Good," he said and smiled at her. She didn't smile back.

She had made her decision and felt relieved about it. Before the week was up she would have placed the fire bomb where it would do the most damage and blown the Sky Lord out of the sky.

After her apparent acquiescence to his sexual blackmail Milo once again became sympathetic and, superficially at least, charming. He offered her another biscuit, saying that they would eat something more substantial after they had slept. Then he

95

took the thin mattress off the wicker-work bed and laid it out on the floor. "You can sleep on that. It will be more comfortable than the bed."

She thanked him and stretched out on it. She felt exhausted but at the same time not really sleepy. She realized that the idea of going to sleep scared her. She was afraid of what she might dream.

He stood over her, looking down. He said, "You can remove your garment if you wish. I won't bother you. I gave you my word."

"I'll keep it on."

He shrugged and undid the fastener on his own pair of baggy overalls. As he stepped out of them she gave his body only a brief, mildly curious glance before rolling over on her side and closing her eyes. It had been an unremarkable body, as male bodies went. Completely hairless, true, but then Minervan men had very little body hair as well. His sexual organs seemed normal, though she was well aware that her familiarity with male sexual organs rested on her one experience with Simon. The only odd thing about Milo's body was that it didn't look very powerful. Certainly not powerful enough to have done what she had seen him do to the heavily-built Buncher.

She heard the bed creak as Milo lay upon it. Through the thin walls she could still hear the murmuring of voices. Somewhere, a long way off, a woman sobbed. She wondered if the lights were ever turned down or off. She could see the glow through her closed eyelids.

The glow from the ceiling lights turned red. She saw leaping flames as Minerva again burned. She heard screams, heard the sounds of the bombs, saw Helen again, dazed and staggering while she clutched an arm that ended in a bloody stump . . . .

Jan opened her eyes. As she feared, the nightmare of the last two days was waiting for her inside her head. Even before she was asleep the images were pushing their way out. If she slept she would have to live through it all over again. But she *was* getting sleepy now. There was no way she would be able to stay awake for very long, despite the unpleasant itching of her skin as a result of that white liquid. Against her wishes her eyes closed again.

*

96

Who was screaming? It was an awful sound; high-pitched and penetrating. It shredded the nerves. Jan looked anxiously around but there was too much smoke. The screaming continued, getting closer. Then, out of the smoke, Jan saw Martha running towards her. The chimp's hair was alight, from head to foot. As she got closer Jan could hear the crackling of her burning flesh. "No!" cried Jan as Martha, in her panic and fear, leapt up at her. She started to scream as well as the chimp's powerful, burning arms hugged her in desperation . . . .

Jan screamed and screamed as she struggled to get free of those arms but she couldn't, they were too strong.

"Shush, amazon," said a voice in her ear. "Calm down, it's just a dream. You're all right . . ."

The feel of the flames on her flesh faded away, though the powerful arms continued to hold her tightly. She realized where she was; in Milo's cubicle, though it was darker now. She stopped screaming.

"For Christ's sake, shut that bitch up, will ya!" a man yelled from another cubicle.

"Feeling better?" Milo asked her gently.

"I . . . I . . . don't know. What's the matter with me?" Her body was shaking violently, her limbs trembling so badly she seemed to be having a convulsion. She was filled with a feeling of nameless terror, as if she was about to fall off the edge of a bottomless abyss.

"It's just a delayed reaction to all you've been through," Milo told her, still holding her tightly. She, in turn, clung tightly to him. She felt that if she didn't hold on to him the force of her terror would sweep her away and she would be lost forever.

"Relax," he whispered. "Breathe deeply and slowly. One . . . two . . . One . . . two . . . ."

Gradually the awful feeling of panic and terror diminished, the trembling subsided. Milo released her. She felt drained; sick. In the dimness she saw him go to his trunk and take out a small box and his canteen. Kneeling before her on the mattress he told her to hold out her hand. When she did so he placed a pill in her palm and said, "Swallow that. It'll make you feel better."

"What is it?" she asked suspiciously.

97

She saw the flash of his teeth in the gloom. "You're already sounding like your normal self. But don't worry. It's just a synthetic hormone that will stimulate your brain into producing more of a specific encephalin. It will calm you down and allow you to sleep peacefully. You'd better take it before I change my mind. Those things are as rare as hen's teeth these days."

She frowned. "But all hens have teeth . . . ."

"Forget it. An archaic saying. Just take the pill."

Doubtfully, she put the pill in her mouth. He gave her the canteen and she washed the pill down with several welcome swallows of water. "I don't feel any different," she said as she gave the canteen back to him.

"You will." He put the canteen and box back into the trunk. He turned and faced her again, remaining on his knees. "Jan," he asked quietly. "What's that you have in your pocket?"

"What?" she asked. For a moment she didn't know what he was talking about. Then she remembered the bomb. Her mind went blank. "Er . . . it's . . . I . . . don't know . . ." she said lamely.

"You don't know what you have in your pocket?" he asked. He leaned towards her and reached out. She didn't resist as he deftly plucked the bomb from her top pocket. She watched him examine it in the dim light. "It's heavy," he said. "So what is this thing you didn't know you had, eh, amazon?"

Oh Mother God, she thought as she watched him handling it, *if he should twist the top . . . .*

"Give it back to me," she demanded, holding out her hand. "And I'll tell you."

He hesitated for a long time before handing the cylinder back to her. "Well?" he insisted quietly.

Something was happening to her. She realized it must be the pill. She was beginning to feel . . . wonderful. All her worries and fears—even her grief—were falling from her like old scabs from a healed wound. She felt both euphoric and pleasantly relaxed.

"Tell me what it is, Jan," persisted Milo in the same quiet, encouraging tone.

Why not tell him the truth, she wondered? What did it matter? But at the last moment she decided not to tell him. Instead she said, "It's a sacred object. Very sacred. All I have left of Minerva. My mother gave it to me."

"Your mother?"

"My mother was a Headwoman in Minerva. Very important. The people you call the Aristos don't know that . . . kept it a secret from them . . . you won't tell, will you . . .?"

She leaned back on the mattress, resting on one elbow. She was feeling very sleepy now. Wonderfully sleepy.

"I won't tell them," said Milo softly. "But what is that object?"

"I'm tired," she said drowsily. "Want to go to sleep."

"In a moment, amazon. First tell me what it is."

"Very sacred."

"You said that. I want to know why."

"It's a rod of authority. One of several given to our fore-mothers by the Mother God." The pang of guilt Jan experienced as she spoke this blasphemy was so slight as to be almost non-existent. "Swore to my mother I would look after it. Protect it with my life."

"I see," he said slowly. "But how did you manage to get it on board?"

"Hid it." She was struggling to keep her eyes open. It felt as if she was sinking into some deep, cosy bed. She felt like a child again; a glow of reassurance was washing over her from some unknown source.

"But how? Surely your own clothes were destroyed."

She giggled. "Hid it in *me* . . . ."

"Oh," he said, understanding. "Of course."

"Sleep now," she said and let her head drop on to the mattress. Within seconds she *was* asleep.

Milo remained where he was, staring down at her. When he was certain she was in a deep sleep he reached over and again removed the cylinder from her overall. He studied it thoughtfully for some time then returned it to her pocket. He got up and went to his bed. As he lay there he concentrated on damping down the sexual desire that the girl's presence had induced. Eventually he slept and for the first time in decades he dreamed of Miranda.

*

The feeling of well-being was still with Jan when she woke up, though not as intense as before. She sat up. Milo was already awake. He was dressed and sitting on the edge of his bed, looking at her. "Feel better?" he asked.

"Yes," she admitted. "Thank you." She looked around. The lights were back on. Then she remembered what had happened just before she'd fallen asleep and quickly felt her pocket. The bomb was still there.

"Don't worry," he said wryly. "I haven't stolen your precious heirloom."

She felt herself blush. "What was in that pill you gave me?" she asked, changing the subject. "Some kind of Old Science drug?"

"A product of Old Science, yes, but not a drug in the sense that you probably understand the word," he told her. "As I tried to explain to you last night, the actual drug that makes you feel better is produced by your own brain. The pill contained a substance that stimulates the specific part of your brain into producing large amounts of the 'drug'."

She frowned at him, trying to make sense of his words. As before, she was unsure if he was deliberately spinning her a tall tale or telling the truth — or what *he* believed was the truth. "You are saying there is a drug in my brain that caused that marvellous feeling I had before I went to sleep last night?" she asked. "But that can't be, otherwise I would have felt like that before."

He gave a small sigh. "You wouldn't have experienced the effect as intensely before because your brain had never before released so much of the relevant encephalin — 'drug' — into your nervous system."

She continued to look doubtful. Milo said, "'You are familiar with the drug called morphine?"

"Yes. It comes from the poppy. A gift from the Mother God. It deadens pain . . . ."

"Well, a long, long time ago scientists discovered that the human central nervous system possessed its own version of morphine, which explained how some people could suffer serious injuries and not feel any pain — at least not immediately. And as research into the biochemical workings of the brain continued more and more substances were discovered that were analogous not only to narcotics and anaesthetics but also to a large variety of other mood-changing drugs. It became apparent that human thought was the end result of a veritable chemical cocktail. Identifying all the different chemical participants and pinpointing their exact function took many years and along the way several interesting discoveries about human nature were made. One of them concerned depression. You know what the word depression means, don't you?"

"Yes, of course. It means to feel sad or miserable."

"Do you feel that way often?"

"Well, not *often*, but sometimes. More so lately . . . ."

He smiled. "But not at this exact moment, right? Even though your present situation is a bleak one you feel mellow, at ease — yes?"

She admitted she did. He said, "The lingering effects of the hormone I gave you. But you are physiologically incapable of experiencing depression of the kind familiar to many pre-Prime Standard people, thanks to the genetic modification your ancestors underwent. In the days before the genetic era many were prone to a condition known as manic depression. The condition was regarded as an illness — the result of either a psychological flaw or a physical one. It was then considered 'normal' not to suffer such a state of mind; that the *natural* state of the human mind was a kind of emotional equilibrium with an innate leaning towards an underlying feeling of well-being and vague optimism, depending on exterior circumstances, of course."

"But that's natural, isn't it?" she asked.

"That's the point," he said. "The scientists had made the discovery that Nature had ensured that human beings were continually drugged up to the eyeballs, in a manner of speaking, in order to cope with life. The *normal* ones, anyway. The abnormal ones, those prone to manic-depression or other chronic mental problems, did indeed suffer from an organic malfunction in the brain, but their brains were failing to produce *enough* of the neutrotransmitters to ensure that they possessed the somewhat rosy, if distorted, outlook on life experienced by 'ordinary' people. As a result these abnormal individuals apparently experienced a more *objective* viewpoint of reality, given the human condition as it is . . . ."

She shook her head wonderingly. "You do talk a lot of nonsense."

"Well, that's exactly what a lot of people said when this theory was first made public — that it was nonsense. It is human nature for an individual to believe that his, or her, perception of reality is objective. But the sad truth is that our perception of anything — and everything we think and feel — is at the mercy of our genetic programming, which in turn controls the manufacture of all the hormones that in their turn dictate the play of the chemical activities within our brains. Even our very perception of time itself is a product of these processes. The human concept of time is a biologically-induced illusion; there is no such thing as linear time, instead time is . . . ." He looked at her and didn't continue. "Forgive me," he said wearily. "My need to be able to *talk* to someone again got the better of me. I keep forgetting that for all your native intelligence you're still a savage, like the rest of them in this place."

"I'm no savage!" she protested.

"No? So you understand what I'm saying?" he asked, teasingly.

"Well, not much of it," she admitted. "But I do know that you are wrong about the mind. It is part of the Minervan creed that the mind is *separate from the body*. It is the property of the Mother God and when we die she reclaims it. She will either keep it as a part of her in paradise or if it needs a further spiritual cleansing she will send it back to Earth to live out another life."

"So much for Minervan theology," he sneered. "Heaven and Earth reduced to a giant laundry."

His words infuriated her. "It makes more sense than all that rubbish *you* speak!"

"My poor little amazon, you yourself are a product of all that so-called 'rubbish'. As I told you before, your very own Minervan genegineers saw to that. Your ancestors were modified past the specifications set down in the Prime Standard ruling.

102

Both physically and mentally you are different, not only from the pre-gene era women of the past but also the women on this airship. Your female ancestors, thanks to the genetic tinkering with the hormonal balances, became not only bigger physically but slightly more masculine in emotional outlook. Your men subsequently underwent a more drastic modification. The end product was a smaller, non-agressive, non-competitive, non-threatening human male — in short the feminist ideal of what a man should be."

"It's unthinkable that any Minervan would ever make use of genetic engineering but it's true, I admit, that Minervan men were changed," said Jan.

"By magic, eh?"

"The Mother God changed them. After the Gene Wars a group of them came to Minerva and begged forgiveness. They also begged for sanctuary. The Headwomen asked the Mother God what they should do. The Mother God spoke to them and said she would transform every man who truly begged forgiveness, and their sons would be transformed as well and their sons too and so on . . . ."

"Like I said, by magic." Milo stood up and slowly stretched, raising his arms straight above his head. "But have it your way. At least we agree that Minervan men aren't normal men. *Nicer* men, maybe, but not normal. And the big drawback for your early Minervans is that the idea didn't catch on outside the Minervan state. Sure, a lot of men, who supported the Minervan ideal of a feminist state, gladly volunteered to be modified, but the majority of the world's male population didn't show any inclination to join the queue.

"The problem was that to rewire a man's brain to the point where all the unwanted masculine traits could either be tuned down or eradicated completely you had to radically alter his sexuality — the hormonal programming for masculine sexuality and masculine behaviour traits are one and the same. So your transformed Minervan man, though still physically male, was very undersexed compared to the average untransformed man. Which is why they became known as 'eunuchs', and even worse, by the outside world."

"They're not eunuchs," said Jan quickly.

He raised his eyebrows. "You speak from personal experience, do you?"

She felt her face grow hot. "That's none of your business."

"On the contrary, everything to do with you is my business now, little amazon. But no matter. Tell me instead how you felt about Minervan men in general."

She shrugged her shoulders. "I liked them. My father I *loved*."

"As much as you loved your mother?"

"Well, no . . . ."

"What was the main difference between Minervan men and women? I don't mean the obvious physical differences — I mean temperamentally."

Jan frowned. "Well, I suppose the men were less . . . less *complicated* than all the women I knew. Their attitude to life could be a little annoying at times — they were always cheerful, placid, happy . . . ."

Milo gave a triumphant grin. "Which proves my point, and goes back to what I was saying about the manipulation of mental states. Your genegineers were obliged to up the dose of those natural happy drugs we've all got in our heads as a way of keeping your men contented with their changed lot in life. You Minervans may not have actually cut their balls off but you neutered them just the same."

"All I know is that I'd rather be with a Minervan man than with *you*."

He grinned down at her. "You don't find me stimulating company?"

"No Minervan man has ever raped a woman in the whole history of Minerva."

"Have I threatened to rape you?"

"Yes," she said coldly.

His grin turned into a scowl. "Oh, not *that* again." He gestured that she should get up. "Come on. We'll go and get some food. There's only an hour or so before we'll be taken up top to go to work."

She got to her feet. "What *is* our work? I heard the overseers say that I was going to be a glass walker. What is that?"

"I'll tell you after we've eaten. I don't want to kill your appetite."

Chapter Eleven:

"Don't look down if it disturbs you," said Milo.

"I can't help it," Jan told him weakly as she clung to the support bar with all her strength. It was almost as bad as it had been in the wicker basket hanging beneath the *Lord Pangloth*. They were crammed with several other slaves into a glass-sided box that was slowly rising within a vast, sagging cavern like the stomach of some gigantic animal.

What intensified Jan's feeling of vertigo was that the glass cage and its heavy human cargo was supported by two strips of narrow black tape that looked as substantial as hair ribbons. Jan couldn't understand why the tapes didn't snap under all that weight and Milo's brief and puzzling explanation that the tapes were made of an extra-strong material that came from beyond the sky gave her no solace at all.

"Relax and enjoy the view," said Milo cheerfully. "It's quite a remarkable sight, you must admit. I've been seeing it for three years but it never fails to impress me."

Jan forced herself to look around. She shuddered. The great, flesh-like walls were undulating slowly as if alive. "I don't understand. There's nothing keeping it all up. Why doesn't it collapse on us?"

"I've already tried to explain to you," said Milo. "We're surrounded by gas. Helium. Millions and millions of cubic feet of it. You can't see it because it's invisible, like air. This gas bag, and all the others like it, is what keeps the *Lord Pangloth* flying. Think of it as like being inside a giant version of a toy balloon."

"A what?" she said blankly.

"Ah yes. I forgot. No toy balloons. Not even kites allowed. The law of the Sky Lords . . . ." He rubbed his chin. "Okay then, think of it as being like a giant soap bubble. You do know what a soap bubble is, don't you."

She gave him a disdainful look. "Of course I do. But it doesn't *look* like a soap bubble. Soap bubbles are round."

"And so would this be if it was completely inflated with gas. It isn't, though, because when a Sky Lord goes higher the surrounding air pressure drops and the gas in the cell expands. If you put too much gas in the cell when it's at a low altitude the gas would rupture the cell at a higher altitude. Understand?"

"I think so."

He chuckled patronizingly and made to ruffle her hair but she ducked. One of the other slaves sniggered, but he soon went silent when Milo turned and looked at him.

Jan said to Milo, "You gave me a week to decide, remember? You promised not to touch me in the meantime."

"I was being friendly, that's all," he said, sounding hurt.

"Some friend," she said bitterly.

The glass cage was almost at the top of the gas cell. Jan saw what seemed to be an inverted glass dome attached to the ceiling of the cell. As they neared the dome an opening appeared in it and the cage, still climbing up its impossibly thin twin lengths of black tape, entered. The dome swung shut beneath the cage and then Jan saw another opening appear in the material of the cell itself. "Gas lock," explained Milo. "Prevents the gas from escaping."

The cage came to a halt in a dimly lit space above the gas cell. The doors of the cage slid open. "Out!" ordered Benny. The slaves spilled from the cage. Jan stared about wonderingly. The grey and shadowy space between the floor and the low ceiling seemed to stretch in all directions forever. A maze of struts and spidery girders connected the two surfaces.

"We're between the inner and outer hulls," said Milo quietly.

"No talking!" yelled Benny. "Get your gear and get topside, glass walkers!" He came up to Jan. "Amazon, you can use Milroy's gear. He sure won't be needing it again."

Several of the slaves laughed as they headed towards a row of wooden lockers standing nearby. Milo led Jan to one and showed her how it opened.

"What happened to Milroy?" she asked as she gazed at the bewildering collection of objects within the locker.

"He was careless," said Milo. He pulled out a quilted jacket and handed it to her. "This goes on first. You'll need it. It's going to be cold out there."

It was too big for her but Jan was grateful for it. It was already much colder up in this strange place than it had been way down in the slave's quarters. Milo was meanwhile pulling other things out of her locker. "Put this on over the jacket," he instructed, giving her a kind of harness made of leather. She allowed him to help her do up its many fastenings, trying to ignore the feel of his hands when they touched her body. She wondered what the metal loops on the harness were for. Next came a pair of boots with thick soles made of a strange rubbery substance, then a pair of leather gloves. Both boots and gloves looked well-used and had a pungent odour. Then Milo handed her a large coil of cord with metal clips at each end. He showed her how to carry it over her shoulder, with the aid of a loop on the harness. Finally he gave her a stick with a clump of cloth strips on one end.

She stared at it. *It's a mop*, she told herself disbelievingly. What was she supposed to do with it — clean the outside of the Sky Lord? The idea was absurd. Surely the hull was kept clean by rain showers and the wind.

"Move it, you lazy bastards!" roared Benny, moving among them. "Last one topside will get a kiss from my razzle stick!"

Jan cringed mentally at the memory of the unbearable pain she'd experienced when the thing had touched her before. She looked desperately towards Milo who had gone to a locker at the end of the row and was hastily donning his own equipment. She hurriedly joined him. "Where are we supposed to go?" she asked.

He jerked his head. She looked and saw a ladder extending down from the ceiling. The others were already moving towards it. Benny was pushing a lever at the base of the ladder. A panel in the upper hull slid open and Jan saw bright sunlight and felt a rush of cold air. She went to the ladder, anxious not to be the last up it but every time she tried to get on it one of the other slaves

107

blocked her way. She began to feel panicky. Anything would be better than to feel the effects of that magic stick again.

But they continued to block her way until the last of the other slaves, grinning, ascended the ladder ahead of her. She glanced apprehensively towards Benny and then realized that Milo was holding back behind her, waiting for her to go up. With relief she got on the ladder. As she climbed she looked back over her shoulder. Milo was following. Benny was scowling at him but made no move to touch him with the pain stick.

Had Milo deliberately put himself at risk on her behalf or had he known Benny was only bluffing, she wondered? But then she emerged through the hatchway and all such thoughts vanished. For a few moments she was so disorientated she froze on the ladder but then she felt a sharp tap on her leg and Milo said curtly, "Out, amazon. Plenty of time for sight-seeing later. Too much time . . . ."

She slowly climbed the rest of the way out and stood beside the hatchway, bracing herself against the stiff wind that blew over the airship's hull. *Airship*. She had forcibly to remind herself that she was indeed standing on top of the airship. So immense was the hull she had got the impression she'd been magically transported to some other world. She couldn't see the ground, all she could see was the curving, alien landscape of the Sky Lord's vast back in all directions.

Feeling insignificant and vulnerable she went and took a firm hold on the rail that formed a large circle around the hatchway area. The other slaves, oblivious of the view, laughed and joked loudly over the whistling of the wind. "Quite a sight, eh?" asked Milo, joining her at the rail. "I know how you feel. I felt the same way when I first came topside. But you'll get over it."

Jan didn't believe a word he said. She couldn't imagine him feeling the way she felt at the moment, nor did she imagine she would ever get used to being a flea on this giant's smooth and shiny back. She looked more closely at the surface of the hull. It seemed to be covered with countless close-fitting pieces of hexagonally-shaped, dark grey glass. She remembered watching the Sky Lord from the ground and thinking that its upper half was covered in fish scales. She asked Milo what they were.

"Sun-gatherers. At least that's what these sky people call them. Actually, they're . . . ."

He was interrupted by Benny yelling at them to get moving. The slaves started to head out on to what seemed to be a kind of pathway, bounded by low hand rails, that appeared to stretch along the spine of the hull all the way back to the huge tail fin. Jan figured that the towering structure of the fin was at least a third of a mile away, but distances were hard to judge in this bizarre landscape.

She kept hold of the rail as she and Milo followed the others on to the pathway. Benny brought up the rear. He was whistling.

"The sun-gatherers are what used to be called solar cells," Milo continued. "They absorb the sunlight and convert it into electrical energy. That's where the power comes from for the Sky Lord's engines, for the heating and light — everything. When they finally all give out the sky people will be, as we used to say once upon a time, up shit creek without a — "

"Give out? What do you mean?" she asked.

He gestured at the glass pieces. "These are Old Science. The members of the Sky Lord's Guild of Engineers, the nearest thing to intelligent people on board this giant bag of gas, can't duplicate them. They contain a genetically engineered substance that is similar to the chlorophyll in plants. Very efficient and in theory will continue to work indefinitely, but I wouldn't bet on it. These airships have been knocking around the world for hundreds of years now and the wear and tear is really beginning to show. I wouldn't be surprised if a large percentage of these cells are no longer functioning properly, or maybe have become disconnected from the power grid. The engineers don't even know how *that* works so until the lights go out one day they won't have a clue about the real situation . . . ."

"Okay, hold it!" ordered Benny. "This is it, section five. Where you work today, glass walkers."

Jan looked and saw a large figure '5' daubed to the left of the pathway. The red paint covered several of the 'sun-gatherers'. Jan asked Milo, "Don't tell me we're supposed to clean all these things?"

"Can you think of any other reason to be out here with mops?" he said with a grin.

"But why do they *need* cleaning?"

"Fungus. There's a particular species that likes to make its home on the glass. The air-borne spores lodge in the cracks between the cells. Eventually the fungus covers the whole cell, preventing it from absorbing the sunlight."

Jan looked down at the glass segments in front of her. "They look clean to me," she said.

"*These* may be but this isn't where we'll be working. Come on . . . ." He helped her over the railing. The other slaves, and Benny, were already over and heading towards the left 'horizon'. As she walked after them with Milo she almost immediately became aware of the curvature of the hull under her feet. Walking along the footpath had created the impression that the hull's surface was perfectly flat. A queasy feeling stirred in her stomach. She didn't want to go any further from the path but knew she had no choice.

"See those two carrying those tanks?" Milo asked her, pointing at two male slaves who were carrying bulky metal cylinders on their backs. "They'll spray the affected areas with solvent ahead of us then we simply wipe it off."

"So why aren't they spraying yet?" she asked anxiously.

"Because we haven't reached the allotted area yet. All this part of the upper hull — the easily accessible sections — are taken care of by other slave units. But Guild Master Bannion's glass walkers get the more difficult jobs. That's why Bannion is rich and we live better than most of the other slaves."

"We live *better*?"

"Believe it, we do."

They were now on a definite downward slope but there was no sign of the group slowing their pace. How much further could they go before the slope became so acute they would all lose their footing and start to slide down the side of the hull?

"How much further?" she asked Milo worriedly.

"Quite a way, I'm afraid."

"But surely we can't go much further," she protested.

"Why do you think we're carrying these ropes?"

"Oh Mother God . . . ." she sighed.

Jan had been curious as to where Milo planned to obtain the food he'd mentioned. She'd become more curious as she followed him down the rows of flimsy cubicles and into the main communal area. The pair of them attracted angry glares from the few other slaves already up but no one said anything. Milo led Jan to the spiral stairs. "Up you go," he said.

She was surprised. "We can just *leave*? I thought we were prisoners here."

"We're prisoners, all right, but we can go where we like on board the *Pangloth*. As long as it's anywhere bearing the sign." He pointed at the black star on his cheek. "Bannion must have told you that when he branded you."

"Oh, yes, I think he did," she said as she mounted the stairs. "But I wasn't paying much attention at the time."

"That's understandable. Meeting Bannion for the first time is not a pleasurable experience for any slave. I imagine it must be much worse for a woman."

"Yes. And I remember now something else he told me — that if I turn out to be clean he'd like to get to know me much better." They were now walking along the tunnel Benny had brought her down. Milo said, "What he meant was that if whichever slave you slept with didn't turn into a mass of cancers from some sexually-transmitted virus he would give you the honour of letting you become one of his personal slaves. Not a bad job. Plenty of good food and other luxuries. Of course you'd have to endure certain indignities, like getting his whip across your backside at frequent intervals. Bannion enjoys hurting women. Apart from making money I would say it's his chief pleasure in life."

Jan remembered the girl with Bannion. The thought of being like her was revolting. "How can anyone *enjoy* hurting someone else?" she asked Milo.

"That's an interesting question. The evolutionary value of sado-masochistic traits has attracted a lot of speculation but I shall spare you my own theories . . . Let's just say that you will find staying with me a much more agreeable fate."

111

Another question had occurred to her. "You're willing to make love to me right away. Why aren't you afraid of getting a disease from me, like the Guild Master is?"

"Because he's a superstitious cretin, like most of the sky people. The chances of your community harbouring any of the fatal viruses are very remote these days but the belief lingers on among these fools. The only really dangerous places still are the cities. Even though there are no people some of the plague spores were designed to live indefinitely. The ground itself is unhealthy."

Jan said, "There haven't been any plagues in Minerva for a long, long time. Very occasionally someone will die from the fungus but that's all."

"So you see, I'm not being brave by wanting to sleep with you. Just rational. And I think it's irrational that we should wait the full week."

"You promised," she told him. "We made an agreement."

"And I'm not breaking it. I'm simply asking you to reconsider. Surely you too will do the rational thing and accept my demands. It would be irrational of you to do otherwise."

She said nothing and they spent the rest of the journey in silence. Their destination turned out to be the enclosed 'town' that the Sky Warrior, Tanith, had escorted her through the day before. There weren't so many people about this time, which she presumed was due to the earliness of the hour. Nor was she subjected to the abuse she'd received on the previous occasion. She wondered why. She was still the same 'disease-ridden earthworm' that she'd been the day before. What had changed? Was it Milo's presence? Or was it the star-shaped brand she now displayed on her cheek? Most likely it was because everyone knew she was now the property of Guild Master Bannion . . . .

Milo stopped at a stall selling melons. The woman running the stall was obviously not happy about serving Milo — she scowled at him and muttered something under her breath — but she took his money just the same.

As he gave her the melon to carry she said, "Where did you get the money?"

112

"From Bannion. He gets paid a lot of money for our services and he pays us a pittance. Just enough to stay alive on, plus the occasional luxury." He stopped at another stall. This one sold long tubes of what Jan suspected were made of dried meat.

"I'm not eating any of that," she told him.

"You won't be. It's for me. One of those rare luxuries I told you about."

They stopped at three more stalls where he bought some unfamiliar-looking vegetables, some wizened fruit — oranges and pears — and finally some bread. Then they returned to the slave quarters. The communal area had filled up in their absence. Women were cooking at the stoves while the men were seated around the low tables or reclining on the dirty straw matting. The chatter that had filled the air as they'd descended the stairway vanished as soon as they'd reached the bottom. The feeling of hostility was palpable, but no one made a move against them as she and Milo walked by.

"Hope you weren't expecting a hot meal," said Milo softly. "But I think it would be wise to keep out of the way of the others until things cool down a bit."

She agreed with him. The less contact she had with the other slaves the better she felt.

Unimpressive as the food was she was grateful for it and told Milo so when she'd finished eating. He shrugged and cut off another sliver from the tube of dried meat. "You're welcome."

"I'll make it up to you."

"I certainly hope so," he said, looking directly at her. His meaning was clear.

"I meant I'll repay the money."

"There's no need to — once our arrangement comes into practice." He put the sliver of meat into his mouth and chewed contentedly, his eyes still on her.

She looked away. Her gaze fastened on the painting on the wall. "Who did that?" she asked, anxious to change the subject.

"I did."

She stared at the swirling colours and shapes. "What's it supposed to be?"

"If you mean what is it supposed to represent the answer is

nothing. It's an aid for, well, relaxation. By concentrating on it I can more easily enter a neutral state of mind. Which means I trigger a set of those neuro-peptides I was telling you about — those natural happy drugs in our brains."

"I see," said Jan slowly. The painting looked anything but relaxing. To stave off what she feared might be another of his long, nonsensical lectures she asked him where he'd lived before coming on board the *Lord Pangloth*.

"On the ocean," he answered. "In a sea habitat."

"A what?"

"Call it a floating town. Used to be a lot of them once upon a time. Mine was probably one of the last in existence. The oceans have their own form of blight. They've become too dangerous. Too dangerous for human life, anyway."

She asked him in what way.

"Squids, for one thing. They've practically taken over out there, thanks to the damn Japanese."

She told him she didn't know the meaning of either term.

"The Japanese were, and maybe still are, an island race," he told her. "They loved eating squid. Squids are a kind of fish. A primitive kind with very soft bodies and lots of tentacles. Look like something out of a bad dream but to the Japanese they were a delicacy. Well, not to just the Japanese; other people ate squid as well but the Japanese were obsessive about it. Their favourite kind of squid was a species called *surumeika*. They bred these in huge squid farms in the seas around their islands. Then they started playing around with their genes to produce larger, faster-growing *surumeika* . . . and the inevitable happened."

"Which was?"

"Some of them got out of the farms and into the open sea. They bred with natural *surumeika* and the resulting hybrid was a new species of super-squid. Fast-breeding, tough — and smart. This new squid has thrived at the expense of most other types of fish. But the *surumeika* are not the only hazards out in the oceans and finally we had to admit defeat and move to what we mistakenly thought would be safer waters close to shore . . . ." He shook his head sadly.

"*Lord Pangloth*?" she asked.

114

"Yes. Out in the ocean we rarely saw Sky Lords. If one was spotted we did the same as when a bad storm threatened the habitat — we submerged it a few hundred feet below the surface. At that depth we were safe from bombs as well as storms. Thankfully the art of making depth charges has been lost by the armourers of the Sky Lords. But when we were forced into shallow waters we could no longer protect ourselves in that way. We couldn't descend deep enough, so when *Lord Pangloth* appeared, told us we were now within his territory and demanded tribute, we had no choice but to try and fight back."

"Why didn't you pay his tribute?"

"We were in the same situation as your people were. We subsisted mainly on fish and plankton farming and were barely able to feed our own population, so we couldn't spare any food. Once we had machines that could extract certain ores and chemicals from the sea water but most of those no longer functioned. They had been cannibalized for parts to keep our most precious machine working — a solar-powered unit that converted sea water into fresh water. So we resisted. We had some primitive cannon and harpoon guns that we'd been using against the *surumeika* and the giant sea worms but it was useless. The lasers destroyed the shells and harpoons like they destroyed your rockets.

"And, of course, we were a sitting target for the Sky Lord's bombs. The habitat's flotation chambers were ripped open and down it went. I was one of the few survivors. I got picked up and I've been here ever since."

"Three years, you said."

"Yes, three years. And it seems like thirty. But I know one thing for certain — I'm not going to spend *another* three years in this aerial zoo."

That's true, she said to herself as she thought of the bomb concealed in her overalls. Hastily she said, "How long did you live on that floating town?"

"Since I was born. Nearly two centuries ago."

Her eyes widened with surprise. "That means . . . ."

"Yes," he said, "I'm nearly at the end of my allotted span. By my reckoning I'm one hundred and eighty years old. Which means, as you were about to observe, that I have a minimum of fourteen

115

years of life left, and a maximum of nineteen. It was thoughtful of our re-designers to provide us with the five year 'uncertainty' period at the end of our lives. It would be in extremely poor taste if we knew the exact day that we were due to genetically self-destruct, relatively painless though the process may be." He smiled bleakly.

"I've never met anyone as old as you before," Jan said as she gazed at him with new interest.

"No? But surely you have," he said, puzzled. "There must have been people in your town who lived out their full span of life."

"No. Not now, anyway. Avedon is . . . *was* . . . one of the oldest. She was over a hundred. But my mother said that when she was a young girl she remembered many Minervans who reached their day of Passing Over."

He made a face. "Trust you Minervans to call it that. I suppose it's another sign of the times, though, that your people weren't making it to the target year. The increasing harshness in living conditions down there on the ground is boosting the rate of natural wastage. Then again, I have yet to meet anyone as old as me up here. The Aristos may be a different kettle of fish. They sure don't put themselves at risk if they can help it so I expect their average survival rate is high."

She was regarding him thoughtfully. "That's why you know so much about the old days — because you're so old."

He laughed. "I'm not *that* old. No, history was my hobby. We had a well-stocked library of electronic records on the habitat. And there was plenty of time to study. Life on the habitat used to be fairly safe and uneventful — up until about thirty years ago when all that accumulating genetic shit passed its critical mass and suddenly we were up to our eyeballs in squid, mutated seaweed and those damn sea worms . . . ." He stopped, picked up the canteen and took a long drink from it, as if trying to wash away the sour taste of his memories. When he put the canteen down he was smiling again. "I'm surprised you think I know 'so much' about the old days — I was under the impression you thought I spoke nothing but rubbish and nonsense."

She didn't rise to the bait. Instead she said, "Doesn't it worry you? Being so close to your day of . . . of Passing Over?"

"Sometimes," he admitted. "But not much. Not yet at least. I'm sure it will in ten years time, if I live *that* long. Then I'll start cursing those damn twenty-first century politicians and their two hundred year ruling. When you think we had the secret of immortality in our grasp and did nothing with it . . . Madness. And now we've lost it."

Her expression was a sceptical one. "Could we really have been made immortal?"

"Indeed. In the same way that the human life-span was extended from an average of seventy years to two hundred. It's the same mechanism — the genetic prevention of cell maturation. The secret was discovered through cancer research. Unlike normal cells, which usually die after fifty divisions, cancer cells are immortal. They can keep on dividing forever because they never reach maturation and therefore the molecular clocks within their nucleii are not activated. When the genes responsible were identified it was possible to apply the changes to normal cells — except that instead of our cells being immortal their maturation has simply been delayed."

"Was anyone ever made immortal?"

"Oh yes. Many people underwent the necessary genetic modification. The rich and very powerful. It cost a lot because it was absolutely forbidden by international law. And the penalties for all concerned were very severe. But, of course, a lot of people were prepared to take the risk."

"So there might be immortals still alive?"

"No. The ones that survived the Gene Wars were killed in the purges that followed. As the perpetrators of the Gene Wars and the immortals tended to be one and the same the mobs killed two birds with one stake."

"Stake?"

"It was a fad at the time — driving wooden stakes through the hearts of suspected immortals. Originated, I think, from vampire folklore. Of course, a lot of people who probably *weren't* immortals died the same way. They were confused times."

There was a loud clanging sound. Milo frowned, then started to put the remains of the food away. "That's the signal. Time for us to go to work. But first we may have some trouble

117

with Benny and the other overseers." He reached down and helped her to her feet. "Just stay close by me and let me do all the talking."

She looked worriedly into his disconcertingly mismatched eyes. "What's going to happen?"

"Nothing. I hope."

Chapter Twelve:

They had been waiting for them. The other slaves *and* the overseers. As Milo and Jan entered the communal section the slaves parted to let the three black-clad overseers through. Benny led the way. His two companions looked familiar to Jan and she guessed she'd seen them in the Guild Master's headquarters. Benny stopped in front of Milo and put his hands on his hips. The pain stick dangled a few inches from his right hand. He said, "So what the hell are you playing at, Milo?"

"Playing at?" Milo asked with exaggerated innocence.

"With *her*," said Benny, inclining his head towards Jan. "I gave her to Buncher. So how come you've got her?"

"Why, Buncher gave her to me, Benny. We came to an understanding."

"That's a damned lie!" One of the male slaves had stepped forward. Jan recognized him as being one of the three who had confronted Milo outside the latrine. "He did something to Buncher; *made* him hand the amazon over, somehow."

Milo regarded him calmly. "I did nothing to him. Show me a mark on Buncher's body that he says I put there." Milo glanced around. "Where is friend Buncher anyway? Let *him* make these accusations if they are going to be made."

"Buncher won't come out of his cubicle," said another slave. "Keeps to his bunk. Been coughing up blood too."

Milo turned back to Benny and spread his hands.

118

"Well, there you are then," he said. "No wonder Buncher lost interest in the amazon. He's not feeling well."

Benny stared hard at Milo. "So Buncher just came up to you and said, 'Here, Milo, my old friend, take my amazon'?"

"Not exactly. I asked him for her. We haggled and, as I told you before, we came to an understanding."

"You *paid* Buncher for her?"

"No. I've agreed to do him a few favours in return," said Milo. "What kind of favours?"

Milo shrugged. "That will depend on Buncher."

Jan watched Benny's face closely. His suspicion, and open dislike of Milo, was plain to see. But there was something else. A wariness. A hint, even, of fear.

"If you wanted her," persisted Benny, "why didn't you say anything to me when I brought her down?"

"I hadn't made up my mind," said Milo easily. "Besides, even if I had asked you I doubt whether you would have given her to me, Benny. Am I right?"

Benny ignored the question. "Why did you want her, Milo?"

Milo turned and looked Jan up and down and then he drawled, "Well, I should think that's obvious, Benny." This got a response from the other slaves but Benny's angry, sweeping glare quickly silenced the sniggers. When he turned back to Milo Jan saw that he was barely keeping his anger in check. He wanted to lash out at Milo but something held him back. "Milo," he rasped. "You know your days are numbered, don't you? The next wrong step you make and Bannion is going to make you take the long drop." There were mutters of approval from many of the slaves.

"I find that hard to believe," replied Milo with a confidence that Jan envied. "I'm too valuable an asset for Bannion to dispose of so casually. I do the work of at least three of any of his other glass walkers. Nor have I ever done anything wrong. I've never been disobedient to you or any other overseer, nor have I ever brawled with any of my fellow slaves. Correct?"

"You've just never been *caught* at doing anything," said Benny, his scowl deepening. "But people around you have a funny habit of getting hurt. Sometimes fatally."

"I can't be blamed for other people's bad luck."

"Word is you cause that bad luck. Word is you're a sorcerer."

Milo laughed. "But, of course, an intelligent man like you, Benny, laughs at such rumours. You're a Freeman and the silly talk of superstitious slaves is beneath your contempt, isn't it?"

Benny didn't know how to answer that one. Finally he growled, "You've got one last chance, Milo. Remember that. And I'm going to be watching you."

"As I have nothing to hide you are welcome to watch all you want," Milo told him.

Benny made a grunting sound and started to turn. "Oh, one thing, Benny," said Milo. Benny turned back to him. "What?"

"Does this mean I get to keep the amazon?" Milo asked politely.

Benny glanced at Jan. He seemed to have forgotten she had been the point of the whole conversation. He frowned, then gave a sneering grin. "Sure. Why not? Enjoy her, Milo. Enjoy her while you can."

After that Benny and the other two overseers divided the slaves up into three groups. Jan wasn't surprised that she and Milo ended up in Benny's group. Then, after leaving the slave quarters, the three groups went off in three different directions. Jan had been intrigued by the journey up through the Sky Lord, though there had been little to see except bare corridors and narrow spiral staircases. Then they had arrived at the glass cage and the nightmare ride up through the vast gas bag had followed.

One of the things that Milo had explained to her during the ride was the meaning of the large sign next to the entrance to the cage. It has been an illustration of a flame with a black line across it. "It's forbidden to bring anything capable of causing a flame or even a spark beyond the lower section of the Sky Lord. That whole section is sealed off from the gas cells but from here upwards there's always the danger of hydrogen leaks. One spark could cause a tremendous explosion."

Jan immediately became more aware of the weight of the bomb in her breast pocket. "What happens if someone forgets?" she asked as the cage had climbed up its narrow thread like a spider going up its web. "I mean, if they forget they're carrying a flint or something?"

"The penalty is death by torture. And that applies to the Aristos as well as the slaves and Freemen. I will spare you the details of how the sentence is carried out. You're already looking a little green. Don't you like heights?"

"No," she answered and tried to put the bomb out of her mind. It was too late now, anyway.

" . . . THEREFORE MAKE THE SIGNAL THAT YOU ARE READY TO OFFER UP THAT WHICH IS RIGHTFULLY MINE. (*click*) FAIL TO DO SO AND MY RETRIBUTION WILL BE SWIFT AND TERRIBLE . . . TERRIBLE . . . TERRIBLE . . . TERRIBLE . . . ."

Lord Pangloth's familiar words didn't sound so loud and intimidating from Jan's vantage point on the upper surface. She was a long way down the slope of the hull but there was still a vast curving grey expanse below her which was blocking off her view of the ground directly beneath the Sky Lord as well as muffling *Lord Pangloth*'s speech to his subjects. When Jan had learnt that the Sky Lord was stopping to pick up tribute from a farming community she had become very excited, hoping that it was another of those lost parts of Minerva that Milo had told her about. But he said it wasn't—Minerva lay far to the south and they had been travelling north.

Jan was feeling more confident as she scrubbed at the sun-gatherers with her mop. She now trusted the harness and cord enough to work with both hands; before she had kept one hand tightly gripping the cord, in case it should suddenly start to slip through the loops of her harness despite the locking mechanism.

She stood with her feet braced against the hull, which at this point was angled steeply at about forty degrees, and with her body leaning backwards. If she looked up she could see her cord disappearing over the curve of the hull to its distant anchor point. Some fifteen feet to her right Milo was working level with her. To her left, and slightly below her, was another slave. They were spread out along the hull in a ragged line, slowly making their way downwards. The procedure was to work sideways as far as the lines permitted and then descend further down the lines to a fresh section of the hull. The slaves with the solvent sprays had gone on ahead, soaking the sun-gatherers with the foul-smelling liquid.

121

"Everything okay?" Milo called to her. Even though the Sky Lord had come to a halt there was still a swift wind blowing over the hull and it was hard to hear him. "I'm fine," she called back though the muscles in her legs, back and arms ached intensely. She wondered how long this ordeal would continue. She also wondered what was happening on the ground and what the community being taxed by the Sky Lord was like. All Milo had had time to tell her was that it was a farming community and quite large. If she looked over her shoulder she could see rolling hills in the distance that appeared to be free of the blight. She hoped that the ground dwellers didn't have anything planned along the lines of Minerva's abortive attack on the Sky Lord. She felt vulnerable enough dangling as she was on her thin length of cord without finding herself in the middle of a battle.

She had cleaned as much as she could of this section; it was time to descend further down the line. Sticking the mop handle under a strap of her harness she took a firm grip on the cord with her right hand and prepared to release the brake mechanism with her left. She told herself not to worry. Even if she lost her grip on the line the brake mechanism, as Milo had explained to her while showing her how the system worked, would close automatically when the line started to move too quickly through the loops of the harness.

She released the brake and slowly started to step backwards down the slope of the hull, feeding the line through the loops a few inches at a time. She had marvelled at the agility Milo and the others demonstrated as they moved about the hull, but then they'd had more practice.

When she decided she'd descended far enough she set the brake and then pulled her mop free. At that moment an unexpected gust of wind pushed her against the hull, and she almost dropped the mop as she put her hand out to prevent herself banging her face against the sun-gatherers. Then it happened . . . .

Her line went slack. She started to slide downwards.

She screamed. She let go of the mop and tried to dig her fingernails into the hull in the hope of getting a purchase on the narrow gaps between the sun-gatherers, but the thick gloves

122

made it impossible. Nor could she slow her descent by applying the supposedly 'non-slip' soles of her boots. The angle of the hull's slope was too acute. She began to pick up speed.

The faster she fell the more time seemed to slow down, giving her ample opportunity to feel the increasing heat through the gloves; to examine her rippling reflection on the passing sun-gatherers with its wide 'O' of a mouth; to listen to the terror in the high-pitched scream that was coming from that same mouth.

The angle of her slide became increasingly acute and then suddenly she was falling vertically and she lost her tenuous contact with the hull. Nothing now but empty air until she hit the ground.

Thump. An awful jarring sensation that sent the air whooshing out of her lungs, cutting off her scream. Confusion. Had she hit the ground already? But she was still alive . . . .

She saw a flash of silvery-grey hull, then blue sky, distant hills. She realized she was spinning on the end of her line. It must have got snagged by something on the hull! But her feeling of relief was only momentary as the hopelessness of her situation sank in. The line could pull free long before anyone could figure out a way of rescuing her.

She extended her arms carefully and managed to slow her rate of spin. She saw that the hull was a depressingly long distance away from her. She was well below its mid-point and it was now curving inwards. She could see a row of large windows but they might as well have been a thousand miles away for all the good they could do her. She could also see one of the huge thrusters. It was level with her but about fifty yards away towards the tail of the airship.

The line jerked and, thinking she was about to fall again, panic squeezed Jan's heart and she shut her eyes. But then she realized she was moving *upwards*. Someone had hold of her line and they were pulling her back up.

Progress was slow and punctuated by a series of jolting stops. With every jolt she thought she was about to fall again, but it didn't happen. She forced herself to stay calm, taking a series of deep breaths, and told herself she would soon be safe. She tried not to look down but couldn't help it. The town below was a sickening distance away. She tried to distract herself by studying it and its surrounding lands. It was smaller than Minerva but more haphazardly laid out and the buildings seemed crudely constructed. But there was no wall around the town and the farm lands were plainly untouched by the blight. Apart from wheat fields she saw what appeared to be extensive vineyards.

Her shoulder bumped into something. She looked and saw that she was in contact with the hull again. She turned so that she was facing inwards and tried to get a grip on it with her hands and toes as she continued to be hauled upwards. She failed, but it made her feel less helpless to be doing something instead of just dangling on the line.

The slow journey continued. She passed the outermost curve of the hull and then she saw what had saved her. Milo. Somehow he had covered the fifteen feet of space between them and reached her rapidly falling line before the end of it had shot by. He'd grabbed it (she didn't want to think of how little line there'd been left when he reached it) and then started pulling her up. She knew he was much stronger than he looked but she couldn't imagine how he had managed to halt her fall without having both his arms pulled out of their sockets . . . .

The other slaves had stopped work to watch but none of them had gone to his assistance. On the contrary, when Jan appeared into view they began to jeer and catcall. Jan's dislike and distrust of them suddenly boiled over into pure hatred. Whatever worries she'd had about the harm she would cause the Sky Lord's slave population when she succeeded in setting her bomb off disappeared. They would deserve everything they got.

As the curve of the hull became less acute she was able to gain a purchase on the sun-gatherers and take some of the strain off Milo. She was close enough now to see the effort it was costing him etched on his face. They were now only yards apart. He gave her a forced grin. "Hello again, amazon," he called to her. "Enjoy the view?"

She even managed to smile back at him. "Very nice," she gasped. The gap between them narrowed. Then he had hold of her arm. Relief swept over her. She was only dimly aware of him tying her line to his harness. "Here, put your arms around my

124

waist and hold on," he instructed. She did so. The jeers from the other slaves intensified. Milo began to haul himself up his own line. Clinging to him, her face pressed against his back, Jan did her best to get footholds on the sloping glass.

"What happened?" she asked him.

"At a rough guess I would say Benny cut your line," he told her over his shoulder. "He was the only one up there."

"But why?"

"To get at me. Teach me a lesson."

"You saved my life."

"Just. It was a near thing."

The slope of the hull decreased to an easy twenty-five degrees. Milo told her it was safe to let go of him. They were nearly at the point where the lines had been anchored to small metal loops protruding from the hull. She could see Benny standing about ten yards away, his face grim.

Keeping a firm grip on Jan's arm, Milo continued towards him. "Ho, Benny, all in a day's work, eh?" he called cheerfully.

The overseer said quickly, "Her line snapped. Nothing I could do, was there?"

"Oh, I think you did enough, Benny," said Milo in the same cheerful tone. He let go of Jan and went over to the loop that Jan's line had been attached to. He squatted down and examined the short length of line that remained. Then he looked at Benny.

"I say it snapped," growled Benny. "You want to say different, Milo?"

Milo got to his feet and walked towards him. "I agree, Benny. It snapped. Problem is, the amazon dropped her mop over the side. I think it might be a good idea if you went down and fetched it."

The colour went from Benny's face. He took a step backwards, reaching for his pain stick at the same time. "You keep away from me, Milo!" he bellowed, fear breaking through into his voice.

Milo stopped and raised his hands. "It's all right, Benny. I'm not going to touch you."

"You threatened me! I heard you! You know the penalty for that!" Benny was pointing the pain stick at Milo.

"Me? Threaten *you*?" asked Milo, sounding astonished. "The very idea is absurd. I was merely suggesting you attempt to recover a missing tool. I know how fussy Guild Master Bannion is about such wastage. After all, I imagine he's going to be more than a little annoyed that he almost lost his new slave on her first day."

Benny lowered the pain stick. "I'll tell him her line snapped. He'll believe me."

"Of course he will," Milo assured him, smiling.

Milo entered the cubicle and sat down in the wicker chair. He looked at Jan, who was lying on the bed, and gave her a smile of self-satisfaction. "I saw Bannion. Told him what happened. He's not happy."

"He believed you?" she asked, surprised. "I would have thought he'd have accepted Benny's version."

"He did — officially. He can't be seen to take a slave's side against the word of one of his overseers. Be bad for discipline. But he knows those lines don't just snap and he's been losing too many slaves that way. It's become a common method among the slaves of settling scores and Bannion is pissed about it. The last thing he needs is an overseer getting into the act as well. He's not happy that Benny tried to kill a valuable slave — you — just to get even with me. So our friend Benny is in for a hard time."

"Good," she said, with feeling.

"Oh, and something else to cheer you up. Buncher died during the day, so I've just heard. Coughed up a few pints of blood and keeled over." Milo put his hands behind his head and leaned back. His expression was serene. "That friendly little hug I gave him must have put a splinter of rib into one of his lungs."

Jan stared at him.

That night, after the lights had dimmed and they had gone to bed, Jan lay awake on the mattress and wondered what to do about Milo. She owed him her life. If he hadn't somehow caught the end of her line — and she still couldn't understand how he had managed to reach it in time — she would now be lying dead back in that town, her body nothing but pulped flesh and bones.

Not only had he saved her but he had enabled her to persevere with her plan to destroy the Sky Lord. If she had died all chance of Minervan vengeance on the destroyer of her town, family and friends would have died with her.

And that put her in an awkward dilemma. Because she now owed him so much she felt an obligation to give him the only thing she had that he wanted — her body. Several times she'd been on the verge of waking him and telling him her decision but she hadn't gone through with it. The thought of having sex with him scared her. Her only previous experience of making love to a man had been her one time with Simon. It had been strange and interesting, if not particularly pleasurable, but not painful or distressing in any way. However she had known Simon well and had been in control of the situation. He had, after all, been a Minervan male. Making love to an 'unchanged' man like Milo might be very different. The thought of him inside, possibly hurting her, and she not having the power to do anything about it, frightened her.

But the other thing was that she was scared of Milo himself. He may have saved her life but there was something about him that disturbed her profoundly. She remembered the accusations that both the slaves and Benny had made against him — that he was a sorcerer. It was easy to believe. She glanced over at his apparently sleeping form. He just wasn't big or muscular enough to have done the things she had witnessed him do. The way he'd halted her fall . . . the way he had actually crushed Buncher to death, finally, by a simple squeeze round his shoulders.

Jan shuddered and turned away. No, she would not offer him her body despite her debt to him. She would have to find some other way of repaying it in the time left before she achieved her goal of setting *Lord Pangloth* alight.

Chapter Thirteen:

It had taken all of her resources of willpower to go out on to the hull again the following day and trust her life to that thin line, even though Milo had assured her that the new overseer — Benny had been absent — was unlikely to repeat Benny's mistake. As she'd cleaned the sun-gatherers, her fear had threatened several times to overwhelm her and become pure panic. She'd wanted to close her eyes and just cling to the hull, crying, but she forced herself to keep working. She had to remain part of a glass-walking squad — she couldn't afford the luxury of a complete breakdown. She had to become totally familiar with the environment of the upper hull, and especially that limbo land between its two skins. It was vital to the plan she had begun to formulate as to how she would plant the incendiary.

By the second day it wasn't so bad out on the hull even though Benny had reappeared. He was subdued, his face puffy, and he walked stiffly. Whatever punishment had been inflicted on him by Bannion had, for the time being at least, tamed him.

On the fourth day after the incident Jan was feeling confident and excited as she stepped into one of the glass cages with the others. She had finalized her plan of action. If all went well, tonight would be the night . . . .

The particular glass cage they were riding didn't travel up through the centre of one of the gas cells like the first one. Instead it operated in an area *between* two of the cells. "We're travelling up through one of the transverse frames," explained Milo, pointing at the passing hexagonal patterns of spidery metal-work. "They form the basic skeleton of the Sky Lord. There's a transverse frame between every two gas cells. The elevator was moved here because the cells on either side are full of hydrogen. The Guild of Engineers feared that there was a chance the elevator mechanism might produce the odd spark if it was left in the cell."

The news that they were surrounded by hydrogen both disturbed and cheered Jan. It boded well for her plan, she told herself. She deliberately wouldn't think beyond the moment of setting the bomb and activating it. At the back of her mind was some unformed idea of getting out on to the hull and running as far away from the point of ignition as possible, but after that it was all a blank. She knew that her chances of survival were negligible.

Jan had learnt a lot about the Sky Lord during the previous few days. One important fact was that nearly two thirds of the huge gas cells were filled with the inflammable hydrogen now. Helen had been right. Milo confirmed that whenever helium was lost, either by accident or natural leakage, it was irreplaceable, whereas hydrogen could be manufactured from water. Milo also told her about the origin of the Sky Lords; his account bore only a marginal similarity to the Minervan stories of those long ago events. Jan was beginning to realize, with extreme reluctance, that the Minervan version of history had many gaps in it, while Milo's appeared to form a seamless whole. She didn't want to believe him but was becoming increasingly fascinated by what he had to say.

According to Milo the Sky Lords had originally been called Sky Angels. They had been built by the organization known as the United Nations for a dual purpose. One was to provide a cheap and clean means of transporting cargo between countries, mainly the countries of the poorer 'third world'; the other was to provide relief in times of natural disasters — they could ship in vast amounts of emergency supplies to areas stricken by famine or, in the event of earthquakes and floods, act as floating sanctuaries for the victims of the disasters, providing beds, food and shelter within their huge dormitories.

Thus it was only natural, in the chaotic aftermath of the Gene Wars, that the survivors should attempt to escape the plague viruses and other threats by retreating to these great sanctuaries in the sky. The trouble was that a lot of people had the same idea and for a time fierce fighting raged in and around each of the Sky

Angels as the various groups struggled for possession. In the process two of the airships were destroyed. Finally the victors emerged from the carnage and life on the Sky Angels stabilized. But when the emergency supplies that each of the airships carried began to run out the people in them were obliged to turn their attention to the ground again. They needed food and other raw materials and so they forced those still living on the ground to provide it for them. The reign of the Sky Lords had begun.

At first there was no organization. The Sky Lords were rivals for the same food-producing lands and great air battles between these behemoths of the air were common. When another two Sky Lords had been destroyed a truce was agreed. This was followed by a conference between the rulers of each Sky Lord and the world was divided up into territories for the remaining airships. The idea was that each Sky Lord would never move out of his allotted territory and this rule had been followed ever since. But according to Milo it was unlikely to hold for much longer . . . .

"The blight has got the upper hand across the world now," he had explained. "Too many of the ground communities are going under. When a Sky Lord discovers his official territory no longer contains enough food-producing communities to supply his needs it's obvious he's going to start poaching in the territories of the Sky Lords. It's rumoured that there have already been aerial clashes between Sky Lords. Eventually it will turn into a full-scale war." He seemed pleased at the prospect.

She said, "It's so stupid. Men will go on fighting each other while the Mother Earth dies around them. Why don't the Sky Lords and the ground people work together to try and stop the spread of the blight before it's too late?"

"Old habits are hard to break," he replied. "The sky people have traditionally regarded the ground dwellers as less than human. For them suddenly to start co-operating with the 'earthworms' on an equal basis at this stage is mere wishful thinking. Besides, I don't see what the Sky Lords could do to help stop the blight."

"Those lights that burn. The beams that destroyed our rockets — surely they could be used to burn the blight lands clean?"

"Well, they *could*," he admitted slowly, "but as I told you, those laser weapons aren't under the control of the sky people. They only operate automatically, and only against non-living dangers to the Sky Lord." Then he'd given her a patronizing smile and said, "Anyway, what's a good little Minervan doing considering the use of devices created by Man's Science, eh?"

She had replied stiffly, "If such devices were put to the task of purifying the world I'm sure the Mother God might consider that Men weren't completely beyond redemption."

Jan received an unpleasant surprise when she climbed out on to the hull. There were several Sky Warriors standing about in the area surrounding the hatchway. They were all armed with their usual long-barrelled rifles and were scanning the skies. At the first opportunity Jan asked Milo the reason for their presence.

"Hazzini," was his reply. "We're flying over Hazzini territory at the moment. Will be for the next twenty-four hours or so. See, those are their nests."

She looked and saw, ahead of them, a number of tall structures rising up from a row of low, blight-covered hills. They resembled huge, twisted tree trunks. Jan realized with a shock that they had to be hundreds of feet high.

"What are Hazzini?" she asked as she hooked the end of her line into a hull support. Today they were working on the bow of the Sky Lord and the view this position offered was spectacular.

"You never had any Hazzini raids on Minerva?" Milo asked.

"Not that I know of," she called back.

"Well, you'd certainly know if you had. I guess Minerva was out of their range. Think yourself lucky. Hazzini are genetically engineered killing machines, pure and simple. One of the big corporations created them for use as a private army way back. Basic genetic material was from the insect kingdom. The things have wings. Most can't fly this high but you get the occasional odd high-flier, so I'm told."

"Oh," she said. They were closer to the 'nests' now and she could see just how enormous the structures were. There were ledges protruding from the sides of the things and she thought she could see black dots swarming across them. Milo and she,

131

like the other 'wipers', were waiting for the squad spraying on the solvent to get far enough ahead before they started work. The *Lord Pangloth* had, as usual, slowed down for the sake of the various slave squads out on the hull, but even so the rush of air sweeping over the bow was quite powerful and Jan had difficulty in keeping her balance. "So the Sky Warriors are guarding us then?" she asked Milo.

He laughed. "Us? Who cares about a bunch of slaves? No, the Warriors are there to guard the hatches and other possible points of entry on the hull. And you'll notice that our friend Benny has left us to our own devices today."

She looked back over her shoulder. The overseer had stayed with the group of Warriors around the hatchway. "You think we're in danger from these creatures?" she asked. She looked down towards the ground again. The black dots were in the air now and some were growing uncomfortably large.

"I've worked over Hazzini territory lots of times," said Milo, "and never seen one of them get even close to us. But if you believe the rumours there have been instances in the past when glass walkers have been snatched off the hull by Hazzini."

"Are they intelligent?"

"If you mean self-aware, I would say no. But they're certainly cunning. They're programmed to do two things — kill their enemies and reproduce — and their designers provided them with enough built-in ingenuity to be very efficient at both. And as they're also designed to live on practically anything, they can eat even the most toxic fungi. So they're thriving in the blight lands. My guess is that the world will eventually be covered with blight and Hazzini . . . ."

Jan spent an uncomfortable day out on the hull, constantly looking behind her in case one of the Hazzini had managed to fly as high as the *Lord Pangloth* but though there was a lot of activity every time the airship flew over a Hazzini nest none of the swarming black dots far below them seemed to come any closer.

The presence of the Hazzini on the ground made Jan have second thoughts about her plan to detonate the fire bomb that night. But she told herself that she was just looking for an excuse to postpone the moment of no return. The aim was to destroy the

Lord Pangloth and all those on board — what difference did it make how the sky people died? Whether they died by fire, by falling to the ground, or became victims to the Hazzini, it was all the same. Nor could she allow the fact that the Hazzini would reduce her own slim hope of survival to vanishing point to influence her. No, she had no choice — it had to be tonight. With working conditions so difficult Jan's body was a mass of aching muscles by the end of the long shift. During a short break in the middle of the day she had complained to Milo that the sky people were foolish not to make use of chimps as hull cleaners. "They'd make perfect glass walkers," she'd told him as they'd sat side by side. "Be a lot quicker than us too."

"True," he agreed. "But the sky people never make use of any of the 'altered' animals. Against their religion. They consider them to be unclean — tainted. Yet another part of the cultural fall-out from the Gene Wars. You Minervans weren't the only ones to develop some strange ideas about the Old Science."

She ignored the gibe. She was too exhausted to get angry with him. "We didn't make use of any Old Science, true, but there was no law against using the animals. It wasn't their fault they'd been altered. Once, long ago, we had all sorts of animals in Minerva but by the time I was born we only had the chimps. The others had all become unreliable. Even the male chimps couldn't be trusted any more. We had to cage them up when they reached a certain age."

"Interesting," he said. "But it's only to be expected. There was no way the genetic engineers could ensure long-term stability in their designer chromosones. Mutations can't be prevented so bugs are going to get into the program. More and more throwbacks will occur. Like you."

"Like *me*?" she said, surprised.

"Of course. You're unusually small for a Minervan. You're obviously a throwback. Oh, I'm sure that in all other ways, apart from your size, you're a genetically sound Minervan — you certainly have the typical Minervan physique and features: androgynous body with long legs, small breasts, muscular build, olive skin and a very attractive face. It's probably just the genetic material relating to your growth that's affected, but it would be interesting to see any of your children that resulted from a union with a non-Minervan male."

His clinical appraisal of her body annoyed her, even though she had been vaguely flattered by the reference to her 'very attractive' face. But what hurt most of all was his mention of her having children. *No chance of that,* she thought grimly. *No chance of anything after tonight.*

There was a considerable distance between the hatchway and the place where the glass cage was waiting to take them down, which suited Jan's plans perfectly. She lagged behind the strung-out group of slaves as they made their way through the structural confusion that was the environment in the space between the two hulls. Milo had told her that the clutter and chaos of the *Lord Pangloth's* interior was the work of the succeeding generations of sky people. "For years they've been making their increasingly clumsy repairs," he said. "And various other alterations, such as converting cargo storage areas into living quarters. I doubt if one of the designers of the original Sky Angels would recognize the interior of any of the Sky Lords today."

Jan seized her chance. She ducked behind a slanting girder then quickly retreated into the protection of the shadows. Moving as quietly as possible she intended to put as much distance between herself and the others before her absence was discovered. It was Milo who worried her the most. He would surely be the first to see she was missing, and he was certain to be the most persistent in searching for her.

The further she ran the darker it got. Only the areas regularly used had been provided with illumination. She halted and crouched down, listening. She could hear the voices of the slaves receding into the distance. Then came silence, disturbed only by the creaking of the hulls. She continued on. Because she was heading towards one side the curvature of the floor soon became more acute and finally she was obliged to stop again for fear of slipping and hurting herself in the dark. She clung to a strut, panting. Then she heard a distant shout. It was her name. They were looking for her.

She had no idea how long she waited there in the almost total blackness. At one point one of her searchers seemed to get quite close. Or at least his voice sounded loud as he shouted her name. She was sure it was Milo. If anyone found her it would be him. His sorcerer's powers probably enabled him to see in the dark . . . .

But Milo didn't find her, and when all became silent again she knew she had achieved the first part of her plan. She started moving again, having to feel her way along. She retraced her steps a certain distance, until the slope became less acute, then tried to proceed towards the bow.

She was disorientated now. She would have to establish the position of the forward hatchway before she would know exactly where she was. She headed in what she hoped was the right direction. She was relieved when she eventually saw the glow of lights ahead of her. Then, to her dismay, she heard the murmur of voices. She dropped to a crouch and proceeded cautiously. She saw that she had indeed found her way back to the hatchway but a group of Sky Warriors were sitting around the ladder, their helmets off.

For a moment Jan thought they had remained to search for her but then she realized they were still on guard duty because of the Hazzini.

Having pinpointed her position she headed back into the darkness again, moving parallel to the pathway between the hatchway and the spot where the glass cage emerged from its shaft. Her destination was one of the entry-points into the network of catwalks beneath the inner hull that permitted inspection of the membrane of the gas cells. When Milo had told her about these a couple of days ago, pointing one out, she knew she had found the perfect place to set off the bomb.

She had intended to go down the nearest entry-point but with the Warriors at the hatchway she would have to use one much further away.

When Jan decided she was a safe distance from the Warriors she lifted the thin, circular hatch of the entry point she had chosen. A short ladder extended below. She climbed down. At least the inspection tunnels were well-illuminated by the strange 'cold' lamps that Milo had told her contained living cells. She closed the hatch and began to move along the tunnel, her body bent forward to avoid hitting her head on the ceiling. The walls of the tunnel were actually the membrane of the huge cell whose top she was crossing like some tiny insect. It gave her a queasy feeling to think that below the thin metal mesh of the catwalk floor, and the membrane pressed against it, there was a drop of over a thousand feet.

She came to a halt. Here was as good a place as any. Jan took off her overalls, squatted down and removed the bomb from her vagina. She had been obliged to conceal it within herself again after Milo had warned her of the spot checks carried out by Warriors to see if anyone was carrying anything capable of producing sparks or flames in the forbidden area. There was the chance, of course, that they wouldn't recognize it for what it was but she couldn't afford to take that chance. There had been no checks during the last four days, however, and now it didn't matter.

Jan unwrapped the device and gazed at it. She remembered her mother's words — twist the end in the direction of the arrow. Simple. Then she would jam it between the mesh and the surface of the membrane. Thirty seconds later it would detonate, spewing out burning liquid. The cell membrane, she had learned from Milo, was very tough — like all the components of the Sky Lord that had been made in that factory in space she still couldn't really believe in — but she was confident the contents of the bomb would burn through it. And on the other side of the membrane waited millions of cubic feet of hydrogen . . . .

She took a deep breath, gripped the cylinder firmly in her left hand and prepared to twist the top with her right.

She couldn't.

She tried to. She kept trying to. Tears mingled with the sweat running down her cheeks but she just couldn't make her hand do her bidding. She couldn't twist the end of the cylinder. She couldn't be responsible for the deaths of all the people on board the *Lord Pangloth*, no matter how much she hated them. Oh yes, she had no qualms about helping to fire rockets at the Sky

136

Lord from the roof of the tavern but that had been different. That had been war; a fight for survival. And she hadn't been alone. There was Milo to consider as well. Jan didn't like him, and he was quite possibly a sorcerer, but she did owe him her life. It wasn't fair to him that she had given him no warning of what she'd planned to do. She had thought of doing so but, of course, if she had he would have stopped her.

And then there was herself. She didn't want to die.

Jan bowed her head and began to sob. She had betrayed her mother. Alsa. Minerva . . . .

Finally she stood and dressed and put the bomb in her pocket. She would have to dispose of it somehow. Flush it out of the latrine, perhaps. As Jan made her way back to the entry-point she tried to think up a story that would explain her disappearance. Maybe she could say she went back to fetch a piece of forgotten equipment and got lost . . . .

She climbed out through the entry-hatch. *Now what*, she wondered bleakly. Go and give herself up to the Warriors by the hatchway? No, she wasn't ready to see anyone just yet. She wanted to be by herself. She would head towards the cage shaft and wait until the others arrived to start the next day's shift. She had no idea how many hours away that would be but she was too depressed to care.

A flicker of red light in the darkness ahead distracted her from her pain. Jan frowned, wondering what it was. Engineers doing repair work? But surely, if that was so, the whole area where they were working would be well-illuminated. She went closer, not caring if she made a noise or was spotted. It didn't matter now.

The nearer she got to the source of the flickering red glow the more puzzled she became. It seemed to be at floor level. She also got colder. There was a stiff breeze coming from somewhere. An open hatchway? But there wasn't one in this part of the hull.

The red light was making a sizzling sound. Then she saw sparks fly out. *Sparks.* The significance of this suddenly hit her. Someone was using naked flames in the forbidden area. If there was a leak of hydrogen . . . .

The light flared and in the expanded red glow she got a glimpse of a figure crouched beside the light. The figure wasn't human.

137

Jan was now less than twenty feet away from the flickering light. She started to back away, once again trying not to make a sound.

Clang.

She had collided with a support strut. It reverberated with appalling loudness. The red light abruptly winked out. She turned and ran. And almost immediately collided with another obstacle, bounced off it and fell. She lay there, listening for any sound of approaching footsteps. She heard none, but there was a strange rustling sound that was growing louder. And it was coming from the ceiling.

She got up and started running again, one hand held out in front of her for protection. She had a good idea now what was pursuing her. *A Hazzini*. And maybe more than one. The brief glimpse she'd received of the thing was more than enough to convince her that Hazzini were definitely bad news.

There was light ahead of her. Jan was approaching the narrow illuminated section again. She made a decision. When she reached the pathway she would turn left towards the hatchway where the Warriors were waiting.

Something dropped down from the ceiling in front of her. She skidded to a stop. It was about nine feet long. Its body was segmented. Folded, transparent wings hung down its sides. It had six limbs. It was using the two rear ones to stand on. One of the forelimbs held a bulky object that was glowing slightly. Two of the other forelimbs shot forward. One grabbed her by the upper arm; the other seized her by the ankle. She screamed as the razor-sharp claws dug into her. She was jerked off-balance and fell on her back. The thing loomed over her, still holding her firmly. She could feel blood pouring from her arm and ankle. She screamed again as the Hazzini dipped its head towards her and she got a clearer look at it. It was as if the head of a horse had been crossed with that of a mosquito. Instead of ears, hairy antennae sprouted from behind the eyes, which were far too intelligent to belong to any insect. Its colour was a mottled black and grey and there were tufts of spiky black hair protruding in a random pattern all over it.

Jan struggled, but she was held fast. The head came still lower and she gagged as the odour of the creature washed over her. Then, through watering eyes, she saw the 'mouth' of the thing split into three segments and a tube appear out of it. What looked like the teeth of a saw extended from the tip of the tube. The whole tube was slowly rotating.

I'm dead, thought Jan, though she still struggled frantically. *This is my punishment from the Mother God for failing to avenge Minerva . . . .*

The rotating tube continued to emerge from the mouth. The teeth on the tip glistened with fluid. Jan guessed it was poison, or some sort of digestive chemical. But whatever the thing was about to do to her, the outcome would be the same.

Then she remembered the bomb.

With her free hand she plucked it out of her pocket, gripped the end between her teeth and twisted it sharply. It made a satisfying *click!* Then, with all the force she could muster, she jammed it up the end of the descending tube. The Hazzini's head flinched back, then shook from side to side, trying to dislodge the blockage. *Thirty seconds!* was the silent scream that echoed in Jan's mind.

The creature's efforts to dislodge the bomb became more frenzied. It gripped its feeding tube with its free hand, or claw. At the same time it dropped the device it had been holding. Then it released Jan's shoulder, so that three of its four front limbs were engaged in the task of trying to clear the blockage. But the fourth claw maintained its grip on her ankle.

Jan rolled on to her stomach, grabbed hold of a strut and tried to pull herself free, but the thing tightened its grip until she could feel the bones crunching under the pressure. She screamed and almost blacked out from the pain.

How many seconds left?

The creature flipped her over on to her back again and pulled her closer to it, even as it continued simultaneously to shake its head and claw at its mouth. She saw that the end of the bomb was no longer visible in the tube and guessed that the Hazzini had involuntarily sucked it in. But would it explode in time to save her? Then came a sound like a massive, muffled fart. The Hazzini's entire body gave a convulsive shudder then went rigid.

Smoke began to pour out of its mouth and then from other, hitherto hidden, orifices. *Skreeeeeeee!* screamed the dying, perhaps already dead, Hazzini in a pitch so high it was barely audible. The pressure went from Jan's ankle. She began to scramble backwards away from the thing. She wasn't fast enough. The claw that had held her ankle lashed out, opening up her body all the way from the base of her throat to her lower belly. Then, with black smoke pouring out of it, the Hazzini toppled over with a loud crash.

Jan felt as if she'd been plunged into ice water. She tried to sit up but then saw how badly she'd been hurt and lay back on the hard deck, wrapping her arms about herself in the hope of keeping her body from falling apart.

When black oblivion finally closed in on her consciousness it was very welcome.

Chapter Fourteen:

Jan thought she looked ridiculous and said so.

"Nonsense!" cried Mary Anne in her high, trilling voice. "You look absolutely beautiful!" Then she added, in a lower tone. "All things considered."

'All things considered' meaning, thought Jan wryly, that for a physically deformed amazon, not to mention a tainted earthworm, she was passable. Though *passable* was not a word that Jan would have used to describe her present appearance. She continued to stare at her image in the full-length mirror. The only thing she liked about it was the lovely shade of deep blue of the gown she was wearing. The gown itself was bizarre, as was her shape. Thanks to the variety of constricting undergarments that Mary Anne had insisted she wear, her waist was ludicrously narrow; but below it the gown ballooned out over her hips, forming a bell-shape that extended all the way to the floor.

If she was totally concealed from the waist down the situation was almost entirely opposite from the waist up. The tight-fitting fabric on her upper torso was cut low at the front in a deep curve that exposed her breasts almost to her nipples. But even with the halter she was wearing, designed to push her breasts upwards, there was no way she could match the expanse of mammaries being displayed by Mary Anne standing next to her. These people, Jan decided, definitely had some kind of odd obsession about breasts.

To complete her bizarre appearance were the billowing sleeves of the gown, the black ribbon around her throat, the white powder on her face, the red dye that stained her lips and the jewelled tiara on her hair. Mary Anne surveyed her handiwork with a satisfied smile. "Even your own mother wouldn't recognize you," she assured Jan.

"If my mother had ever seen me looking like this she would have run me through with her sword," Jan said grimly.

"Ooo, don't say that!" cried Mary Anne, looking shocked. "You must put that awful amazon way of life you led out of your mind, Jan. That's all far behind you now. Instead, look forward to your future with us. From now on your life is going to be very different."

"It certainly seems so," agreed Jan softly. Once again she experienced a strong feeling of unreality — as if she was in a dream. These feelings had come often during the last twenty-four hours since she had been brought into the Aristo section of the *Lord Pangloth*. But then she'd been having similar feelings ever since regaining consciousness after being attacked by the Hazzini. She glanced down at her exposed chest. The scar had faded to a thin white line. The crude stitch marks were almost gone as well. But perhaps she was really dead after all. Maybe this was all a dream that the Mother God had created for her as an ante-room to Paradise. The meals she'd had, the scented baths, the luxurious bed she'd slept in — all had had a feel of paradise about them.

"I'm still alive?" had been her first surprised words, in faint whisper, when she'd opened her eyes and seen Milo leaning over her.

"Barely, little amazon," he'd told her, with a smile. "The members of the Medic Guild on *Pangloth* are little more than butchers but at least they are capable of stitching up wounds, even one as long as yours. None of your internal organs were damaged. It was the loss of blood, and shock, that almost killed you. But the worst is over. With your powers of regeneration you'll pull through all right. And won't even have a scar to show for it."

She had murmured, "The Mother God is with me," and fallen into a deep sleep.

The next time she woke Milo had given her some water to drink from his canteen. She became aware of her surroundings. She was back in his cubicle. She tried to lift her head to see what condition her body was in but she was too weak. "I . . . don't . . . feel any pain," she whispered.

Milo held up a device she recognized. A hypodermic needle. There had still been a number of them at the hospital in Minerva. "I've been injecting you with a hormone that activates your internal pain killers. Cost me a lot to get it. A Freeman in the village has a direct supply route from one of the Aristo pharmacies."

"Thank you . . . ."

"My dear little amazon, don't mistake my generosity for altruism," he said, grinning. "Remember our agreement. I have almost as much interest in you in getting that young body of yours back to normal."

She'd managed a faint smile.

"So do you feel strong enough to tell me what happened?" he asked.

"Got lost . . ." she whispered. "Wandered around . . . for hours. Then saw . . . Hazzini. Chased me. Clawed me . . . Thought it had cut me in two . . . ." She couldn't go on.

He ran his fingers though his non-existent hair and regarded her silently for awhile. Then he said, "Do you know that you are a heroine? The general assumption is that you came across the Hazzini, grabbed its Old Science cutter and incinerated it with it."

She frowned. "Cutter. . . ?"

142

"The thing it had used to cut through the outer hull, and was about to cut through the inner hull with when you interrupted it. The theory is that a Hazzini nest selected their best flyer, equipped him with a cutter that they must have found in some old ruin, and instructed him to sneak into the *Pangloth* and sabotage one or two of the gas cells so that the *Pangloth* would drop in altitude and be within reach of the other Hazzini. Trouble is that the creature didn't realize that the cell it was about to penetrate was full of hydrogen. The Hazzini would have got quite a surprise when the *Pangloth* had fallen out of the sky in a ball of flames and landed right on top of a bunch of their nests."

He suddenly clutched her shoulder, his eyes cold.

"I know what really happened up there. And I know what you planned to do. You and the Hazzini had a similar goal in mind that night," he told her harshly.

"What do you . . . mean?"

"You know what I'm talking about. It involves that precious Minervan relic of yours — the 'rod of authority' that you were going to protect with your life. You appear to have lost it."

"Have . . . I . . . ?" She was finding it hard to think now. She wanted to go back to sleep.

"Oh, stop pretending. I was suspicious of the thing all along but I gave you the benefit of the doubt. And in return for my trust you planned to incinerate me along with everyone else when you set off your bomb. For sheer ruthlessness you Minervans can probably teach the Sky Lords a thing or two."

"No . . . no . . ." she protested weakly, trying to shake her head. "I couldn't do it . . . when the time came. Couldn't. So I gave up . . . ."

He stared hard at her. Finally he said, "I suspect you're telling the truth." His expression then softened. "So having given up your mission you then blundered into the Hazzini. You must have used your bomb to kill the thing. The idea of you grabbing that cutter from the grip of a full-grown Hazzini and using it on him is absurd."

"Yes . . ." she said and told him what she'd done. He started to smile again. "Right up his proboscis, eh? How apt. If he'd penetrated you with that thing he'd have sucked you inside out. Human blood is a delicacy for the Hazzini."

"Will . . . will they find the pieces . . . of the bomb?" she asked.

"Don't worry. No one performed an autopsy on the creature's body. It had obviously been burnt to death and the cutter was lying nearby. When the Warriors, who heard your screams, arrived on the scene they jumped to the obvious conclusion. The Hazzini has been dumped overboard, so there's no chance now of anyone else discovering the truth."

"Good . . ." she murmured. She couldn't keep her eyes open.

"Sleep," he told her and she did.

There was a knock on the door hidden by the pink drapes that covered the walls and the ceiling. "Yes?" called Mary Anne. Ceri, Mary Anne's hand-maiden, entered the dressing room through a gap in the drapes. Ceri, like Jan, was an ex-slave and wore the same tattooed circle around the black star on her cheek. But though an ex-slave, Ceri wasn't a Freewoman either; Mary Anne had said she was a Bondswoman and as far as Jan could see this was just another term for slave. The difference was that being a slave in the Aristos' section of the Sky Lord was far preferable to being a slave anywhere else on the ship. She had liked Ceri at first sight. The hand-maiden was a slim girl with very fair hair and green, attractive eyes. Her face displayed both intelligence and sensitivity, two qualities that Jan already knew were in short supply on board the Sky Lord. But she had to admit she rather liked Mary Anne as well, even though the woman was patently stupid.

Ceri inclined her head respectfully towards Mary Anne and said in her soft, pleasant voice, "Prince Magid wishes to know if you and your guest are ready yet, Mistress. He is waiting in the saloon."

"We'll be out shortly, Ceri darling," Mary Anne told her.

As Ceri withdrew Mary Anne fussily tucked a stray hair back under Jan's tiara. "Not long now before your moment of glory," she said breathlessly. "You must be feeling very excited."

144

"Oh, *very*," said Jan and smiled at Mary Anne's reflection in the mirror.

Prince Magid, *Lord Pangloth*'s High Chamberlain, looked just as absurd to Jan as he had when she'd seen him on the day of her capture. With his long, somewhat skinny legs clad in red-and-orange striped tights and his voluminous, puffed-up jacket, he reminded her of some bizarre bird. And she found it hard not to smile whenever she glanced at the bright green leather box that covered his genitals. Knowing the thing was called a 'cod piece' didn't help.

He was standing at one of the windows with his back to them as they entered the saloon. He turned and said, in his usual reedy voice, "Ah, here you are at *last*." Fingering his pointed beard, and with his other hand resting on the hilt of his ceremonial sword, he made a great show of inspecting Jan, walking all around her and making odd noises through his nose. She considered how easy it would be to grab him by the throat, whip out his sword and stick it through his heart. But apart from a brief satisfaction such an action would achieve nothing, so instead she gazed out at the magnificent view through the row of outward slanting windows that made up one entire wall of the saloon. The sun was setting behind a distant mountain range and clouds were lit up in a brilliant red.

"Well, I suppose she'll do," said Prince Magid reluctantly.

"Oh, Phylus, I think she looks absolutely splendid!" cried Mary Anne, clasping her hands together.

"For an *amazon* she is suitable," he said pointedly. "Now let us go. We don't want to keep Prince Caspar waiting."

"You mean you don't want to keep Lady Jane waiting," she said with a sniff. Prince Magid glared at her and she visibly wilted under the intensity of his look.

As she accompanied the pair of them along the wide, carpeted corridor Jan said hesitantly, "Ah, Prince Magid, I thought I was going to meet Lord Pangloth himself tonight . . . ."

He gave an exaggerated sigh and said, condescendingly. "There *is* no Lord Pangloth, girl."

*

145

It was the fourth or fifth period of wakefulness. "What are you doing to me?" Jan asked as she surfaced out of the deep well of sleep. Milo was bending over her.

"Calm yourself. I'm just changing your dressing, that's all. I've given you another shot of pain-blocking hormone so you won't feel much."

"Want to see," she said trying to raise her head.

"I wouldn't advise it."

But, stronger now, she was able to lift her head and look down along her exposed body. "Oh Mother God . . ." she sighed and let her head drop back on to the hard pillow. What she had seen was a ragged incision running down between her breasts all the way to her lower stomach. The sides of the incision were held together by crude, black stitches which looked as if they'd been inserted by someone who was very drunk at the time. Jan felt that if she sneezed or made some other too-violent movement the stitches would break and her body would simply open up, spilling out her intestines and other organs . . . .

"Mother God," she murmured again and closed her eyes tight. She tried to take very shallow breaths.

"It's not as bad as it looks," Milo told her.

This information did nothing to cheer her. "Leave me alone and let me die."

"No, really. You're healing fast, which is to be expected. The stitches can come out in a few days."

"No!" she cried, alarmed. "Those stitches are all that's keeping me together!"

She found Milo's ringing laughter quite hurtful.

But Milo was right. Three days later Jan was strong enough to get out of bed and, with Milo's help, walk all the way to the latrine. She was also able to switch from the strong broths he'd been feeding her to solid foods.

She was glad to be partly mobile again because she'd come to resent both her total reliance upon him and the enforced intimacy this had produced. At the same time she had to admit that he hadn't taken even the slightest advantage of the situation and was actually a very skilled and efficient nurse. But once again Jan found herself sliding even deeper into his debt and she didn't

146

like it. Eventually she would have to repay him, but the price was getting bigger all the time.

She was grateful, though, for his company as she lay there recuperating. He'd explained that he'd been excused duty to look after her. The order had come from the Aristos, not Bannion, he stressed. "You're the flavour of the day with them," he told her. "It's something we might be able to take advantage of . . . ."

On the fifth day Milo pronounced her sufficiently healed for the stitches to be removed. Because the supply of pain-blockers had been exhausted Jan found it an uncomfortable experience. She shut her eyes and put her thumb between her teeth, trying not to cry out.

After what seemed hours Milo said, "I'm finished." She raised her head and looked. The long wound had changed drastically in appearance since that first day. It still looked red and ugly but it had definitely healed to the point where it now seemed to be just a superficial incision. The wounds on her ankle and upper arm had similarly healed. "Thank you," she said.

"My pleasure." He said it in a teasing tone of voice. Then Jan became aware that he had left his hand resting on her left thigh. She suddenly felt naked and exposed under his gaze. She pushed his hand away and hurriedly pulled the thin blanket up to her chin.

He regarded her discomfiture with amusement. "Now that you've changed your mind about blowing up the *Lord Pangloth*, and me along with it, I see no reason why you shouldn't fulfil your side of our little agreement. Can you?"

After a long pause she said, in a small voice, "No . . . ."

"Good. When you're completely well I shall expect your full co-operation." He got up from the bed. "Now try and get some more sleep. I'm going to the village to buy food. I won't be long."

It took some time before Jan was able to slip into a troubled sleep. When she woke it was to find the gross and wheezing bulk of Guild Master Bannion looming over her.

Chapter Fifteen:

What the Aristos enjoyed, at the expense of the other in-habitants of the *Lord Pangloth*, was the luxury of space. That became clear to Jan soon after her arrival in the Aristo section of the airship, but was confirmed beyond doubt when she entered the 'Grand Saloon'. The room was huge. It was hundreds of feet in length and, at its broadest end, equally wide. Jan realized it was located in the bow of the Sky Lord, probably not far below the airship's actual nose. Two rows of tall windows, much bigger than the one in Magid's quarters, converged at a rounded point at the far end of the room. Jan could see wisps of white cloud passing by the windows.

There must have been about three hundred people present but so vast was the floor space that the room didn't seem the least bit crowded. The majority of the people, judging by their clothes, were Aristos but there were a large number of ser-vants, or slaves, passing among them carrying trays of drinks or food. As Jan stood at the top of the short staircase, flanked by Prince Magid and Mary Anne, she again felt a wave of unreality wash over. The feeling intensified when the crowd below her all turned in her direction and silence fell over the hall-like room.

Then someone started to applaud and before long everyone, apart from the servants, were clapping. With a sense of shock Jan realized they were applauding *her*.

Prince Magid touched her elbow, a signal that she should move forward. She did so. Magid and Mary Anne accompanied her down the stairs. When they reached the bottom the assembled Aristos, still applauding, split into two groups so that a wide corridor was formed between them stretching all the way to the end of the room. In front of where the rows of windows met to form their rounded point stood a small dais. On it were seated two figures; a man and a woman.

Jan knew who they were. The man was Prince Caspar. The woman was his mother, Lady Jane. As far as Jan could gather they reigned supreme within the Sky Lord.

She had been surprised to learn that Lord Pangloth didn't exist. There *had* been a Lord Pangloth a long time ago. Several, in fact, but from the small scraps of information that Magid had reluctantly given her on the way to the Grand Saloon it appeared that the Pangloth dynasty had been wiped out centuries ago by a rival Aristo family. She wondered if the present day Aristos were still prone to similar power struggles.

As she passed among the clapping Aristos, with Magid and Mary Anne one step behind her, Jan saw that Prince Caspar was much younger than she had expected. In fact he was nothing more than a youth and she guessed he was her age or even younger. He was also, she observed with interest, the prettiest male she had ever encountered. His long, angular face was framed with shoulder-length black hair, his smoothly textured skin was very white, and he had brown eyes that she could only describe as enormous.

Lady Jane, seated further back on the dais, was an older version of her son. She had the same long, handsome face with its immaculate cheekbones and very white skin, but her eyes were blue instead of brown. And unlike her son's, they were cold eyes.

When Jan, Magid and Mary Anne reached the dais Prince Caspar and his mother stood. Both were dressed entirely in black except for the white lace collar and cuffs worn by the Prince and a blood red jewel that hung between the breasts of Lady Jane. The Prince raised his arms and the clapping abruptly ceased. He looked down at Jan and smiled. It was a beautiful smile which stirred something somewhere inside her. She smiled back. Then she felt Magid poke his finger sharply into her back and she remembered what she was supposed to do. Awkwardly, she dipped her knees and bowed her head as Mary Anne had instructed her to do.

Prince Caspar said, "Jan Dorvin of Minerva, all of us here owe you a great debt of gratitude. If it hadn't been for your act of bravery against the Hazzini intruder the *Lord Pangloth* might well have been destroyed." He spoke in a soft but clear voice. "We therefore take pleasure in pardoning you for all past crimes against us and grant you both freedom and the honorary status of an Aristo. This means you will enjoy all the rights and privileges of being one of us, with the exception of being able to marry into an Aristo family. Welcome, Jan Dorvin. And thank you."

"Thank *you*, your Highness," said Jan in as sincere a tone as she could manage.

Prince Caspar raised his arms and the applause resumed. Jan dipped her knees and bowed again. She tried to fight back her tears. She was filled with shame. *Mother God forgive me*, she prayed. *It wasn't my fault. I didn't mean to save the* Lord Pangloth!

While Jan was being presented at court Milo was lying on his bunk and dreaming . . . .

His armoured flipper had landed on the gravel courtyard in front of Kagen's mansion. As he got out, a two-legged cyberoid paused and turned in his direction for a few moments then, satisfied, resumed its patrol alongside the wall. Kagen himself, accompanied by a blank-faced clone warrior, came hurrying out of the house to greet him. He was obviously very excited. Milo watched his approach with wry amusement. Kagen had had himself modified to the extent that no physical trace of the old Kagen remained, but his gait betrayed him. He still walked like the fat man he had been. The *litte* fat man.

"Glad you could make it, Haze. You won't be disappointed!" he said as he shook Milo's hand. "Come and see . . . ."

"Didn't think it was going to work," he said breathlessly as he ushered Milo in through the front entrance. "Lost the first three foetuses during the growth acceleration process. Struck lucky with number four. The white coats celebrated for a whole week straight."

Kagen took Milo down into the basement. The journey ended at a metal door guarded by another clone warrior. Kagen pressed his palm on the indentilock and the door slid open. It was dark beyond. "She doesn't like the light," he explained. In the dim

150

light from the corridor Milo saw the outline of a figure sitting on a bed. A woman and, by the look of it, quite ordinary in shape. Two arms, two legs, one head . . . .

Then Kagen turned the light on.

The woman – girl, really — gave a cry and covered her eyes with her forearm. Milo stared at her.

"Unique, eh? A real collector's item," said Kagen proudly.

Her skin was transparent. Beneath it, clearly visible, were pulsing arteries and veins, layers of fat deposits, muscle fibres . . . .

"Girl, take your hand away and look this way!" commanded Kagen.

Reluctantly she did so. Frightened eyes stared out through transparent lids. Two green pools of life set in what appeared to be a flayed, raw skull.

Kagen turned to Milo. "Well, what do you think of her?"

Milo woke and sat up. He clutched his head and moaned. Then he leaned forward and threw up on the clean floor of his cubicle.

Jan was relieved when the twittering Mary Anne finally said good night and left her alone in her bedroom. She removed the rest of her underclothes — Mary Anne had helped her out of the garment called a corset — and then put on a robe made of the sheerest material she had ever felt before. She sat on the soft bed with a tired sigh and stared out at the starless night through her single window. The presentation at court had exhausted her. All that smiling and being polite to the Aristos while her inner voice had kept repeating to her 'These are the people who murdered your mother, your father, all your friends . . . the people who destroyed Minerva.' *But I have no choice!* she had argued back. *I must do as Milo said and take advantage of the situation. He has a plan.*

She had been terrified that day when she'd woken up and found the huge Guild Master in Milo's cubicle. At first she'd thought she was alone with the creature and feared the worst, but then saw Milo and one of the overseers behind him. She feared that Bannion had come to take her away with him but instead he was only on an errand. An errand for the Aristos. Pompously, he told her that Lord Pangloth had graciously decided to reward her for her heroism by granting her freedom. When she was well enough she would be taken to the quarters of the Lord Chamberlain, Prince Magid, which would be her new home for the time being. Then he'd patted her on the cheek and said wistfully, "What a waste, my dear. I had other plans for you."

When he'd manoeuvred his bulk out through the cubicle's narrow entrance she had stared with astonishment at Milo. He looked cheerful. "Congratulations," he said and sat down in the wicker chair.

"I don't want to go and live with the Aristos," she told him.

"You want to stay here as a slave? You want to keep working as a glass walker and end up as Bannion's plaything?"

"No," she'd admitted. "But . . . ."

"Ah, I know what it is. You don't want to leave *me*."

"Rubbish," she said, then regretted having spoken so quickly. But Milo was still smiling. His reaction puzzled her. "You don't seem very upset about my imminent departure. I thought you had 'plans' for me too."

"And I still do. But they're no longer the same ones."

She frowned. "I don't understand."

"I no longer have plans for your body, but for your new exalted position in our airborne society. You're going to be in a position to do me a great deal of good."

"Like what?" she asked, suspiciously, having visions of herself smuggling various luxury items out of the Aristo section for Milo.

"Like enabling me to achieve what I've been trying to do for the three years I've been on board this thing. And if you do that I promise you two things that are closest to your heart."

"And they are?"

"Your freedom; and vengeance on the *Lord Pangloth*."

There was a tap on Jan's door. She groaned under her breath, presuming that it was Mary Anne coming back. But when the door opened she saw it was Ceri. She was dressed in a white shift and her hair was tousled. Jan guessed she'd come from her bed. "The Mistress asked me to see if you needed anything," she told Jan. "From now on you are to regard me as your servant."

152

"I don't need anything, thanks, and I'm certainly not going to treat you as my servant," Jan said firmly.

"I find it's best to do as the Mistress says," said Ceri. "It makes for a quieter life."

"Does she mistreat you?"

Ceri gave a slight shrug of the shoulders. "No, not physically. But she can be very tiresome when she doesn't get her own way."

"What about Prince Magid?"

Again the slight shrug. "It's best to keep him happy too," she said cryptically.

Jan patted the bed beside her. "Come and sit down. I'd like to talk to you awhile. Unless you're anxious to get back to your own bed."

"No." Ceri came over and sat down. They looked at each other. "You're very pretty," Jan told her.

"Thank you. So are you."

They were silent for a time then Ceri asked, "Did you enjoy yourself tonight?"

Jan made a face. "It was an ordeal. The Aristos are strange people. Everyone I talked to only talked about themselves. They'd ask a token question — usually asking if I'd fully recovered from the attack — and that was the only interest they showed in me; the rest of their conversation was about their problems. Not that they seemed to have any *real* ones."

"No, they live in a world of their own. Anything that lies outside of it is of no interest to them. They spend their time playing games, watching their 'entertainments', having sex and flattering Prince Caspar and his mother," said Ceri. "Were you presented to them, by the way? To the Prince and Lady Jane?"

"Oh yes. And later I had a brief chat with him. He's invited me to their private quarters tomorrow night for dinner. I don't want to go but I suppose I have no choice."

"What was your impression of him?" Ceri asked.

"Very beautiful. For a man . . . ." The implication hung in the air between them. Jan suddenly realized she had an over-powering urge to embrace Ceri. She badly needed the comfort of another woman's arms around her. It had been so long . . . .

She gave way to the impulse. She leaned forward and hugged Ceri, burying her face against her neck. "Hold me, please," she begged.

Ceri put her arms around Jan but not tightly. They stayed in this position for awhile and then Ceri said quietly, "You want me to sleep with you?"

"Oh yes, yes," sighed Jan. "More than anything."

Ceri gently disengaged herself from Jan's arms, stood up and pulled her white shift up over her head and dropped it on the floor. She wore nothing beneath it. She stood there and looked at Jan. Then she said coolly, "You are certainly learning fast."

"What do you mean?" asked Jan, puzzled by her attitude.

"Learning how to treat me as a servant. At this rate you'll make a fine Aristo."

Jan gasped. "You think . . . you think I'm *forcing* you to have sex with me?"

"Aren't you?"

"No! Of course not!" Jan was shocked that Ceri could have thought that of her. "I just assumed you *wanted* to."

"I'm not a Minervan, Jan," Ceri said quietly.

Comprehension dawned on Jan. She put her hand to her mouth. "Oh, I didn't realize. I mean, I just . . . ." She felt embarrassed. "You don't like women? I mean, you don't sleep with women?"

"I sleep with women. When I *have* to. And since I've been working for the Aristos I've slept with quite a lot of women. And a lot of Aristo men too."

"You mean they *make* you?"

She shrugged. "Let's say I have no choice in the matter. Unless I want to return to being a common slave again. At least the living conditions are better here."

Jan didn't know what to say. Her emotions were in confusion; she felt embarrassed, hurt; indignant on Ceri's behalf . . . and still sexually aroused. She said hurriedly, "Please put your shift back on. I'm sorry for the misunderstanding."

"That's all right." said Ceri as she bent down and picked up the white sleeping garment. As she slipped it over her head and pulled it down Jan said to her, "Please stay, though, and talk to

154

me a while longer. But only if you want to, as my friend. Not because you think you have some obligation to."

Ceri gave her a searching look then smiled. "I'd be happy to stay for awhile, as your *friend*." She sat back down on the bed beside Jan.

Jan said, "How long have you been on the *Lord Pangloth*, Ceri?"

"Three years. Before that I lived at sea. On a sea habitat. Do you know what that is?"

"Why yes. The slave who, well, befriended me — he lived on one as well. He said it was like a floating town." A thought occurred to her. "Maybe you both lived on the same one! Do you know a man by the name of Milo?"

At the mention of Milo's name Ceri's expression darkened. "Milo? That's the man who befriended you?"

"Yes. You know him then? He's a strange man, but he saved my life. More than once, I suspect."

"I know Milo all right," said Ceri with a slight scowl. "And I don't like him. It was thanks to him our sea habitat got destroyed. He finally convinced the Council that we should move close in to shore. It was true that conditions had worsened out in the ocean but we could have survived out there for many more years to come. Don't ask me what his motive was but ever since he arrived at the habitat he kept trying to persuade people that the habitat needed to be moved close to the mainland."

Jan was puzzled. "Since he arrived? He told me he was born in your floating town."

"He told you that?" Ceri shook her head. "No. He arrived about ten years before the *Lord Pangloth* sank us. He was in a strange, floating capsule. It was sealed and apparently very hard to break into. There were three bodies in the capsule with him. They'd been dead for weeks. Milo was in a deep coma and it was presumed he would soon die as well, but he suddenly regained consciousness."

Jan frowned. "I wonder why he lied to me? I don't understand . . . ."

"Milo was a hard one to understand, I grant you that," said Ceri. "And no one really liked him, but because he knew so

155

much, especially about machinery and electronics, he was a welcome addition to the community. Until he lured us to our destruction, that is. I lost everything. My parents. My husband . . . ."

"We have much in common then," Jan told her softly. She wanted to touch Ceri again but decided it would be wise not to. Her thoughts turned back to Milo. "He told me so many things. I wonder how many of those were lies too."

"What sort of things?"

"Oh, about the past. Early history. About before the Gene Wars and the like. He said he got it from the history machines you had in your sea town."

Ceri shook her head. "Another lie. All we had left in our library were some technical manuals and novels on tape, and a few holographic fiction movies. No historical stuff left at all."

Jan was about to ask what the terms 'novels' and 'holographic fiction movies' meant when an awful thought occurred to her. "There's something else he told me . . . you've got to tell me he was telling the truth about *that*."

Ceri regarded her with concern. "What's the matter? You've gone pale."

"Milo said that my town was only *part* of Minerva," said Jan anxiously. "He said there were other parts that I didn't know about . . . towns just like my own. He *was* telling the truth, wasn't he?" She stared at Ceri with pleading eyes. Ceri looked down at her hands which lay clasped together on her lap. "I'm sorry, Jan," she said quietly. "I know of no other surviving parts of Minerva. Your town was the only one."

Jan sucked in air then expelled it with a single, convulsive sob. She started to tremble. The knowledge that Minerva continued to exist in another form had been of profound importance to her. It had provided her with the will to keep going, knowing that somewhere the spirit of Minerva was being kept alive by others of her own kind. But now . . . .

Now she again had to deal with the awful realization that she was the last living Minervan woman. Her body shook as she cried. It was too much to bear.

Dimly, she became aware that Ceri was holding her, rocking

156

her gently back and forth in her arms. "Hey, come on Jan, take it easy," she heard Ceri croon in her ear. "Everything is going to be all right. Jesus, you're just a kid, aren't you . . .?"

Jan clung desperately to her. After a long time her sobbing stopped but she continued to hold on to Ceri. Eventually Ceri said, "Come on, Jan, time you went to bed."

Reluctantly, Jan let go of her. She didn't want to be alone but she couldn't make any more demands on Ceri. She watched as Ceri pulled back the bed covers for her then meekly slid under them. To her surprise Ceri slipped into bed beside her.

"Wha . . .?" she began but Ceri put two fingers on her lips and said, "Shush. What I'm doing is what I *want* to do. As a *friend.* All right?"

Jan smiled. "All right."

"No more talk," said Ceri, taking her in her arms.

Milo was leaning on the railing, staring down at the blight land that the airship was passing over. He looked round when Jan emerged on to the narrow, open observation deck where they had arranged to meet. He grinned as he looked her up and down. "Fancy dress suits you," he told her with amusement.

"It was the simplest thing I could find to wear," she said coldly. She was wearing a plain, full-length grey and black gown and, despite Mary Anne's protests, was wearing nothing underneath it. She couldn't stand that constricting underwear and had made up her mind to only wear it on formal occasions.

Milo regarded her plunging neckline with obvious appreciation. "You're healing well. I can hardly see the scar."

She folded her arms across her chest.

"So how did it go last night? Were you a social success? Did you meet Lord Pangloth?" he asked eagerly.

"Milo, our arrangement is off. I don't know what you want but I'm not going to help you get it. I never want to see you again. I never want to speak to you again. That's the only reason I came here today — to tell you that."

He looked surprised. "What's eating you? What happened last night?"

"I found out that you lied to me. There are no other 'lost' parts

157

of Minerva. My Minerva was all that was left. And it's gone. Everything you told me was a lie."

Milo shrugged. "It seemed the best thing I could do for you at the time."

"It was *what*?" she asked in astonishment.

"You were in a bad way emotionally. Close to losing the will to live. You needed something to boost you up — give you hope and all that — so I told you what can be described as a remedial lie. And you've got to admit it worked."

Jan clenched her fists. She wanted to smash that arrogant, smug expression from his face. "You bastard — you don't know what you did to me!"

"I did what I thought best. And I still think it was the right thing to do. Now, enough of this foolishness. You must stick to our agreement. I told you what was at stake. If I succeed we'll both have our freedom and the *Lord Pangloth* will be in *our* power."

She gave a bitter laugh. "You think I'm going to believe anything else you tell me now? Mother God, it was probably *all* lies. Everything you said, about the past — about *your* past."

He shook his head. "No, I swear it wasn't."

"Really. That's not what Ceri told me."

His eyes became wary. "Ceri?"

"You might remember her. You lived in the same floating sea city. She certainly remembers you. She doesn't like you very much."

"Yes, I remember her," he said slowly. "You've spoken to her, then?"

"We've become very good friends. She told me how you were found in a capsule with three dead bodies just ten years before you were captured by the *Lord Pangloth*. A rather different story to the one you told me."

He sighed. "All right, I admit I lied there as well, but only because you wouldn't have believed the truth if I'd told you it."

"And what is *that*?" she asked sceptically.

"That capsule was an emergency survival pod. It came from a spaceship that had crashed into the sea."

"A spaceship?"

"A craft capable of travelling through space. From planet to planet. The spaceship had come from the planet Mars."

"Mars?" she said blankly.

He pointed upwards. "Mars. You've heard of the planet Mars?"

"Yes, of course. Are you saying . . .?"

"Yes, I am. I come from Mars."

PART II

The Perfumed Breeze

Chapter Sixteen:

Jan leaned over Prince Caspar and playfully tickled his bare chest with a lock of her now long hair. "Come on, my Lord and master, time for you to get up."

Keeping his eyes closed Caspar brushed the hair away. "Why should I get up? It's too early," he groaned.

"Have you forgotten again? It's another Duty Day for you in the control room. We're due to arrive at Bandala in a few hours."

"Oh shit," he muttered. Then, "I don't care. What does it matter if I turn up or not. Gorman is really in charge down there."

That's true, thought Jan, though she was surprised to hear Caspar actually admit it. But he probably didn't believe this deep down — his self-deprecating words had just been for effect. "Nonsense, my Lord," she told him, running a caressing hand over his chest. "You are indispensable in the control room and you know it. Gorman and his engineers are but clever hands ruled by your noble head."

He opened his eyes. She never tired of looking into his eyes. "Flatterer," he told her. But he didn't sound displeased. Flattery *always* works, Milo had once told her. The human ego has no emotional defence against it even when the rational part of the mind recognizes it for what it is.

Jan kissed him on the mouth. "I speak the truth and you know it, my Lord." Caspar responded by putting his arms around her and hugging her tightly to him. Then he rolled them both over on the bed until she was pinned beneath him. "Again . . . *already?*" she gasped.

"It's your fault," he said hoarsely as he entered her. "It's that amazon smell of yours . . . It excites me so."

When Caspar was finished he rolled on to his back again and

was silent for awhile. Then he said, "You'll accompany me to the control room today?"

"Of course I will, my Lord."

"You like visiting the control room, don't you?" He opened his eyes and looked at her.

Jan was instantly wary. "Yes, sire. I told you — I find it very interesting."

"Women don't find such things interesting. Machinery and the like. What's your real reason?"

She felt a flicker of panic. Had he somehow divined the truth? Had some action of hers made him suspicious? Trying to keep the nervousness out of her voice she said, "What do you think my real reason is, my Lord?"

He gave a knowing smile. "You are having an affair with one of the engineers. They are rugged, muscular men — the sort that an amazon probably finds very attractive. Tell me which one it is. Is it Gorman himself?"

She relaxed, but not completely. "There is only one man in my life, my Lord, and that is you. I swear it. How could there possibly be *room* in my life for any other man when you fill it so completely?"

Caspar looked thoughtfully at her, then nodded. He believed her, but he was still puzzled. "Then what attracts you to that dreary place?"

"I told you, my Lord. I find it interesting. I'm an amazon, remember, sire, and not like normal women."

Slowly his puzzled expression cleared. He accepted this explanation. *Idiot*, she thought. He propped himself up on one elbow and smiled at her. "It is because you are not like normal women that I have kept you as my exclusive companion for so long," he told her.

Jan knew that was true too. As Milo had said, she had a novelty value for the Aristos. But how much longer would the situation last? It had been nearly six months since she had been with Prince Caspar and his mother and she knew that, for all her 'amazon' novelty, Caspar would sooner or later tire of her. Lady Jane was certainly showing signs of boredom. Only small signs so far, true, but it was only a matter of time.

164

From that first night when she dined with Prince Caspar and Lady Jane in their private quarters Jan had realized that both son and mother had an equal sexual interest in her, but whereas Caspar was quite open about it Lady Jane was being more subtle. Jan correctly deduced that any relationship she had with the mother would have to be kept from the son.

When she'd told Milo the situation he had calmly suggested that she sleep with both of them. "Exploit the situation as much as you can. From what you tell me Lady Jane is the power behind the throne. She will be as valuable to us as the Prince."

"You're asking me to prostitute myself for you," she said bitterly.

"No, whatever you do will be for yourself as well. I've told you what the prize will be if I succeed in my aims."

"*If* you're telling me the truth."

"You have no choice but to believe me, Jan. I'm your only hope."

"I've heard *that* before," she told him disdainfully. But to herself she had to admit it was true; he was. But whatever slim hope he offered was getting slimmer all the time. Despite her many 'games' on the keyboard of the device that the Engineers said was a useless relic but which Milo believed held the key to his scheme, she seemed to be no closer to achieving what he wanted. Nor did it help that he wouldn't confide in her what his scheme actually entailed. "It's best you don't know, little amazon. For your own sake. Just in case you let something slip during a session of pillow-talk with their Royal Highnesses."

She had protested that she would never do such a thing but it was to no avail. He would tell her nothing more.

Prince Caspar got out of bed, stretched languorously, then admired his naked reflection in the full-length mirror. Jan admired it too; he had a beautiful body. If only, she mused, he wasn't so hopeless in bed with it. If only he had a fraction of the love-making skills possessed by his mother. But then Lady Jane was much older — over a hundred, she'd admitted — and naturally was much more experienced.

He went into the bathroom. Jan hoped it might be one of those

165

rare days when he would actually take a bath but she knew that was unlikely. Water was plentiful in the Aristo part of the airship but they didn't take advantage of it, preferring to soak themselves, and their clothes, with sickly-sweet scents.

Jan got up too and looked at her own reflection in the mirror. Unlike Caspar she didn't like what she saw. I'm getting soft, she thought. No, she had *become* soft. Not fat, just soft. Her muscles had smoothed out and the flesh of her torso, arms and legs had become featureless and bland. *And* pale. No wonder Lady Jane was losing interest in her. That wild — even dangerous — looking 'amazon' that the jaded Lady Jane had found so sexually titillating six months ago had practically vanished.

When Jan had finally learnt the meaning of the word amazon — it had been Ceri who'd told her — she'd been vaguely amused but not offended. She didn't mind that Minervans were compared with a mythical tribe of ferocious women warriors, even if the comparison was meant derisively.

Caspar emerged from the bathroom wearing his favourite robe. It was made of black fur, the hide of which hadn't been properly cured and its underlying pungent odour could be easily detected through the perfume. "I'll be leaving for the control room directly after breakfast. Be ready by then if you want to come with me."

"I will be, my Lord," she told him and picked up her own robe from the foot of the bed. She was just putting it on when he opened the door to admit Dalwyn, Caspar's personal manservant and bodyguard who had been on duty outside Jan's bedroom all night. Dalwyn was a big, good-looking man who seemed utterly devoted to Prince Caspar. He made it clear to Jan he resented her relationship with the Prince and though she went out of her way to be pleasant to him he was openly hostile to her. This morning was no exception. Her smile and friendly greeting to him drew nothing but a surly glare. As usual Prince Caspar pretended not to notice.

She sighed when the door had closed behind them both and glanced at the clock on the wall. It would be an hour before he finished having breakfast with Lady Jane. No need to rush. She sat on the bed and pressed a button on the bedside table. Ceri appeared almost immediately. Persuading Prince Caspar to make Ceri her personal servant was, in Jan's opinion, her most positive achievement since becoming the Prince's lover. Neither Mary Anne nor Prince Magid had been pleased with this development but they had to bow to Caspar's will.

Jan motioned Ceri to be seated in one of the bedroom's armchairs and said, "I'm exhausted."

"Another job well done?" asked Ceri dryly.

"I think I can safely claim that," Jan said. "Mother God, he has incredible sexual stamina. It's a pity he's so useless at making love."

Ceri studied her for a while then said hesitantly, "May I ask you a personal question?"

"You, of all people, should know you can ask me anything you want," Jan told her with a smile. "What do you want to know?"

"How . . . how do you feel when you make love to the Prince?" Ceri asked her seriously.

"How do I *feel*?" Jan raised her eyebrows. "Do you mean do I *enjoy* it?"

"Well . . . yes."

She shrugged. "Well, yes, I do get some physical pleasure from him, in spite of his incompetence."

"And in spite of him being a man?"

Jan gave Ceri a sly smile. "You want to know how I, a Minervan, can bear to make love to a man, yes? But I've told you before, I'm sure, that Minervan women didn't sleep exclusively with women. In fact younger women like myself were actively encouraged to experiment with men so that we would be familiar with the experience when the time of breeding came."

Ceri frowned. "Yes, but basically you *prefer* sleeping with women, don't you? I mean, surely you get more satisfaction from Lady Jane . . .?"

"Well, yes. But that's mainly because she's much more sexually skilful than Caspar, not just because she's a woman. But I get no real *emotional* satisfaction from either of them. Yes, I find both of them attractive, despite of *who* they are and

167

what they are — but I shut *that* out of my mind when I'm with them — but I have no love for them. It's *you* I love, Ceri."

Ceri winced. "I thought we'd agreed not to discuss that again."

"You brought up the subject of my sexual preferences, not me," said Jan. Since that one night, the day of her presentation at court, Ceri hadn't slept with her again. She had made it clear that their love-making on that occasion had been a one-off event. It had been a special act of friendship but, given her freedom of choice, Ceri preferred not to sleep with women. She allowed Jan physical contact with her — hugs, even kisses — but nothing more. And Jan had been in an agony of frustration ever since. "I wish you'd reconsider, Ceri," pleaded Jan. "If people love each other it doesn't matter what sex they are. And I *do* love you!"

Ceri looked uncomfortable. "Please, Jan, don't talk this way. You don't really love me. It's just because I'm the first real friend you've had since coming on board the *Lord Pangloth*. And because you're a Minervan, and young. You're infatuated, that's all, but it's not *real* love."

"I think I'm the best judge of my own emotions," Jan told her firmly.

"*No* one is the best judge of their *own* emotions," said Ceri.

Jan made a groaning sound. "That's the sort of thing Milo would say."

As usual Ceri scowled at the mention of Milo's name. "If you did love me you'd heed my advice about that creature . . . ."

"Don't change the subject," said Jan quickly. She was only too well aware of how Ceri felt about Milo. She remembered the time when she'd recounted Milo's story to her. Ceri had been incredulous. "He said he's from *Mars*?"

"Yes. And he was very convincing."

"You mean you believe he's an alien from outer space?" Ceri had laughed.

"Well, I wouldn't be surprised if he had been but no, he says he is human. There's a colony on Mars, he says, which was established before the Gene Wars and that's where he was born."

Ceri had frowned. "There are stories of such a colony, and of habitats in space, but surely, without support from Earth, they'd have died out years ago."

"Well, according to Milo the colony on Mars is still flourishing."

Ceri had remained sceptical. "So how did he get to Earth, and why?"

"He came in a spaceship that crashed in the sea. But as to *why* he won't say yet."

Ceri had shaken her head in disbelief. "So why didn't he tell *us* all this stuff about Mars? Why did he lie to us about coming from another sea habitat?"

"He said he had his reasons."

"Yes, I'll *bet* he did. Jan, I don't know how you can be so gullible! You know how much he's lied to you in the past. And now you're willing to trust him again; willing to partake in some crazy, downright dangerous scheme involving the machinery in the control room?"

In anguish, Jan had said, "I have no choice, don't you see? I have to trust him again! He has promised me the means of vengeance on the *Lord Pangloth*! I won't have peace of mind until I do!"

"But you told me that when you had the chance to destroy the *Lord Pangloth* you couldn't go through with it. I'm not complaining, mind, but what makes you think you'll be able to do it if Milo provides you with a second chance?"

Jan had shaken her head. "He's not talking about destroying the airship but taking *control* of it somehow."

"But he won't tell you how?"

"No," Jan had admitted. "Not yet."

Ceri had given her a despairing look. "I'm beginning to think your first opinion of Milo was the correct one. That he's a sorcerer. He certainly seems to have performed sorcery on your good sense."

Nothing had happened since then to alter Ceri's opinion of either Milo or Jan's involvement with him and Jan had given up trying to argue with her. "We're talking about *us*, not Milo," she told Ceri.

169

"Not any more we're not," said Ceri firmly. She stood up. "When the Prince finishes his ritual breakfast with his beloved mother he will expect to find you all dressed and ready to go. Come on, I'll run you a bath. And while you're taking it I'll go fetch you some food."

Jan looked at her and sighed.

The doors of the elevator slid open and Prince Caspar entered the control room. Jan, keeping a dutiful few steps behind, followed him. The twelve Engineers in the room were all standing stiffly to attention. They raised their right arms, the fists clenched, in salute to the Prince as he took his seat on the throne on the dais at the rear of the control room. Jan took her place beside the throne, her arm resting across its back, while Dalwyn remained by the elevator doors.

"Resume your duties," Caspar told the Engineers and they immediately relaxed and turned their attention to their instruments. Gorman, the Chief Engineer, approached the throne. He was a small man with a bland, unreadable face. As usual his grey uniform, with its black Engineering Guild insignia — a bolt of lightning across a circle — on the left breast, was neatly pressed and a pair of binoculars hung from his neck. "We're on schedule, sire," he said.

"Good. Carry on, Chief Engineer," said Caspar, the lack of interest clear in his tone of voice. Jan knew he found his control room duties boring. She also knew that he was completely ignorant, like all the Aristos, of the actual mechanics involved in running and operating the *Lord Pangloth*. Without the Engineers, who were well aware of how indispensable they were, they would be helpless.

Gorman gave a bow to Caspar. "Very well, your Highness." As he straightened his eyes met briefly with Jan. Once again she got the feeling he could see straight through her; knew her every secret. She had noticed him surreptitiously watching her when she had been 'playing' with the device that was the object of Milo's interest even though she thought she'd allayed his suspicions long ago by telling him that she liked the 'pretty colours' that appeared on the screen when she pushed the various buttons.

Gorman returned to his customary position immediately behind the two seated helmsmen. The control room was a glass blister protruding from the hull at the bottom of the bow. Only the walkways and equipment partially obscured a 360 degree field of vision.

Jan was able to recognize now just what in the control room dated back to the airship's original builders and what had been added, or altered, by subsequent generations of Engineers. It was also easy, now, for her to realize that the more recent the modification the more primitive it appeared to be in comparison to the original equipment and fittings.

Milo had been fascinated by her descriptions of the state of the control room after her first visits to it. "It sounds as if," he told her, "thanks to their meddling over the years, they've bypassed more and more of the functions of the central computer in order to feel more in control. But obviously the computer is still exerting its influence over much of the running of the *Lord Pangloth*. There is no way a human pilot could fly something of this size without the assistance of a computer. Just maintaining the ship's trim would be beyond *ten* human pilots working together. The computer must be constantly making adjustments; to the thrusters, to the temperature of the gas in the individual cells, to the stabilizers and elevators . . . ."

"We are approaching Bandala," announced Gorman. "We will be directly overhead in exactly five minutes."

Jan peered down through the curving transparent wall. The airship was passing over rugged hill country. Parts of the hill slopes were richly forested but even at this high altitude the blight had gotten a secure grip on the land. The blight, she had learned, thrived best at low altitudes and high temperatures.

Bandala was a remnant of a state that had been exclusively black. Like Minerva it had shrunk to a mere fragment of its former size but unlike Minerva it wasn't a producer of grain and other foodstuffs but metal and timber. There was an iron ore mine within its shrunken borders, as well as smelters, foundries and several small factories. The latter were capable of making a limited range of metal and wooden artifacts.

Jan watched with interest as a wide valley full of buildings

171

came into view. Bandala was much bigger than Minerva had been, both in terms of the area that it covered and the number of buildings it contained. Some of the buildings had long chimneys from which smoke was rising. As with Minerva every available space was covered with vegetable gardens. Jan knew it was part of the traditional contract between Bandala and the *Lord Pangloth* that the Sky Lord actually provided the Bandalans with supplies of grain, as they had lost their distant farm lands ages ago.

She also knew that the Bandalans had been very dissatisfied with the meagre load of grain that the Sky Lord had deposited on its last trip but the Sky Warriors had told them it was all that was available. And they were telling the truth. Minerva wasn't the only food-producing community that had been lost to the *Lord Pangloth* recently. Two others had been overrun completely by the blight within the last year and the Sky Lord's grain surplus had been drastically reduced as a result.

"With your permission, your Highness, I shall halt the vessel and descend to hailing distance," said Gorman to the Prince. Caspar nodded and Gorman gave a curt command to the helmsmen who both pulled sharply back on four large levers. Jan felt the floor vibrate slightly and heard the thrusters roar their protest as they went into full reverse power to bring the mile-long airship to a gliding halt above the valley. Some of the thrusters, she knew, would be swivelling to hold it steady in that position no matter how strong a wind was blowing.

More terse commands from Gorman, more manipulation of levers by the helmsmen. Another tremor ran through the floor as the *Lord Pangloth* began to descend. It dropped about a thousand feet, then Gorman gave the order to stop. "Hail them," he said. Another Engineer pressed a switch on a console and once again the voice of 'Lord Pangloth' boomed out.

Jan knew now that it wasn't the voice of the last Lord Pangloth. Its owner, long since dead, had been chosen for the task simply because he possessed an impressively deep voice. His words, spoken long ago, had been trapped inside a machine. "Think of the machine as a kind of echo trap," Milo had said when attempting to explain the principle to her. But however it worked, the machine was showing increasing signs of breaking

172

down. 'Lord Pangloth's' voice was accompanied by much loud hissing and crackling.

The speech ended. Smoke rose from an empty square in the centre of the valley. The signal of acquiescence. The airship began to descend again. Then Jan noticed that Gorman was in conversation with his second-in-command. Gorman was pointing downwards. Jan looked but could see nothing out of the ordinary. Puzzled, she glanced at Caspar, but he was engrossed in polishing his big ruby ring on the fabric of his trouser leg.

"Your Highness . . ." Gorman had turned to the Prince. "Something is not right . . . ."

"What do you mean?" asked Caspar, uninterestedly.

"Look, sire," said Gorman, pointing. "Three large structures that I am sure were not here on our last visit."

"What, you mean those water tanks? But surely they've always been there?" said Caspar.

"There were two before. Now there are *five*," said Gorman. "And the three new ones are much bigger than the others. The combined water capacity of these additional tanks is far beyond the needs of Bandala's population."

The objects of Gorman's concern, Jan saw, were large, cylindrical structures made of wood. They were built high up on the slopes of the valley walls.

Caspar studied them with a frown then said, in exasperation, "Oh really, Gorman! So the earthworms have built water towers they don't need—so what? Why should we be concerned by such a demonstration of their stupidity?"

"I don't know, sire," admitted Gorman. "But after the experience with Minerva I believe that in these, er, unusual times extreme caution is called for." Gorman then gave Jan a pointed look. "I think we should return to a safer altitude until we're sure."

Caspar sucked noisily on his ruby rings. He hated making decisions. He also didn't like to stay in the control room any longer than necessary. But to ignore advice from Gorman was never wise . . . . "Oh, very well, Gorman," Caspar said testily. "Do whatever you want. But if this delay proves to be a complete waste of time I'm going to be *very* displeased."

"Thank you, sire," said Gorman, unperturbed. He turned and

snapped out an order to the helmsmen. There was an increase of sound from the thrusters. The *Lord Pangloth's* descent slowed. Jan saw that the summits of the surrounding hills were now level with the control room.

"Take us up, fast," ordered Gorman.

But it was too late. The three new 'water tanks' were opening up like vast, wooden flowers, revealing that they contained not watr but something very different.

Chapter Seventeen:

"All units to battle stations!" yelled Gorman into the microphone connected to loudspeakers throughout the airship. "We are under attack!"

"What *are* they?" asked the Prince as he stared wide-eyed at the three rapidly rising objects.

"Balloons," said Gorman. "Hot-air balloons. And damn *big* ones."

Two of the balloons were rising on the *Lord Pangloth's* port side, the third was to starboard. The 'water tanks', it was obvious now, had been flimsy wooden constructs concealing the large balloons, which Jan estimated were about eighty feet from top to bottom. They were level with the airship's lower hull and she could see plainly the structures hanging beneath each balloon. They were big wooden cages filled with men, ropes, boxes and objects that were presumably weapons. At the centre of the cage sat a huge stove that men were furiously feeding with pieces of coal and wood. The stack of each stove disappeared into the open neck of the towering balloon above.

"Shoot them down!" cried the Prince. "Blow them out of the sky with the cannon! They have no right to be up here! They are breaking the first law of the Sky Lords!" He had risen to his feet and his face had gone very red.

"They are moving too fast for the cannon," said Gorman. This was true. The three balloons were ascending much faster than the *Lord Pangloth* and would soon be out of sight to those in the control room. Gorman leaned over the microphone again. "All units of riflemen — open fire!"

Instantly Jan heard the crackling of gunfire. She saw a man in one of the wooden cages fall backwards. The others took cover where they could. Jan saw puffs of smoke along the side of the cage. The Bandalans were firing back, but then came flashes of light. The *Lord Pangloth's* automatic defences — the lasers — were designed to destroy threatening objects even as small as bullets.

"Can't we rise any faster?" cried the Prince.

"No, sire," answered Gorman. "The thrusters are at full power. We're raising the temperature of the gas in the cells which will give us extra lift but it will be some time before that takes effect."

The three balloons had now passed out of sight. The sound of rifle-fire continued.

"What do those stupid earthworms think they're doing, Gorman?" demanded the Prince.

"I don't know, yet," confessed Gorman. Jan had never seen him looking so concerned. She realized he was now helpless, with no way of knowing what was going on outside. Everything had been designed to deal with events happening on the ground; Gorman and his men were not prepared for dealing with threats that came from above. Nor was the loudspeaker system any help. Gorman could issue orders *to* the rest of the ship but communication worked one way only. The original system had long since fallen into disrepair and the only way to get a message *into* the control room was to have it physically delivered. And by the time any messenger arrived the Bandalans would have no doubt already done whatever they planned to do.

"Sire, I'm going to order full ahead. It's too dangerous to stay in the area," Gorman told the prince.

"What?" Casper looked astonished. "You mean *flee*? No, out of the question, Gorman. The *Lord Pangloth* will never run away from a bunch of earthworms . . . ."

175

"Consider it a *temporary* retreat, sire," said Gorman with strained formality. "We shall return when we are in a safe altitude and suitably punish the Bandalans."

"No," said Caspar, his voice cracking with anger. "A Sky Lord would never . . . ."

His words were drowned out by a large explosion. There were cries of alarm from some of the Engineers as the deck began to sway back and forth. Then Jan saw pieces of wreckage dropping from the sky on the starboard side of the airship. Fragments of charred and burning wood . . . bits of rope . . . blackened objects that she realized were parts of bodies. Then, more slowly, the burning, twisting balloon canopy of one of the hot-air balloons. Ripped apart, it flapped downwards like a giant piece of burning rag.

The Engineers began to cheer. The Prince rounded on Gorman with a triumphant grin. "See, Gorman! So much for the earthworms! You said our cannons couldn't hit them but they have!"

Gorman was still watching the falling canopy, his expression grim. He said, "Sire, one of our shells could not have produced such a massive explosion. The only other explanation is that the Bandalans were carrying explosives of their own. And that means the other two balloons are similarly equipped. I repeat, sire, we must leave the area immediately."

Prince Caspar's look of triumph drained away. "You think there is a chance the Bandalans could harm us?"

"I do, sire. Let me give the order to proceed full ahead."

Caspar chewed his lower lip worriedly, then nodded. "Very well, Gorman, but I'm holding you responsible."

"Full ahead!" Gorman snapped to the helmsmen.

They pushed levers. The control room juddered as the *Lord Pangloth*'s thrusters changed direction and started to drive the mile-long vessel forward.

Then came another explosion. Seconds later the deck again began to tilt, but so violently this time that several of the Engineers lost their balance. Jan would have fallen too if she hadn't been holding on to the back of the throne. Caspar wasn't so fortunate and was pitched off the dais to land on his hands and knees behind Gorman. Gorman helped him up as one of the Engineers yelled, "Sir, we're losing altitude! Instruments show a major rupture in Cell number Seven!"

White-faced, the Prince clung on to Gorman and cried at him, "My God, they've blown us up! We're on fire!"

"Cell Seven contains helium, sire! Or rather it *did*. . . ." Gorman tried to pull free of the Prince's convulsive grip. "Everyone remain calm!" he yelled, more for the Prince's benefit than anyone else. "How fast are we losing altitude?"

"Just over a foot every second!" called back the Engineer who was monitoring a row of altimeters. "Seventy feet a minute."

"Sir!" cried one of the helmsmen. "If we keep descending at this rate we're going to hit that next range of hills ahead of us."

"Gorman, do something!" cried the Prince, still gripping his arms. "I order you to do something!"

What Gorman did was to give the Prince such a violent shove that he fell backwards and landed heavily on the deck. Caspar's first reaction was one of stunned amazement, then his expression changed to one of naked fury. "Kill him!" he ordered Dalwyn, who was already moving towards Gorman. "He dared to lay hands upon me."

Dalwyn grabbed Gorman by the throat but seemed unsure of what to do. He looked enquiringly to the Prince. "Kill him!" yelled Caspar again, getting to his feet and reaching for his ceremonial sword. "Or I will myself!"

The scene formed a bizarre tableau within the control room, with everyone frozen except the Prince, who was drawing his sword and advancing on Gorman. Then Jan saw that Gorman was giving *her* a pleading look . . . .

She saw immediately what he had in mind and hesitated only a moment before stepping forward and crying, "My Lord, don't kill him yet! You still have *need* of him!"

The Prince turned to her, his face a mask of rage. "What?" he demanded. "What are you talking about, girl? This filth assaulted me. He *must* die."

Jan stepped close to him and clasped his face between her hands. "My master, listen to me, please," she pleaded. "I know he must be punished but not yet. The *Lord Pangloth* is in serious

177

trouble and only you and the Chief Engineer working *together* can save it. You *must* let him resume his duties, and *fast*. Every second counts, my Lord. Look!" She made him turn and look ahead. The range of high hills were looming dangerously close.

Caspar stared at them for several long and tense moments, then let his sword drop back into its scabbard. "Dalwyn, release him. Gorman, do what is necessary."

Dalwyn let Gorman go. Pausing only to rub his throat Gorman said calmly. "Helmsmen, reverse thrust, then give us full power straight up."

"And did our beloved monarch have him executed afterwards?" asked Milo cheerfully.

"No. Lady Jane talked him out of doing anything so drastic. He's been suspended from duty and restricted to his quarters. I heard there's going to be some sort of trial, but they need Gorman too much to kill him, or even keep him suspended from duty for very long."

"The Aristos needed *them* too, but look what they did . . . ." He indicated the columns of black smoke that were still visible above the distant valley of Bandala.

"They did argue a lot before they came to the decision to bomb the Bandalans," she said. "Lady Jane was the voice of reason again but she was out-voted. Many of the Aristos were hysterical . . . they wouldn't listen to her."

"So they destroy the one place within their ever-shrinking empire that supplied them with metal, not to mention most of their gunpowder." He laughed. "That kind of thinking brings empires to a hasty end."

"I told you, they were scared," said Jan. She wrapped her arms around herself. It was cold out on their usual meeting place, the small observation deck, and her thin garment gave her no protection. "Probably more scared than when we Minervans attacked. We didn't do any damage but the Bandalans certainly did."

"They did indeed," agreed Milo, almost gleefully. "Even I was becoming a little worried about the outcome."

It had been a close thing, as Jan realized when she had later learned what had happened. Gorman had been right that the three balloons had been carrying large amounts of explosives. A lucky hit with a bullet had set off the explosives in one of the balloons but the other two succeeded in rising up and over the *Lord Pangloth*, where they then dropped large grappling hooks towards the hull. A man perched precariously on each hook prevented them from being destroyed by the automatic lasers.

Both grappling hooks got a purchase on the hull, a considerable distance apart, and the Bandalans were then able to haul their balloons down along the ropes, at the same time making the balloons less buoyant by shutting off the supplies of hot air.

Each cage contained about ten men. One group survived for only a short time, having come down near a large unit of Sky Warriors, but the second group was more fortunate, landing a long way from the nearest hatchway. By the time Sky Warriors reached them they had succeeded in detonating their crate of gunpowder, ripping a large hole in the hull and also puncturing, possibly beyond repair, one of the gas cells, allowing its irreplaceable supply of helium to escape into the atmosphere. If, of course, they'd happened to have set off their explosive above one of the hydrogen-filled cells the *Lord Pangloth* would have been doomed. As it was the airship had sustained serious damage and might even be permanently crippled if it proved impossible to repair Cell number Seven and fill it with hydrogen. At the moment the *Lord Pangloth* was still listing slightly to port and was flying only at a thousand feet, the best altitude it could manage.

Milo sighed. "And with all those distractions you missed a perfect opportunity to test those new sequences of symbols I gave you for the terminal."

She glared at him. "Distractions? I thought we were about to crash. And if it hadn't been for Gorman we would have. The last thing on my mind was your precious box of lights."

"I keep telling you — my 'box of lights' holds a key that will allow us to unlock a source of great power. You could have tried afterwards, when the emergency was over and everyone was squabbling as to whether to bomb the Bandalans or not."

"I was too busy with the Prince, trying to keep him calm. He

179

was still demanding that Gorman be executed. But don't worry, I'll try again at the next opportunity. With Gorman out of the way for the time being it'll be easier for me. He's the only one who keeps watching me when I'm playing with your box of lights. I'm sure he suspects something."

Milo shrugged. "From what you tell me you saved his life. Even if he gets his old post back his attitude towards you will be different."

"I doubt that. He's cold, like you. He follows his own secret set of motives and doesn't let personal feelings get in the way. *Just like you.*"

He laughed and put his arm around her bare shoulders. "How could you accuse me of being cold. You know how I feel about you."

She pulled away from him. "Don't. Yes, I know how you feel about me. First you needed me for sex, now you need me for something else, but as soon as you don't need me at all I will be nothing to you."

"*All* human relationships are based on need — on selfishness. And all human emotions too. Selfishness equals survival. To believe otherwise is to indulge in romantic self-deception."

"So you admit that as soon as you stop needing me I'll be expendable?" she asked him coolly.

He smiled at her. "Jan, I can't imagine a time when I *won't* need you."

"I'm sure a lot of women have heard you say those same words during your long life. And where are they all now, I wonder. All dead and forgotten by you, no doubt."

He looked pained. "You've become a cynic terribly fast."

"I've had a good teacher. And now I've got to go. The Prince is showing one of his favourite Entertainments to his inner circle tonight and he wants me to be there."

"The Aristos are going to spend tonight watching old movies?" asked Milo in surprise. "After all that's happened today and with the *Lord Pangloth* in the state it's in?"

"That's *exactly* why. They want to retreat back into their cosy, insulated world as soon as possible. They want to pretend that today never happened."

But even though she knew this Jan still found the atmosphere at the Prince's screening party that night very strange. No one mentioned the Bandalans' near-successful attack, no one discussed what might happen if the *Lord Pangloth* couldn't be repaired; instead there was only small-talk about nothing in particular, jokes and forced laughter. They *were* pretending everything was the same as usual. And maybe, she suspected, they even believed it.

After the food had been eaten and a lot of drink had been consumed they all settled down in their fur-covered seats and faced a wall that seemed to be made of black glass. Jan sat beside the Prince. He put his hand on her upper thigh and began stroking it through the fabric of her gown. She could tell that he was sexually keyed up and took it as another reaction to the day's traumatic events. She guessed that he would be very active in bed that night.

The lights went out and the wall of glass vanished. The 'Entertainment' had begun.

The first time she had seen one Jan had been profoundly shocked, much to the amusement of the Prince and his friends. It had been a disconcerting experience to see the glass wall suddenly turn into a gateway that led straight to the centre of another world — a world that looked more *real* than her own one, where the colours were richer and the people larger and more attractive. She had gasped with fright and clutched at the Prince's arm. "What's happening?" she had cried.

He had chuckled and told her to be quiet. "Watch and enjoy. It's only an Entertainment." So she had forced herself to sit still and to watch the disturbing sights visible through the gap where the fourth wall had been — people whose faces suddenly became enormous, dizzying flights over strange landscapes and vast cities made of towers of glass full of coloured lights, fights between groups of people using weapons of horrible power, things made of metal that talked like men . . . By the end of it she felt as if her head was going to explode from the sheer *amount* of different, unbelievable things she had seen.

The next day Jan was anxious to talk to Milo and to get his explanation for the phenomenon she had witnessed. "It was a holographic movie," he told her. "The 'glass wall' projects images in three dimensions. Produces one hundred per cent realism, so I'm not surprised you were knocked for a loop by it all."

She asked him where the images had come from. "They're stored—preserved—on a tape, but don't ask me to explain how. Probably date back to the early twenty-first century. What was the movie about?"

She hadn't known the 'Entertainment' had been *about* anything. All she'd seen were apparently unconnected images adding up to chaos. Milo then asked her what clothes the people had worn. "They were dressed very much like the Aristos . . . and, oh yes, they *sang* a lot."

"They sang?" he asked, then laughed. "I know the period that was made now. Mid-twenty-first century. Part of a long series of musical fantasies. Became incredibly popular but I never understood why. I thought they were banal crap. Still, the ancestors of the Aristos must have thought highly of them. Wouldn't surprise me if they modelled their own clothing on the styles in the series, which is why the Aristos are still going around in fancy dress." He found this thought very amusing and laughed for a long time but Jan was still puzzled.

"I don't understand," she said. "Those images, were they of the past before the Gene Wars? Were there really huge cities of glass on other worlds?"

"I'm afraid not, Jan. None of it was real. It was all a fantasy. One of a series, like I said, set in a never-never future about a pseudo-medieval empire that ruled the galaxy."

"Oh," she said. She was a little disappointed. "But the whole thing had seemed so *real*. How was it done? And where did those beautiful people come from? And when they sung they had such beautiful voices too . . . ."

"Those people never existed, Jan. Like the glass cities and everything you saw, they were generated inside a computer. Think of them as incredibly realistic paintings . . . paintings that can move and talk . . . ."

Jan hadn't believed him then and even now, as she watched the very same Entertainment for about the thirtieth time, she still found it difficult to accept that these beautiful people had never lived or breathed; that they were the product of some ancient mechanical brain.

Even so she normally enjoyed watching it — she was now capable of discerning the 'plot' — but tonight she couldn't keep her attention on the spectacle. She kept remembering Milo's final words to her that evening. "You must increase your efforts with that computer terminal. I have the strong feeling that time is running out. I don't believe in omens as a rule, but today's near-catastrophe seems a kind of warning to me. that the *Lord Pangloth*'s days are numbered."

Jan knew what he meant. She shared the same feeling that, from now on, the *Lord Pangloth* and everyone in it were living on borrowed time.

These premonitions were proved correct exactly a week later. On the morning that the *Lord Pangloth* encountered the *Perfumed Breeze*.

Chapter Eighteen:

A difficult manoeuvre was being carried out. The *Lord Pangloth* was hovering very close to the surface of a lake in order to take on board a large amount of fresh water. The water, being pumped up through a long, weighted hose, was needed not only to replenish the normal supplies but also for conversion into hydrogen gas. A large amount of the gas would need to be produced in the airship's electrolysis plant to inflate Cell number Seven which, it was hoped, had now been successfully repaired.

The manoeuvre was difficult because as more water was pumped on board the airship naturally became heavier, and to compensate for this the temperature in the gas cells had to be adjusted to provide more lift. So delicate was the operation that Gorman had been temporarily released from his quarters to supervise it. The atmosphere in the control room was very tense as a result, which provided Jan with the perfect opportunity to try the computer terminal again. Milo had provided her with yet another series of permutations of what he called the 'access code' and she was having trouble keeping all the numbers in her mind.

She was so engrossed in what she was doing that she wasn't aware at first that something was wrong. It was only when she heard Caspar call out Gorman's name that she became alerted to the fact that there was an emergency; until then the Prince had been pretending that Gorman wasn't present. She looked up from the frustratingly blank screen and saw that everyone was staring out through the port side of the control room. And then she saw it . . . .

For a few moments she thought the spherical object was another hot air balloon but then she realized that she was seeing another airship travelling bow-on towards them at the same low altitude.

Another airship?

Everyone in the control room, with the exception of Jan, was talking at once. Over the babble of voices she heard Caspar's uncomprehending cry to Gorman: "Gorman, how can it be possible? How could the earthworms have built an *airship*?"

"I don't think that has anything to do with earthworms, sire," said Gorman as he studied the approaching airship through his binoculars. "That's another Sky Lord."

Caspar looked as if someone had just kicked him very hard in the backside. And he wasn't the only one, Jan noticed.

"But that's impossible!" Caspar finally managed to splutter.

Gorman was ignoring him. "Pumping crew, cease operating and reel in," Gorman called into the microphone. Then, "Helmsmen, take us up immediately. Don't wait for them to reel the hose in . . . ."

Jan looked again at the approaching Sky Lord. It was much bigger now and she estimated that it was less than two miles away. She could also see details on the round face it presented to them. The lower half was luridly coloured and, like the *Lord Pangloth*, it had giant eyes painted on its sides.

"Full elevation at full speed!" ordered Gorman, and Jan had to clutch on to the back of Caspar's throne as the *Lord Pangloth*'s bow began to rise sharply as the airship surged forward.

184

"All units to battle stations!" Gorman yelled into the microphone. She could hear his amplified voice booming in other parts of the *Lord Pangloth*. She could hear sirens and alarm bells as well.

"But what's another Sky Lord doing in *our* territory?" cried the Prince.

Gorman ignored him. He was again watching the intruder through his binoculars. "That's not the *Lord Matamoros*, that's for certain."

The *Lord Matamoros*, Jan knew, was the Sky Lord whose territory lay immediately to the south of the *Lord Pangloth*'s.

"Why aren't we turning, Gorman?" demanded the Prince. "Turn and attack the intruder!"

Gorman lowered his binoculars and looked at Caspar. "I advise caution, sire. The intruder has the advantage on us, and from the way it was bearing down on us it has some definite plan of attack in mind."

"So why don't we just attack *it*?" cried the Prince in exasperation. "Gorman, I command you to turn and attack the intruder!"

Jan saw a muscle twitch in Gorman's cheek and anticipated a repeat of the events a week ago. But Gorman maintained his self-control and said carefully, "Sire, just *how* do you suggest we attack the intruder?"

The Prince looked blank. "Why, we simply close in on him and open . . . ." He didn't continue. Awareness had dawned in his eyes.

Gorman nodded. "Exactly. His lasers would stop our every shell and bullet."

"But . . . but . . . ." protested Caspar as he grappled with the problem. Gorman waited patiently. When it was clear that no illuminating shaft of wisdom would be forthcoming from the Prince he said, "There is nothing we can do to cause the intruder damage."

Jan, who never spoke in the control room unless spoken to first, decided that the unusual circumstances warranted her breaking of the rule. "Chief Engineer," she said, "just as we can't hit the intruder with bullets or shells neither can he hit us."

Caspar whirled in her direction. "Hah!" he cried. "The

185

amazon is right! We have nothing to be afraid of!" He turned back to Gorman. "So what reason do we have to run?"

Gorman looked at Jan briefly before answering the Prince. "Possibly no reason at all. But from the confidence of his approach I feel it wise to give him the benefit of the doubt. He may have developed a means unknown to us of attacking another Sky Lord."

They all turned to watch the intruder, which was now to the rear of the *Lord Pangloth*. It was turning to give chase and Jan saw that its bright colours extended all the way along its side. She also saw that it had a huge red circle painted on its tail fin.

"The *Perfumed Breeze*," murmured Gorman.

"You know its name?" asked the Prince sharply. "Where is it from? What's its territory?"

"It's one of the Sky Lords of the Orient. In the Far East. It's come a long way."

"But *why*?" demanded the Prince.

Gorman shrugged. "Whatever the reason I think we can safely assume it is unconnected with any feeling of goodwill towards us."

"Sir, the intruder is gaining on us!" announced one of the Engineers.

"I'm not surprised," said Gorman. "With Cell Seven only partially inflated we're a lot slower than him." He glanced around at the clear blue sky. "Not even any cloud for us to hide in . . . ."

"What can we do?" asked the Prince.

"We can't outrun him so we're going to have to out-manoeuvre him," said Gorman. "Helmsmen, hard to starboard!"

And so began a game of aerial cat-and-mouse that was to last for nearly five hours. But despite all of Gorman's skills the outcome of the dual became apparent early on — all he could really do was delay the inevitable . . . .

During the five-hour period several of the higher-ranking Aristos came down to the control room, including Lady Jane and Prince Magid. Lady Jane took in the situation very quickly and, after asking Gorman a couple of brief, terse questions, stood silently beside Jan, her expression grim. Prince Magid, however, like Caspar, pestered Gorman with useless questions and suggestions.

Finally, at half-past three in the afternoon, the *Perfumed Breeze* was flying alongside the *Lord Pangloth* less than five hundred feet away. The intruder was close enough for the many people crowding her decks and upper hull to be clearly visible. But so far there was no sign of any overt aggression from the other airship.

"Can't we open fire on them?" asked the Prince wistfully. "I know it would be a waste of time but at least it would be a *gesture*."

"A gesture they might consider to be provocative," said Gorman. "Not to mention a waste of valuable ammunition."

"I agree," said Lady Jane quietly. "Let's wait and see what they want with us."

"Now what?" muttered Gorman with a frown. The *Perfumed Breeze* was picking up speed and pulling ahead of the *Lord Pangloth*. Then, in what seemed to be an act of madness, the other airship started to cut in front of the *Pangloth*. There were cries of alarm in the control room. "We're going to collide . . . !" screamed someone.

"Full reverse!" cried Gorman. "Quickly!"

The thrusters roared, but the gap between the *Pangloth* and the other airship that now lay immediately across its bow continued to shrink at a frightening rate. Jan and Lady Jane clutched each other. Jan shut her eyes and waited for the impact. It didn't come. She heard Lady Jane give a long sigh.

Jan looked and saw that the hull of the other airship was still a couple of hundred feet away. Then it began to slowly recede as the screaming thrusters pushed the *Lord Pangloth* into reverse. But then Jan saw people *leaping* from the other airship, from almost every deck. They were suspended from what appeared to be large, triangular-shaped pieces of brightly coloured material.

Gorman snatched up the microphone. "All rifle units, open fire at approaching targets! Open fire!"

187

The air between the two Sky Lords was rapidly becoming filled with the brightly coloured, fluttering triangles and their black-clad passengers. There were hundreds of them.

"What kind of parachutes are they?" cried Caspar. "They don't fall, they float!"

"They're not floating — they're *gliding*," said Gorman. "It's what I feared. The masters or master of the *Perfumed Breeze* has devised a method for attacking another Sky Lord. Our laser defences won't work against them . . . ."

As the attackers drew closer several of them were hit by rifle bullets and fell, screaming, from their gliders, which went cork-screwing through the air out of control. But the majority of them flew on unscathed and were soon out of sight to those in the control room as they headed for landing sites on the upper hull.

Then came a wave of larger gliders. These each had two people suspended beneath them, precariously perched on a wire cradle and gripping a bar which obviously controlled the glider's direction.

Jan thought she saw something glinting behind a couple of the approaching, larger gliders — like the strand of a spider's web caught by the sun. Gorman had noticed it too. "Helmsmen, take us down, *fast* . . . ."

But as the *Lord Pangloth* started to descend, so did the intruder, keeping an exact pace. Gorman slammed his fist into his other palm with anger and frustration, then he turned to one of his men and said, "Pryce, go topside and check on the situation! *Quickly*, we must know what's going on!"

As the man hurried up the spiral staircase beside the elevator, which was reserved exclusively for the use of the Aristos, Jan saw that black lines seemed to be growing towards them from the other airship.

"Cables," said Gorman bitterly when the Prince asked him what they were. "The last batch of gliders were trailing out thin wires as they came. Now they're being used to haul over heavier cables. They aim to tether us."

"Enough of this!" Prince Caspar suddenly shouted. He drew his sword, waved it with a flourish and headed towards the elevator. "I am going up to fight these scum! Who is with me?"

None of the other Aristo men made a move to follow him. Lady Jane stepped forward. "Caspar, don't be reckless. You mustn't put your life in danger needlessly. Let the Sky Warriors handle it."

"Why should they have all the fun? No, I'm going topside."

"No, Caspar," said Lady Jane, more loudly. "You must remain here. I may need your protection."

This made him hesitate. "Oh, *Mother* . . ." he whined. "You don't need *my* protection, You're perfectly safe here. But I'll leave Dalwyn with you if you're really worried . . . ."

"I want *you* to stay with me, Caspar," said Lady Jane. "It's your duty."

Caspar stamped his foot on the deck. "But I have to *do* something, mother! I just can't wait here doing nothing!"

"I agree with you, sire," interceded Gorman. "I suggest we order the forward batteries to open fire on the *Perfumed Breeze*." Everyone looked at him. "But the lasers . . . our shells won't reach their target," said the Prince.

Gorman shrugged. "Probably not, but at this range there may be a chance. But even if none do the resulting explosions and laser flashes may sever some of those damn cables."

"Do it then!" commanded the Prince. "Give the order."

Gorman picked up the mike. "Attention forward batteries. Open fire at will! Open fire at will!"

About fifteen or twenty seconds later there came a dull boom as one of the cannons was fired. Then, to the astonishment of every one in the control room, they saw an explosion on the hull of the intruder. The shell hit near a thruster and when the smoke cleared there was a jagged-edged hole some twelve feet across in the hull.

"No lasers!" cried the Prince amid the cheering. "Their lasers can't be working!"

Gorman was already yelling into the mike. "Attention all batteries! Open fire! Open fire! The target is undefended! I repeat, *the target is undefended!*"

They waited expectantly for the sound of more cannon fire. But it didn't come.

"What's the matter with those fools?" erupted the Prince. "Why aren't they firing?"

"I think I know why," Gorman said, grim-faced.

"That settles it," said Caspar. "I *am* going topside. I'm going to take personal command of one of the batteries and blow that gang of pirates out of the sky myself!"

But before he could move there came the clatter of footsteps on the spiral staircase above. It was the Engineer who Gorman had sent to see what was happening.

"Bad news," he gasped as he came down the stairs. "The invaders are inside the *Lord Pangloth*. There are hundreds and hundreds of them. They fight like demons. Our Sky Warriors are no match for them."

Prince Caspar stepped forward and grabbed the man by the shoulder. "What sections of the ship have they penetrated?" he demanded.

"I'm not certain — everything is so confused up there. People running from the invaders one way, and meeting people fleeing from the opposite direction. But I heard someone say that the invaders are definitely inside your Lords' and Ladyships' quarters, sire."

Oh Mother God, thought Jan when she heard this, *Ceri*.

"We're done for," muttered Prince Magid.

"Not necessarily," said Gorman. "We are still in control of the nerve centre of the *Lord Pangloth*. And if we seal the hatchway and disable the elevator we should remain in control."

"But what good will that do us?" asked the Prince. "We're helpless! Look at those cables! If we tried to flee we'd just drag those pirates along with us."

"But there's nothing to stop us from going forward, sire," Gorman told him.

"You mean, *ram* them? But we'd destroy ourselves as well."

"I suggest we use the *threat* of ramming the *Perfumed Breeze* to force the invaders to negotiate with us," said Gorman. "If they think we're just bluffing, well then — " he shrugged — "better to die by our own hand than to be butchered by these orientals."

There was silence in the control room for a few moments then Caspar nodded his agreement. "You're right, Gorman. Have your men seal the entrance immediately."

But before anyone could make a move there came again the clattering of footsteps from the top of the spiral staircase.

190

Presuming that the first of the invaders was entering the control room Caspar and Dalwyn drew their swords and rushed forward.

A blood-soaked figure came into view. He was wearing shredded overalls and was carrying a sword the like of which Jan had never seen before. At first she didn't recognize the blood-spattered man. As he reached the bottom of the stairs she gasped with surprise. It was Milo.

Chapter Nineteen:

Milo stopped at base of the staircase, looked around and grinned broadly. "Forgive the intrusion, your Royal Highnesses, but I'm on a rather important errand. I did intend to be here sooner but the traffic up there is murder."

The Aristos and the Engineers stared uncomprehendingly at Milo. Then Dalwyn spotted the brand on Milo's cheek. "He's a slave!" he cried.

"An *ex*-slave, I'd say, judging by the mess upstairs." Then he spotted Jan. "Hi Jan!" he called cheerfully. "I hoped I'd find you here. Where's the terminal?"

As Jan pointed Lady Jane said to her, "You know him?"

Jan nodded. "His name is Milo. The one I told you about. The one who, er, befriended me."

Milo was looking at Prince Caspar and Dalwyn, who stood before him with their swords drawn. "Out of my way, your Worshipfulnesses. I don't want to harm you but I need to get to that terminal over there."

"Slave," commanded the Prince. "Put down your sword or suffer the consequences."

"I'll say it one more time — out of my way. It won't be long before the Japs get down here and I've got a lot to do before they do." He raised the strange sword.

"Dalwyn," said the Prince, "kill him."

191

Dalwyn lunged at Milo.

Milo didn't move; he *blurred*. At the same time there came a sickening sound of sharp metal chopping through flesh and bone and Dalwyn's head was suddenly racing through the air. His headless body, meanwhile, toppled to the deck and lay there twitching. To Jan it seemed, for a few moments, as if it was trying to get up again but then it went mercifully still. She looked at Milo. He was still grinning. His eyes had an insane look to them. "Next!" he said, to Caspar.

"He's a sorcerer!" gasped someone.

Caspar was staring fearfully at Dalwyn's decapitated corpse. Slowly he lowered his sword and backed away from Milo.

"That's the spirit," said Milo approvingly and bounded towards the terminal. People collided with each other in their efforts to keep well away from him. He surveyed the console with satisfaction then turned. "Jan!" he said beckoning to her. "Here. I need you."

Jan remained still. The apparition that she knew as Milo terrified her. Her suspicions had been correct all along. He *was* a sorcerer. No human being could move that fast.

"Jan!" he called again, impatient now. "Don't just stand there, you idiot! Come here!"

"You'd better go to him," murmured Lady Jane, giving her hand a reassuring squeeze.

Unwillingly, Jan stepped from behind the throne and went across to him. He eyed her quizzically. "For a moment there I thought you'd gone across to the other side. Here . . ." He handed her the strange sword, still covered in Dalwyn's blood. "You hold it with both hands — yes, like that. I want you to protect my back while I work. Anyone comes near, you give a yell and take a swing at them." Then he turned and began punching the keys on the console, ignoring her completely. She didn't know what to do. She turned and looked sheepishly at the others. They stared back, some accusingly.

What would have happened next Jan had no idea, but then came sounds of fighting from above. There were shouts and screams and the clanging of metal hitting metal. The body of a Sky Warrior, bearing hideous wounds, suddenly came sliding on its back down the spiral staircase. It was followed by a rush of men. They were of small build, and wore bulky, brightly-coloured robes, armour and helmets. And they were wielding the same sort of swords that Jan was now holding.

Caspar and several others went to meet them and very quickly the scene became one of total confusion. Milo glanced over his shoulder at the melee. "I'm relying on you, little one," he told Jan over the noise. "Protect my back — I need more time."

Jan's mind was in a whirl. She didn't know what she was doing, or what she *would* do. Too much was happening at once — everything was out of control . . . .

She saw Caspar receive a wicked slash across his forearm. His sword dropped from his hand and then he was borne down under the weight of three of his small attackers. They obviously wanted to capture him alive. She could see their faces now. They had smooth, bland features with curiously-shaped eyes that seemed somehow stretched.

More and more of the invaders were pouring down the stairs into the control room and Jan saw that the defenders would soon be overwhelmed. As she waited for the first of the attackers to head in her direction she saw Gorman standing nearby, watching the fighting with a calm expression. Then he turned his attention to her. "What is he doing?" he asked, gesturing at Milo.

"I don't know," Jan said.

"I think you *do*," he told her. "I knew all along you were up to something. Well, whatever you and that demon had planned, it's too late now." He turned and headed towards the helm controls. Jan realized what he planned to do.

"Milo! The Chief Engineer! He's going to ram the *Lord Pangloth* into the other airship!"

"What?" He wasn't listening to her. He was too engrossed with the console. She repeated her warning at the top of her voice. Without looking round, Milo said, "Then kill him."

"Kill him? Me?"

But he was ignoring her again. Jan turned and saw that Gorman had reached the controls. Hesitantly, she started after him. She wondered what to do. She couldn't kill him in cold blood; maybe she could knock him out with the flat edge of the blade . . . .

Before she could reach him, however, one of the invaders leapt forward. Just as Gorman began to manipulate the first of the levers the attacker slashed him across the back of his neck with his sword. Gorman slumped forward across the controls.

Jan turned back to Milo and saw three invaders converging on him. He seemed oblivious of their presence. "Milo!" she cried. "Behind you!"

Almost reluctantly, Milo turned from the console. The nearest of the three invaders was already rushing at him, sword raised. Milo *blurred* again. Then, somehow, the attacker was on the deck, writhing, and Milo had his sword. The sword flashed downwards . . . .

Then he was facing the other two. They rushed him together, letting out high-pitched cries, their swords held ready. Again Milo blurred. Both attackers fell. One died swiftly, his throat sliced open; the other sat contemplating uncomprehendingly the mass of steaming intestine that lay between his legs.

Other invaders were converging on Milo now but, with the evidence of his prowess impossible to ignore, they moved much more warily. Milo gestured to Jan. "Here, quickly!"

As she stepped up beside him he again handed her the sword. "Keep them off me," he ordered. "I need just a little more time."

"Are you crazy?" she said hoarsely. "I can't do what you just did!"

"Just *look* as if you can. Bluff, girl, *bluff*." He turned back to the console.

Jan faced the half-circle of converging invaders. Their expressions were fierce but their eyes were watchful, cautious. She held the sword the same way they were holding theirs, in both hands and with the blade raised at an angle in front of her right shoulder. She tried to look fierce as well, but she had no idea what to do if one of them should lunge at her. She was used to an entirely different style of fencing — the invaders' method was all hack and slash and she doubted her chances of parrying even a single one of their blows.

All the other fighting in the control room had ceased. Most of the Engineers lay dead but the Aristos, with a few exceptions, had been taken alive. Jan glimpsed Lady Jane on her knees

194

between two of the invaders. In front of her lay another invader, her dagger protruding from under his chin.

The half-circle was closing in on her. Then, with a nerve-shattering yell, one of the warriors lunged at her. She parried the downward blow of his sword more by instinct than skill, then jumped back just in time to avoid a vicious sideswipe that would have cut deep into her waist. "Milo . . ." she cried as the warrior lunged again.

"Eureka!" she heard Milo exclaim behind her just before the two blades met with a ringing clang. This time she knew it was pure luck that she managed to prevent her skull being sliced in two. And now the warrior's blade was flashing at her from an angle she had no chance of blocking.

She was wrenched backwards with a jolt. At the same time the sword was snatched out of her hands. The next thing she knew Milo was in front of her. And then he wasn't — he was suddenly to her right. The warrior who'd attacked her was falling backwards, arms flung wide, his metal breast-plate split open to reveal a gory chasm in his chest. The other warriors had no time to react before Milo was moving through them. They might as well have been ears of wheat rooted to the ground for all the hope they had of avoiding his whirling blade. Blood sprayed into the air and mingled with their death screams.

Then it was all over. Corpses — some butchered beyond all semblance to humanity — lay scattered about in large pools of blood. Milo was in focus again. He lowered his sword and looked around the control room. The remaining invaders and their Aristo captives regarded him in fearful silence. He turned to Jan. Wiping blood from his face he grinned at her. The insane look was back in his eyes. Distended veins pulsed at the sides of his neck and temples. "I think I've got their attention," he told her. Turning his back on all the others he went to the console. Jan saw that the screen was full of lines of symbols and letters. A blip on the top right-hand corner of the screen was flashing urgently. "There it is," said Milo triumphantly. "Just what I needed to know. Step One has been accomplished; now the going may get a little difficult before we succeed with Step Two. Watch your eyes."

195

His last words confused her until, in another blur of movement, he brought his sword down on the console. There was an explosion of sparks as the blade cut through it. Jan gasped, then said, "Why did you destroy it?"

"I have all I need to know from it. I don't want someone else learning the same thing."

He turned as footsteps sounded again on the spiral staircase. Jan turned too. More of the invaders were coming down into the control room: warriors, but also one man who, to judge by his ornate armour and jagged winged helmet, held high rank. The warriors parted as he strutted forward, barking out questions. He came to an abrupt halt when he saw the corpses strewn in front of Milo. He stared at Milo, then barked out more questions to the surrounding warriors. One pointed at Milo and said something to the newcomer in a deferential voice. The newcomer's eyebrows, which were thin black lines, slowly rose. Then he said something that was obviously a command. The warrior who had answered his questions suddenly looked very unhappy and reluctantly took a step forward.

Milo sighed. "The officer wants to see for himself. Bastard." The warrior lunged at Milo with a yell. Milo killed him. The newcomer looked suitably impressed. Then his expression turned to surprise as Milo addressed him in his own language.

The exchange was a short one. It ended with the officer nodding violently, then turning and heading back towards the staircase at a run. As he bounded up the stairs, followed by two of his warriors, Jan said wonderingly to Milo, "You speak their language?"

"Only a bit. Had to learn it for business reasons a long time ago. Back when the Japanese dominated the international economy."

"Japanese?" she asked.

"Yep. That's who this lot are. I told you about them before. They're the ones who liked eating squid so much. Also xenophobic as hell. One of the few nations that didn't fragment after the Prime Standard ruling . . . ." He was interrupted suddenly by Lady Jane saying in a calm, clear voice, "You, demon, sorcerer or whatever you are!" One of the two warriors

196

holding her immediately gave her a hard slap across the side of her face but she continued to speak to Milo: "Why don't you kill the rest of these yellow monsters?"

Milo smiled at her. "Why should I, your Royal Ladyship?" he asked mockingly.

"Help us regain control of the *Lord Pangloth . . . uh!*" Her head rocked back as she was struck again, harder, but she kept talking, "Help us, and you can name your price. Anything at all . . . ." She was struck again. Blood began to trickle from a split in her lower lip.

"I'm already making a bargain," Milo told her jovially, "but not with you. You and the rest of your group of costumed fools are already extinct. You've been extinct for a long time, you just didn't realize it. But now you're about to find out . . . ." More officers were coming down the stairs, led by the one who'd spoken to Milo. Orders were shouted and the Aristos were herded towards the stairway. The officers approached Milo but halted at a respectful distance from him. One, more ornately dressed than the others, addressed him in a series of short, staccato words. Milo answered him, then pointed at the smoking ruins of the computer terminal. The officer looked at it and then back at Milo. He frowned, then gave a curt nod of his head. He turned on his heel and strode off. The other officers followed him, with the exception of two who remained to watch Milo and Jan.

"What's happening?" she whispered to him.

"As I said, I'm making a bargain. For our lives."

"What about Ceri?"

"Ceri? Oh, your little friend from the sea habitat. What about her?"

"Can't you include her in the bargain you're making?" Jan asked pleadingly.

His teeth showed white against the blood drying on his face. "Why should I? You've told me she loathes me. Besides, she won't be killed by the Japs. She's not an Aristo or a Sky Warrior. She's probably been raped by now but that's the worst that'll happen to her."

Jan flinched. "Please, I beg you, Milo. Try and save her. I don't want to be parted from her . . . ."

197

"Ah, so she's stirred up your Minervan blood, has she?" he asked. "Well, I'm sorry, it's out of the question. Just count yourself lucky I'm including *you* in the deal."

More of the invaders were entering the control room but these new arrivals, judging from their dress, weren't warriors. And by the way they excitedly examined the equipment and controls they were the invader equivalent of the *Pangloth*'s Engineers. And by the way they occasionally cast fearful sidelong glances at Milo and the butchered corpses lying about the deck they were aware of who he was and what he was capable of.

About ten minutes later the original officer returned and, after talking briefly to the other two, gestured at Milo that he should follow him. "Come on," said Milo to Jan. "Keep close to me and stay calm whatever happens."

Escorted by the three officers and six warriors they went up the spiral staircase. There were a lot of bodies lying about on the next level as well, but they were all Sky Warriors. From somewhere far off came screams and shouts, but the fighting was definitely over in this part of the *Lord Pangloth*.

Milo and Jan were taken a short distance along the main corridor that led from the entrance to the control room and then ordered into an Engineer's latrine. The door was slammed shut behind them but no attempt was made to disarm Milo.

"Phew . . ." he said and his body suddenly sagged. He dropped the sword to the floor and went to one of the basins. Leaning on its edge he began to splash water on his head and face. His body seemed to shrink as Jan watched.

"Are you all right?" she asked.

"No, but I will be, as soon as I get some food. I burned up a lot of my fuel reserves with all those fancy fun and games." He drank a lot of water, then stripped off his ruined overalls and began washing the blood from his body.

"*Are* you a sorcerer?" she asked, remembering the terrifying speed with which he had cut through that whole crowd of warriors.

"Me, no," he answered casually. "But I guess you could say I'm the *product* of sorcerers. They gave me a super-charged metabolism. My chemistry isn't like yours — radically different as you are from a pre-Standard Prime you're still basically, well, er . . . human."

"And you're *not*?"

"Technically speaking, no."

"Where was this done to you? Mars?"

He shook his head. "No, a long time ago. Before Mars."

"*Before* Mars?" she asked, puzzled. "What do you mean?"

Milo yawned. "Later. I'll explain it all later. Right now I need some sleep." And to her amazement he lay down on the floor and, using his rolled-up overalls as a pillow, closed his eyes.

"How can you sleep at a time like this?" she cried.

"Because I have to. Need to recharge . . . won't take long . . . pick up sword . . . wake me if any . . . ." Then he was asleep.

Jan stared at him for a time, then did as he said. She picked up the sword, sat down facing the door, her back against a wall and the sword resting across her thighs. She felt exhausted as well, but knew she was far too tense to sleep. And also too worried about Ceri.

About two hours passed. During that time there appeared to be a lot of activity outside. The *Lord Pangloth* shuddered on several occasions and the deck listed each time but she had no idea what this signified.

At the end of the second hour Milo woke abruptly, got up, and quickly donned his tattered and blood-stained garment. "All quiet?" he asked Jan.

"No, but no one's come in here," she told him. "How do you feel?"

"Better. But I still need food." He went to one of the basins and drank more water.

"You were making funny sounds. Towards the end of your sleep," she told him. "And twitching."

"Dreams. Bad ones." He splashed water on his face, wiped it away then straightened up. He looked at her and smiled. It seemed forced to her. Whatever he had dreamed had shaken him. "How are *you* feeling?" he asked.

"Not too good," Jan admitted. "What do you think is going to happen to us?"

"That depends on how good a job I can do convincing whoever controls this bunch of children of the Rising Sun that I have something to offer them that they want."

"Which is what?"

"I told you — information."

"Yes, but about *what*?" she asked impatiently.

Before he could answer there were sounds outside the door. Milo gestured urgently for the sword. She quickly handed it over to him. The door swung open with a bang. An officer stepped warily into the room. Jan wasn't sure if she'd seen him before or if he was someone new. She had trouble telling these people apart. Four warriors followed him inside. He gave Milo a brief bow of his head and said something very quickly. Milo nodded.

"We're to go with them," Milo told Jan. "We're being honoured with an audience with the top gun himself, their warlord."

They were led outside and taken up into the Aristo section of the ship. The corridors had been cleared of casualties but there were still pools of congealed blood everywhere she looked. The invaders seemed to be everywhere too, hurrying back and forth along the corridors with the air of people on very important errands. Of the original inhabitants of these quarters, the Aristos, there was no sign. Jan guessed thay had all been confined somewhere. Once again she wondered worriedly about Ceri . . . .

Their destination, she soon realized, was the Grand Saloon, but when she and Milo were ushered inside she saw that it had undergone a major transformation. Coloured banners hung from the ceiling and the floor area had been partitioned off by portable cloth screens on which had been painted scenes of mountains, lakes, unfamiliar-looking trees and other things that Jan didn't recognize.

"The decorators have moved in already," muttered Milo.

Their escort gestured them to continue forward. Warriors slid aside the screens as they approached. They progressed through four sets of dividing screens before they entered the final section.

On the dais where Caspar had sat on his throne sat a different man on a different throne. Behind him hung a red banner on which a strange black lizard was depicted spitting fire. At his feet sat two women dressed in peculiar robes, their faces painted a startling white.

But Jan's attention was fixed on something else. On either side of the warlord's throne was a spear, and on each spear a severed head had been set.

Jan stared first into the sightless eyes of Prince Caspar and then into those of Lady Jane.

Chapter Twenty:

"You wanted vengeance," murmured Milo in her ear as they approached the dais, "well, there it is, in the raw."

Jan said nothing. Her gaze was fixed on Caspar's face. She felt sick. Then the officer in charge of their escort cried something that was obviously the command to halt. They were still about fifteen feet from the dais. Their escort bowed deeply as the man on the throne slowly rose to his feet. He was much taller than the other invaders. The square cut of his robe, like the robes of the warriors, made him look bulkier than he really was, but even so he was an unusually big man. The average Minervan woman would have looked minute beside him.

He looked down on them. The slits of his eyes offered no clue to either his thoughts or his mood. Then he said, in perfect Americano, "Well, well, Milo Haze, it's been a long time. Where have you been hiding yourself these last four centuries?"

Surprised, Jan glanced at Milo and saw that he was looking mystified as well. Then he frowned as he stared hard at the giant invader. "I know you?" he asked.

"We met a few times at bio-tech conferences. Naturally you wouldn't recognize me now. I have, of course, *changed* somewhat." The tall man gave a brief, thin smile. "You, on the other hand, have changed little. On the *outside* at least. From what my samurai tell me of your actions you've undergone a very sophisticated enhancement."

Milo nodded. Then, in a wondering tone, he said, "So you're an immortal too . . . ."

"I am indeed. And until today I was under the impression I was the last alive. My name is Shumi Horado. Do you recall me now?"

"Horado . . ." said Milo slowly. "The Horado Corporation. Yes, I do. You were a small man then, balding . . . ."

The warlord smiled thinly again and touched his chest with his fingertips. "All is vanity, is it not, Mr Haze? I gave myself thirty extra inches of height and a full head of hair. While *you* chose baldness and eyes that don't match, plus all your other enhancements. And at the risk of being impolite, it is the latter we must discuss first. You'll notice that, as an act of faith, I have let you retain that sword you no doubt took by force from one of my warriors. But just in case you harbour any thoughts of using it on me — and I'm sure you don't — let me assure you that I *am* protected."

He clapped his hands. Immediately a screen on each side of them rolled back, revealing warriors holding what seemed to be very small rifles. "Automatic weapons," said the warlord. "I would say they are the only ones still in working order. I found a cache of them perfectly preserved about eighty years ago. So let me warn you that no matter how fast you can move, Mr Haze, you'll be dead before you reach me."

"I have no intention of any such action," Milo said. "My violent activities with this weapon were designed merely to attract your attention. Though, of course, I had no idea who *you* were. As you must have been told, I have a proposition for you."

"Yes, so I was informed." The warlord clapped his hands again. This time servants emerged from behind the screens carrying small folding stools which they placed behind Jan and Milo. The warlord indicated they should sit down, then returned to his throne. "But before we discuss business, Mr Haze, let us observe some of the old formalities. You and your companion will join me in a cup of *sake*." He clapped his hands for the third time.

Jan's feeling of bewilderment increased as a servant presented a small cup containing clear liquid. What was going on? How did Milo come to know this frightening giant? What was all that talk about being immortal?

She glanced again at Prince Caspar's head on the spear. His mouth hung open in a silent scream. His lips had gone very white. Not so many hours ago she had been kissing those lips . . . .

There were other heads. When the screens had been rolled back she had seen that there was a whole row of spears lined in front of the windows on either side. Other screens prevented her from seeing how far the rows of disembodied heads extended but she guessed they went all the way along the sides of the Great Saloon. If that was so then every Aristo was now dead.

She took a sip of the drink. It was bitter and made her eyes water. But the wave of warmth it sent through her body was welcome.

"Your young companion, who is she?" asked the warlord.

She realized, with a start, that he was referring to her.

"Her name is Jan Dorvin. A Minervan. One of the last. The *Lord Pangloth* destroyed her town. She is now under my protection. Whatever agreement we come to between ourselves applies to her as well."

The warlord gave a slight shrug. "Whatever you wish." He stared at her. "A sturdy creature," he commented. "Not to my taste at all." He turned back to Milo. "I remember that your reputation with women in the old days assumed the dimension of mythology. One rumour that I heard later astonished even me. About a woman called, let me see, was it Miriam?"

"Miranda," said Milo stiffly.

"Was there any truth in the rumour?"

"Yes. It was true."

The warlord chuckled. "As I said, all is vanity, but *that* is taking it to extremes. What ever happened to her?"

"She died."

"Forgive me," the warlord inclined his head. "I see that the subject is still a sensitive one for you despite the passing of so many years. Let us talk instead of how you managed to survive all this time."

"I got off the planet," said Milo. "Managed to get a seat in one of the last shuttles before the off-Earth communities imposed their quarantine. Went to the Belvedere space habitat."

"Belvedere. Ah yes, the first and biggest of the habitats," said the warlord. "It still exists? I used to listen in on transmissions from Belvedere and the other habitats years ago but our radio equipment has long since fallen into disrepair."

"Belvedere still exists. So do the other three habitats and the Martian colonies. The lunar colonies died out long ago. There was no way they could become self-sufficient, and the other off-Earth communities couldn't spare the resources to assist them."

"And how long did you stay on Belvedere?"

"As long as I could. Until I ran into the inevitable problem. The problem of being immortal, of course."

"The Belvederians didn't have a liberal attitude in that area?"

"On the contrary. And besides, if they discovered I was an immortal they would automatically have identified me as a high executive in one of the gene corporations or a head of state. I'd have been executed one way or the other — either as an illegal immortal or a war criminal."

"So your solution was?" asked the warlord.

"There is regular, if not frequent, traffic between the off-Earth communities. I did a few of these trips as a volunteer crewman to one of the other space habitats — Creuse City. Then, when an opportunity came up to do a trip to the Mars colony I took it. It was a long voyage." Milo sighed. "What I did I had to do. My survival was at stake." He looked at the warlord. "You understand?"

"I do indeed."

Milo glanced briefly at Jan then continued. "There were six of us on board. I was the only one to reach Mars alive. My story was that an emergency decompression — caused by a micro-meteor penetration — killed the others. I happened to be doing maintenance work in the airlock at the time and was wearing my suit. My story was believed."

The warlord said, "But how had your situation improved? With Belvedere and the Martian colony in radio contact the Martian colonists would have known who you were and, most important, how *old* you were."

"I switched identities with one of the other crew members. As far as the Belvederians were concerned I was dead."

"And the deception was never discovered?"

Milo shook his head. "The Belvederians wanted the survivor sent back to Belvedere to take part in a court of enquiry but I asked for political asylum on Mars. There are political differences, you see, between Mars and Belvedere. The Martians refused to extradite me, saying that the results of their own enquiry on the tragedy should be enough to satisfy the Belvederians."

"And so you remained on Mars."

"For as long as I could," said Milo. "Until, finally, the same problem arose. I was getting within a few years of my 200th birthday again."

"And your solution on this occasion?"

"Much the same as before. I campaigned for an expedition to Starshine, the last of the space habitats to be established. It was to be a trading mission. We knew they had succeeded in synthesizing a wide range of drugs that we'd long ago run out of on Mars. We, on the other hand, would take them plant seeds to improve the crop strains in their hydroponic gardens. The expedition wasn't really necessary, of course, and drained the colony of much-needed resources, but by then I had attained a position of some influence."

The warlord gave an approving nod.

"The ship never reached Starshine," said Milo. "I couldn't allow it to. Starshine and Belvedere had formed an alliance. There was a lot of traffic between the two and I couldn't take the risk of encountering someone from Belvedere or Starshine who had been alive when I'd left the habitat a hundred and sixty years before. Unlikely but a distinct, and dangerous, possibility."

"So what misfortune befell *this* expedition?" asked the warlord.

"A rupture in the main fuel tank. No way could we reach Starshine, but we did have enough fuel to nudge ourselves towards the Earth and let its gravity do the rest. But the ship wasn't designed to enter the Earth's heavy atmosphere and broke up on the way down. I and some of the crew landed in the

205

sea in an escape pod. We drifted a long time and the others, not possessing my, er, special qualities, died. I was picked up by a sea habitat. I lived on it until it was attacked by the *Lord Pangloth* and I was captured. And that's it, until *you* arrived."

Jan knew he was not telling everything. Ceri had said that it was Milo who had convinced the sea habitat people to move closer to land. Why? He must have had a reason.

The warlord considered Milo carefully. Then he said, "And during your time on the *Lord Pangloth* you have discovered something that you feel will be of great value to me. I confess I am curious as to its nature."

Milo smiled at him. Jan knew that smile. It was the one she didn't like. "Before I tell you," said Milo, "I want to hear of *your* adventures over the years."

The warlord made a nonchalant gesture with his hands. "Mr Haze, compared to you I have lived a life of infinite dullness since the Gene Wars. Once I established myself on the *Perfumed Breeze*, admittedly an achievement of some difficulty and much regrettable bloodshed, I was out of danger. With total power in my hands my immortality was no longer a problem. The traditional Japanese predilection for obedience towards authority worked in my favour, of course. And I helped the situation by cultivating my own modified version of *Bushido* which, among other things, conferred godhood upon myself. My subjects therefore *expect* me to be immortal. The advantage, Mr Haze, of living within a society that has culturally regressed as opposed to living with your outer space technocrats."

"You were fortunate," agreed Milo.

The warlord glanced in the direction of Prince Caspar's severed head, then gestured at the long row of Aristo heads. "It is curious, is it not, that these Americanos also appeared to have regressed culturally? I am at a loss, I admit, to understand why they seem to have adopted a vaguely medieval European lifestyle when such a society would not be in the American cultural memory. Perhaps, as an Americano yourself, you can explain this mystery to me."

"Old movies," said Milo dismissively. "You're right, it's not a genuine cultural regression. All the furniture and other crap came out of old movies." He went on to explain to the warlord about the series of fantasy 'entertainments' that Jan had seen.

The warlord laughed. "How typically Americano," he said. Then he reached over to Lady Jane's head and brushed her cheek with his fingertips.

"Stop that!"

No one was more surprised that Jan herself when she heard her voice ring out. An unsettling silence followed as the warlord slowly turned his head towards her. She heard Milo sigh, then say, "Please excuse my companion. Her manners leave much to be desired. Also, she knew the deceased on your left, er, intimately."

The warlord turned his gaze to Milo. "A Minervan captor was on intimate terms with one of the rulers of the *Lord Pangloth?*" he asked, sounding mildly surprised. "How did that occur?"

"Well, it's a long but rather interesting story . . ." began Milo.

Jan felt another rush of anger. They were still talking as if she wasn't there, and though the warlord intimidated her, and she knew it would be wise to act with caution in his presence, she couldn't help speaking out again: "Isn't it enough that you've murdered all these people? Do you have to treat their remains with disrespect as well?"

Again the warlord's head swivelled slowly in her direction. Another long silence, punctuated only by Milo's barely audible mutter of, "Jesus . . . ." Then the warlord said to Jan, "Girl, for your impertinence I could order you to be taken from here and taken to a room where you would be tied to a wooden frame. Your skin would then be flayed from your body. Every *inch* of your skin. The operation would be performed with great finesse, your skin being removed in one complete piece. Your raw flesh would then be covered in salt and your skin replaced around your body and sewn up. You would then be brought back in here to me and, if I considered your apology to be suitably contrite, I would favour you with a quick death. One clap of my hands is all that it would take to initiate the procedure . . . ." He raised his hands, held them apart for several long moments, then let them fall back to his lap. "However, I will be merciful, for two reasons. One is that you are under Milo Haze's protection and it would be

207

inhospitable of me to put him in such an awkward position. The second is that you are ignorant of your proper place, as a woman, in my domain and were therefore unaware of the gravity of your offence against me." He turned back to Milo. "Please continue with what you were about to say."

As Milo quickly recounted the events surrounding Jan's attempt to blow up the *Lord Pangloth*, her subsequent encounter with the Hazzini, and her resulting adoption by the Aristos, Jan waited for the frantic pounding of her heart to subside. She had no doubt that the warlord had been a hair's breadth away from carrying out his threat.

When Milo finished, the warlord turned to her again and her flesh went cold under his relentless gaze. Whether there was now a touch of new respect for her in those expressionless eyes it was impossible to tell. He spoke, "You had the temerity to rebuke me for the execution of these people — your former enemies — and yet you were prepared to destroy the entire airship and everyone on it."

She opened her mouth to reply then abruptly closed it.

"You may speak," he told her.

Warily, she said, "I couldn't do it when it came down to it. I couldn't kill all those people in cold blood."

"While I *can*, is what you are implying." He shook his head. "You misjudge me. I am not a cruel man. But I had no choice but to eliminate the *Lord Pangloth*'s ruling class. There was no alternative. And I assure you that, on the whole, they died quickly and cleanly. As for this seemingly barbaric display — " he indicated the heads on either side of him — "it is simply the most effective way of showing representatives from the various factions of *Lord Pangloth* society that the old order has been irrevocably swept away and that even the idea of any further resistance to me is futility itself."

He turned back to Milo. "Do you ever suspect that you might be going insane?"

Milo looked startled by the question. It was some moments before he answered, picking his words with obvious care. "Insane? Do I give you the impression I might be. . . ?"

"The question was directed more towards myself than you,"

the warlord said. "There are times when I think I might be insane and I was wondering if it might be a side-effect of immortality. What is your opinion?"

"I haven't noticed any signs of mental instability in myself," said Milo slowly. "Nor do I see why immortality would lead to insanity, though perhaps when one has lived for thousands of years one might suffer from emotional strains of an unknown nature. Or perhaps one may become simply bored with life itself."

"Boredom," said the warlord thoughtfully. "Yes, I do get bored on occasion but it's more my tendency towards solipsism that vaguely worries me. I imagine it's to do with my rarefied way of life. I have been so long acting out the role of god in my kingdom here, with no equal whom I can confide in, that I am slowly coming to accept the role as reality. What do you think?"

Again Milo seemed to pick his words with care. "I suppose there is a danger of that. But the fact that you can be objective about it all shows that you haven't succumbed to the delusion."

"Not *yet*, anyway," said the warlord with a slight smile. "And I must tell you, Mr Haze, that I am finding today's encounter with you very diverting. And, no doubt, your presence is providing good mental therapy for me. It is also amusing to talk Americano again after so long. Do you know, I can remember when your language was called English."

"So can I," said Milo. "I can even remember England. In fact I paid a visit to London only a month before the disaster."

"Ah, yes," said the warlord, nodding. "That reactor. Chernobyl, it was called, wasn't it?"

"No. That was the one in Russia. Years before. I can't remember the name of the English one. The difference was that the Russian accident didn't do too much damage to Russia thanks to the prevailing weather conditions. In England the weather conditions were the exact opposite and the crap came straight down all across Southern England."

"Such a misfortune," agreed the warlord. "But compared to the ravages of the blight today the destruction of one small country shrinks in importance."

"The blight is just as bad in your part of the world?"

"Worse. Which is why the Sky Lords in the East are at war with each other, and why I am over here."

"I had been wondering why you have made such a long journey," said Milo.

"I had no choice. As you must be aware, the *Perfumed Breeze*'s laser defence system no longer functions. It broke down completely several years ago. And my rival Sky Lords in the East discovered this. It would have only been a matter of time before the *Perfumed Breeze* fell victim to a successful attack from another Sky Lord. So I decided to risk the long flight to another continent where the *Perfumed Breeze*'s vulnerability would be unknown. My plan was to attack the first Sky Lord I encountered and hope my samurai could overwhelm it before the defenders realized I had no laser protection." He gave a shrug of his padded shoulders. "The plan worked. By the time the *Pangloth*'s warriors discovered they could fire shells with impunity into my airship it was too late. My men had reached the guns."

"A close shave though," said Milo.

"True, but I must admit I never doubted the outcome." He smiled. "You see, further evidence of my growing self-delusion of omnipotence."

"So what will you do now?"

"Establish my base on the *Lord Pangloth*. Most of the original inhabitants — those who have survived — will be transferred to the *Perfumed Breeze* where they will, of course, be under my strict but humane control. Then, with my fleet consisting of two ships, I shall take steps to enlarge it further until I control enough tribute areas to ensure the long-term survival of my people — and myself."

"Makes sense," said Milo approvingly. "And I hope we can come to an arrangement where my companion and I can share in this bright future of yours. As payment for what I have to offer you, naturally."

"What form do you see this payment taking?"

"Well, I prefer to see it as a gift. As to its form — " Milo glanced about the Grand Saloon — "it's all around you. The *Lord Pangloth* itself would be quite suitable."

210

After a long pause the warlord said softly, "And what could you offer that would be worth a whole Sky Lord in return?"

"Why, a *brand new* Sky Lord, of course," Milo answered brightly. "A Sky Lord still in its, so to speak, wrapping paper. All new and shiny and full of precious helium. It will perform much more efficiently than any of the existing Sky Lords, all of which are slowly falling to bits, as you well know. And no doubt it will be full of working Old Science devices as well. It will be a virtual flying treasure trove, and it will be all yours."

The warlord said dryly, "And where exactly do you have this virgin Sky Lord concealed?"

"Not a Sky Lord, a Sky *Angel*," corrected Milo. "And her present home is, naturally, in Paradise." Milo grinned and pointed upwards.

Chapter Twenty-One:

"Are you seriously going into partnership with that . . . that *creature*?" Jan asked.

Milo continued to stuff food into his mouth, using the two implements he'd referred to as 'chopsticks' with dexterity. She waited impatiently for him to answer, pacing up and down the small Aristo servant's room they'd been given to use. Finally Milo gave a satisfied belch and said, "Ah, marvellous! To eat Japanese food again after all these years. Are you sure you won't have more? You've only eaten a bit of rice."

"I'm not hungry. Besides, all the other dishes have meat in them."

"No, not all." He picked a bowl up off the table and held it out to her. "This is fish."

She looked at the glistening white chunks of flesh and grimaced. "Fish meat is still meat."

"True," he said, and put a piece of it in his mouth. She looked

211

away in disgust. "Are you going to answer my question?" she demanded.

"All in good time," he told her. "So why don't you just sit down and try and relax. Today's events have come to a very satisfactory conclusion."

"For *you*, perhaps."

"And you too. For one thing you've still got your skin, despite your best efforts to lose it. I could have killed you myself when you started your crazy yapping."

"I couldn't help it. He made me furious the way he touched Lady Jane's head, like it was just some toy of his."

"Lady Jane was past caring, so why should it bother you?" asked Milo as he ate more of the fish.

"Don't you have any respect for the dead?" she asked coldly.

"I don't have much respect for the living, so why should I treat the dead differently?" he said and smiled.

Jan looked down at him and nodded. "Yes, you're no different from him, really. You're both murderers; he just does his killing on a grander scale."

"That's no way to speak to your protector," he replied brightly. "If it hadn't been for me you'd be suffering the agonies of the damned right now. He meant what he said about flaying you, you know; he wasn't just trying to scare you."

"Yes, I know," Jan said and shivered. She wrapped her arms around herself.

Milo gave her a leering grin. "It would have been a tragedy if he'd had his threat carried out. Your skin is one of your best features. A pity, though, that you have chosen to cover most of it once again. I much preferred you in Aristo garb."

"Well, *I* didn't." When she and Milo had been brought to this cabin she had asked him to put in a request with their escort for a change of clothing. At first they had brought her a complicated gown similar to the ones worn by the women who'd been seated at the feet of the warlord. They had been puzzled when she'd refused it and asked instead for man's clothing. The second time they brought her the garments she was now wearing; loose fitting jacket and trousers, both in black. The only problem was that there were no buttons or other fasteners on the jacket and the only means of keeping it closed was a cloth belt which was inadequate for the task. Still, the clothes felt very comfortable after the constraining Aristo gowns and dresses.

Milo finished the fish and picked up another bowl. "Seaweed," he said approvingly. "Now this you *can* eat without violating any of your Minervan principles."

"I told you I don't have any appetite. I'm too tense, and *worried*."

"What is there to be worried about? We're in no immediate danger, we have food, shelter and a warm bed. And everything is going as I planned."

"I'm not worried about me so much as about Ceri," she told him. "Why can't you do as I asked and see if you can find out if she's safe?"

"Because I've asked enough favours from the warlord and his minions for the time being. I don't want to push my luck by pestering him over the whereabouts of a servant girl, even if she *is* your little bedmate."

"She is *not*," snapped Jan, feeling her face redden.

Milo laughed. "You should see yourself, amazon. The full flush of love. My, what an active sex life you've led these past few months — with Prince Caspar, Lady Jane *and* your precious sea nymph. How different from that sexually reticent little Minervan first encountered the day you came on board the *Lord Pangloth*."

"*You* know why I slept with Caspar and Lady Jane," she said angrily. "And you're wrong about Ceri. Yes, I admit I'm in love with her, but we're not lovers. It's her choice, not mine."

"You've *never* slept with her?" he asked with a knowing smile.

"That's none of your business."

"I thought so," he said and laughed again.

Jan fought to keep control of her temper. "Milo, *please*. I'm begging you to help me find out what's happened to her."

Milo put down his chopsticks — all the bowls were empty now —and eyed her speculatively. "Very well," he said finally. "But in return I want to make love to you. Now. On there." He pointed at the bed. "What do you say?"

The thought of being in intimate contact with Milo caused a spasm of revulsion to pass through her body. Her automatic reaction was to cry *no* but she held back — she had to think of Ceri. After a long hesitation she said, thickly, "If that's what you want, I'll do it."

He narrowed his eyes. "Why do I detect such extreme reluctance? What is it about me that you find so unpalatable? You were, after all, able to overcome your Minervan sexual mores when it came to sleeping with Prince Caspar, a man who had a large share of the responsibility for destroying your people. Do you, perhaps, find me physically offensive? It can't be my smell because I don't have any."

Jan *did* find him physically offensive, but she couldn't say why exactly. And it wasn't just his body, but him in total. The more she knew of him the more he unsettled her; the more her conviction grew that he was right when he described himself as no longer being human. He seemed to take pride in this fact, but it awoke in her an atavistic fear . . . and a sense of revulsion.

"Well?" he asked, impatiently.

"Look, I'm willing to make love to you in return for you finding Ceri, so let's leave my personal feelings out of it. You've never shown much regard for them before, so why start now?" She began undoing the knot in her cloth belt.

Milo held up a hand and said wearily, "Don't bother. I was just testing you. For fun. I used up so much of myself today that my libido is as dead as a flat battery. I could no more make love to you now that I could fly. Nothing personal."

She felt a simultaneous rush of relief and disappointment. "What about Ceri then?"

"Forget her," he said coldly. "If she's still alive she's no doubt been transferred to the *Perfumed Breeze* by now." He gestured at the lights of the other Sky Lord visible through the small window. The two great airships now floated side by side, secured by a network of cables. Flimsy wooden gangways connected the two hulls and earlier Jan and Milo had watched an exodus take place as streams of the *Lord Pangloth*'s defeated subjects were herded along these gangways into the *Perfumed Breeze*.

"You bastard," said Jan, her eyes stinging. "You cruel bastard. How can I forget her? She means everything to me."

Milo poured himself a glass of the drink called *sake*. He drained the cup, then said to her, "You're going to have to be realistic. I'm risking my plans by even including you in them. There is no way three of us could make it."

"Make it? Make it where?" she asked, frowning.

"Down to the ground. We're going to jump ship. Not yet, of course, but in two days' time when we're approaching the ruins of the Armstrong spaceport."

Jan was confused. "But why? I thought that was the place you wanted to reach. You told the warlord the communication device was located there."

"You're still so naive, Jan, in spite of everything," he said with a sigh. "Do you think I would actually trust that man? As soon as he got what he wanted he would order my execution. I can imagine how it would happen too — he would invite me to have a celebratory meal or drink with him and suddenly those warriors of his with the automatic guns would appear and riddle me with bullets." Milo smiled approvingly at the thought. "Besides, he is clearly operating with most of his lights out."

"What?"

"I mean that his suspicions about his increasingly tenuous hold on reality are correct." Milo poured more sake into his cup.

"I don't understand," Jan said. "All that you told him about the Sky Lord you saw up in the sky — wasn't that true?"

"Oh yes. Every word."

Milo had described to the warlord how he and the other people on the spacecraft from Mars had made their discovery. "It was after I had sabotaged the main fuel tank and the decision had been made to give up any hope of trying to make it to Starshine and to head for Earth instead. We were still about 15,000 miles away when we picked up a large object ahead of us on our radar. It was so big we thought it might be another habitat, even though there was no record of a fifth space habitat being built. Then our computer dredged up the solution to the mystery from its files. The object was Paradise, the name given to the huge factory facility where the Sky Angels had been constructed."

"An argument broke out among us," Milo had continued. "The majority wanted to use some of our remaining precious fuel to alter course and intercept Paradise. The idea was that the facility might contain stores of fuel that we could use. I argued against it, of course, because the last thing I wanted was to continue the journey to Starshine. But I was out-voted and had no option but to let the others do as they wanted.

"I had to admit, when we finally got into a matching orbit with the facility and drew closer to it, that Paradise was an impressive sight. A vast skeletal cylinder about a mile and a half in length and surrounded by an array of solar receptors. But the really astonishing thing was what we could see inside it — a Sky Angel.

"Then we got another surprise. As we got nearer to it we got a radio call from Paradise asking who we were. For a terrible moment I thought the place was inhabited, but it turned out to be a computer sending the signal. We identified ourselves and asked permission to dock, but when we couldn't produce — not surprisingly — the correct authorization code the computer denied us permission.

"Meanwhile I was digging around in my dim memories about Paradise and getting some results. I remembered that Paradise had always operated almost completely automatically. There had been a few human supervisors around, but the construction of the Sky Angels had been done by robots under the control of a central computer.

"I also remembered that the facility had been abandoned well before the Gene Wars, when the demand for further Sky Angels seemed to have disappeared due to improving conditions in the Third World, thanks to the gene revolution. But I certainly didn't remember anything about a finished Sky Angel being left in the facility.

"The only possible solution to the mystery was that the computer had continued with its construction program after the humans had gone. The facility was certainly alive on every level — the electromagnetic anti-meteor umbrella was still functioning and when we got closer we observed spider-like robots scuttling about the factory and on the hull of the Sky Angel itself. Also, when we made an attempt to dock on the facility the computer carried out evasive manoeuvres, making docking impossible. As we were running out of fuel we had no choice but to give up and continue onwards towards Earth, much to my relief.

"But in the years since then I've thought a lot about that virgin Angel up there. And something occurred to me. That computer running the facility is waiting for a signal from Earth telling it to send its finished Sky Angel off to its destination. The descent procedure, I remember, is also automatic. So, send the right signal, wait awhile, and then, lo and behold, a brand new Sky Angel will descend towards you from the sky. The problem, of course, is finding the right signal and the means of sending it."

"And you believe you have a solution?" the warlord had asked Milo.

"I do now," Milo replied. "Another thing I remembered about the Sky Angels was that they were controlled by a United Nations command centre. All I had to do was discover the whereabouts of the place, travel there and then beam the appropriate command up to Paradise."

"But how do you know this command centre is still capable of functioning after all this time?" the warlord asked.

"Because I've established contact with it. Or rather with the computer running it. That's what I was doing in the *Pangloth*'s control room when your warriors arrived. Ever since I was brought on board this airship I'd been trying to devise a method of getting access to the control room. I thought there was a chance that the *Pangloth*'s computer still had a communication link with the command centre. Trouble was I couldn't think of a way, but then my little companion here came along and ingratiated herself with the Aristos. Through her I discovered a working terminal in the control room, which was very encouraging, but none of the variations on the possible access codes for getting a response from the command computer bore fruit. Either the command computer was ignoring the signal, or the signal wasn't getting through because of faulty equipment on either the *Pangloth* or at the centre. I realized the hit-and-miss approach through Jan was going to take forever — I still needed to get to that terminal myself."

217

"And when you and your *Perfumed Breeze* arrived on the scene today," Milo told the warlord, "I at last had the perfect opportunity. It didn't take me long to try all the various codes, and I received a response from the centre's computer, just as I hoped. So I asked it where it was and it told me. The command centre is located at the Armstrong spaceport, which is only about twenty-four hours' flying time from here on the East coast. Once we've come to an arrangement I'll give you the exact coordinates."

The warlord asked, "But when we reach this command centre, how will you discover what the signal is that will bring the new Sky Lord to Earth?"

"That information will be stored somewhere in the centre's computer. Given time I'm sure I'll be able to coax it out. So what do you say, Shumi Horado, warlord of the skies; do we have a deal?"

The warlord had, of course, said yes.

". . . But if everything you told him was the truth, you'll just be *giving* him the new airship for nothing," said Jan, mystified.

"Ah, well, not *everything* was the truth," Milo said, with a smile. "The command centre isn't at the Armstrong spaceport, it's actually in a nearby city. At the top of a building called the Sky Tower. I remember it now. Very distinctive. Should be easy to find once we get to the city."

Jan's shoulder's slumped. Fatigue was suddenly overwhelming her. She sat down in a chair and said wearily to Milo, "And just *how* are *we* going to reach this city?"

"We're going to fly there."

"Oh really? In what? Do you have a *third* Sky Lord salted away somewhere?"

"We're going to fly to the city in one of those Jap gliders."

"Oh Mother God, you're serious . . . ."

He nodded.

"They looked incredibly dangerous."

"Nonsense. They're great sport. I used to fly in similar gliders once upon a time just for fun. We called them hang-gliders. Of course, that was before I had myself immortalized. Couldn't take the risk then . . . ."

"What risk? You said they weren't dangerous."

"Well, accidents happen. When you become immortal your attitude to taking risks changes. You have more to lose."

"I can imagine," she said dryly. Then another thought occurred to her. "You intend for us to enter a *city*! What about the plague spores?"

Milo shrugged. "It's a risk we'll have to take. But with luck we won't have to touch down on the ground. We'll land right on the Sky Tower."

"A *risk*. You've just told me you avoid taking risks," she pointed out.

"It's not possible to avoid all risks in this life," he said blandly.

Jan gave him a suspicious look. "Why do I get the feeling that *I'll* be the only one at risk from the plague spores? Would I be right in thinking that your immortality comes with a totally effective immune system?"

"I doubt if such a thing is possible," he replied, "But yes, I do admit that my immune system is more efficient than yours. But don't worry, the chances of our encountering an active plague area are probably very remote."

"That's not what I've heard," she muttered.

Milo yawned. "Anyway, that's the reason why you might as well put Ceri out of your mind. The glider will only take two of us."

"I'm *not* going to put her out of my mind," Jan said firmly.

"Very well then. Stay behind here if you like. I'm sure you will enjoy life as a geisha girl, tending to the wants of Horado's samurai. If you thought life as a woman under the Aristos was bad enough, wait until you experience the Japanese variety."

Jan didn't need to be told that. The little she'd so far seen of life in Horado's society was enough to convince her that women had no status at all at any level. They were totally subservient to the men.

"Well?" asked Milo.

"No, I don't want to stay here," she admitted. "But I can't just abandon Ceri. I *can't* . . . ."

Milo ran his fingers over his scalp and frowned. "Look," he said eventually, "I can't guarantee it, but maybe there's a chance we can buy her off Horado later."

"How do you mean?" she asked hopefully.

"Well, when we get control of our Sky Angel maybe we can do a deal with Horado. Offer him some Old Science technology in return for your sea nymph?"

"You really think he'd agree to that?"

"I don't see why not," said Milo. "But remember, I'm not guaranteeing anything."

Jan stared hard at him. "Milo," she said slowly, "I want you to *promise* me — *swear* to me on whatever you hold sacred — that if everything goes as you plan you will *try* to do what you just said about Ceri."

Sighing, he said, "Very well, you have my sincere promise. Now let's put an end to this talk and go to bed. I still need a lot more sleep." He stood up and began to remove the kimono. "You can share the bed with me if you like. As I told you, I'm presently incapable of sex, so you can rest easy."

"If you don't mind," she told him. "I'd prefer to sleep by myself. On the floor."

Milo shrugged. "Suit yourself." Wearing nothing but a loin-cloth-like undergarment, he climbed into the single bed then reached up and dimmed the lights.

Jan remained in the chair. After a while she said, "Milo, why are you taking *me* with you."

"We're partners, remember. We have an agreement. You helped me and now I'll help you."

"Somehow I don't think you've ever made a habit of keeping your side of any bargain. You don't *need* me any more, so you could easily leave me here."

"Who says I don't need you any more?"

"Milo, I'm never going to be your lover."

After a silence he said, "We'll see. Stranger things have happened."

Jan sat there in the darkness for some time, then she spoke again. "Milo?"

"What is it now? I'm trying to sleep."

"The warlord. He mentioned a woman. Miranda. Who was she?"

Milo didn't answer for a long time. Then he said, "She was someone special to me."

"You were in love with her?"

"There's no such thing as love, but, yes, I cared about her more than I've ever cared about anyone else apart from myself."

"What made her so special to you?"

"Because she was me."

Chapter Twenty-Two:

"Are you mad? You can't stay *here*! It's too dangerous! We've got to leave, and soon. The morons have already destroyed my corporation headquarters! They'll come here next!"

Milo and Miranda were in the Sea Room. Holographic screens created the illusion of being on the beach of a tropical South Sea island. Sound effects and concealed heat lamps added to the illusion. Miranda, wearing the jacket and trousers from a man's ancient, and very valuable dinner suit, was reclining languidly in a hammock strung between two palm trees. She sucked on the straw protruding from the replica coconut then said calmly, "I mean it, Milo. I'm not coming with you. I'm staying. I'll be safe here, for the time being at least. The estate is well-defended. After that, well, I don't know where I'll go. But I'll survive somehow."

Milo stared at her in disbelief. "What's got into you? You know you couldn't survive on your own. You're coming with me and that's that. So get up and start packing a bag."

She made a slurping sound through the straw, then said, "Milo, you don't seem to be taking in what I'm telling you. I'm saying that I don't want to be with you any more. Do you understand?"

"What are you talking about?" he demanded. "You can't live without *me*! I'm your whole life! For God's sake, I *created* you!"

She suddenly flung the fake coconut at his head. He ducked and it hurtled across the beach and vanished into one of the holographic projections. Then came the sound of breaking glass. Miranda jumped out of the hammock and pointed an accusing finger at Milo. "Yes!" she screamed. "Say it again! Tell me yet again what I owe you! That's all I've heard during my short life — that the great Milo Haze took a rib from his own perfect body and created the perfect woman. The perfect woman for Milo Haze, that is! A woman made in his image!" Her face had become contorted with rage and her chest was heaving violently.

Milo was startled by the intensity of her anger. "All right, all right . . ." he said soothingly. "Take it easy. You've been under a lot of stress recently and it's understandable you're upset. I know you don't know what you're saying. You still love me as much as I love you." He stepped close to her, put his hands under her open dinner jacket and caressed her breasts. Miranda knocked his hands away and moved backwards.

"I don't love you! And you don't love me! You only love yourself!" she cried scornfully. "That's the whole point! The whole point of my existence! When we're in bed we're not really making love together — there's just you masturbating with yourself."

"Don't speak this way, Miranda," he said coldly.

"Isn't science wonderful?" she continued in the same scornful tone. "Once all a man needed was his hand but now, for a mere billion dollars or so, he can get something like me — a female clone of himself, nurtured in an artificial womb, subjected to accelerated growth and force-fed with hand-me-down memories, all within a span of six years. The ultimate jerk-off apparatus for the man with an over-sized Narcissus complex. Yes, that's what I call progress!"

Her words stung him. "Miranda, I don't see you that way. You're as real as I am . . . ."

"Oh, thank you very much," she said sarcastically. "Coming from you that's a real compliment."

Milo took a deep breath. He wanted to grab Miranda and shake that smug, condescending expression off her face, but he knew it would be unwise to lose his temper. This strange attitude of hers had to be some temporary emotional aberration which he should be able to talk her out of if he kept calm. He said seriously, "Miranda, we have a special relationship — a unique one. We have a relationship closer than any other couple alive."

222

"If we're as close as it's possible for two people to be then God help humanity," she said mockingly.

"You can't deny it!" he told her. "You love me just as much as I love you. You have no choice, you were . . . ." He didn't go on, realizing he'd made a mistake.

She finished the sentence for him. ". . . *conditioned* to love you. Yes, I'm well aware of that, Milo. And I did love you once. But the conditioning doesn't work any more. It doesn't work because you're no longer the same man."

"What are you talking about?"

"I'm talking about all those 'enhancements' you've under-gone. They've had a cumulative effect on you. They've changed you in ways you didn't anticipate. In fact, I'm beginning to feel you're not even human any more."

"What crap!" he cried. "You must be drunk!"

"No, I'm not. I'm telling you the truth. You've passed over some invisible dividing line between being human and being something else. You've re-designed yourself right out of the human race, Milo."

"Nonsense! I admit I've changed, but I'm still human!" he told her fiercely.

"Human?" she asked. "What human being can't feel pain? What human being is incapable of feeling fear? Panic? Terror?"

"So why does the absence of those human flaws make me *less* human? Why should humanity be defined by the ability to experience pain, fear and terror?"

"I can give you lots of reasons, but the main one is that if you can't feel pain or fear yourself you can't empathize with the rest of us who can. And that makes you no longer one of *us*. You've cut yourself off from the rest of humanity."

Milo shook his head. "No, no, you don't understand. I remember only too well what it was like to suffer from those afflictions of so-called humanity. But just because I'm free of them now doesn't make me inhuman. If anything, I feel even more pity for the rest of you! You don't know what you're missing, Miranda. Since my last series of enhancements I feel completely liberated. And you could have been like me too if you hadn't been so stupid."

"I thank you again for the gift of immortality, Milo, but all those other gifts you offered were of no interest to me."

"One day you'll regret that you rejected them," he told her coldly.

"That day will never come, Milo, I promise you. I may be just a genetic echo of you but I am still human. And I want to stay that way."

He felt his control of his temper start to slip. It took all his strength of will to keep his hands off her. "I keep telling you — I *am* human. *Super*human, yes, but basically still human."

"You may think you are, Milo, but you're not. You can't see what you've become. The human personality is the product of an infinitely complicated and sophisticated biological process and science has a long way to go before it unravels them. You can't just chop great chunks out of the system — as your genegineers did with you — without destroying something vital . . . ." Miranda nodded agreement with herself. "Yes . . . yes . . . that's it. In a sense you've *killed* yourself, Milo." Suddenly she laughed. "It's ironic, actually. All that money and effort to turn yourself into a superman, but by doing so you've committed a form of suicide. You're walking around thinking you're immortal but you're dead inside and the ants are already feeding on your soul."

"Shut up!" he exploded, raising his hand as if to hit her. "I won't listen to this superstitious crap! Now, for the last time, are you coming with me or not?"

"No, Milo. Because I just can't *stand* being in your presence any more. It's not just your altered personality, it's physical as well. Those 'enhancements' of yours again, they've screwed you up on some subtle level. I'm telling you the truth when I say that you physically revolt me. And I mean that with every one of *your* cells in *my* body."

Milo slowly lowered his hand. He stared at her for a long time in silence, then turned and strode off down the 'beach'. He passed through one of the holographic projections and then out of the door. He took the elevator straight to the flipper garage on the roof. One of the smaller house cyberoids met him as he entered the garage. "Good evening, Mr Haze. Are you going out?"

224

"Yes," he said curtly as he headed for his flipper. He had no fixed plan in mind, only a vague idea about getting out of the state. After that? Well, with the way the newer plagues were spreading maybe he should think about getting off the planet itself.

"It's a pleasant night for a flight," said the cyberoid, following him.

"Certainly is," said Milo and smiled bleakly. He was about to climb into his flipper when a thought occurred to him. He looked at Miranda's flipper parked on the other side of the garage then pointed to it. "Disable that vehicle," he ordered. "Open the maintenance access panel and destroy the drive unit."

"But sir," said the cyberoid in its flat, polite purr. "It is part of the property I am programmed to protect."

"And I'm overriding your programmed instructions. Do as I say."

"Very well, sir." The cyberoid walked over to Miranda's flipper, opened the rear access panel to the drive and extended its articulated manipulator inside. There came the sound of metal being crushed. Satisfied, Milo was once more about to get into his own flipper, but again he paused. He could hear something. A distant murmuring?

No. It was more like the angry buzzing of hornets. He went to the garage doors and pressed the manual control button. As the doors slid open he stepped out on to the roof. He could hear the sound more clearly now. He knew what was causing it, but he summoned the cyberoid out on to the roof to confirm his opinion. "People," said the cyberoid in answer to his question. "Many of them. They're coming this way."

"Yes," said Milo. He went to the parapet and stared out across his gardens towards the wall, which sparkled with the different coloured lights of his defence system.

"Are you expecting visitors, sir?" the cyberoid enquired.

"No, but my wife is. They're her responsibility." He hurried back inside the garage.

"How many guests is your wife expecting? From the sound of it the approaching group numbers many hundreds."

225

"Don't worry, I'm sure Miranda will be capable of entertaining them all. She likes giving big parties," Milo told the cyberoid as he got into the flipper. The armoured hatch slid shut and Milo ordered the vehicle's computer to take the flipper up to an altitude of a thousand feet and then hover.

From that height Milo, via the sensor monitors, got a clear view of what was happening. The cyberoid had under-estimated the crowd's numbers. There were thousands of them coming through the woods towards the north wall. Milo guessed they had come from Luxton, the nearest big town to his estate. He'd heard that the place had been hit by the plague.

He had one of the monitors zoom in on a group of them. He saw they were all carrying weapons. Guns, axes, garden utensils even. Milo smiled to himself. He was reminded of a visual cliche from the old horror movies — the horde of angry peasants on their way to burn down the castle of the local vampire or mad scientist. All that was missing were the burning torches.

The broad and ragged front line of the approaching mob was now only about a hundred yards from the wall. Milo decided to make it easier for the attackers. He patched into the house computer and gave it the coded command that would override all previous commands and freeze the defence systems, with the exception of the cyberoids who acted as self-contained units. Then he leaned back in his seat and prepared to watch the show.

It didn't take them long to get into the grounds. First came a number of explosions that breached the wall in several places, and then the mob poured through the gaps and into the gardens. There it encountered the first real opposition; three of the estate's large outdoor cyberoids who met the rush of humanity with a devastating mixture of machine-gun and laser fire. Hundreds of the attackers died in the first thirty seconds, but there were so many of them coming through the wall that the cyberoids had no real chance of stopping the invasion. They were quickly overwhelmed by the sheer weight of bodies, toppled off their feet and then, helpless, battered and smashed into shapeless lumps of metal and plastic. The mob surged on towards the house.

A perverse whim caused Milo to patch into the house's interior audio-visual surveillance system. He saw that Miranda was still in the Sea Room, but the special effects had been shut down and she was staring out of one of the front windows. He spoke her name and she turned towards the surveillance unit that he'd activated. "Milo?" she asked anxiously. "Is that you? What's happening? Why aren't the defences working?"

"Must be a malfunction," he told her. "Or maybe it's sabotage. You don't have much time. Get your flipper right away. Don't wait to pack anything."

"Where are you?"

"About a thousand feet above the house. Come and join me. Fast."

She glanced one more time out of the window, then ran from the room. Milo smiled with satisfaction and cut the connection. There came the sound of another explosion. He looked and saw smoke rising from the front of the house. They would be entering the ground floor now. It wouldn't be long . . . .

He aimed one of the sensors at the garage doors on the roof. And waited.

Miranda emerged through them about a minute later, looking upwards. He zoomed in on her face. Her eyes were wide with fear. He guessed the mob must be close behind her. He imagined what she must have felt when she discovered her flipper wasn't functioning. He smiled again.

She ran out on to the garage roof, waving her arms frantically. She could obviously see his lights. Then came flashes of gunfire in the garage. The house cyberoid doing its duty, guessed Milo. Or perhaps it was trying to serve the 'guests' canapes from a tray and couldn't comprehend why it was being fired upon. The thought made Milo laugh aloud.

The first of the mob came through the garage doors. A man, carrying an automatic rifle. A woman followed him. She was wielding a machete. Others emerged . . . .

Miranda ran, but there was nowhere for her to go unless she jumped off the roof. They trapped her in a corner, surrounding her. She continued to wave frantically at him. Milo leaned forward and switched off his flipper's lights. Then he watched the screen intently as Miranda was torn to pieces. It was only when

227

there was nothing left of her to be seen among the rampaging mob that he realized he had a throbbing erection.

He took the flipper down in a swooping dive. He was above them before they knew what was happening. His lasers and guns soon killed all of those on the roof. Then he dropped a bomb on the house and flew off towards the south.

Chapter Twenty-Three:

Flickers of lightning illuminated the taller towers of the distant city in brief flashes. Jan was awe-struck. She had never seen a city before and the sheer size of this one impressed her profoundly. How could buildings have been built to stretch so far into the sky without collapsing at their bases? And to think that all those buildings had once been full of people. It was hard to imagine that so many people had ever lived at the same time.

"There must have been thousands and thousands of people living there," she said to Milo.

"What?" he said distractedly. He had been uncharacteristically silent for the last few minutes as he leaned on the railing and stared broodingly at the city. She repeated her words and he answered, "No, more than that. It had a population of over six million."

"Six *million*?" She shook her head in disbelief.

"It's true. I knew that city well. The last time I saw it it was alive. All those towers shone with lights. Traffic moved in the streets. Flippers moved in the sky . . . ." He went silent again.

She guessed he was reliving memories from all those centuries ago and felt briefly sorry for him. "That big tower, in the centre. Is that the one we have to reach? The Sky Tower?"

"Shush," he cautioned her and glanced over his shoulder towards their ever-present escort, two silent samurai who were standing some ten feet away from them on the open deck. Jan and Milo had, in theory, the warlord's permission to go wherever they wanted within the public sections of the *Lord Pangloth*, but whenever they left their cabin they were followed by two warriors. Milo had told Jan that he doubted if they could understand Americano; he was fairly certain that only the warlord had any familiarity with the language, but they couldn't afford to take the chance of speaking openly in front of them.

"Speak in a whisper," he told her, leaning his head close to hers. "Yes, that's the Sky Tower. I only hope it doesn't spark off any old memories in our friend Horado's mind."

"When do we leave?" Jan asked. The city already seemed a long way away and the thought of flying all that distance in one of the Japanese gliders made her stomach flutter queasily. And with every passing moment the city became more distant as the *Lord Pangloth*, having made a wide detour round it, now flew northwards towards the place known as the Armstrong Spaceport.

"When it gets completely dark," whispered Milo.

"But how will we see where to go?" she asked worriedly.

"Didn't I tell you? I can see perfectly well in the dark."

She was past being surprised by anything about Milo. She simply nodded and said, "Yes, but I can't."

"Don't worry. I'll be doing all the steering. You just follow my instructions and everything will be fine. Our only problem is that storm up there in the hills. Let's just hope it's moving in the other direction."

"What about our other problem?" she asked, shifting her head slightly to indicate their solemn-faced escorts, who were pretending to be watching the city instead of them.

Milo glanced briefly at them and shrugged. "No problem. On the contrary, they'll be of help to us. Well, *one* of them will be." He didn't elaborate and she didn't pursue the matter. She knew that she would find out what he had in mind soon enough. Let him enjoy his little dramatic game in the meantime.

The city grew ever more distant and soon Jan had trouble in making out its towers during the intermittent flashes of lightning. What she could see clearly were the lights of the *Lord Pangloth*, which was following the *Perfumed Breeze* at a distance of about a

229

mile. Her thoughts turned inevitably to Ceri — was she on the *Lord Pangloth* or was she still on the *Perfumed Breeze*? Was she safe? What was happening to her at this very moment?

Asking herself these questions only aggravated her anxiety about Ceri, and Jan tried to put her out of her mind. She looked at Milo, who was again staring silently into space. This prompted another line of anxious self-questioning: what was she doing putting her life yet again in the hands of this strange creature whom she already knew couldn't be trusted? The more she learned about Milo the more he mystified and disturbed her. And still she couldn't tell how much of what he told her of the old days was the truth and how much was invention concocted for reasons of his own.

What he'd told her about the woman called Miranda, for example, was very difficult to accept: that she had literally been himself in female form, a clone grown from one of his cells that had been genetically engineered to alter the Y chromosome. In this way Milo had been able to marry himself. "A marriage made in a heavenly test tube," he had said with bitter humour. Jan got the impression that the relationship with his clone had not turned out as he had intended, but despite her continued questioning he refused to tell her any more about Miranda. She remembered he'd told the warlord tersely that Miranda had died, and she wondered about the full circumstances surrounding the clone's death.

"It's time," murmured Milo.

His words caught her by surprise. "What are . . .?" she began but Milo was already moving towards their two guards. He said something to them in their language. It sounded to Jan like a question. The two guards frowned and then glanced at each other as Milo continued to approach them. Then he *blurred . . . .*

The guards had no time to draw their swords. Jan saw one of them fly backwards. He bounced off the wall behind him and fell to his knees, blood pouring from his nose. Milo had hold of the other one by his head. He wrenched the man's head round with frightening strength. The vertebrae in his neck made a ghastly sound as they were twisted apart. Jan looked away. When she turned back the guard was lying face-down on the deck and Milo was bending over the first man. He brought the edge of his hand down on the back of the man's neck. The guard slumped forward and lay still. Milo undid the warrior's weapons harness and tossed it, with the sheathed swords and knives, at Jan's feet. Then he picked the dead man up, carried him to the railing and, without displaying the least effort, flung him into space. The darkness swiftly swallowed up the man's falling corpse. Milo went to the other body and began to strip it.

Everything had happened so fast that Jan felt disorientated. One moment there had been two living, breathing human beings with them on the small deck and now, within the blink, it seemed, of an eye, they were both dead; and one of them was plunging through the night air towards the ground . . . .

Milo was putting on the dead warrior's clothes and armour. He looked at Jan and said, "Pick up those weapons. You're going to need them." She did as she was told. He put on the man's helmet and grinned unpleasantly at her. "How do I look?"

"Everything's too small on you. You won't fool anyone . . . not for long, anyway," she told him.

"I didn't expect to get there and back completely unnoticed," he said unperturbed. "Especially carrying a glider along the corridor. But the disguise will give me a slight edge and that's all I need. See you soon . . . ." He picked up the near-naked body and tossed it over the railing as effortlessly as the first one, then hurried down the deck and disappeared through the hatchway.

Jan sighed, then turned and leaned on the railing, trying to conceal the weapons with her body in case one of the Japanese should venture out on to the deck while Milo was gone. Underneath her jacket was a water bottle and a bag containing a number of rice cakes. She knew that the next ten minutes or so were going to be very long ones. Milo had estimated that was the amount of time it would take him to reach the nearest of the glider storage areas, steal one and get back to the deck. She wondered what she would do if he never returned. Use one of the knives on herself? Jump? Anything would be better than to fall into the hands of the warlord, who would undoubtedly be furious at being betrayed by Milo.

As expected, the time passed with agonizing slowness. Her palms began to sweat and the slightest sound made her start. Where was Milo? Surely more than ten minutes had passed by now . . . .

She gave another start. The sound of someone coming. At a run. Milo emerged through the hatchway. Under one arm he was carrying a folded-up glider, in his other hand he was holding a sword. Jan's first thought was that the glider looked too ridiculously small to be capable of supporting two people, then she noticed the blood on the blade of the sword.

Milo's eyes held the wild look she had seen before. He grinned crazily and said, "Bit more difficult that I expected. Left something of a mess back there but the survivors have probably sorted themselves out by now and are hot on my trail. We don't have much time." He sheathed his sword and began to unfold the glider. To Jan it seemed magical the way the thing just grew and grew — sections of tubular metal expanded to four times their original length; the silken cloth of the wing itself seemed endless . . . soon the glider's wing span extended the full length of the small deck. Milo suddenly kicked at the railings, splintering them. A couple more kicks and the railings were gone. Jan backed away from the edge. The idea of jumping into the black void supported only by a flimsy arrangement of silk, hollow metal poles and wires grew even less attractive.

"Quickly!" urged Milo. "Get your weapons on and then get into this harness." He was already climbing into his own leather harness, which was attached by wires to the centre of the glider. She hurriedly strapped on her swords and knives then got into the harness. It fitted around her thighs and waist. The glider, at this point, was resting on its rear wing tip; from the centre, where the harness wires were secured, extended a triangle made up of the three metal poles. "Take hold of the bar — like this," said Milo as he grabbed the pole that formed the base of the triangle. Jan did likewise, her heart thumping painfully.

"After we launch keep your body straight and do whatever I tell you. Understand?"

"Yes," she replied with a dry mouth.

"Right, step to the edge and get ready to jump as hard as you can when I give the signal."

They moved to the very edge of the deck, the silk wing standing almost upright behind them. "On the count of three," said Milo, bending his knees in readiness to jump. Jan did the same. Her long hair was caught by the wind and blown across her face. The silk fabric of the wing began to flap.

"One . . . ."

Angry shouts behind them. The Japanese had arrived.

"Two . . . *three!*"

The knowledge that the deck was about to fill up with furious Japanese warriors overcame any last-moment doubts Jan had about jumping. She put every effort she could into her leap from the edge of the deck — but just as she and Milo jumped there came the crash of gunfire and she felt a bullet pass close by her ear.

More gunfire, but by then she and Milo were hurtling downwards through the cold night air. For several moments Jan thought they were falling out of control, but no; she then realized they were in a downward, gliding swoop. They were *flying*.

"Shift your weight to the left!" ordered Milo.

"What?" The glider was levelling out now. The air was rushing by so fast her eyes were watering. Not that there was anything to see anyway.

"Shift to the left — towards me!" shouted Milo. "Now!"

She did as he wanted. She felt his body move in the same direction. The glider dipped to the left, then she realized they were turning. Moments later he yelled, "Okay, stop! Straighten out again!" She did so. "Good," he said. "At least we're going in the right direction, but we need more height if we're going to reach the city. Let's hope we encounter some updrafts."

As they flew on Jan discovered that she was beginning to enjoy the experience. Flying in silence like an arrow through the night air . . . .

"Shit," grunted Milo.

"What's wrong?"

"Got a rip in the wing. Bullet hole, or a sword slash." She looked over her shoulder, but though she could just make out the shape of the wing above them in the darkness she certainly couldn't see any rip in the fabric. "Is it a problem?" she asked.

"Not yet, but it's getting bigger."

"Oh." Her feeling of exhilaration had gone. She peered downwards, trying to see how far they were above the ground.

"Shit," said Milo again. "We're not going to make the city at this rate."

"Are we going to crash?"

"I doubt it, but we may have a long walk. And that's blight land below us."

Jan had no idea how much time passed before she felt a violent jolt and almost lost her grip on the bar. She heard Milo yell "Hang on!" and then the glider stood on its nose and plunged downwards. She screamed.

They seemed to fall thousands of feet before the glider unexpectedly straightened out again. "You okay?" Milo called.

"I think so," she said shakily. "I thought we were finished."

"These things are designed to pull out of dives automatically. Trouble is, we've lost even more height now, thanks to that pocket of turbulence, and I can't see how— " The ripping sound was clearly audible over the flapping of the wing and the rush of the air. Then the glider dipped violently to the right. It didn't dive this time but went into a spiral. Milo was yelling something, but she couldn't hear what.

It could have been hours later or merely seconds when the glider crashed into something and Jan received a blow on the forehead that sent her consciousness spinning off into the void . . . .

When she came to she found she was suspended upside-down by her harness. She couldn't see anything. "Milo?" she groaned. There was no answer. She reached blindly out for him but couldn't find him. What had happened? Where was she? The glider seemed to be facing nose down, but was it on the ground or stuck in the branches of some tall tree? She felt her face. It was sticky — with blood, no doubt — and there was a lump on her forehead just above the hairline. "Milo!" she called again, more loudly this time.

Something coughed in the darkness. The sound was familiar to

Jan. It was the sound the big cats often made as they prowled around the walls. She remembered where she was. In the blight lands. And, apparently, alone. Milo had abandoned her. Or he was dead.

She drew her short sword. It provided a modicum of solace but she still felt ridiculously vulnerable and exposed, hanging there upside-down. She probed about with the sword and found Milo's empty harness hanging nearby. Then she made contact with one of the tubular metal poles. With difficulty she managed to grab hold of it. As she did so the glider shifted slightly and there was a tearing noise. As she'd suspected the thing appeared to be caught in the branches of a tree. But she still had no idea how high up she was. One thing was certain, though; it wouldn't take much, from the sound of it, to dislodge the glider from its precarious perch.

Jan came to a decision. She had no choice but to try and jump to the ground before the glider fell, taking her with it. She sheathed the short sword and reached out for the glider's cross-bar. She gripped it firmly with one hand and with the other began to undo the straps of her harness.

As the last fastening came free the harness slipped open and she was suddenly falling. Desperately she grabbed for the bar with her other hand.

Got it! She gave a grunt as her body swung round, putting all her weight on her arms with a violent jerk. Then she swung there, legs dangling in space. She felt down with her toes, hoping to touch the ground. But it wasn't there. How far away was it? Five feet? Ten? Fifty? It was the difference between a sprained ankle, broken bones or death.

Get it over with, Jan told herself. She took a deep breath and let go of the bar . . . .

As she fell she drew up her knees, instinctively beginning to curl up into a ball.

She fell and fell . . . .

I'm going to die!

She plunged into something very soft, but though the substance broke her fall the impact was still sufficient to knock the breath out of her. She rolled head over heels though the stuff and ended up lying on her back, frantically trying to suck air into her lungs. Whatever she'd landed in was all over her face as well, which made trying to breathe even more difficult. As she scraped it off the foul smell told her what it was . . . .

Fungus!

"Ugh," Jan groaned with disgust. She sat up and hurriedly brushed the stuff from her clothing. Then she stood up and took a tentative step. Immediately she sank to her knees in the springy, repulsive substance. She wanted to be sick, then she told herself that the fungus *had* saved her life. Without it she would have surely broken her neck, not to mention every other bone in her body.

Then it occurred to her that if she had survived the fall from the glider then Milo must have as well. But where was he? Probably a long way from here already, she thought bitterly. Maybe he had given her up for dead, or had he just decided that she would slow him down on foot? Either way, he had abandoned her.

She heard that feline cough again. It was closer now. She drew the longer of the two swords, holding it with both hands, and faced in the direction where she thought the big cat was. She remembered, with a superstitious chill, the black panther at the gate. The one that had brought about Carla's death. Surely it couldn't be the same one . . . .

Another sound. Right behind her.

Jan started to turn, but she knew it was already too late.

Chapter Twenty-Four:

"Careful with that thing, you idiot!" warned Milo tersely.

"Milo! Thank the Mother God . . . ." Jan lowered the sword as relief flooded through her. "I thought you'd abandoned me."

He stepped close to her. She could just make out his shape in the darkness. "I did," he told her.

"You did?" she asked, surprised. "But you came back . . . ."

236

"Don't ask me why," he said coldly. "I don't know myself. Just don't make me regret my decision."

Another cough from the big cat. *Very* close now. "Milo . . .?"

"Yes, I can see it. A tiger. Sabre-tooth. Big. About twenty yards away." He lowered his voice. "It's just spotted us. Gone into a crouch. We're down-wind of it, so it hadn't got our scent."

Jan was irrationally relieved that the big cat wasn't a panther, even though she was well aware that a sabre-tooth was even more deadly. Then she heard Milo moving away from her. "Where are you going?" she asked anxiously.

"Nowhere," he answered softly. "Just a few yards in front of you. I'm now standing with my back to the cat." She heard him slowly draw one of his swords.

"But why have you got your back to the tiger?" she asked, alarmed. "You won't be able to see him coming."

"Be quiet!" Milo ordered.

She obeyed. All was silent at first and then she heard a slight sound of movement. In her mind's eye she could see the sabre-tooth coming through the sound-absorbing fungus. Any moment now and he would be in range to spring. She tensed, ready to run. Then came a swishing sound followed by a loud *thunk*. She heard something heavy landing in the fungus very nearby. A powerful animal smell washed over her. "Milo . . .?"

"I'm still here. But the cat isn't."

"What happened?"

"I beheaded it."

"But how did you know when to strike? You had your back to it."

"I can hear just as well as I can see in the dark. Audio enhancement. That poor pussycat made as much noise coming though that fungoid mush as a cyberoid falling down a staircase. Now come on, let's go and find you some shelter. No use trying to cover any distance to the city tonight. You'd probably blunder into a whip tree." She felt him grasp her wrist and allowed herself to be led through the impenetrable blackness. Progress, however, was difficult, thanks to the fungus. It was like trying to wade through a lake of viscous liquid and very soon Jan's legs were aching. "Where are we going?" she asked.

237

"I'm looking for a suitable tree," he told her. "Most around here are dead and rotten thanks to the fungus."

She remembered his comment about blundering into a whip tree and said nervously. "Can you see well enough in the dark to spot a whip tree?"

"Let's hope so," he said and chuckled.

Jan didn't find it amusing. Whip trees were notoriously deceptive. They mimicked other species of trees so closely that it was impossible to tell them apart; that is, until the whip-like tendrils cracked through the air towards the unfortunate victim, who was then dragged by them towards the trunk, where giant thorns were already emerging to impale him and slowly absorb all the fluid from his body. "Where did whip trees come from?" she asked Milo.

"Like so many other things out here in the blight they were created by genegineers."

"But *why*? Why would anyone deliberately create anything so horrible?"

Milo laughed and said, "The Mother God created man, didn't she?"

"You don't believe in the Mother God, I know. You're making fun of me."

"True. But to answer your question, the whip trees were created by genegineers working for a very rich man called Planus. He wanted a novel way of dissuading trespassers from entering his extensive estates. The whip trees aren't really trees. They're a hybrid of animal and vegetable. Neither one nor the other." He paused then added, "Like me."

"Like you?" she asked, puzzled.

"Yes. Neither one thing nor the other." There was bitterness in his voice. "Someone once told me that a long time ago. I didn't believe her. But what the hell, I survive, and that's what counts. That's what *everything* is all about."

Not understanding what he was talking about Jan didn't answer. He continued and she realized he was talking more to himself than her. "Survival. The reason for everything, yet it remains the basic mystery. Why should complicated molecules have developed the ability to replicate? Is it the automatic outcome of natural chemical processes? The automatic outcome of matter's innate, chemical desire to persist in a form that is mathematically harmonious . . .?" Milo suddenly tightened his grip on her arm. "Look!"

"Look where?" She asked nervously. "You know I can't see anything."

"Upwards, you fool. Look at the sky."

She did so, and saw a cluster of lights moving overhead. "The *Lord Pangloth!*" she gasped.

"Or the *Perfumed Breeze.* Obviously the warlord is not giving up so easily. He must have his heart set on getting a shiny, new Sky Angel."

As they stared upwards a beam of intense, white light suddenly stabbed downwards from the dark mass of the airship. It touched the ground about a hundred yards in front of them, illuminating the ghostly outlines of fungus draped trees and huge, free-standing fungoid growths. Then the beam of light began to track back and forth. "Quickly, this way," urged Milo, leading Jan towards a nearby fungus that resembled a giant mushroom. They crouched down under its drooping cap. The beam was sweeping in their direction now. "Keep still . . . don't move a muscle," he told her.

Jan had every intention of remaining perfectly still . . . until a cold and slimy thing dropped on to the back of her neck. She gave a cry of alarm and turned to see a thick, white worm crawling over her shoulder. When she felt another one drop on her neck she screamed and stood up. "No . . ." warned Milo, but it was too late. The impact made the cap of the mushroom explode into powdery fragments, leaving them exposed to the fast-approaching beam of light.

"Stupid bitch!" snarled Milo as he reached up and pulled her down beside him. "Lie flat!"

But then Jan saw that the ground was now covered with large, writhing worms. They had apparently been inside the mushroom's cap, feeding on it, probably. "Oh, Mother God . . ." she groaned and tried to stand again but Milo pushed her face-down on to the pulpy ground. "Be still or I'll kill you," he hissed . . . She could feel the worms writhing under her as

239

they were crushed by her weight. Bile rose up in the back of her throat . . . .

The beam of light was coming through the trees straight towards them. They had no chance. And then, when it was less than fifty feet away, there was a harsh cry and suddenly something on two legs was illuminated by the beam. Nothing human, Jan saw, but one of the reptiles that walked upright on its hind legs. A small one.

Screeching with alarm, the reptile took flight and the beam followed it, or tried to as the creature sped off through the distorted scenery of the blight land. Gradually the beam faded in the distance. So too did the whine of the airship's thrusters, and Jan was in total darkness again. It was only then that Milo spoke. "I should leave you here for that," he said, his voice cold and flat.

She felt ashamed. "I'm sorry, Milo. I acted like a child."

"No. You acted like a stupid woman."

Anger flared up in Jan but she bit back her words of protest. She had no right to defend herself. She *had* behaved stupidly. Finally she said, haltingly, "Well, *are* you going to leave me?"

There was no answer from Milo. The silence went on so long she began to think that he had already gone, moving so quietly she hadn't heard him go. Then, unexpectedly, she felt his hands grab the cloth of her Japanese jacket. He slammed her backwards and then his weight was on top of her. "You owe me," he told her coldly.

Automatically, she started to resist but then she stopped struggling. Again, he was right. She *did* owe him, monster though he was. And she knew that without him she would never get out of the blight land alive. There was no choice but to let him have what he wanted.

So she didn't resist as he roughly stripped her of her weapons harness and clothes and then, equally roughly, entered her. She lay there on the putrid fungus and the cold slime of the crushed worms' bodies, trying to rein back the physical revulsion she had for Milo and hoping that it would all be over quickly.

It wasn't. She realized, eventually, that she should have anticipated that Milo would be unlike poor Prince Caspar in his love-making; the eager and over-excited Caspar could never last

240

very long before firing off his juices inside her but Milo wasn't liable to such lack of self-control. On the contrary. As Milo had had so many of his bodily functions improved by those long-dead genegineers she guessed that his sexual prowess had been similarly 'enhanced'. He took her again and again in a variety of positions, climaxing every time but coming erect again almost immediately.

She tried to let herself go — tried to give herself over to the experience — but though her body responded to a certain degree her mind remained locked off from what was happening to her. Even when she tried to pretend it was Prince Caspar making love to her with a cold skill he had never achieved before she failed to overcome her basic revulsion. So instead she simulated enjoyment — as she had sometimes done with Caspar — crying and moaning and shuddering in a way that she hoped would convince Milo.

Finally he climaxed with an intensity that went far beyond his previous orgasms, giving a piercing scream as his body underwent a series of convulsive muscle contractions. Then he slumped down beside her and Jan could hear him panting. She waited for a time then said, "That was wonderful . . . ."

The slap that came out of the darkness took her completely by surprise. It seared her cheek and rattled her teeth. Then, before she could react, Milo's hands gripped her neck. "Bitch," he hissed. "Who do you think you're dealing with? Do you think you could ever fool *me*?"

Not since the time in the wicker cage with the other captives had Jan spent such an uncomfortable night, perched precariously as she was high up in a fork in the tall tree. It was impossible to sleep because she knew if she did she would have surely fallen. She had almost fallen when relieving herself. Even eating and drinking had been a risky operation as she really needed both hands to hold on to the tree.

Adding to her discomfort were the state of her clothes, which remained sticky and smelt putrid, and the soreness around her throat that made swallowing painful. For several terrifying moments she had been convinced that Milo was going to kill her, but just as she began to lose consciousness he'd let go of her throat and told her brusquely to get up and get dressed. Since then he'd said very little to her, apart from announcing that he'd found a suitable tree and giving some words of advice on how to climb it.

One of the rare occasions he spoke was when they heard something very large approaching the tree. "What is it?" she'd called anxiously to him. Milo, who was on a branch a short distance below her, replied that it was a particularly large reptile.

It was so heavy it made the ground shake and Jan had to hold even more tightly on to the tree. She could hear other trees being knocked down and guessed that the creature was so enormous it was simply creating its own path through the blighted forest. "Milo . . .!" she'd cried, expecting the thing to knock their tree over at any moment. But he'd called back, "Don't worry, it's going to miss us. Just."

Milo was right. Jan had a brief impression of an impossibly large bulk passing by very close and then the sounds of its ground-shaking footsteps began to recede. "It must have been *huge*," she said.

"It was. Biggest dinosaur I ever saw. A brachiosaurus, by the look of it . . . not that any of those things are real dinosaurs. Their genetic base isn't even reptilian, it's mammalian. Canine, in fact. Yeah, those so-called dinosaurs are really just overgrown dogs . . . ." He gave a harsh laugh and then became silent again.

Apart from that close encounter with the giant beast they had no trouble with any other creature during the long night, though from all the cries and shrieks that could be heard at regular intervals it was clear that this area of the blight land was well populated with *something*. Jan felt very relieved when it finally began to grow light. Her back and neck were stiff and her limbs ached from the strain of maintaining a grip on the tree.

The dawn illuminated a depressing but familiar scene. Blight land in all directions. Fungus everywhere. Hanging from the trees like pieces of rotting shroud, rising from the ground in various bizarre shapes. Some of the growths were of different colours — Jan saw several giant puffballs that were bright red — but most of the fungus was a dirty white. It was a colour she associated with death and decay. The air smelled of decay too, a strong odour of mustiness which she knew came from the fungus. And it would get worse when the fungus was warmed by the sun.

"I'm going down," she told Milo. "Another minute in this tree will drive me crazy."

Her muscles protested strongly as she began the long climb down to the ground. She expected Milo to descend ahead of her, but instead he moved out of her way and then began to climb towards the top of the tree. "What are you doing?" she asked, pausing.

"Want to get my bearings. Got disorientated last night. Should be able to see the city from the top."

Jan continued down. On the ground she walked off a short distance and relieved herself behind a rotting tree. When she returned Milo was there. His expression was grim. "Not good. We flew further off course in that damn glider than I thought."

"How far away is the city?"

"Too far. I could just make out the towers on the horizon. It's going to take us days to get there travelling through this mess." He took out a rice cake from the pouch inside his jacket and began to eat. Between bites he said, "Trouble is, we don't have enough food or water."

"*I* don't, you mean," she said, remembering what Ceri had said about Milo surviving in the sea while his companions had died of thirst and starvation. "You don't need food or water to stay alive. Ceri told me."

He frowned at her. "It's true I can slow down my metabolism, in the same way I can speed it up, but that means going into a form of hibernation. I can't walk and hibernate at the same time. I need nourishment and water just as much as you."

"So what can we do?"

"Just keep going and hope something turns up. Maybe we'll run into some marauders or wanderers and I can kill them for their supplies. But somehow I doubt if we'll see any other humans this close to the city."

Jan took out her water bottle and shook it. It sounded less than half full. She had one mouthful and put the bottle back inside her jacket. "Any sign of the Sky Lords?"

He nodded. "The *Perfumed Breeze* is cruising about some ten miles to the east. The warlord must have taken *Pangloth* on to the Armstrong spaceport to check out my story just in case it wasn't all lies. I only hope he doesn't realize that we were attempting to reach the city. That might trigger off some buried memory about the Sky Tower. Then again, he wouldn't think anyone could be so mad as to enter a city."

"Yes,"she agreed sourly. "Who else but us could be so mad?"

For the first time that day Milo smiled and seemed like his old self again, but his change of mood was only temporary and he lapsed again into grim silence as he led the way towards the distant city.

Trudging along behind him through the foul-smelling fungus, Jan wondered about her relationship with him. It had changed, thanks to the sex of the previous night. He had finally got what he wanted, only it hadn't satisfied him. What *had* he wanted then? Not just sex with her. Had he somehow expected to transform her through the act of love-making? Into what? A genuine lover, even though she had already warned him she could never be that to him? That was likely. He had believed, in his arrogance, that he could possess her through the power of his penis alone. Or maybe it wasn't as simple as that. Perhaps, despite denying the existence of love, he hoped she would fall in love with him.

Well, however differently he felt about her now it did not bode well for her future survival. He must realize that there was no chance of her changing her attitude towards him and that meant he might now regard her as a disposable item; something that could be easily abandoned at the first sign of serious inconvenience.

The morning passed without incident. They heard many sounds in the surrounding woods but nothing overtly threatened them. They did encounter a whip tree, but as it had only recently trapped some fresh prey it presented no danger, being clearly visible for what it was. The prey — a large wolf-like animal — was held against the trunk in an obscene embrace by the tree's tentacles. Already the wolf's body was caving in under its fur as the spikes of the trunk slowly sucked it dry.

"Why are the whip trees never attacked by fungus?" Jan asked Milo as they detoured around it.

"As I told you before, they're not really trees. But apart from that they were designed to be pretty difficult to kill. They're full of toxins. Too deadly for even the toughest fungi to infest."

They stopped around noon for a rest. Jan flung herself down thankfully. She was worn out from struggling through the fungus and her muscles throbbed with pain. It was uncomfortably hot too. The storm clouds of the previous night had vanished and the sun beat down unimpeded on the blight land.

"Mother God . . . the stink . . ." she groaned. It wasn't just the fungus, it was her as well. Her slime-encrusted clothes smelt appalling in the heat and she would have given anything for a bath. She thought with nostalgia of the bathroom in her quarters on the *Lord Pangloth* and wryly berated herself for such weakness.

She was terribly thirsty as well. She took out her water bottle. She had intended only to have a couple of mouthfuls, but before she knew what she was doing she had finished the remainder of the water. She sighed inwardly. How was she going to spend two or three days travelling without another drink of water? She glanced towards Milo, who was lying on his back. Would he share his remaining water with her? Best not to ask him just yet.

Ten minutes later and Jan felt herself begin to drift off to sleep. She knew it was a dangerous thing to do out in the open like this but surely Milo would let her know if anything dangerous appeared.

A sound made her return to full wakefulness. She listened intently. Yes, there it was again! She hadn't imagined it.

It was a *splash*.

She sat up. "Milo, did you hear that?"

He didn't answer. She looked at him. He appeared to be asleep. Good. She would handle this on her own. It would be good if she could announce to him on her return that she had found a source of fresh water. It would help to compensate for her stupid behaviour of the previous night.

She stood up quietly. There was another splash. It came from somewhere to her left. She began to head in what she hoped was the right direction. As a precaution she drew her short sword . . . .

She'd gone, she'd estimated, about fifty yards when suddenly the claustrophobic clutter of rotting trees and fungoid growths came to an end and she found herself standing in a clearing. In the centre of the clearing was a small lake. It was almost perfectly round and Jan wondered if it was artificial.

Whatever its origin it looked marvellous to her. As she approached it she felt a strong desire to tear off her clothes and plunge straight into its mirror-like surface.

She froze. The surface of the small lake was perfectly flat and there was no stream either entering it or leaving it. So what had caused the splashing? Raising her sword defensively she glanced around the clearing. No sign of anyone else in the vicinity. She looked back towards the lake and advanced towards it warily. She froze again as a large bubble appeared on its surface and then broke with a splashing sound. She immediately relaxed. The mystery had been solved.

But what was causing the bubbles? Gas, perhaps? Coming up through the ground on the bottom of the lake? Or could it be formed by rotting vegetation under the water? She went to the edge of the lake and peered into it. It seemed deep, its sides dropping away steeply. Jan frowned as she wondered if the water was safe to drink. It looked so enticing . . . .

She went down on one knee, cupped her free hand and dipped it into the water. It felt surprisingly cold. She tasted the water cautiously with the tip of her tongue, then swished a small amount of it back and forth in her mouth. It seemed okay. She would risk a couple of mouthfuls.

A louder splash than usual made her look up. There, in the centre of the lake, a head had appeared. It was frog-like in appearance and coloured a dark green. It had large, bulging eyes and a very wide mouth. The mouth grinned at her. Jan sprung upright and was about to run when the mouth opened and a great length of tongue shot out of it at amazing speed. The end of it was around Jan's left leg before she knew what was happening. She was jerked violently off her feet and dragged inexorably into the edge of the lake.

She hacked blindly with her sword. The blade made contact with something, sliced through it and suddenly she was no longer being pulled into the water. Frantically she scrambled out of the lake. Looking over her shoulder she saw the head had vanished, but the water in the centre of the lake seemed to be boiling. She started to run. At the same time there came an explosion of water from the lake. She glanced over her shoulder again and saw that the creature had leapt out of the lake. It was huge, with powerful hind legs. She saw the muscles tense as it prepared to leap again . . . .

She knew she didn't have a chance. The creature sailed straight over her head and landed with a thump some five yards ahead of her. It spun round to face her as she skidded helplessly to a halt.

It was massive. Even squatting it loomed over her. The great mouth opened again. She saw blood trickling from its corners. "Smart-ass," the frog-creature growled. "You hurt me. Gonna take weeks to regrow that four foot of tongue . . . ." He reached out one of his fore-limbs towards her. The long fingers on the human-like hand were tipped with vicious-looking claws. "Gonna teach you some lessons 'fore I eat you, woman. 'Fore I finish with you, you gonna be beggin' me to have my supper just to get it over with . . . ."

The creature suddenly stiffened and let loose a bellow of pain. It whirled around and Jan saw a large and deep gash across its upper back. A shape blurred beside the creature as it turned. She saw the flash of a sword. The creature bellowed again as one of its fore-legs was lopped off.

Milo, she realized.

The sword flashed again and again and soon the creature was on its back, hind legs kicking feebly as blood pumped out of several fatal wounds. Milo came into focus and began wiping his stained long-sword. He gave her a look of contempt. "Stupid, stupid woman. You've been trying so hard to get yourself killed I'm going to let you succeed the next time. You're absolutely useless . . . *what the hell* . . .?"

The metal net that had dropped neatly over Milo's head took them both equally by surprise.

Chapter Twenty-Five:

The wooden cage, mounted on two big wheels and hauled by a team of sick-looking bullocks, trundled slowly through the blight land. Jan and Milo weren't the only prisoners. There were three others in the cage with them. Two of them were male, one a female. They were all dressed in dirty robes that covered everything but their faces. They wore the same expression of sullen resignation. Under their thick black beards the men appeared to have identical features and Jan presumed they were twins. They were good looking, but in a way that Jan found too aggressively masculine. In fact it seemed to her that they *reeked* of pure masculinity on some physical level. The woman, on the other hand, was possessed of an almost beatific beauty; the bone structure underlying her flawless white skin appeared to Jan to be as fragile as egg shells. Unfortunately she was deformed by a pronounced hump on her back which protruded clearly through her bulky robes.

Their captors were of an unusual appearance as well, some more so than others. Jan stared again at the man keeping pace beside the wheeled cage. His face was marred with deep furrows and the flesh hung loose on his neck and beneath his chin. His thin hair had streaks of white in it as if he had attempted to dye it in the manner of the Minervan Headwomen.

All of their captors had similar markings on their faces, but this particular man was the worst affected. Jan wondered if it was the result of some kind of ritual scarring and had asked Milo this, but he was still refusing to speak. He just lay silently within the tight confines of the metal net, his expression unreadable. She guessed he was furious with himself at being taken by surprise so easily by this bunch of bedraggled-looking men. But it had all happened so quickly: the metal nets had seemed to come from nowhere.

While Jan had been staring in astonishment as the net dropped over Milo and cords attached to it pulled him off-balance, another net was flying through the air towards her. Very soon she was in the same position as Milo; lying helpless on the ground with her arms pinned to her sides. And then the bedraggled men with the strangely scarred faces were surrounding them, laughing and giving cries of triumph. They were armed with spears, pitch-forks and axes — all rusty — but had no guns as far as Jan could see. They spoke Americano, but with an odd accent that made understanding them difficult. One word cropped up again and again. *Ezekiel.*

Jan had heard that word many times since their capture and now realized it was someone's name. From what she had been able to decipher of their conversation Ezekiel was their leader. And apparently he was going to be very pleased with them when they returned with their five prizes. Or, as one of their captors had put it, ". . . these five abominations in the eyes of the Lord." Jan hadn't liked the sound of that.

They travelled without a stop right through the night. Jan managed to sleep for several hours, in spite of the discomfort. Fortunately they had removed the net from her before putting her in the mobile cage. They had tied her hands behind her, and her feet together, as they had the other prisoners with the exception of Milo. Jan doubted if she could have stood to remain within the cruel confines of the metal net for more than a couple of hours and felt increasingly sorry for Milo, though as usual he gave no sign of being in pain.

On waking up with a terrible thirst Jan had asked the nearest of their captors for some water, but he laughed and gave the side of the cage a whack with the shaft of his spear. "You think you're thirsty now, unclean one?" he said in his barely penetrable accent. "Just wait until Ezekiel sends you to hell where you belong — then you'll know *real* thirst!"

With the morning came glimpses over the tree-tops of the towers of the city, revealing to Jan that they were now much closer. She estimated that the outskirts were probably only about ten miles away. Then, at around mid-morning, the cage and ragged escort arrived at their destination. After passing through a gap in a wall made of metal netting covered with camouflage they entered a small settlement. For the first time since being thrown into the cage Milo struggled into a sitting position and began to display an interest in his surroundings.

It was a dismal place. The buildings, made of fungus-riddled wood, were squat and ugly. The atmosphere was made even more dismal by the camouflaged netting that hung over the whole of the settlement, keeping it in a state of permanent twilight.

They came to a square in the centre of the ramshackle little town and the mobile cage was halted. People were coming out of the buildings and very soon the cage was surrounded by a sizable crowd. Then Jan got a close look at some of the people and gave a gasp of fear and revulsion.

They were *living corpses*! Their withered skin hung from their bones in what appeared to be an advanced state of decay; their faces were so disfigured they scarcely resembled human beings! It was impossible that people could look like that and still be alive. They had obviously fallen into the hands of a nest of sorcerers who were using magic to keep these unfortunate creatures alive!

Unconsciously, Jan moved closer to Milo. He laughed cynically. "What's the matter?"

"Those creatures . . . Mother God, what *are* they? Have they been dug out of their graves and reanimated by sorcerers?"

Milo laughed again. "You're having your first look at an affliction that every human being was prone to once upon a time, provided he or she lived long enough. It's called 'old age'. These people must be the remnants of one of the big fundamentalist communities. They considered genetic enhancement to be 'unnatural' and against the will of God. They preferred to rot slowly like this over a period of many years. Pretty sight, isn't it? If it wasn't for those genengineers you despise so much, the same fate would be in store for you."

Jan covered her face with her hands. "No, I don't believe you! The Mother God wouldn't be so cruel!"

"Maybe She wouldn't be, but God the Father was, or Nature or the blind forces of chance — depending on what you want to believe rules over the cosmos . . ."

"*Ezekiel!*"

A great shout had risen from the crowd, and then a parting formed among them. Ezekiel had arrived. Ezekiel was like nothing Jan had ever seen before. It was made of metal and consisted of a large, box-like head, about five feet wide, and two huge legs that ended in great clawed feet. As it moved it clanked noisily and Jan saw that it left deep footprints in the ground. "Jesus," she heard Milo whisper. "I don't believe it . . . after all these years . . . ."

The thing halted beside the cage. It stood some ten feet high, which was the same height as the cage on its wheeled platform. There was a cluster of metal tubes mounted on top of the metal box and a mechanical arm attached to one of its sides. Jan then saw something that resembled a pair of large binoculars, mounted on another mechanical arm, emerge from the front of the box. She shivered as the binoculars scrutinized her, then did the same to the other four prisoners. Then the thing spoke.

"I am Ezekiel, the Hammer of the Lord. I am the instrument who will send you to your rightful place in Hell, for your presence here sorely offends the Lord." Its voice was loud but flat; without any range or emotion. It made the skin over Jan's spine tingle unpleasantly.

The thing then took a step backwards. "Open the cage. I will inspect these accursed ones."

As the crowd drew away to form a wide space around the cage two members of the escort opened the cage door and began to drag out the prisoners. Soon all five were lying on the ground in front of the thing called Ezekiel. It motioned towards Milo with its mechanical arm. "Why is that one wrapped so securely?"

One of their captors stepped forward. "Oh, great Ezekiel, Hammer of the Lord, he is a demon of a rare sort. We saw him move so fast the eye could not catch up with him. In this manner he was able to kill the great frog demon of the Round Lake."

The binoculars were extended on their long arm towards Milo. Then the thing said, "You are right to be cautious. Stun him before removing the net. Then use metal shackles on his limbs."

"Yes, great Ezekiel." The man turned, took a club from his belt, leaned over Milo and gave him two hard cracks with it on the side of his head. Milo grunted and went limp. Jan hoped he wasn't dead. But surely, she told herself, it would take more than that to kill Milo.

She stopped worrying about Milo when she saw another of their captors bend over her with a knife in his hand. But it was not her flesh he was intent on cutting open, merely her clothing. Very soon she was naked, but still securely bound. "On your feet," ordered the man and pulled her roughly up. The other three prisoners had been similarly stripped. Jan stared at them in astonishment. The two men were normal from the waist up, but from the waist down they were covered in thick, matted fur. And instead of feet they had *hooves* . . . .

There were gasps and angry mutterings from the crowd. The metal creature cried, "Behold! They are in the very image of their master!"

Jan was noticing other things about the two men-animals. They both had small horns protruding from the sides of their foreheads . . . and their sexual organs were so large as to be almost absurd. But it was the girl who got her full attention. She had a flawlessly beautiful body, marred only by the two wings covered in white feathers that sprouted from her shoulder blades.

Ezekiel pointed at her and said loudly, "Witness the deviousness of the Dark One! He has created a demon in the image of one of the Lord's servants! But do not be deceived!" Then it was Jan's turn. She was made to turn round so that Ezekiel could inspect every inch of her body. Finally the thing said, "I can find no sign of Satan's work upon her. Why have you brought her to me?"

One of their captors said, nervously, "She was with the man who moved like a demon, great Ezekiel. She must be tainted in some way."

"Ah, yes, the man," said Ezekiel, turning its binoculars towards Milo. At that moment a wizened creature, all bent and gnarled like a tree, came through the throng carrying an armful of chains and shackles. With a shock Jan realized she was female. The pathetic creature threw her burden down beside Milo. Immediately two of the men unwrapped the net from him, cut his clothes from him and then put the shackles on his wrists and ankles. Ezekiel studied him for a long time. "I can find no sign of Satan on this one either," he said finally.

"But great one, we saw him. All of us. He moved as only a demon could move."

Ezekiel inclined its head in an approximation of a human nod. "It is well known that not all the signs of the Dark One's work are on the outside. But before I impose the Lord's wrath upon him I must question him. Put him back in the cage. The girl too. I will question them when he regains his senses."

Rough hands lifted Jan and she was thrust through the opening of the cage. She barely had time to roll out of the way before Milo was flung in after her. The door was slammed shut and bolted.

"As for these others, who are accursed in the eyes of God, they shall be broken on the wheel and thus sent on their way to suffer eternal torment in the undying fire of hell!" cried Ezekiel. "Bring forth the wheels . . . ."

Several members of the crowd hurried away and returned shortly, rolling along in their midst five wheels that were as large as the ones supporting the cage. Jan watched as they were each mounted on to tree stumps that had been cut to an average height of about three feet. The bonds of the three prisoners were then cut. The two males struggled as they were forced down on their backs across the wheels, spread-eagled, and their hands and feet tied to the rims. The winged girl, however, submitted to the same treatment without any sign of resistance. She had given up all hope, Jan saw, and her heart ached for her. Her wings had been cruelly pinioned beneath her and one protruded down through the spokes of the wheel. Jan couldn't comprehend how anyone could wish to harm a creature of such exquisite and fragile beauty.

"Denizens of Babylon," said Ezekiel as it loomed over them. "By rights you should be burnt at the stake but fire would alert the evil giants that stalk the skies of our existence here. Thus you shall be released to meet your master in a more merciful manner than you deserve. But I am sure God will forgive me."

One of the creatures who Jan still thought of as living corpses offered Ezekiel a large hammer. Ezekiel grasped it with its single arm and raised it high. Then it brought the weapon down very

253

hard on the shin of the winged girl, shattering it. The girl gave a shrill scream of agony. Ezekiel proceeded to shatter her three other limbs with equally vicious blows of the hammer. Jan, horrified, turned her head from the sight. To her surprise she saw that Milo's eyes were open and he was watching the scene intently. She also saw, with a feeling of disbelief, that he had an erection.

Disgust overwhelmed her. "Mother God, you're *enjoying* this!" she cried accusingly.

"Quiet!" he whispered. "I don't want them to know I'm awake yet."

Jan's mind whirled with sick confusion as she tried to comprehend this new aspect of Milo's character. Behind her came the thuds of more bone-breaking hammer blows and one of the males began to scream. She could still hear the shrill cries of the girl. She put her fingers in her ears but she couldn't block out the sounds. More thuds of the hammer, the splintering of bones, more screaming . . . .

She glanced again at Milo and saw he was looking at her now. His lips were moving. Jan took her hands away from her ears. ". . . I said, it may be a horrible way to die but it's relatively quick," Milo was saying softly. "Unless you're very unlucky."

"How can it be quick?" she asked. "He's just broken their arms and legs. They'll linger in agony for days. And so will we."

"No. The shock should kill them. Shock is a drastic reduction of blood pressure. There'll be massive haemorrhaging into the tissues around the breaks and even now the three of them should be entering a state of deep shock. Soon their blood pressure won't be sufficient to keep their brains supplied with oxygen and they'll die."

"I'm sure that information will be a great solace to me when they tie me to one of those wheels," Jan said bitterly. "Also of solace will be the knowledge that as my arms and legs are broken you will be deriving physical pleasure from my agony."

Milo gave a slight shrug. "I admit I have strong sado-sexual tendencies but I assure you that watching you die would give me no pleasure at all."

"Well, that *is* a relief," she said with heavy sarcasm. "Esp-

ecially as it was only two nights ago that you tried to kill me
yourself . . . ."

"Shush," he warned. "Here they come."

She turned and saw that Ezekiel was leading the crowd back to
the cage. The three victims were groaning and twitching feebly
on their wheels but already seemed to have lapsed into uncon-
sciousness. Maybe Milo had been talking sense, she decided.
The thought that the agony to come would be brief lessened
slightly the knot of terror in her stomach.

"Ah, the demon is awake again," said Ezekiel, peering at Milo
with its binocular-like device through the wooden bars of the
cage. "Now you will answer my questions. Are you a creature of
Babylon? Does the Dark One give you the power to move faster
than any of the Lord's natural creations?"

"Why should I answer any of your questions, Ezekiel?" Milo
asked the machine casually. "You will only believe what you
want to believe. Why should I waste my breath?"

"If you don't answer my questions voluntarily you, and your
unclean companion, will be *forced* to speak," said Ezekiel. "And
I promise you that the torture you will endure will be a thousand
times worse than the pain of being broken on the wheel."

"And who gives you the authority to decide these matters?"
Milo asked the metal creature who called itself Ezekiel.

"The Lord God gives me the authority!" Ezekiel replied
loudly. "For thus saith the Lord God; when I shall make thee a
desolate city, like the cities that are not inhabited; when I shall
bring up the deep upon thee, and great waters shall cover thee;
when I shall bring thee down with them that descend into the pit,
with the people of old time, and shall set thee in the low parts of
the earth, in places desolate of old, with them that go down into
the pit, that thou be not inhabited; and I shall set glory in the land
of the living; I will make thee a terror, and thou *shalt be* no
more: though thou be sought for, yet shalt thou never be found
again, saith the Lord God!" There were murmurs of 'Amen'
from the crowd.

Milo, with difficulty, stood up. "Your name is not Ezekiel," he
told the creature firmly.

"I *am* Ezekiel, the hammer of the Lord!"

"You are nothing but an ancient, clapped-out *cyberoid*! What's your operating number and the name of your owner?"

The binoculars on the end of the arm twitched. "Wha-what did you say?" asked Ezekiel, its voice faltering.

"You heard me, cyberoid!" called Milo. "Your number and the name of your owner. You are required by law to tell me!"

Ezekiel rocked back on its massive legs then tried to speak again, but all that came out were a series of meaningless sounds. Milo laughed and flexed his arms. The manacles around his wrists fell apart with a *snap*. As he bent down and gripped the chains around his ankles he said to Jan, "Rusty as hell." The chains shattered in his hands. Then he blurred. The wooden bars of the cage exploded outwards and there were cries of fear from the crowd. Then gasps as they saw Milo seem to materialize on the back of Ezekiel's great box of a head. Milo was wrenching at something. A metal panel opened with a screech of protest. He plunged his hand inside and Ezekiel screamed. It was a flat, emotionless sound, like his speech, but Jan could sense the awful agony it represented. On hearing this the group of ragged people started to wail in terror. Some fell to their knees, others turned and ran.

Milo threw his head back and roared with laughter. He wore the maniacal expression Jan had seen before in the control room. He was larger again and radiated power . . . and something else. Milo finally withdrew his hand from the interior of Ezekiel's head and slowly the creature's scream faded away. Milo beamed down at Jan. "Impressive, eh?"

She gazed back at him in silent wonder. And fear.

"Now, my dear old cyberoid," Milo told the machine, "You are going to reach into the cage and gently sever the bonds of my companion. Mark her in any way and I'll boil your brains. Do it!"

Ezekiel trembled, then slowly it extended its mechanical arm. Jan flinched when she saw a blade extend from one of the metal 'fingers'. But Ezekiel cut through her bindings without touching her. When he'd finished Milo cried, "Don't just sit there. Come and join me. This clunky old piece of machinery is going to give us a free ride all the way to the Sky Tower!"

Jan hesitantly climbed down from the cage and moved to the rear of Ezekiel. Milo reached down and helped her up on to a narrow ridge that ran along the back of the creature's head. There were handholds as well. When she was beside Milo he slammed his hand on the top of Ezekiel's head. "Cyberoid! Your number and the name of your owner!"

Very slowly, as if each word was being squeezed out of it, the creature said, "My operating number is 0008005. My master is Hilary Du Cann of the Phobos Corporation."

"That's better," said Milo approvingly.

Ezekiel made a groaning sound. "But that was . . . long ago. The master is dead . . . and I have a new name . . . it is . . . ."

Milo reached into the recess in the top of Ezekiel's head. Jan saw a spark jump between the ends of two broken wires. Ezekiel screamed again.

"You have *no* new name!" Milo thundered. "You are still 0008005 and the property of Hilary Du Cann!"

"Yes! Yes! Please, no more pain!" begged Ezekiel.

"There'll be no more pain, 0008005, but only if you cooperate," Milo told the machine creature.

"I will! I will!"

"Fine. For a start, you will give me your command override code."

"I . . . I *can't*! It is not permitted . . . for unauthorized personnel to have access . . . Arghhhh!"

Jan winced as Ezekiel made its awful sound for the third time. She looked at Milo. He was grinning with pleasure.

"The code . . . the codeword is . . . Mozart-McCartney. Overriding command must be followed by 'Mozart-McCartney' . . . ."

Milo laughed. "Good. Then listen well, I am overriding all previous commands. I am your new master. My name is Milo. You will obey my every command. *Mozart-McCartney*. Do you understand?"

"Yes," said Ezekiel. "You are my new master. Your name is Milo. I will obey your every command."

"Did you hear that?" Milo yelled at the people cowering on the ground. None of them answered. Some whimpered. Milo smiled

257

at Jan. "Our fortunes have taken a change for the better, eh?"

"So it would seem," she answered shakily, "But I don't understand *how*. Why is this machine now obeying you?"

"It's not a machine, it's a cyberoid. It has a human brain inside it . . . well, *most* of a human brain."

"You mean this was once a *man*?" Jan asked in dismay.

"No. Its brain came from an unborn foetus grown in some laboratory. It would have been conditioned to obey the orders of its owner, but as cyberoid conditioning could never be one hundred percent guaranteed they had a safety factor built-in . . . a device linked directly with their pain centres. The device could be activated by a specific radio signal in the event of a cyberoid going out of control. I've activated this one's manually." Milo pointed at the wires inside the recess. "I've also revived its old conditioning. It *should* be completely cooperative from now on, but just to be certain I'm going to keep within reach of the pain activator." He slammed his palm down on Ezekiel's head again. "Listen to me, 0008005. You will order your followers here to fetch us clothing. Preferably cleaner than the rags they have on. And our weapons. They will also fetch us food and water and the means to carry both. Do you understand?"

"I understand, Milo."

"Then do it."

Ezekiel repeated Milo's instructions to the cowering and shocked group surrounding them. After some nervous muttering three women were despatched to fetch the required items. One returned shortly and deposited a bundle of clothing in front of the cyberoid. Milo said to Jan, "Go down and get dressed. I'll stay up here and make sure our friend behaves himself."

Jan climbed down off Ezekiel's back and warily moved around it, keeping an uneasy eye on its massive legs. She still didn't trust the machine creature, in spite of its new-found docility. She examined the clothes. They were anything but clean and smelt bad, but nothing like as bad as the garments that had been cut from her. She selected a pair of baggy pants with fewer holes than the others, a shirt made of a coarse, heavy material and a pair of battered leather boots. As she was dressing the other two women returned bearing her and Milo's weapons, two water bags and a sack which presumably contained food. The two women — one of whom was nothing but a bent skeleton covered in withered skin — nervously put their burdens within Jan's reach and hurriedly backed away. Like the others they kept casting looks of shocked disbelief at Ezekiel.

When she'd finished dressing and put on her weapons harness she climbed back up on to Ezekiel with the food and water. Milo showed her how to put the wires together inside Ezekiel that would cause him extreme agony, then descended to dress and pick up his own weapons. Jan looked at the three strange beings on the wheels. She shuddered at the state of their shattered limbs but was relieved to see that they were either unconscious or dead. She hoped it was the latter.

Milo rejoined her. She said to him, "You could have saved them too. Why didn't you?"

"Those toys?" He glanced briefly at them. "No. The timing would have been wrong. I had to take the cyberoid by surprise."

"You could have done it, Milo," she told him coldly. "But you wanted to see the girl suffer and die, didn't you?"

"Believe whatever you want. It's no matter to me. But just remember that *you're* still alive and those toys are dead. Or soon will be."

Yes, *I'm still alive*, she thought, *but for how much longer*? "Why do you call them toys?"

"Because that's what they were. Or rather their grandparents or great grandparents were. *Sex* toys, created to provide sexual pleasure for their owners. Many of the toys didn't breed true but the ancestors of these three obviously did." He suddenly slapped the top of the cyberoid's head. "Now, 0008005, it's time we got moving. But before we go, a question — are any of your weapons in operating order?"

"Yes. Not my guns. I have no ammunition for them. But my laser is still functioning."

"Good," said Milo, pleased. "That house, thirty degrees on your left. The one nearest to us. Fire your laser at it."

The bundle of metal tubes on the top of the head swivelled round. Jan saw a bright red line of light form between the end of one of the tubes and the ramshackle building that Milo had

259

indicated. Almost immediately the whole structure burst noisily into flames. The people moaned in terror. Milo, plainly enjoying himself, instructed Ezekiel to set fire to another building. As this one began to catch alight there were screams from inside. A door flew open and children of various ages, and a number of younger women carrying babies, came pouring out. All, to Jan's eyes, looked starved and in bad health. "Stop!" she cried to Milo as the cyberoid continued to fire at the building. Milo ignored her. Only when the building was completely in flames did he direct Ezekiel to turn the laser on another ramshackle structure. Soon most of the settlement was on fire, the flames spreading to the camouflaged netting above.

"Was all this necessary?" cried Jan over the crackle of burning wood and the screams of the fleeing inhabitants.

"Why waste your sympathy on these scum? They were about to murder you just to placate their God." He banged his fist on the cyberoid's head again. "Right, 0008005, let's get moving. Head towards the city. You know which direction it's in?"

"Yes," it replied and began to walk.

Very soon they were out in the bright sunlight again. Behind them the grim settlement of Ezekiel's people blazed furiously, sending up a column of black smoke above the blight land.

The cyberoid swayed violently from side to side as it walked and Jan found it difficult to hang on to the small handholds, which Milo had told her were there for the benefit of maintenance engineers. He also told her that Ezekiel must have access to some functioning power source somewhere which enabled him to recharge his fuel cell. It was probably located in the city.

After they had been travelling about an hour Jan was relieved when Milo suddenly ordered the cyberoid to halt. "What's wrong?" she asked as Milo peered intently into the trees on their left.

"I saw something glinting. Like glass. It's gone now."

"I didn't see anything."

"No, you wouldn't have," he said smugly and then directed Ezekiel to veer to the left.

They hadn't gone far when the dead trees thinned out and they entered a large clearing. In the centre of it was a jumble of white stones scattered over a considerable area.

"Looks like the remains of a villa. A big one," he said as the cyberoid approached the outskirts of the ruin. "I wonder what it was I saw flashing around here?" He ordered the cyberoid to stop. "You get down and check the place out," he told Jan. "I'll stay up here and make sure our fundamentalist tin-can doesn't get any funny ideas." Gratefully, Jan got down from the machine-creature's back. "I'm going for a pee first," she told Milo and headed for the nearest of the stone blocks. She had almost reached it when a cry made her turn . . . .

She was just in time to see the cyberoid pluck Milo off the back of its head with its mechanical arm, fling him to the ground and then crush him under one of its great metal feet.

Chapter Twenty-Six:

"And I will set my glory among the heathen, and all the heathen shall see my judgement that I have executed, and my hand that I have laid upon them!"

Ezekiel roared out these words as it kept stamping on Milo. Jan started back towards them then stopped; it was plain there was nothing she could do to help Milo. His body was already a shapeless mass of bloody meat. He had to be dead.

Milo the immortal. Dead.

Ezekiel stopped stamping on Milo's gory remains. The binoculars on their metal stalk turned in Jan's direction. The collection of tubes on the cyberoid's head followed suit. Jan flung herself on the ground. The red beam burnt through the air above her. She rolled, scrambled to her feet and ducked behind the block of stone.

"I am Ezekiel, Hammer of the Lord!" roared Ezekiel and she heard the sound of its great feet as it approached.

Keeping the stone block beneath her and Ezekiel she ran deeper into the ruins. She ducked and weaved around the scattered masonry, hoping to lose the cyberoid in the maze, but Ezekiel's roaring voice grew louder. "Therefore *as* I live, saith the Lord God, I will prepare thee unto blood, and blood shall pursue thee; sith thou hast not hated blood, even blood shall pursue thee!"

Jan ran faster. She ducked round another corner . . . .

. . . and found herself in a cul de sac.

Broken walls and stone blocks formed a kind of alleyway that ended in a blank expanse of white stone that was too high for her to scale. It was too late to back-track; Ezekiel was too close. She was trapped.

The consciousness that was observing Jan was not human and it was observing her with an objectivity that was chilling in its absoluteness. Though it had organic components within its system these components were entirely synthetic — the product of a long-vanished laboratory — and lacked the attributes common to all natural life. The entity literally had no emotions; no fears, no desires, no curiosity, no empathy at all with the world it observed through its myriad sensors. It had been programmed to preserve itself, but did not possess the innate drive to survive shared by all natural organisms forged in the genetic furnace of evolution. It was just *mind*, pure and simple, and therefore not really alive.

But dormant within its system of electronic and organic components was another mind, and this one was human. Or rather, it *had* been. The first mind deliberated on the problem for several nanoseconds and decided the situation warranted activating the other mind . . . .

"Ashley. Wake up."

"What?" (— *irritably* —)

"Look."

The other mind looked. Then it (— *said* —), "Jesus H., what are you waiting for, lame-brain?" (— *excitedly* —) "Let her in!"

When Jan saw an opening miraculously appear in the wall in front of her she didn't pause to think but plunged through it — and almost instantly collided with another wall. To her dismay, she found herself in a small, narrow room and the only door was the one she'd come through. She turned and saw Ezekiel striding down the alleyway. "And the Lord said unto him, Go through the midst of the city, through the midst of Jerusalem, and set a mark upon the foreheads of the men that sigh and that cry for all the abominations that be done in the midst thereof!" Jan searched frantically for some way of closing the opening but there wasn't any.

Ezekiel halted outside and bent down. "And to the others he said in mine hearing, Go ye after him through the city, and smite: let not your eye spare, neither have ye pity." It reached in through the opening with its mechanical arm. Jan pressed herself against the wall. "No!" she cried. "Leave me alone!"

The opening abrubtly closed and there was a *clang* as the end of Ezekiel's arm, sheared through, fell to the floor. Then the floor itself began to sink rapidly beneath Jan's feet and she realized that the whole room was descending into the ground in the same manner as one of the elevators in the *Lord Pangloth*. It seemed to her that the room travelled a long way before it slowed to a halt. She held her breath as the opening reappeared, letting in bright light. It took a few moments for her eyes to adjust to the light, then she saw that she was looking into a large room that was as lavishly furnished as any of the royal quarters on the *Pangloth*.

"I'm sorry. The light is obviously too bright for you. I'll dim them. It's been so long since they've been used." It was a girl's voice, friendly and reassuring. Jan stepped into the room but couldn't see anyone. The lights dimmed and then, suddenly, there she was standing in the centre of the room. Jan couldn't understand how she had missed seeing her before. As the girl approached her Jan got a shock; for a moment she thought it was Ceri, but then she saw that though the resemblance was very strong, the girl wasn't Ceri's double. Her eyes were brown instead of blue and her hair was much lighter.

She stopped some five feet away from Jan and smiled warmly. She wore strange clothes: a very tight pair of blue trousers cut low on the hips, an equally tight yellow shirt, the front of which was tied in a knot that revealed her midriff. Her feet were bare. "Hi, I'm Ashley! What's your name?" said the girl brightly.

Jan told her her name, then asked if she could sit down. She had started to tremble. Reaction was setting in.

"Oh, of course!" said Ashley. "Sit wherever you like, Jan."

Jan collapsed on to a well-upholstered couch and wrapped her arms around herself. Ashley, she noticed, remained standing. "Why was that cyberoid trying to kill you?" she asked Jan.

Jan shook her head wearily. "I don't know. It was mad, I think. That's what Milo said on the way here . . . that it had gone insane over the years . . . Milo said it was very, very old . . . Milo . . . ." She just couldn't accept that Milo was *dead*. It was impossible!

"Milo was the man the cyberoid killed before he started chasing you?" Ashley asked her gently.

"Yes. You saw it happen?" Jan asked her, surprised.

"No. I watched a replay. Was he your husband?"

"No . . . not my husband," said Jan and smiled wryly. She wondered what Ashley meant by 'replay'.

"Your lover then? Your boyfriend?"

Jan sighed. "No. He wasn't even my friend, not really. He was just *Milo* . . . and now he's gone. I can't get over the shock. And I don't know what I'm going to do now." To her own surprise she started to cry. She knew she wasn't crying for Milo; she was crying for herself. "I won't be able to survive in the blight lands without him."

"You can stay here, Jan," said Ashley. "For as long as you like. It's been so long since I had any company."

"You live here by yourself?"

"Yes. Except for Carl, and he doesn't count. He's not really a male; he's just a computer program, but I call him Carl to make him seem a little more human. Not that it works . . . ." She gave a wistful sigh, then her face brightened again. "Please say you'll stay here! It would make me so happy!"

Jan wiped her eyes and looked around the large room with its low ceiling. Then she looked back at Ashley. She felt something was not quite right with her but she couldn't decide what it was. "What exactly is this place?" she asked.

"A shelter," the girl replied. "Originally it was built as a nuclear bomb shelter but years later my parents had it refurbished as a shelter against the Gene Wars." Ashley's expression grew sad. "It didn't save them though. One of the later designer plague viruses penetrated the filters and other protective barriers and they died. In there. . . . " Ashley turned and pointed at one of several closed doors leading off from the room.

"But *you* survived," said Jan, feeling increasingly puzzled. Her feeling that there was something very strange about Ashley was growing stronger.

"Oh, yes, I survived. And I guess I always will." She didn't sound pleased at the prospect.

Jan had a revelation. "You're an immortal!" she cried. "Like Milo!"

"Your friend was an immortal?" asked Ashley, surprised. "I thought they had all been killed off centuries ago. Anyway, he's certainly not an immortal now, is he?"

Mystified, Jan said, "But you must be an immortal. You said your parents died during the Gene Wars. And you don't look any older than me."

"How old are you?" Ashley asked with what sounded like genuine interest.

Wishing that the girl would stick to the subject Jan said, "I'm eighteen . . . no, I must be nineteen now." She realized her birthday must have occurred two or three months ago, but she had lost track of the time.

"I'm younger than you, then. I'm only seventeen. And I'll always be seventeen. Sweet seventeen." She gave a wistful sigh again.

Jan began to wonder if Ashley was crazy. Perhaps she was just a refugee from the blight land, like her, who had entered this strange underground place by accident and was now creating fantasies about her past. As she deliberated on the best way of handling Ashley if she was indeed insane, Jan said, "Where do you get your food and water from? And would there be enough for both of us if I was to stay here?"

"Oh," said Ashley and put a finger to her lips. "I hadn't thought of that. Just a moment, I'll ask Carl." For a very brief moment her eyes went blank, then she smiled at Jan. "Carl says he can activate the food synthesizer again. The basic organic fuels are in the deep freeze and will have to be thawed, which will take some time, but he can get you some water right away. There's an underground stream down there." She pointed at the floor.

Jan stared at her. She *was* mad. "Er . . . this 'Carl' person just spoke to you and told you all that?" she asked hesitantly.

Ashley nodded. "We have a direct link."

"I see," said Jan as if that explained everything. "So there is food and water here." Mention of water made her aware of a raging thirst, and she hoped the water wasn't another of Ashley's fantasies. But the girl appeared physically healthy, at least, so she must have been getting food and water from somewhere. Yet, oddly enough, she hadn't mentioned eating or drinking herself. "Ah, don't you and Carl need food or water?" she asked, trying to humour her.

"I told you, Carl is a computer program. Programs don't eat or drink." She gave a nervous giggle.

"And what about you?"

Ashley bit her lip and looked uncomfortable. She didn't answer.

"Well?" persisted Jan.

"I suppose I'd better tell you," said Ashley sadly. "You would have found out sooner or later."

"Found out what?"

"This." Ashley walked over to where Jan was sitting on the couch and held out her right hand to her. Puzzled, Jan went to take hold of it . . . .

. . . and her hand passed straight through Ashley's as if it wasn't there.

"See?" said Ashley and sighed.

Jan shrank back on the couch and stared at her with terrified eyes. "You're a ghost!" she cried.

"Well, sort of."

Jan stared about frantically. The luxurious room had suddenly become a frightening place. She was trapped inside it hundreds of feet below the earth with this dead *thing*. "I want to leave! Please let me go!" she pleaded.

"Oh shit, I was afraid you'd react this way," said Ashley, backing away from the couch. "Look, I'm not the sort of ghost you seem to think I am."

"You're not dead?" Jan asked nervously.

"Oh, I'm dead all right," Ashley admitted brightly. "Or rather, the *original* me is. I'm just a recording."

"A what?"

"You know, a recording. A copy. There was once, centuries ago, a real, live girl called Ashley Vee and a copy was made of her mind and stored in a computer. And I'm that copy."

"But I can *see* you," protested Jan.

"What you can see is a holographic projection controlled by the computer. You do know what a hologram is, do you?"

Jan remembered the 'entertainments' of the Aristos. Milo had called them holographic projections, and they had been remarkably realistic too. She relaxed slightly. "So you're not a ghost . . .?"

"Not a *real* one. Only an electronic one. So please don't go. There's nothing for you to be afraid of. Please say you'll stay."

Jan didn't know what to do. The knowledge that Ashley wasn't a supernatural apparition was comforting, but at the same time she still found her presence unnerving. The holographic people in the 'entertainments' had appeared real too but they hadn't carried on conversations with you. "Who did . . . this . . . to you? And why?" Jan asked hesitantly.

"My parents," Ashley answered. "I had this dangerous hobby, you see. Glider flying. Do you know what a glider is?"

Ruefully, she said, "Only too well." And she told her of the escape from the *Lord Pangloth* in the Japanese glider.

"Oh, I don't mean hang-gliding. My glider looked like a plane, with a cockpit and everything. It was called Pegasus, and it had a wing-span of over a hundred feet. I could go up thousands of feet in it. It was beautiful. But my parents were right. I crashed it. And died."

"You mean you can remember being *killed*?" Jan asked, shocked.

"Oh no. The last update on the recording occurred two weeks before I was killed, so I have no memory of the last two weeks of

267

'my' life, including the crash itself. Anyway, fearing that I was going to kill myself, my parents wanted to preserve me in some way. Their original intention was to implant the recording of my personality and memories into a clone of myself, but though they were rich they weren't powerful enough to arrange to have me cloned. At the time I was alive it was highly illegal, you see. So they settled for second best. A hologram. Me."

Jan was silent for a time as she stared hard at Ashley. The illusion was perfect. It was hard to believe she wasn't made of flesh and blood. Then she said, "What's it, well, *feel* like? Being what you are, I mean."

Ashley frowned. "Well, that's kind of hard to put into words. But I can tell you it's sure not the same as being alive . . . as being *real*."

"But you think, and you have feelings, don't you?" Jan asked.

"Oh yes, I can think. At least, I *think* I can think. It's hard to be sure. The same with feelings. I *think* I have feelings but they're not the same as what I had when I was alive. Do you know what I mean?"

"No," admitted Jan.

Ashley sighed. "It's difficult to explain . . . it's as if my feelings were *imitation* feelings. Unreal. Yes — " she gave a nod " — I definitely feel unreal. But then that shouldn't be surprising . . . I am, after all, just an electronic shadow of my former self." She smiled at Jan then added, "But I'm fading, I know it. The human bits of me. I'm afraid I'll eventually end up just like Carl. And, God, he's *boring*."

Jan was trying to imagine what it must be like for Ashley but it was beyond her capability. "How long have you been, er, like this?"

"Just a sec, I'll ask Carl." And then without a pause she said, "Four hundred and thirty-nine years."

"That long? How awful! How do you spend your time down here? You must get very bored."

"I do, when I'm awake. Most of the time I'm asleep. Well, not really asleep — I don't dream or anything — I'm actually shut down. But when I'm awake I can make time go very fast, which helps. To talk to you I've had to really slow down my thought processes. I haven't had subjective time to go this slowly since my last visitor."

"When was that?" asked Jan.

"Oh, about eighty years ago. His name was Vic. A very pretty boy. He took shelter in the ruins to escape some marauders who were pursuing him. He stayed here for ten years then he got sick and died. He didn't like it down here, which was a shame. That's him over there." Ashley turned and pointed. At the same moment the lights brightened and Jan saw, lying on the far side of the room, what appeared to be a pile of bones.

Jan was shocked. "You just left him lying there?"

"What else could I do? I kind of lack substance, as you've already noticed," Ashley said and laughed. "There used to be a couple of servo-mechanisms that kept the shelter clean but they broke down ages ago."

A worrying thought had occurred to Jan. "You said Vic wanted to leave here. Why didn't he?"

"Oh, Carl wouldn't let him, of course. Carl acts as my protector, you see. He doesn't want knowledge of the shelter's existence to get out, so he never lets my visitors leave."

Jan said, "You mean he's not going to let me leave either?"

Ashley nodded gravely. "I'm afraid so. You aren't going to be upset, are you?"

Chapter Twenty-Seven:

"You know what I miss most of all about being alive?" asked Ashley.

"What?"

"Flying. Flying my glider was the greatest. I loved it so much, being up there in the sky."

"Anything would be better than being stuck down here," Jan said with feeling. She had only been in the shelter twelve days and already the place profoundly depressed her. At first she had appreciated the sanctuary it had provided from the dangers of the blight land, especially Ezekiel, as well as the food and drink — as bland as the latter had turned out to be — but very quickly she had grown restless and uneasy. It was the fact that she wasn't allowed to leave that aggravated her dislike of living in the shelter. If she had a free choice she might have been prepared to spend a month or more down there fairly happily. As it was she had become desperate to return to the surface, even though she had no idea of what she would do if she did manage to get back up top. She sighed.

Ashley looked at her with concern. "I'm sorry you don't like it down here." Today she was dressed in very short trousers, which she called, appropriately enough, 'shorts', a white vest and white shoes and socks. She called these garments her 'tennis outfit'. A couple of days previously Jan had asked her why she appeared in different clothes each day. Ashley had shrugged and said, "It added to the sense of realism for my parents. I was photographed holographically in lots and lots of different clothes, you see, and they're all stored in the computer, along with me. Besides, I like to look attractive even now. Mom used to say I was a vain little exhibitionist but I *was* pretty, wasn't I?" And she twirled around to show herself off. Jan had said, bleakly, "Yes, you were. Very." The fact that Ashley's beautiful body was as insubstantial as a shadow was beginning, she had realized, to get under her skin in more ways than one. And her more than passing resemblance to Ceri didn't help matters. Another reason for leaving the shelter and returning to the surface . . . .

"I don't like being a prisoner. If only I was allowed out for a few minutes of fresh air every day I probably wouldn't mind it so much down here."

"Jan, you know if it was up to me you could come and go as you like, but Carl's in charge and he doesn't trust you."

"I know that." Jan had tried speaking to Carl directly on several occasions. It was an unnerving experience, talking to a disembodied voice that *sounded* human but was frustratingly *un*human in its responses.

"Anyway, why do you want to risk going topside again? That crazy cyberoid is probably still looking for you."

"You told me Carl hadn't seen any sign of him for over a week."

"Not in the vicinity of the villa, but there's a limit to Carl's sensor range. The cyberoid could still be lurking nearby in the woods."

"I suppose so," said Jan, worriedly. She had nightmares still about Ezekiel. She would be running through an endless stone maze with the cyberoid close behind her yelling its crazy words about death and vengeance while leaving bloody footprints behind it. The blood was Milo's . . . .

"What about Sky Lords? Any more sightings?"

"I'll ask Carl," said Ashley. "Yep. One of them passed almost directly overhead a couple of hours ago."

"*Damn.*" Carl had made sightings of either the *Lord Pangloth* or the *Perfumed Breeze* almost every day since she had arrived. The warlord was not giving up. She shivered at the thought of what he would do to her if she fell into his hands again.

"See?" said Ashley, as if reading her mind. "You're much better off staying down here. With me. Now come on, stop looking so glum and tell me more about your adventures."

Ashley had demonstrated an inexhaustible curiosity about Jan's life and Jan had obliged by spending hours telling her about Minerva and the events following the bombing and her capture. "Adventures? I haven't had any adventures. I've been through an *ordeal.*" *Which is still going on*, she added under her breath.

"Well, they sound like adventures to me" Ashley told her. "Go on, tell me again about Prince Caspar. He sounds dreamy."

Jan sighed. "What more can I say about him?"

"Tell me what happened when you were in bed together."

Jan couldn't help feeling mildly shocked. "Why do you want to know that?"

Ashley smiled mischievously. "Why do you think?"

"I don't want to be impolite," said Jan slowly, "But I don't understand how you can be interested in sex when you don't have, er, a body."

"But I told you before — I still have feelings. Well, like I said, they're more the *memory* of feelings than the real thing . . . ."

"Feelings, yes," said Jan with a frown. "That I understand, I think, but sex is, well, an *appetite*."

"Oh yes, I have appetites. I mean, they're just the same as feelings, aren't they?"

"I suppose so," said Jan doubtfully.

"My appetites got recorded along with the rest of me," Ashley told her. "They didn't think of that when they made me what I am. It wouldn't have mattered if I'd been transcribed into a cloned body, but being what I am it's impossible, of course, for me to satisfy any of my appetites. At first it was really awful; I was hungry all the time. But then a technician made some adjustments and kind of dulled my appetite for food. The scientists said they couldn't just remove all my appetites without the possibility of eradicating parts of my personality completely."

Jan was trying to imagine what it would be like to be a mind without a body. She tried to imagine being hungry for over 400 years while knowing you would never have the chance to eat again. "You poor thing," she said.

"Oh, I'm used to it now," said Ashley cheerfully. "Besides, like all my other 'feelings' my appetites are slowly fading away and one day I won't have any at all."

"But now you still have, er, sexual urges?"

"Yeah. Kind of. It was a bit of a problem when Vic was here. I told you he was really pretty, didn't I?" She glanced wistfully at the bones by the wall. "It was a bit of a problem for him too. Not being able to touch me made him go crazy at times."

Jan felt a twinge of sympathy for the dead Vic. "Did you ever have a lover? When you were alive, I mean?"

"Oh sure. I had two. One was my gliding instructor. He was over thirty but he was dreamy. We did it once in his training glider, fifteen thousand feet up. Marvellous!" She shook her head in wonder at the memory. "So come on, tell me all about what you got up to with your Prince Caspar. I want to hear *everything*!"

Another three days dragged by. Jan felt increasingly oppressed by the shelter, which consisted of five separate rooms. Apart from the main one, the living room, there were two bedrooms — one of which contained the bones of Ashley's parents — a kitchen and a bathroom. That, at least, was the accessible area of the place, but Jan knew there were hidden areas containing various machines, including the projectors that created Ashley's holographic image, which could appear in any part of the shelter. The power source for all the machinery, Carl had informed Jan, came from heat deep within the earth.

In the hope of persuading Carl to let her out Jan spent more and more time talking to 'him', much to Ashley's annoyance. He persistently refused to discuss the reason for her containment but was willing to provide any other kind of information she required. More to alleviate her boredom than anything else she asked about the old world before the Gene Wars, curious to see if Milo had been telling the truth or merely spinning more tall tales. In response, Carl dimmed the lights and a glowing screen appeared suspended in the air. Carl then announced he would replay a series of news transmissions from the periods concerned, which prompted a groan from Ashley. "Oh God, it's like being back at school . . . ."

For two days Jan watched fascinated as she watched the images and listened to the different voices from the past. At first it was hard to follow what was going on — many of the words were meaningless to her — but eventually she began to comprehend the overall picture. It seemed to fit with what Milo had told her, and the little she had learned from Ceri.

Long before the Gene Wars the world had been faced with two serious threats; the first had come from nuclear weapons, which had originally been controlled by the two big empires of the latter half of the twentieth century, the Soviet Union and the United States of America. When, at the end of that century, these weapons had spread to many other countries these two empires got very nervous. Then came the 'Little Armageddon' war in the Middle East, where nuclear weapons were used for the first time since the Second World War. This settled the minds of the rulers of the two empires and led to the formation of the Soviet-American Alliance at the beginning of the twenty-first century.

The Alliance's first act was to declare all nuclear weapons banned. There was much opposition to this ultimatum, not only from countries who'd possessed their own nuclear arsenals for a long time, such as a country called France, but also from the Federation of Islamic States who had been the victors in the 'Little Armageddon' war.

The Alliance reacted ruthlessly to this opposition. Using a few of their own nuclear weapons with what the commentator called 'surgical precision', in harness with their 'orbiting beam weapons', they 'cauterized the problem areas'. When the dust cleared the Islamic Federation was once again a collection of individual countries and France had been reduced to a purely agricultural economy. The other nations saw the point of the Alliance's argument and handed over their nuclear weapons. When the Alliance was satisfied that no other such weapons existed, nor the means to manufacture them in future, it destroyed its own nuclear arsenal and remaining nuclear reactors. The nuclear age was over.

The other great threat had appeared in the early nineteen-eighties, though it had probably been around unnoticed for a long time before that. It was a plague caused by a type of virus that normally only affected animals — a 'lentivirus'. The theory was that the virus had jumped the 'species barrier' from a species of African monkeys to humans.

Whatever the origin of the virus it spread rapidly and by the end of the twentieth century had infected one in every ten people on the planet. It was literally decimating the world's population. And being a lentivirus it possessed genetic characteristics that made it very difficult to combat. The genegineers — called 'microbiologists', Jan noted, in these early reports — tried for years to create a safe vaccine but without success.

A parallel line of attack on the virus had been going on for some time by other genegineers. They had been trying to build their *own* virus — a synthetic 'hunter-killer' virus using altered genetic material from the plague virus itself. A virus is a genetic parasite — it invades a cell and hi-jacks the cell's own DNA in order to replicate itself. The hunter-killer virus would, in theory, not only seek out and destroy the plague virus within an infected system but also penetrate infected cells and insert modified DNA into the cells' nucleii that would neutralize the DNA created by the invading plague virus, thus preventing further replication. That was the theory, but to turn it into working reality involved major breakthroughs in the mapping and manipulation of human DNA. The enormity of their task was succinctly summed up by one startling image — that if you were to lay all the DNA in a single human being end to end the chain would reach the moon and back 8,000 times.

Finally, however, they did succeed — their synthetic virus acted as both a cure and a super-vaccine and the plague was quickly eradicated.

But the major breathroughs that had been achieved in human genetic engineering on the way to creating the synthetic virus had other important repercussions for the whole human race: in the same way that the virus had been used to cure infected cells it was now possible to make all manner of modifications to human DNA. It could be altered to improve the immune system, to eradicate diseases like cancer, to increase the human life span . . . all the modifications that were eventually incorporated into the Standard Prime.

At the same time genetic engineering in other areas had also made tremendous progress — new strains of cereal had been created that were disease resistant and could grow in arid conditions; the 'bio-chip' had replaced the silicon chip, resulting in much more efficient computer systems; new forms of bacteria had been created to perform a whole variety of industrial functions, from producing cheap fuels to making things like imitation wood pulp that could be turned into paper; there were the biological fuel cells and synthetic chlorophyll that turned the sun's rays into electricity . . . .

The list of wonders seemed endless. It seemed as if all the traditional scourges of humanity would be eradicated forever. The genegineers had brought the world to the verge of a true Golden Age.

But it was not to be.

According to the long-dead voices that accompanied the images on the floating screen it was the creation of the Standard

Prime genetically-altered human being that led indirectly to the Gene Wars. Up until then, and for some time after that, the United Nations possessed real power, as it was backed by the Soviet-American Alliance. It had enough power to enforce its rulings on those areas of micro-biological research and genetic manipulation that were forbidden but, as Milo had told her, the coming of the Standard Prime caused the break-up of the bigger nations into independent states. The disintegration of both America and Russia into smaller states meant, of course, the end of the Alliance and, in turn, the end of the power that had been wielded by the United Nations.

In the chaos that followed it was the multi-national corporations, most of which relied on genetic engineering patents for their wealth, who emerged as the true holders of power. And with the United Nations effectively finished as a law enforcing agency it meant all the restraints on genetic engineering were gone. The corporations could now do whatever they wanted.

Even before then there had been rumours of the rich and powerful experimenting in forbidden areas. There were tales of incredible creations hidden behind locked doors; of billionaires stocking their private islands and estates with all manner of exotic creatures — sexual fantasies made flesh by the genegineers; and there were stories that certain heads of states and corporations were building up secret armies composed of terrible beings who were nothing but living weapons.

All these rumours turned out to be true.

With the United Nations and the Alliance gone the corporations began to war amongst themselves. The independent states were draggd into the conflict, having to pledge allegiance to one corporation or the other. The Gene Wars had begun.

After a decade of fighting using their genetically engineered armies, the Wars entered a new and more deadly stage when one of the corporations initiated germ warfare — something that all the corporations had originally sworn not to do. It was the beginning of the end.

The first targets were agricultural ones — cereal crops and the like. Then came fungi engineered to eat vital parts of electronic systems, as well as practically everything else. Finally the inevitable happened — the unleashing of the designer plagues specifically engineered to kill people.

Millions and millions died. Whole cities became deserted virtually overnight. Civilization collapsed.

Carl informed Jan at this point that there were no more news tapes.

Jan had been profoundly moved by what she had seen during her two days of watching the screen, but what had most affected her had been a report on Minerva shortly after it had been established as an independent state. Jan wept as she saw what Minerva had once been and what a sad remnant of that once great society *her* Minerva had been. She also saw, reluctantly, that the early Minervans *had* made use of Old Science. In fact, as Milo had told her, the very creation of a society where women could overthrow the natural inequalities imposed by their sex rested on the work of the genegineers.

But though it went against all she had been taught by her religious teachers, she found she could now come to terms with this knowledge. The important thing was the ideal behind Minerva itself and she felt a huge weight of responsibility descend on her as she realized that she had been cast by fate, or the Mother God, to be the last, living embodiment of that ideal. It was up to her to keep it alive. Not only alive but to see it somehow flourish again . . . .

Some hope of that, she thought bitterly.

As two more days passed Jan began to suspect, from the evasive way Carl reacted to her requests to be set free, that it might not be him that was keeping her prisoner but *Ashley*.

The idea made sense. Ashley seemed to have control over Carl in all other areas. She was determined to keep Jan with her but blamed the situation on Carl so as to not attract Jan's anger. Presuming that this was the case Jan realized she would now have to concentrate on trying to persuade Ashley that she should be set free.

But how?

It was the morning of the sixteenth day and Jan was in the

bathroom cutting her hair. She had decided that the long Aristo style was too big a nuisance and that it would be better to have it cropped short. She was staring at her reflection in the mirror when a possible solution to her problems occurred to her. She froze as the plan unfolded in her mind like a seed sprouting. The seed grew . . . it put down roots, leaves spread and, finally, a flower opened its petals. *She had the solution.*

Chapter Twenty-Eight:

Trying to conceal her state of intense excitement, Jan walked back into the living room and said calmly, "Ashley, are you there?"

"Of course," came Ashley's voice and she materialized in front of Jan. Today she was wearing a long back dress that left one breast bare. She looked very beautiful. "What do you want to talk about?"

"Flying."

Ashley's face lit up. "My favourite subject!"

"I know. What would you say if I told you there's a chance you could fly again?"

Ashley stared at her. "What do you mean? There's no possible way I can fly again. I'm trapped down here. Like you. No, I'm more trapped than you. I'm in a computer. You *know* that."

"Yes. I've been learning a lot about computers. First from Milo and now from Carl. I told you about Milo's plan, didn't I? How he intended to enter the Sky Tower in the city and use the computer within it to summon down the Sky Angel from space?"

"Yes, yes," said Ashley impatiently. "But what's that got to do with *me*?"

"You and Carl can be separated from the computer, can't you? The essential bits of you, I mean. The programs."

"Of course. We're on the same piece of software. Why?"

278

"The type of computer here — are its parts interchangeable with other computers? Such as the ones in the city?" Jan asked her.

"Most likely," said Ashley. Then after a pause she said, "I've just asked Carl and he said yes. All the bio-chip computer systems were compatible."

Jan said, "So if I were to take your 'software', take it into the city and insert it in the computer in the Sky Tower you and Carl would come to life again — inside *that* computer?"

"Yes," said Ashley doubtfully. "Provided that the computer there was still working. . . ."

"It is. Milo established that from the *Lord Pangloth*'s control room."

"So?" Ashley shrugged. "What good would it do me to be transferred to this other computer? I wouldn't even have my holographic projection facilities."

"I haven't finished yet. Once inside that computer you and Carl would be in control of it, right? You would be able to take over its functions?"

"Yes," said Ashley with an impatient sigh. "Provided you removed the original software first."

"Good. Then you and Carl could do what Milo planned to do. Make the Sky Tower computer send the signal that would bring the Sky Angel down from space?"

"Well, Carl could, I suppose," said Ashley, frowning. "But I still don't see the point."

"If I had access to the Sky Angel I could then take your software from the tower's computer and insert it in the Sky Angel's. And what would happen then?" Ashley didn't answer for some time. Jan guessed she was in communication with Carl. Then, with eyes wide with excitement, she said, "I could become linked up with the Sky Angel's every sensor. I could control its every movement. I could *be* the Sky Angel!"

"That's what I thought," said Jan with satisfaction.

"So what are we waiting for?" cried Ashley. "Let's leave right away. I'll show you how to remove the software."

"Calm down," Jan cautioned. "You must know that everything I just told you is out of the question."

Ashley looked stricken. "Why? *Why* is it out of the question?" she demanded.

"Well, for a start I can't leave here, can I? Carl won't let me."

"Oh, is that all?" said Ashley, relieved. "Don't worry, I'll soon sort him out."

I thought you would, thought Jan in triumph.

Jan was almost ready to leave. But now that the moment was near Jan was suddenly unwilling to return to the surface. It *was* safe down in the shelter while the surface held nothing but dangers. And even with the weapons that Ashley had supplied her from a hidden compartment in the main bedroom she knew her chances of reaching the Sky Tower were not good. There was also the strong possibility that she would succumb to whatever plague viruses or spores still lurked in the city itself.

When she'd expressed this latter fear, Ashley had conferred with Carl, then said brightly, "Oh, you can wear an anti-contamination suit!" Another previously concealed panel had opened in the main bedroom to reveal a row of hanging, one-piece suits made of some smooth, white material. Jan took one of them out and examined it. It had a hood that would completely cover the head. Like the old clothes of Ashley's that Jan was now wearing in preference to the smelly rags of Ezekiel's people the suit seemed to be in good condition despite its great age. She asked Ashley about this.

"Oh, it's probably to do with the lack of air," she told Jan uninterestedly. "Carl pumps all the air out of the shelter when I don't have, er, visitors. He lowers the temperature too. Go on, put it on."

Jan had obediently climbed into the anti-contamination suit and closed all the seals. She peered out through the visor on the head-piece. Below the visor was a protruding nozzle which admitted air whenever she breathed in. She presumed the nozzle contained filters to keep out harmful organisms. Ashley confirmed this.

"Do they work?" Jan asked her.

"I don't know. The suits were to be used in an emergency. If Mum and Dad had to make a journey out on the surface for some

280

reason. But they never got a chance to use them. The plague got in here first."

"Through the same sort of filters?" Jan asked, her heart sinking.

"I guess so," said Ashley, reluctantly.

"Well, this is a waste of time then," said Jan, and she unsealed the hood and pushed it back so that it hung behind her. She decided, however, to keep the suit on. Its material was reassuringly thick and would offer some protection out in the blight land.

The weapons that Carl had advised her to select from the small armoury were two rifle-like devices. One, he informed her, was a laser. The other fired explosive projectiles which, he told her, were 'smart bullets'. "When you have your target centred in the scope on top of the weapon simply press the firing button. The image in the scope is imprinted on the projectile's 'brain' and it will make all the necessary manoeuvres to reach its target. Then it explodes."

Jan had been impressed. Surely the weapon would be more than enough to deal with Ezekiel if she should encounter the creature.

"I've recharged the power units on both weapons," said Carl, but then added blandly, "The laser should function efficiently but I can't guarantee that the ammunition in the other weapon hasn't deteriorated to the point of being useless."

"Oh, great," Jan had muttered.

Now she stood in the living room, weighed down by both weapons, her sword harness and a backpack containing food and water. "All ready?" Ashley asked eagerly. She looked very excited.

"I suppose so," Jan answered without enthusiasm.

"Carl and I will shut down now. Then a panel will open and reveal the computer console. Carl has told you how to remove the software?"

"Yes."

"The elevator will operate automatically. Carl says there's no sign of the cyberoid, or any Sky Lords."

"Good," said Jan, her mouth dry.

"Right then, here we go . . . Oh, and Jan, you will be *very* careful with the software, won't you? I know I'm not really alive but I still don't want to die. Again."

"Don't worry, I'll take care of you."

Ashley then vanished. There was silence.

"Ashley, Carl?" said Jan.

No answer. She suddenly felt very alone. Then she gave a start as a panel slid open in the wall in front of her with a mechanical whine. She saw a row of lights. She approached the console and pressed the two buttons that Carl had told her to press. A small glass panel slid open in the console and she reached inside and withdrew the software. Jan was surprised to see that it consisted of a small tube about four inches long and one and a half inches in width. She found it hard to believe that it contained all of Ashley's memories, her mind and emotions, not to mention Carl as well. She carefully put it in her backpack and turned towards the elevator. As she approached it the door opened.

She hesitated when she saw Ezekiel's mechanical hand still lying on the floor of the elevator. Then she stepped over it and kicked it out into the living room with the toe of her boot. The door closed.

When the door opened again Jan was dazzled by bright sunlight. Then she gagged as the stench of the fungus hit her. She was tempted to put the hood back on but feared it would restrict her vision and hearing. She wanted to be fully alert for any sign of Ezekiel.

The alley between the stones was empty. She emerged cautiously from the elevator, the laser in her hands. The projectile weapon remained strapped over her shoulder. Slowly she retraced her footsteps of nineteen days ago until the spot where Milo died was visible once again. She hesitated by the great block of white stone, still expecting the cyberoid to leap shrieking into view at any moment.

Finally, she approached the site of Milo's death. There was nothing left of him but bones. Animals had eaten his flesh, insects had stripped the remaining organic matter from his bones.

His bones gleamed.

She squatted down beside them. They weren't ordinary bones. They seemed to be made of a mixture of metal and some other material. None of them had been damaged by Ezekiel's onslaught. Even Milo's skull was intact. It had a bluish sheen to it, as did his other bones.

She reached out with tentative fingers and touched it. Then she came to a decision, hooked a finger through one of the eye sockets and picked it up. It was very light. She stood and, after a cautious scan of the nearby trees, took off her pack and put Milo's skull inside it. Then she shouldered her pack again and headed towards the city.

It was mid-afternoon when she reached the outskirts of the city. She had got that far without serious incident, with the exception of an encounter with one of the big reptiles. It had come lumbering towards her through the trees, but she had fired the laser at it and the thing had abruptly collapsed into a twitching heap when it was still some fifty feet away. There had been no sign of Ezekiel, but Jan couldn't shake off the feeling that it was near. And following her.

The outskirts of the city consisted of the ruins of private dwelling places set in their own rather spacious grounds. The fungus, she noticed, didn't grow in the same profusion as it did in the woods. She paused to rest, sitting down on the remains of a stone wall. She propped the laser up alongside her then took one of the canteens out of the back-pack and had a drink of water.

Some minutes later she decided to push on but before she did she pulled the hood on and sealed it. Maybe it would do her no good at all, or maybe it was too late and one of the designer plagues was already at work inside her body, but it was better than nothing.

As Jan walked she kept turning to look behind her, the laser at the ready. She would give Ezekiel, or anything else for that matter, no chance of catching her by surprise. Occasionally she also looked upwards but the clear sky remained devoid of Sky Lords.

The further she penetrated into the city the less fungus there was. It was as if even those loathsome growths shunned this place of such awful death. It was hot wearing the hood and sweat streamed down her face but she was determined to keep it on. What she would do when she became desperate for a drink of water, or needed to take a pee, she would worry about later.

She was passing vehicles now. Some had wheels but many didn't and she wondered how the latter managed to move about. She peered into their interiors occasionally, but there was no trace left of their long-dead owners apart from scraps of clothing. Yet the upholstery on the seats looked almost new.

The buildings grew higher and closer together as she continued onwards. Jan could still see the upper part of the Sky Tower looming ahead of her but it didn't seem to be getting any closer. With alarm, she realized the sun would be going down soon.

Her footsteps on the strange surface of the roadway echoed back and forth from the walls and façades of the buildings. She kept to the middle of the road, nervously eyeing the darkened doorways and blank windows. The feeling that she was being watched was getting stronger. Jan stopped and listened carefully. Surely if Ezekiel was close by she would hear its heavy tread. But there was no sound at all. She continued on, keeping a tight grip on the laser, which provided a certain comfort.

The sun sank behind the tall buildings. Long shadows filled the artificial valley she moved through. Jan wished Milo was with her, despite everything she had felt about him. She thought of his skull resting in her backpack and wondered again why she had decided to take it. Probably because she felt she owed something to his memory . . . .

Her head was aching. Was it the first symptom of plague? She was thirsty too. If she was sick it wasn't going to make any difference if she removed the hood to drink some water.

She resisted the temptation. Darkness quickly fell and she stopped to remove the recharged flashlight that Carl had provided her with. It was difficult holding it and the laser together, but the powerful beam of light reassured her as she swept it back and forth ahead of her. But the feeling that she was being watched remained.

Jan was exhausted by the time she entered the plaza in which stood the Sky Tower. She rocked back dizzily on her heels as she tilted back her head and stared up at it. How on earth was she going to get to its summit? There were glass cylinders on its side which were obviously exterior elevators, but without any power source they were useless.

As she walked across the plaza, which was covered in different coloured tiles illustrated with drawings of balloons similar to the ones used by the Bandalans, she became aware that a fountain was working. She stopped again and stared at it. As she wondered how it operated after all this time she became even more acutely aware of her thirst.

She turned away from it and continued on towards the Sky Tower. The base of the Tower, she saw, was open on all sides — supported by a series of pillars that appeared to be ridiculously thin to be the foundations of such an immense structure. Jan climbed up some steps and went inside. She swept the beam about. The lobby was empty apart from a circular elevator and a staircase that led up into the ceiling. She went to the stairs and sat down on the bottom one. She intended to rest for a while and then begin the long climb. She hoped that the stairs continued all the way to the top, otherwise she didn't know what she was going to do.

Jan awoke with a start. She hadn't meant to go to sleep. She sat up and felt for the laser and the flashlight. She found the flashlight. The laser was nowhere to be found.

As a flutter of panic began to grow in her stomach she switched on the flashlight. The beam illuminated a large form sitting on the lobby floor about ten feet away. The laser lay beside it.

It was the black panther.

Chapter Twenty-Nine:

The panther's eyes glowed yellow in the beam of the flashlight. It was sitting on its haunches like a house cat, its front legs straight. It seemed to be grinning at her, as it had on that day so long ago.

Jan was overcome with shock. She couldn't understand how the panther could be here in this city hundreds of miles from where Minerva had stood. The Mother God was surely punishing her for some sin she had committed. Punishing her . . .? No . . . *mocking* her.

She considered reaching for the projectile weapon still strapped over her shoulder, but knew that the panther could be on her before she could unstrap it and aim. And there was the possibility that the thing wouldn't even work. She had her swords but, again, in the time it took to draw one of them the panther could easily attack her. She glanced wistfully at the laser by the panther's front foot. The panther glanced at it too then casually put its paw on the weapon. It said, in its familiar sibilant hiss, "Nasssty thing. Don't like. You won't touch."

"No, I won't touch," Jan assured it nervously.

The panther continued to stare at her with its great yellow eyes. Jan considered throwing the flashlight at it as a diversion, but knew that would be futile as well.

Finally she said, "Why are you following me? How did you find me?"

The panther hissed. "Follow you . . .? I not follow you."

"Yes you did," Jan told it accusingly. "All the way from Minerva. Where you killed Carla after I refused to let you into the town."

"Young Missssy talk crazy," said the panther and gave a dismissive snort.

"You're playing with me," said Jan, remembering how she had watched Minervan cats torture mice before killing them. "Why don't you just kill me and get it over with."

"Why me kill missy?" said the panther. "Only kill missy if you try hurt me. This cat only kill *male* people. Always trust *women* people. They have never tried to hurt cat."

Jan frowned in puzzlement. What kind of game was the panther playing now? Then it occurred to her to shine the flashlight beam lower down on the animal's body. She almost laughed aloud with relief at what she saw. Or rather, at what she *didn't* see.

It wasn't the same animal. It was a female.

Even though she was relieved that it was a different panther from the one she had encountered at the gate of Minerva, and a female at that, Jan still didn't trust it. But she was going to wait and see what developed before she attempted any reckless move. The panther had told her she'd spotted her entering the plaza and was curious as to what a human was doing in this 'death place'. Jan, in turn, asked the panther what *she* was doing in the city. Wasn't she scared of the sickness too?

"Been here long time now. Not sick," said the panther. "Mother warn me keep away. Mother's mother warn her. But I old cat. Tired. Hunting not good Out There . . ." The panther turned its head to indicate the blight lands. "Decide to come here. Take chance. Wait, but nothing happen. Water good. Hunting better. Animals come here. No People. You the first."

Jan wondered whether or not to believe the panther. A 'long time' could mean anything in the animal's time scale, from a couple of days to a couple of months. But then, even a couple of days would be more than sufficient for the plague to strike and the panther looked healthy. Jan was hot, thirsty, hungry and desperate for a pee. There was no way she could stay sealed up in the suit for much longer.

"Have you seen a machine in the city?" she asked the panther.

"Maccchine?"

"One that walks on two legs. Like a man."

The panther flicked its thick tail. "No see machine that walks."

Well, that's something, thought Jan. She shifted her position on the uncomfortable stair, taking care to move slowly so as to not alarm the animal. Then she came to a decision. "I'm going to take my weapons off. I don't mean you any harm. Understand?"

"Understand."

She put the torch down on the floor, the beam still pointing at the great cat. Then she slowly unstrapped the projectile weapon from her shoulder and, holding it by the barrel, placed it on the floor beside the torch where it was clearly visible. She then

287

removed her back-pack and weapons harness and dropped them on the floor as well. The panther watched her every move with its unreadable yellow eyes. Jan said, "I'm going to get something out of my bag here. It's not a weapon. Just a water container."

The panther gave a nod. Jan got out one of the two canteens. Then, after a long hesitation, she undid the seals and pulled back her hood. She took a deep breath. *There*, it was too late now. She lifted the canteen and drank.

When she next awoke dawn was breaking over the city of towers. The panther, she saw, was lying about fifteen feet away. It was awake and watching her. It hadn't eaten her while she slept, but that didn't mean it wasn't saving her for breakfast. Jan sat up on her makeshift bed, which consisted of the anti-contamination suit and the back-pack, and said, "Good morning."

The panther made a growling sound deep in its throat. Jan decided to interpret it as a friendly response. Maybe it was purring. She felt strangely cheerful, mainly because she was still alive. The panther hadn't eaten her and she didn't, as far as she knew, have the plague. Not a bad start to the day, all things considered.

She got up and walked out into the plaza. The panther stayed where she was but turned her head to watch Jan as she left. Jan went to the fountain, cupped water in her hands, and drank. The water tasted cold and fresh. She then looked round the plaza, but nothing moved. She felt confident that the clanking Ezekiel wouldn't be able to get close without being detected by the panther. She took off Ashley's clothes — a shirt, trousers, briefs and boots that the dead girl had last worn centuries ago — and climbed into the fountain. The water was shockingly cold as she lowered herself into it, but at the same time it felt marvellously invigorating. She lay on her back in the water and stared up at the Sky Tower. All she had to do was climb to its top, find the computer, insert Ashley and Carl's 'software' into it and then order it to summon down the Sky Angel all the way from its home far beyond the blue sky. Simple!

She didn't reach the top of the tower until the middle of the afternoon. She had been obliged to stop and rest several times, her legs throbbing with pain and her lungs heaving. The panther, who had accompanied her, stopped when she did, though it didn't show any sign of undue exertion. Jan guessed it could have loped to the summit and back down again without any problem.

During one of her first rest-stops she had asked the panther why she was coming with her. By that time they had reached a position of mutual trust — Jan had the laser strapped over her shoulder again. The panther, who called herself *Frusa*, had shrugged and said, "Cat bored. Cat curious." Jan had accepted this. Unlike normal animals the enhanced animals were prone to such human ills as boredom. She'd tried to explain the reason for her mission to the Sky Tower, but she wasn't sure how much the panther understood.

"Thank the Mother God!" Jan cried with relief when she reached the end of the staircase. But then she saw she still hadn't found her destination. The floor she was on was devoid of equipment and was obviously once used simply as a viewing platform, as it was encircled by windows. The Sky Angel's control centre had to be on the floor above, but how was she to gain access to it?

In the centre of the circular floor was a thick metal pillar which appeared to be the only means of support for the uppermost section of the tower. As the panther sat watching, she went to the pillar and examined it. It took two circuits round the pillar before she noticed the outline of the door set flush in its shiny surface. There was also a narrow opening about two inches long which presumably took some kind of key. She tried to prise the door open with her fingernails but it was useless. Out of frustration she kicked it, and jumped back with alarm when a voice said, "Do that again and I'll call the police."

Jan looked around, but apart from Frusa the place was empty. She looked back at the door. The voice had come out of the pillar. Was there someone behind the door? "Who are you?" she asked warily.

"I'm a public information facility and for your information, you being a member of the public, you can't come in here. The summit of the Sky Tower is off-limits to unauthorized personnel." The voice, a man's, sounded testy.

The panther had come over and was sniffing at the door. "Sound like man but no man. No one here," she told Jan.

Jan nodded. She had already guessed that the voice was an artificial one like Carl's, or Ashley's. It was being produced by some kind of machine in the pillar. "Please let me in," she commanded. "I *am* authorized. I'm on an important mission."

"Are you really? What's your authorization code, then?" asked the voice. It sounded vaguely sarcastic.

"Uh, I don't have one, but you must believe me — it's vital that I get into the top of the tower."

"I hear that every day, madam, believe me. Now please be on your way. Visiting hours are almost over. And take your pet with you."

Jan began to feel angry. "Look, machine, or whatever you are, visiting hours have been over in here for quite a long time. Several hundred years, in fact. The city out there is dead. My 'pet' and I are the only living things around for miles. Whatever instructions you were given once upon a time don't matter any more. So I demand you *let me in!*"

The voice didn't answer for some moments, then it said, "The summit of the Sky Tower is off-limits to unauthorized personnel."

Jan groaned, then kicked the door again. The voice said, "That's it, the last straw — I must warn you that I am calling the police."

"Don't hold your breath," muttered Jan. After some deliberation she unshouldered the laser and, warning Frusa to stand clear, aimed it at the lock and fired. Sparks flew and metal sizzled. The voice said, "Well, you're in *big* trouble now, madam!"

"Oh, shut up!" cried Jan as she continued to fire the laser.

She had to cut right through the door before it finally swung open to reveal a tightly spiralled staircase made of some translucent material. The voice, after several more warnings and threats about the police, had fallen silent. Jan experienced a feeling of triumph as she began to climb the staircase. *Almost there!* And she had done it without Milo.

At the top of the staircase she found herself in a small, circular area and facing another door. Jan sighed, anticipating further debate with a mechanical voice, but when she touched a glowing button on the door it slid open without any problem. A stream of fresh air wafted over her and she stepped through the door. That should have alerted her to something being wrong, but she was too preoccupied with her sense of achievement to notice.

Then she saw the three samurai. They had been sitting, cross-legged, around a brazier on which bowls of food were steaming. Their bed rolls and weapons lay scattered about and they had obviously been in the Sky Tower for a considerable length of time. They hadn't been aware of her presence until the door had opened but now they were reacting with alarming speed, grabbing for their swords and leaping to their feet.

Jan lifted the laser and pressed the firing button. Nothing happened. She guessed she'd exhausted its power supply by cutting through the door below. One of the samurai, the nearest, gave a shrieking cry as he charged at her.

She was knocked to one side as something large and very heavy bounded past her. It was Frusa. The leading samurai screamed as she brought him down under her weight. She gave him what seemed to be nothing more than a cuff on the side of the head, but it took half of his face away. Frusa did this without even pausing in her forward rush. She was on the second samurai before he had time even to attempt to defend himself. The third one stood frozen, eyes wide, as Frusa tore out the other man's throat. Then he came to life and raised his sword to hack at Frusa.

Jan threw the laser at him. It hit him on the shoulder, making him stagger sideways. Jan drew her short sword and ran forward, but before she could reach him Frusa struck again, knocking the samurai off his feet with a murderous swipe of her paw. Jan turned her head as the great jaws snapped shut on fragile flesh and bone, cutting off the man's screams.

When she looked again the panther was sitting calmly beside the corpse, blood running down the black fur on its chin. "Thank you," Jan said weakly.

"They men. Cat don't like men. Kill men."

"Yes, you certainly do . . ." Jan said. "How did you know they were here?"

"Smell them. After you go up ladder. Strong man smell."

Jan nodded. That had been when she'd opened the other door. She remembered the breeze as she'd entered and looked around. The summit room of the Sky Tower was like the interior of a giant crystal. The curving walls and ceiling were made of faceted, translucent glass which gave the air a luminous quality. All about were pieces of equipment with glass exteriors which enabled you to see the mysterious patterns created by their electronic nervous systems. Jan spotted where the samurai had gained entrance to the summit room — there was a four foot hole up by the base of the ceiling. On a catwalk below the hole were three folded-up gliders. They had either smashed their way through the crystal or used an explosive charge.

Their presence in the summit room held all manner of grim implications for Jan. It meant that the warlord had remembered the true location of the Sky Angel's control centre, as Milo had feared he would. It also meant that the warlord might already have sent the signal that would bring the remaining Sky Angel down to Earth.

The sound of flesh ripping distracted her. She turned and saw that the panther had begun to eat one of the dead samurai. She grimaced. "What are you doing?" she demanded.

It swallowed a large gobbet of meat and said, "Cat hungry. Cat eat."

"Well . . . can't you do it somewhere else?" asked Jan, trying not to look at what the cat was doing.

The cat hesitated, growled, then dragged the body towards the door. Jan took off her back-pack and then sat down on it. She needed to think. Already she was having doubts about her initial interpretation of the Japanese presence in the Tower. If the warlord had left them behind to ambush Milo and herself, surely he would deployed more than just three men. He knew Milo's abilities. Three wouldn't have stood a chance against him. Nor did they appear to have had guns; they were armed only with swords. Perhaps they were just one of several groups of samurai scattered throughout the city to act as look-outs. Perhaps they were in the Sky Tower just by accident. Hadn't she felt she was being watched ever since she'd arrived in the city? But why hadn't they attacked her? Probably because they were on the look-out for two people. A lone woman would have aroused their curiosity, but they had no way of knowing it was her. Besides, Milo was the important one as far as the warlord was concerned.

Whatever the reason for their presence in the Sky Tower, one thing was certain — it meant that the *Lord Pangloth*, or the *Perfumed Breeze*, would be returning.

She opened the backpack and reached in for the tube that contained Ashley and Carl. As she was feeling for it she touched something metallic and realized it was Milo's skull. She took it out and placed it on the floor in front of her. The empty sockets stared accusingly at her. She tried to analyse her feelings about Milo and his death, but everything was too jumbled up in her mind. The pieces would have to settle before she could even begin to examine how she felt.

Jan smiled sadly at the skull. "Well, Milo, we made it. With a bit of help from a cat." She reached in the bag again and found the tube, then began to examine the different pieces of transparent equipment in the circular room.

Because everything looked so unfamiliar it took her some time to find the part of the computer that housed the software. Then she frowned when she saw, through the transparent top, that the computer contained a whole *row* of similar tubes. Worriedly, she pressed the buttons that ejected the tubes then inserted her single one. Then she waited.

Nothing happened.

Chapter Thirty:

Something made a loud beeping sound on the other side of the room and Jan jumped. She turned. A screen had risen from a console on which a red light was flashing. She hurried over to it with relief. At least a minute had passed since she'd inserted the tube and she had begun to fear that the computer was no longer functioning.

There were words on the screen:"Hi! It's me, Ashley! Ol' lame-brain Carl has been having a bit of trouble sorting things out. Can't activate any of the voice synthesizers yet. Wants you to re-insert as many of the original software tubes as you can back into the mainframe. There's info on them he needs. He wants to copy it on to our software. Hurry, will you? I want to be able to see and hear again. Much love, Ashley."

Not being very good at reading, it took Jan a while before she understood the bulk of the message on the screen. She frowned. "Mainframe? What's that?" she asked.

The words on the screen remained the same. She read the message through again and realized that Ashley couldn't hear her. Then she worked out that the 'mainframe' must refer to the computer where she'd inserted the tube. She returned to it and studied the six other tubes that she'd left lying on its glass top. There was only space in the computer for five now. Did it matter which? Well, she would soon find out, she thought, as she began to push the tubes into the opening. The computer hummed as it took the tubes one by one and drew them deep into itself. Jan became aware of more lights starting to flash on other pieces of equipment. She could feel the circular room of crystal starting to come alive.

The air crackled. Then a voice said, "Ah, that's better! Light and sound! Hi, Jan! Have you missed me?"

It was Ashley. The voice wasn't the same as the one in the shelter — it was neither male or female — but it was unmistakably Ashley. "Hello Ashley," said Jan, looking around for the source of the voice. "You can see me now?" And hear me?"

"Yup. Place is loaded with sensors, inside and out. But Carl couldn't activate them until he got the drill from the other programs. Can you insert the final one now?"

Jan saw one of the tubes starting to emerge from the computer. She took it out and replaced it with the sixth tube. As the computer ingested it, Ashley cried, "Wow, what's been happening in here? Who are those guys?"

Jan guessed she was referring to the dead Japanese. She had been avoiding looking at them as they lay there in their large pools of congealing blood. "They're the warlord's men. They were waiting here."

"Jesus, did you do *that* to them?"

"Of course not. Frusa did."

"Frusa? Who's Frusa?"

"She's a cat."

At that moment the panther, no doubt curious about the sound of voices, came in through the door. "Jesus," said Ashley, that's some cat." The panther sniffed the air and said to Jan, "Hear voice, but no one here."

"There is someone here, Frusa. Her name is Ashley. She's a friend. Ashley, say something nice to Frusa."

"Hello, pussycat. You're real cute. You know, I had a coat exactly like yours once. Oh, but it wasn't *real* fur, it was synthetic."

The panther looked at Jan. "No one here." Then it turned and went back out through the door.

"I'm sorry," Jan told Ashley. "It seems that if Frusa can't smell someone they don't exist."

There was a pause before Ashley replied. "But she's right. I don't exist. Carl wants to talk to you. Bye."

"Ashley . . .?"

"This is Carl." It was the same voice but infinitely different. "I have made contact with the computer controlling the Sky Angel factory facility. I am currently transmitting the sequence of codes which will initiate the launching of the Sky Angel from the facility."

"Oh," she said, taken by surprise. "That was quick. Where did you find these codes?"

"In this computer's memory."

"Yes, of course." She should have known that. "So everything is going fine. The Sky Angel is going to come down here without any problem?" Jan couldn't believe it was going to be so easy . . . .

"All systems are functioning. I can foresee no problem."

"Great. When will it get here?"

"In eight and a half days from now."

"Eight and a half days? That's a long time."

"It has a long way to travel. It will take four days to reach the Earth's atmosphere. Its descent path will bring it down over Australia. It will take another four days to reach here travelling at top speed."

"What's Australia?"

"An island continent in the Southern Hemisphere."

"Why can't you make the Sky Angel come down here instead of in this Australia place that's so far away?" Jan asked.

"The procedure for bringing a Sky Angel down through the atmosphere — intact — is a very complicated one. The mathematics of the procedure are also very complicated and are an integral part of the whole system. For me to alter the system at this stage would be unwise. There may be random factors that the original program is designed to compensate for but of which I am ignorant. I advise you to follow the established procedure."

She sighed. "If you say so." Eight and a half days. What if the warlord returned before then? Or, more likely, other Japanese arrived to relieve the ones who had been here? Well, she had the panther for protection, provided Frusa didn't get bored and wander off. And there was the laser, except that . . . .

"Carl, is there any way you can recharge the laser?"

"No. I have power but not the means to transfer it to the laser's fuel cell."

"Oh," she said, disappointed. That left only the projectile weapon, and Carl had made her dubious about that. Then a question occurred to her. "Carl, where is the power coming from?"

"The sun. There are arrays of solar energy receptors on the outside of the tower."

Sun-gatherers. Jan nodded her understanding, though she wondered why they hadn't become clogged with fungus over the years if there hadn't been anyone to keep them clean. Then again, the city seemed remarkably free of any type of fungi. "Will you let me know when the Sky Angel has actually been launched?"

"Of course."

"Good. Now let me speak to Ashley."

"She's not available."

"Not available. What do you mean?"

"She's incommunicado. She doesn't want to communicate with you. Or me."

"Oh. You mean she's sulking." Frusa's comment had obviously upset her. "Very well, let her sulk." Jan sighed and forced herself to look at the two corpses on the floor. The first thing to do was get rid of them. She wasn't going to spend the next eight and a half days in *their* company. She went downstairs to find the panther. Frusa was on the floor below, finishing her meal. Jan's stomach gave a heave but she managed to keep control of it. The panther regarded her with its unreadable eyes. Jan said, "Um, I don't suppose, when you've finished here, that you'd like to go and eat the other two upstairs . . .?"

"Cat not hungry now. Full belly."

"Oh." Jan thought for a few moments then said, "Well, why don't you, er, put them somewhere for later. For when you're hungry again, I mean."

The panther stared at her. It said, "Like fresh meat. Kill, then eat."

"Oh," she said again. "Well, you see, I really would like to get rid of their remains. I find them . . . uncomfortable. And as I'm going to be in that room for over a week, well, after a while the bodies will . . . ." She couldn't continue under Frusa's unsettling gaze. Jan got the distinct impression that the panther thought she was not right in the head. "It's okay," she told her, "I'll take care of it myself."

She was about to return upstairs when she paused and said, "Frusa, that voice you heard. Ashley's. I know it maybe kind of hard for you to understand but it does belong to a *sort* of real person so next time you hear it I would appreciate it if you would be, er, polite to her."

"Voice came from nothing. No human there. Why talk to nothing?"

"I give up," muttered Jan and left. As she climbed the crystal staircase she wondered if Ashley's comment about Frusa reminding her of one of her old coats was the real cause of the panther's apparent obtuseness.

As she entered the summit room Carl said, "The Sky Angel —
Registration Code A810 JLX — was successfully launched from
the factory facility three minutes ago and is on course for Earth."

"Marvellous!" exclaimed Jan. "Are you actually in control of
it from here?"

"No. It is under the control of the program in its on-board
computer. But I have a direct radio link with that computer. I am
receiving a constant stream of information."

"I see." Jan marvelled at how blasé she was becoming about
Old Science. Here she was, calmly talking to a computer that was
in turn talking to another computer an unimaginable distance
away in outer space. And *that* computer was piloting a mile-long
airship through the void. "Carl, Milo told me once that there was
no air in space. So how does the Sky Angel propel itself? The
thrusters on the Sky Lords depended on air to work."

"The Sky Angel is fitted with rocket motors. They don't need
air to function. When the Sky Angel enters the atmosphere the
rocket motors will be discarded."

Jan thanked Carl for the information and then reluctantly
turned her attention to the grisly task of removing the corpses of
the dead samurai. She solved the problem by wrapping them in
their bed rolls and dragging them, one by one, down the stairs to
the observation room below. From there she dragged them down
a further flight of stairs and left them on the stairs. When she
returned to the summit room she saw the panther licking the
blood from the floor. Whether the panther was doing her a
deliberate favour or not she wasn't sure — and decided not to
ask.

Ashley was silent for several hours. It was dark when she finally
spoke again, and Jan was eating a meal of potato cakes and
synthetic fruit which had been generated by Carl in the shelter.
"Hi, it's me again." She sounded subdued.

"Hello, Ashley. How are you feeling?"

"Okay. Where's the panther?"

"Out on the prowl. Looking for food, and checking to see if
there are any more Japanese about."

"I don't like that animal."

298

"I'm not too keen on it either," Jan admitted. "Reminds me of another panther I once encountered. But I think Frusa can be trusted."

"Hope you're right. For your sake. If she can't find any food out there she might decide to munch on *you*."

"Oh, I doubt that," Jan said uneasily, wishing that Ashley hadn't expressed aloud Jan's own secret fear.

"Carl says the launch of the Sky Angel went okay. It's on its way."

"Yes, I'm very relieved. I only wish it would get here sooner than eight days."

"I can't wait either. I can't believe I'm going to be able to fly again. Carl says the system of sensors in the Sky Angel is very sophisticated. I'll actually be able to *feel* the air as it passes over the hull."

"Sounds delightful," Jan said, glancing up at the gaping hole in the curved ceiling through which a stiff, and increasingly cold, breeze was blowing. Earlier she had gone up on the catwalk and examined it more closely. She saw it was too big for her to rig up some kind of makeshift obstruction across the hole. As she'd looked out she'd marvelled that the three samurai had managed to land their gliders on such a precarious surface.

Further exploration had revealed a door that led out to a narrow, glass-enclosed observation deck which circled the summit dome. She had stared down at the tops of the surrounding buildings, trying to detect signs of other Japanese look-out posts, but saw nothing suspicious.

Another discovery was a door that led into a tube-shaped room. There was a circular door at the end but it refused to open. Carl had later explained what it was.

"That is where the Sky Angels link up with the Tower. The tube extends out and locks into a socket in the nose of the Sky Angel."

"So I'll be able to enter the Sky Angel that way?"

"Yes."

"Why was the connection built in the first place? Why did the Sky Angels come here?"

"This was where they were officially commissioned into service. A christening ceremony was held here in the Sky Tower each time a Sky Angel arrived from space."

"Christening ceremony?"

"They would be given names."

"Oh, I see."

Since then she had been wondering what to call *her* Sky Angel when it arrived. The obvious choice was to call it the *Minerva*, but she also wanted to name it after her dead friend and lover, Alsa.

She mentioned the name problem to Ashley. Ashley said, "Oh, that's easy. You can just name it after me! Call it the *Ashley Vee*. After all, I will *be* the Sky Angel."

Jan was not impressed with this suggestion. "In that case I might as well call it the *Carl*, because he'll be controlling the Sky Angel as well."

"Oh, he doesn't count. I'm the one who's really in charge."

"Yes, I know." Jan remembered the situation in the shelter. She had carefully avoided mentioning the sudden turnabout in 'Carl's' policy regarding visitors to the shelter. It occurred to her that establishing and maintaining control of the Sky Angel once Ashley's program was in its computer might be more difficult than she had anticipated.

She spent an uncomfortable first night in the summit room. The cold and the hard floor made it difficult for her to get to sleep and when she did finally drift off she had a bad dream. She was back in her mother's house in Minerva. There was a knock at the door. She opened it and there was Ceri, unharmed and smiling at her. Jan happily went to embrace her, but as she got closer Ceri's face began to change . . . it became horribly seamed, like the faces of Ezekiel's followers. Ceri cried out for Jan to help her, but Jan could only back away in revulsion. Then the seamed and sagging flesh had begun to fall away from Ceri's face until finally there was only a grinning skull . . . .

Jan had woken up at that point. As she lay there shivering she wondered if the dream meant that Ceri was now dead.

"Jan. Wake up."

"Um . . . What?" she opened her eyes. Everything looked unfamiliar for a few moments, then her memory supplied the necessary information to her consciousness that made the interior of the summit room seem once again all-too-familiar. "Carl . . . what is it?"

"The Sky Angel has just appeared over the horizon. You should be able to see it from here. It's coming from a south-westerly direction."

Jan bounded up from her sleeping roll and ran for the door that led out to the observation deck. The sun had just risen and the sky was clear of clouds. Eagerly, she scanned the horizon. *There!* Something glinting in the sunlight. It had to be her! The Sky Angel. At last . . . .

Four days ago it had seemed that everything was going to end in disaster. Carl had been describing the Sky Angel's descent into the upper atmosphere: "It's entering the exosphere now. Retro-rockets still firing . . . Speed reducing to four thousand, eight hundred and forty miles per hour."

"Why is it moving so fast?" Jan had asked. "Why doesn't it just float down through the air?"

"It has a mass of several thousand tons. Slowing an object with such a mass involves the expenditure of a lot of energy which the rockets are not capable of providing. They do not have sufficient fuel. They will slow the Sky Angel down and the atmosphere itself will be used as the actual brake."

"But I still don't understand why it can't float down," persisted Jan. "It's full of gas, isn't it."

"No," said Carl. "The helium is still in liquid form. There would be no point in starting to fill the gas cells until the Sky Angel enters the lower levels of the atmosphere. Without air density there is no lift . . . Speed now four thousand two hundred miles per hour. Retro-rockets still firing. The Sky Angel will start skimming the upper levels of the ionosphere at any moment . . . ."

"Temperature of outer hull is starting to rise . . . Heat shield functioning . . . ."

"Heat shield?" Jan asked.

"A temporary covering on the outer hull. Ceramic interlock-

301

ing scales. Like glass. To protect the Sky Angel from the effects of the friction. Will be automatically discarded when . . . MALFUNCTION! MALFUNCTION!"

The sudden increase in volume in Carl's voice gave Jan a fright. "What's wrong?" she cried.

"Two of the rocket motors have shut down prematurely," said Carl, his voice back to normal. "The Sky Angel will enter denser atmosphere at too high a velocity."

"But you said the atmosphere itself was going to be used to slow it down."

"The rockets are still needed at this stage. There has been a malfunction in the fuel supply. Blocked line. Or the fuel has leaked from the tanks. Information not available to me yet . . . Speed is still four thousand miles per hour . . . too fast . . . remaining functioning rocket motors not sufficient in power . . . ."

"What will happen?" Jan asked worriedly.

"Heat shield may be burnt off . . . or the intense buffeting may destroy integrity of the hull and the Sky Angel will disintegrate . . . ."

"Oh no!" she cried, dismayed. "Can't you do anything?"

"No. The program in the on-board computer is attempting a compensatory manoeuvre, but I have no control over its actions . . . the Sky Angel is now at an altitude of 350 miles — well within the ionosphere. Hull temperature still rising . . . I have now lost contact with Sky Angel A810 JLX . . . ."

"What do you mean? What's happened? Has it blown up?"

"Condition of Sky Angel unknown. I have lost all radio contact with it. Cause may be intense ionization around the Sky Angel, due to friction, which is interfering with signals."

"What's ioni . . . Oh, it doesn't matter . . . just tell me what's going on!"

"I can tell you nothing."

A minute went by. Another and another. Jan was in an agony of anxiety. To have got this far and then to have lost everything at the last moment . . . .

"I have re-established contact with the Sky Angel," Carl announced, as blandly as ever. "Heat shield is still secure. Speed

302

down to eight hundred miles per hour. Just entering stratosphere. No serious damage has been sustained. Rocket motors being ejected now. Liquid helium being converted to gas. Gas cells being inflated . . . Thrusters activated . . . ."

Jan had given a whoop of delight and wished she had someone to hug.

That had been four days ago. And now the Sky Angel was at last in sight.

Yes, it was clearly visible now and heading straight for the tower. Unlike the Sky Lords it wasn't covered with markings, patterns or giant eyes; apart from where the sun-gatherers glinted in the early morning sunshine its hull was white. Pure white.

Then she saw the other airship. It was well behind the Sky Angel but obviously following it.

A Sky Lord.

And it wasn't alone. There was *another* one, even more distant.

Her stomach began to churn. The two Sky Lords could only be the *Lord Pangloth* and the *Perfumed Breeze*. The warlord was coming.

Chapter Thirty-One:

"Carl!" she cried in panic as she ran back into the summit room. But it was Ashley who answered. "Hi! Isn't it great? In a few minutes we'll be on the Sky Angel."

"Where's Carl?" Jan demanded. "I must talk to him."

"Well, you can't," said Ashley petulantly. "It's my turn to have the voice now. You two talked together long enough."

"Look, you crazy ghost, this is important! There are two Sky Lords right behind the Sky Angel! Tell Carl! He's got to do something!"

"Jesus, there's no need to be rude, Jan!"

"Mother God, help me," Jan groaned. "Look, *you* talk to Carl. Tell him about the Sky Lords."

A brief silence, and then Ashley said, "Carl knows about the Sky Lords. He says that the Sky Angel will arrive here a full twelve minutes before the first of the pursuers. That will give you plenty of time to get on board. With us, of course."

Jan didn't share Ashley's or Carl's confidence. How long would it take for the Sky Angel to link up with the Tower? And then she would have to get all the way from the nose to the control room. How long would that take? She wasn't even sure she would know the *way* to the control room. She ran back out on to the observation deck. The Sky Angel was close enough to look intimidating in its vastness. Its shadow was beginning to fall across the outskirts of the city.

She saw that the Sky Lord behind it was the *Lord Pangloth*, which the warlord had taken over. She gazed at the third airship, the *Perfumed Breeze* — was Ceri on board? Was she even still alive?

She drew a deep breath and returned inside. "Ashley, I *must* talk to Carl!" she cried loudly.

"Oh, all right."

"Carl?"

"I'm here."

"What do I do when the Sky Angel arrives?"

"When it links up to the tower I will give the on-board computer the command to open the entrance and authorize your entry. Then you will take our software from this computer and take it on to the Sky Angel. You will then insert it into the on-board computer."

"Yes, but will I have *time* to do all that before the warlord gets here?"

"That is doubtful," admitted Carl. "But what can the warlord do even when he arrives? The Sky Angel is protected by its automatic defence system."

"Oh, he'll do *something* — don't worry about that," she said grimly. She went and began to gather up her belongings — her back-pack, weapons harness, canteen, remaining food . . . She froze when she heard someone coming up the spiral staircase, then relaxed when she saw it was Frusa.

The panther looked at her and said, "You smell of fear."

"I'm not surprised," Jan said. "Look, I'm going to be leaving here very soon. You can come with me if you like."

"Where go?"

"In a big, er, thing that flies through the air."

"A Sky Lord?"

"Well, yes." Damn panther. "A Sky Angel, actually. Will you come?"

"What cat eat?"

"Eat?" Jan frowned. That was a good question. "Well, I'm sure there will be supplies on board." She *hoped* there would be supplies on board.

"Fresh meat?" asked the panther.

"Uh, I doubt it," admitted Jan.

"Cat stay here."

Jan was secretly relieved. As much as she owed a debt of gratitude to the panther she still felt she couldn't trust her completely. "Very well. Thank you for everything. Take care, Frusa."

The panther made a noise in the back of its throat, then turned and abruptly left. *Strange animal*, thought Jan.

"Jan, the Sky Angel is about to link up with the Tower," announced Carl. "There will be some vibration."

Jan waited. The floor shuddered and she heard a distant *clang*. The Sky Angel was here.

"I have authorized your boarding of the Sky Angel," said Carl. "I will shut down. Remove the software now."

Jan went to the computer. She pressed the button that ejected the software tubes. They emerged with painful slowness. She had to wait for the other five to emerge before she could get the one containing Carl and Ashley's programs. But in her eagerness to take hold of it as it came out of the machine it slipped through her sweaty fingers and fell with a heart-stopping clunk on the floor. Jan stared down at it in dismay, expecting to see it slowly disintegrate. But it looked to be still intact. She bent down, gingerly picked it up and scrutinized it closely. Was it her imagination, or was there now a hairline crack running down its length?

No time to worry about it now. She slipped the tube in her pocket and ran for the door leading into the tunnel.

As the door opened she saw that the tunnel now extended much further. The circular door had disappeared and she realized she could see all the way into the Sky Angel.

She rushed down the tunnel and found herself in a round room with a dais in its centre and three tiers of comfortable seats surrounding it. There was soft music playing. A pleasant, sexually neutral voice said, "Welcome. You are on board Sky Angel A810 JLX. I have been authorized to admit you, but I have not been informed whether you are part of the delegation that will be attending the christening ceremony or a maintenance technician."

"I'm here to christen you," Jan said quickly. "Your name is now *Alsa of Minerva*."

"It is?" The voice sounded puzzled. "But the normal procedure hasn't been followed. By what authority do you — "

"It doesn't matter," Jan interrupted. "I have to get to the control room. What's the quickest way?"

"I'll have an escort take you there," the voice told her.

"What? An escort?" said Jan, surprised. Surely there were no living beings on board.

A door slid open on the opposite side of the circular room and a large metal spider scuttled in on its six metal legs. Jan started to back away from it, drawing her long sword as she did. "There's no need for alarm," said the spider in the same sort of pleasant and reassuring voice as the room. "I'm your escort. Please follow me." It began to retrace its steps towards the open door. After a few seconds hesitation Jan followed it. She guessed it was a machine like Ezekiel, though she hoped it didn't contain a human brain.

She followed the spider, whose body consisted of a shiny metal sphere about a foot and a half in diameter, down a long corridor and then into an elevator. Jan noticed that there was music playing in the elevator as well. As the elevator began to descend the spider said pleasantly, "Beautiful day for the christening ceremony, isn't it?"

306

Jan, who had been regarding the creature with some nervousness, started to laugh.

"Did I say something funny?" asked the spider, sounding pleased with itself.

Still overcome with laughter, Jan couldn't answer.

The elevator doors opened on to another corridor. The same music played here as well. Jan couldn't get over how unfamiliar everything looked on the Sky Angel — without all the alterations, deteriorations and grime accumulated over the centuries in the Sky Lords it was a whole different world. The corridor that stretched ahead of her had a light blue ceiling, white walls and a thickly carpeted floor. There were murals on the walls and the lighting was soft and pleasant on the eyes.

"This way," said the spider, scuttling off.

The doors opened on to a more familiar scene. She recognized the control room, even though it was very different from the one on the *Lord Pangloth*. "Here you are," announced the spider. "Is there anything else I can do for you?"

"No. Just wait here," Jan answered distractedly. She hurried to the rear of the control room and peered out through the curving glass, trying to see how close the *Lord Pangloth* was, but the great expanse of the Sky Angel's hull obscured her view. She looked down and then saw, to her alarm, another huge shadow lying across the city beside the shadow of the Sky Angel. The *Lord Pangloth* had to be very close indeed. She groaned.

"Is there something wrong?" asked the original voice politely.

"I can't *see*," she complained.

"Tell me what you want to see and I'll show it to you," said the voice.

"I want to see in *all* directions at once!"

Banks of monitor screens glowed into life. Jan turned to them. It took a few moments for her to comprehend what she was seeing, then she realized she was getting views being transmitted from different parts of the Sky Angel's hull. She saw that the *Lord Pangloth* was indeed very close. Higher than the Sky Angel, it was descending to a position right alongside her. The *Perfumed Breeze* was still some distance away.

"Where is your software input?" Jan asked urgently, looking

around the control room. A nearby console made a chiming sound and began to flash a green light. Jan went to it, taking the tube from her pocket. She inserted it into the console and waited. "Carl? Ashley?" she asked tentatively. There was no answer.

"Who do you wish to talk to?" asked the original ship's voice.

"The programs on that software I just put into your system."

"That software is inert," the voice informed her calmly.

"What do you mean?" cried Jan.

"There are no active programs on it. It is inert."

Jan groaned in despair. She had damaged it after all. The impact had destroyed Carl and Ashley. She glanced at the screens. What she saw plunged her into deeper despair. Gliders, spilling from the decks of the *Lord Pangloth* and into the air like fungus spores on a windy day in the blight lands.

"Sky Angel!" she cried. "You must leave at once. Disengage from the tower and fly from here at top speed."

"I'm sorry," said the voice, "but I cannot obey your orders without the proper command codes."

Jan wanted to scream with frustration. "You *must* obey me!" she cried. "We will be invaded at any moment. Look! Look at your own screens if you don't believe me . . .!" She pointed at the nearest screen. On it she saw some of the gliders heading for the top of the Sky Tower. They intended to gain entrance to the summit room in the same manner as the other three had done. And from there they could get into the Sky Angel through the connecting tunnel.

"Can you at least close the doors in your bow?" begged Jan.

"Oh, yes, I can do that," said the voice.

"MILO HAZE!"

The voice boomed over the city, echoing from the walls of the towers.

"MILO HAZE! ANSWER ME!"

It was coming from the *Lord Pangloth*. It was the warlord.

"MILO HAZE! YOU HAVE LOST!"

Jan scanned the banks of screens. She saw gliders landing on the upper hull. She turned to the metal spider. "Are you armed?" she asked it. In response it extended a mechanical arm

308

from its spherical body. "I have others if you need them," it assured Jan.

"I meant *weapons*," said Jan. "Do you have any?"

"Oh no," it replied. "No weapons."

She tried to keep calm but it was difficult. Memories of the warlord's description of what it would be like to be flayed alive kept flickering through her mind.

"SURRENDER, MILO HAZE! I WILL BE MERCIFUL!"

"Are there many of you on board?" Jan asked the spider.

"Yes," it said. "There are five hundred maintenance and service mechanicals on active duty with another five hundred in storage."

"Listen to me," Jan said desperately. "People are invading the airship. You and the other things like you must stop them — attack them, kill them!"

"That's impossible," said the spider. "We cannot deliberately harm any human being."

"Mother God, give me strength . . ." groaned Jan. She tried again. "You don't have to harm them, just overpower the invaders, take away their weapons . . . ."

"Such actions might result in injury and therefore can't be considered. I'm sorry."

"You sound it," said Jan and kicked the spider. It scuttled away from her but did nothing else.

"MILO HAZE! DON'T ATTEMPT TO ESCAPE! IT IS TOO LATE!"

That was true, thought Jan bitterly as she stared at the screens. The upper hull was crawling with samurai. *Lucky Milo, to have missed this . . . .*

"Hi! What's happening?"

Jan wondered if she was having a hallucination. "Ashley?"

"Yep, it's me! Large as life!"

Jan couldn't believe it. "You're okay? Carl too?"

"Right as rain."

"I thought I'd destroyed you both! Where were you? The computer here said your software was blank."

"That was Carl's doing. He discovered there were all sorts of safeguards built into the system to prevent unauthorized programs being introduced into the Sky Angel. He had to figure out ways of getting around them. Took a while. Did you miss me?"

"Very much," said Jan with feeling. Quickly, she told Ashley what was going on.

Ashley said, "No problem. Carl and I are in total control of the system now. Carl says we should disengage from the Sky Tower for a start."

"Yes, yes!" cried Jan. "Tell him to do whatever he thinks best."

"What *we* think best," said Ashley.

"Okay, what *you* and Carl think best."

The Sky Angel was already moving. She looked up and saw the top of the tower start to recede.

"HAZE! IT'S TOO LATE! YOU CAN'T ESCAPE! SURRENDER NOW AND I WILL BE MERCIFUL! OTHERWISE YOUR DEATH WILL BE ONE LONG SCREAM!"

The warlord's voice thundered over the city.

"Carl says that the Japanese are entering the Sky Angel," said Ashley.

"I know that. Has he, or do *you*, have any ideas of how to get rid of them?"

"Yeah. The robots. Those spider things."

"I already tried that," Jan told her. "The spider here refused in case people got hurt."

"Carl and I are in charge now," said Ashley proudly. "They'll do whatever we say — we've taken over the central program."

"Then give the word," said Jan urgently. "Fast!"

"It's already been given."

Jan had to duck out of the way as the spider suddenly came to life and charged towards the elevator. It disappeared inside and the door closed. "We're taking the other five hundred out of storage in case we need any back-up."

"MILO HAZE! STOP NOW! MY WARRIORS ARE ALREADY ON BOARD YOUR SHIP. FURTHER RESISTANCE IS USELESS!"

The Sky Angel was now rising above the *Lord Pangloth*. Jan saw the other airship's thrusters swivel their vents downwards in order to ascend as well.

"Let's blow the bastard out of the sky!" said Ashley.

"Nothing I'd like better," said Jan. "But *how*?"

"Oh, didn't I tell you? No, I didn't. Carl infiltrated the system that controls the lasers. We now have full control of them. So what do you say? Do we start shooting?"

It took a few moments for the information to sink in, then Jan realized that the lasers could be made to fire at *anything*. She said quickly, "No, don't fire yet. Is there a way I can speak to the warlord?"

After a pause Ashley said, "Yeah, there's a voice amplification unit here. To be used to communicate with disaster refugees on the ground, says Carl, which is what that warlord is soon going to be himself. Carl is activating it now. Start talking."

"Warlord Horado . . ." she began experimentally, and was instantly shocked to hear her words booming in the same thunderous tones as the warlord's. "Warlord Horado, listen to me. I am Jan Dorvin. I am on my own. Milo is dead. He was killed by a cyberoid weeks ago."

The warlord laughed. It sounded like obscene thunder. Then he said, "Milo haze dead? Killed by a cyberoid? How very droll. . . So now, girl, cease your games and let my ship come alongside."

Jan glanced at the monitor screens. Hundreds of the metal spiders were streaming out on to the upper hull. She saw swords flashing as the Japanese tried to defend themselves. She said to the warlord, "I have the means to destroy you. I have full control of the laser system. Unless you agree to my demands, I will open fire."

The warlord was silent for a short time, then said, "You are bluffing, girl. And at any moment now my samurai will be in your control room."

"Your samurai are being defeated," Jan told him. "There are robots on board this ship. Like the lasers, they are under my control. Will you listen to my demands now?"

Ashley said, "Why bother with demands? Let's just blow him out of the sky."

"I want Ceri, if she's still alive."

"Yeah, but you said yourself that if she was still alive she'd be on the other ship. So let's start shooting. One laser beam and all that hydrogen will go up a real treat."

"Girl, you are an annoyance. My retribution will seem everlasting."

Jan was tempted to do what Ashley suggested, but she couldn't bring herself to give the order. For the second time she was unable to destroy the *Lord Pangloth*. "There are women and children on board. I can't murder them," she told Ashley. "Instead, I want you and Carl to start shooting at the *Lord Pangloth*'s thrusters. Destroy them all."

"Awwww, that's no fun."

"Do as I say," ordered Jan. Here was the first test. Who was really in control of the Sky Angel?

A thin line of turquoise light suddenly appeared between one of the *Lord Pangloth*'s thrusters and an unseen point above the Sky Angel's control room. The metal casing of the thruster began to blacken and curl. More beams of light appeared. Other thrusters on the *Lord Pangloth* began to shrivel, like pieces of fruit thrown on a fire.

The warlord gave a scream of rage.

The *Lord Pangloth* began to go out of control. Neither its helmsmen nor computer could compensate for the sudden loss of so many thrusters along the port side. It went into a tight turn, while at the same time losing altitude.

The Sky Angel, manoeuvring with a speed and grace that the Sky Lords had lost centuries ago, followed the *Lord Pangloth* down. The turquoise lines continued to form in the air. More thrusters became twisted and dead.

"Girl! Girl!" bellowed the warlord. "I will talk with you! Cease your firing. We will bargain together! What do you want?"

"It's too late for that now," Jan told him coldly.

"That's the lot," Ashley informed her. "Every thruster is kaput. Now let's take care of the rudders and elevators as well."

Jan watched as the beams sliced through the *Lord Pangloth*'s great tailplane and side fins like knives. When they were finished the *Lord Pangloth* was completely helpless. It was now at the mercy of the winds. Nose drooping, it drifted over the city. The

huge painted eyes on it bow, which had once created so much
fear in Jan, now looked almost comical to her.

"TALK TO ME, WOMAN! I WILL LISTEN TO YOUR DEMANDS!"

"How are we doing with the samurai?" Jan asked Ashley.

"The ones who got inside are dead," said Ashley. "Some on
the hull escaped in their gliders; those who didn't are dead too."

So much killing, thought Jan bleakly, but there had been no
choice. "Right," she said. "Now let's go and deal with the
Perfumed Breeze."

The commander of the *Perfumed Breeze*, on witnessing the fate
of the *Lord Pangloth*, had turned his ship around and fled at top
speed. But the Sky Angel, with the advantage of a full
complement of working thrusters, caught up with it easily. Its
commander, a Japanese, spoke no English but Carl was able to
broadcast Jan's demands for surrender in perfect Japanese. The
commander refused at first, and fired off a few shells in the Sky
Angel's direction in a token show of resistance. But when the Sky
Angel's lasers incinerated the first of the irreplaceable thrusters
the Japanese commander quickly gave in.

Accompanied by an escort of ten of the metal spiders, Jan
went on board the *Perfumed Breeze*. She expected trouble, but
there was none at all. The commander and his men were
surprisingly submissive, and everywhere she went she was met
with bowed heads and samurai offering her their swords. But the
Americano captives from the *Lord Pangloth*, she quickly saw,
had been living in terrible conditions under the Japanese;
conditions that made her own period of slavery seem humane by
comparison.

As she visited yet another stinking room that served as the
living quarters for up to thirty starved-looking Americanos, she
was surprised when a tall scarecrow of a man covered in sagging
flesh pushed his way forward and fell on his knees in front of her.
"My dear girl, save me, I beg you, from this living hell!" he cried,
wringing his hands. "Remember how I helped you? How I fed
and sheltered you . . . ?"

With a shock, she realized that the man before her was Guild
Master Bannion. She touched the brand on her cheek. "Yes, I

313

remember all right. And in gratitude for all you did for me I won't order my metal friends here to dismember you on the spot." Then she strode from the room. A teacher had told her once that getting one's revenge on someone was always an unsatisfactory experience, but she discovered that it actually felt quite pleasant . . . .

She searched on and on through the *Lord Pangloth*, looking at the thin and drawn faces and asking the same question endlessly. Then finally, in the fiftieth or hundredth stinking, over-crowded room, she found her.

Chapter Thirty-Two:

Physically, the warlord was sitting in his throne room, but his mind was elsewhere, lost in some mental cul-de-sac deep within his skull. The floor of the throne room was tilted both forward and to the starboard. The *Lord Pangloth* was listing badly and still losing altitude. It had first been carried in an easterly direction; then the wind had changed, and it was now drifting over the ocean. If the warlord had been aware of his surroundings he could have turned on his throne and seen, through the great slanted windows of the bow, the grey and choppy surface of the sea getting closer by the minute.

Equally ignored was the body of his chief pilot, which had slid, leaving a trail of lubricating blood, several feet from the spot in front of the throne where the warlord had carried out a crude trepanning operation on him with his long sword.

The pilot had had the unfortunate task of informing the warlord that there was no hope of saving the *Lord Pangloth*. Without the thrusters or the elevators there was no way of maintaining a safe altitude. The lift provided by the gas in the cells wasn't sufficient, mainly because Cell number Seven had

314

never been able to function at full capacity again. Everything that could be thrown overboard had been, including — on the warlord's orders — three hundred 'expendable' people.

From that point on the warlord had retreated within himself and ignored all subsequent, nervous approaches from his anxious officers and servants. They had given up now, and waited for the inevitable with their customary stoicism. None of them even contemplated the dishonourable idea of making an escape from the doomed airship by means of their gliders.

The bow of the *Lord Pangloth* finally made contact with the surface of the sea. It was a brief encounter; nothing more than a kiss, though it shattered windows and ruptured the hull in several places. The next encounter was longer; the third one was for keeps.

Very slowly, the *Lord Pangloth* settled the length of its mile-long body upon the ocean. Its space-born girders screamed at having to endure strains they were not designed to take. Water rushed in through shattered windows and hatches that had not been designed to resist the weight of the sea.

Within its honeycombed lower hull, the Japanese fled the rising waters, which carried not only the threat of death by drowning but other dangers as well, as the first sighting of a long and sinewy tentacle probing its way down a corridor had made only too clear . . . .

The surface of the sea was slowly creeping up along the great windows of the throne room. Water began to spill along the floor, but the warlord still remained oblivious of everything. Even when one of the windows behind him imploded to admit a mass of water, he didn't react. His throne, and his body, were sent hurtling forward. Then the shock of the icy water dragged him, screaming, out of his mental refuge. Automatic survival responses were too strong to resist; he fought and struggled in the churning black water. Then something below its surface took hold of him.

Jan woke early again, and lay there feeling the weight of the future pressing down on her. So much to do; so many responsibilities . . . . Her plans were still vague but the basic idea, which

315

she had discussed with Ceri, Ashley and Carl, was to defeat all the other Sky Lords and bring them under her control in the same way as she had with the *Perfumed Breeze*. Carl had produced a copy of his and Ashley's programs which had been introduced into the *Perfumed Breeze*'s computer system. Carl had already brought the other airship's system back up to full working capacity using the robots and spare electronic parts stored in the Sky Angel. The Americanos and the Japanese on board had no way at all of regaining control of the airship.

She had told the two groups they had the choice of living together in peace on the *Perfumed Breeze* or being deposited on the ground. The Americanos, who outnumbered the Japanese, naturally wanted their revenge on their former tormentors, and Jan had been obliged to leave many of the spiders on board as a temporary measure to keep the two sides apart. A delegation of Americanos had asked why they couldn't move on board the Sky Angel, where there was plenty of living space. Jan told them that she would accept some of the women and their children, to relieve the pressure in the crowded *Perfumed Breeze*, but no men would be permitted on board the Sky Angel, with the exception of the two Minervan men she had discovered, to her surprise and joy, still alive on the Japanese airship.

Conquering all the Sky Lords would probably take years, and after that Jan's plans became even vaguer. She had hopes of somehow harnessing the laser power of the whole fleet of tamed Sky Lords to scour the blight lands surrounding the remaining ground settlements. The Sky Angel contained stores of frozen seeds and animal embryos — it might be possible, with the sky people and the ground dwellers working together under Jan's control, aided by the invaluable Carl, to start reclaiming large areas of land back from the blight.

Her other central concern was how to re-establish a Minervan society. It was vital to preserve and pass on the precious Minervan genes. She would have a baby each from the two Minervan men, but then what? Have the men breed with ordinary women? It would dilute the Minervan genetic mix, but perhaps it would be better than nothing. Minervan genes would be spread.

316

She was abruptly seized with a feeling of nausea. Taking care not to disturb Ceri she hurried out of bed and went into the bathroom. She was sick in the basin. When it was over she washed her mouth out, then splashed water on her face. She saw Ceri appear in the mirror beside her, an expression of concern on her beautiful face. Ceri was almost back to her old self, physically anyway — though her frequent nightmares, and her vehement expressions of hatred towards all men, told Jan that the emotional scars of what she went through at the hands of the Japanese men would take a long time to fade.

Ceri put her arm around Jan's shoulders. "This is the third time in a row you've been sick in the morning," she said worriedly.

Jan gave her a reassuring smile in the mirror. "I'm okay. I feel fine most of the time. I think it's just reaction to all my worries and problems."

"Even so, I think you should have yourself checked out by one of those medic machines."

"I will, when I have the time."

"Do it right away, for *my* sake," Ceri pleaded.

Jan turned and kissed her on the lips. "For you, anything."

She looked at the screen in disbelief. "I can't be pregnant! It's impossible! My breeding time is still almost a year away!" Carl said, "There is no mistake. The machine is in perfect working order."

Jan turned deperately to Ceri. "How can I be pregnant? It's crazy! Even if it were possible for me to be impregnated I haven't made love to any man since Prince Caspar . . . and according to this machine fertilization occurred exactly seven weeks ago . . . ." She stopped. She remembered what Milo had done to her. On that horrible night in the blight lands.

It was *his* child. She knew it.

"Milo," she said dazedly. "He did it. He wasn't human. Who knows how his seed had been altered by his genegineers, or what it was capable of doing to my own reproduction system." She clutched at Ceri and stared with panic into her eyes. "What am I going to do?"

Without a pause Ceri said coldly, "Kill it."

317

Jan shook her head. "No. No, I can't do that. I'll have to have it. Mother God, please may it be a *girl*!"

An hour later Jan had calmed down considerably. She was in the control room, alone. With Carl and Ashley flying the Sky Angel there was no need for any crew. She stared across the desert towards the strange, flat-topped hills on the horizon. The Sky Angel was searching for the *Lord Matamoros*, the Sky Lord which ruled the area immediately to the south of the *Lord Pangloth*'s territories. Carl predicted that interception would occur any day now, and Jan wanted to be in a capable state of mind when the encounter occurred.

She was coming to terms with the knowledge of what she carried within her. Even if the baby turned out to be male, all would not be lost. He would be carrying *her* genes as well as Milo's. That meant there was a good chance he wouldn't be anything at all like Milo.

She thought of Milo's skull, which she kept stored in a locker in her quarters. She could see the grinning jaws, sense the arrogance that Milo displayed even in death, and it made her feel even more determined.

She was going to beat him.

She *had* to, for Minerva.